THE SHADOW SAGA

THE SHADOW EFFECT

DANIEL REINER

PRESS

Published by Vulpine Press in the United Kingdom in 2020

Cover by Claire Wood

ISBN: 978-1-83919-324-8

www.vulpine-press.com

For Karen

PRELUDE

BENEATH BOSTON, 1912

Doctor Quentin Allan Gardiner crept through the dark tunnel as quietly as he was able. The oppressive dampness of a wet Boston Spring seeped down through the earth above, staining the air with the thick smell of loam and making the paving stones slick underfoot. He cursed his heart for beating so strongly, fearing the sound was loud enough to betray his presence. In his left hand, a spool of twine unwound slowly as he advanced. In his right, he held a weapon of sorts. He had eschewed the offer of a revolver, confident that the small, star-shaped piece of soapstone he grasped would be more effective than bullets against anything he might encounter.

Gardiner had started out with a portable light as well, but it was now in a coat pocket, switched off. There was enough illumination coming from an unanticipated source: polished upright columns of quartz, set at irregular intervals in the outer wall, on his left. At first, he'd thought the glow was caused by something *on* the columns— a chemical, or some kind of algae or moss—but no. The faint milky glow was coming from within the mineral itself, providing a series of markers in the gloom. He had counted twelve so far, each being nearly a foot in diameter and at least seven feet tall. The investment of time and money to create them would have been staggering. Who could have done such a thing? And why bury them so deeply? This catacomb was not recent: It was decades old, if not centuries. And so well concealed, in fact, that they would never have found it without the anonymous tip. His colleague who had taken that telephone call, Jebediah Higgins, only said that it had been a woman with an accent, who had hung up after delivering her few hints.

So many mysteries here to solve…

The tunnel had started off with a wide curve to the right, but then twisted fully back upon itself twice, rarely running straight for any distance at all. Taking into account the numerous bends and turns, he was now unsure of how far he'd walked, and in what direction. The entrance was in Copp's Hill Burying Ground, but he could be under the harbor right now, for all he knew.

Upon reaching the next cylinder, he dismissed the concerns about his location. The voices of two men echoed back to him from up ahead, confirming for him that he was in the right place. One belonged to Higgins, who had taken the other fork in the path where it had split near the entrance. The other could only belong to the one whose insanity had drawn them there.

Gardiner had seen Heinrich Bösemann just once, a few weeks prior. Higgins had pointed out the square-faced man from the taxicab they were riding in. There had only been time for a glimpse as the automobile went by, but their eyes had met, as if Bösemann had been aware that he was being watched.

Rounding a sharp bend, he could see that his path terminated in a large chamber, seemingly empty except for a few pieces of decrepit furniture and fixtures for candles. The light from those candles showed the age of the ancient construction around him in great detail—too great for Gardiner's comfort. The walls were terrifyingly old, with some buckling of the stones evident right where he stood. It was a wonder it hadn't collapsed long ago. Hugging the decaying wall, both men were out of sight to his left, though Higgins' shadow was visible.

"…a crime to live where I choose?" asked Bösemann. The words were well pronounced, but colored by a lifetime of German.

"The police may have something to say about it," replied Higgins.

"Police?" There was a laugh. "Are you here to collect taxes?"

"We both know why I'm here."

"I do find it unleidlich—ah. It is *unpleasant* to lie to a gentleman. You don't appreciate my pet. Is that it?"

"Your *pet* has murdered three women! It has no business on this planet, and your crimes against humanity have earned you a death sentence."

"Kill me then. You could do so easily."

"As can you."

"Yet neither of us shoots. Why is that?"

"He was waiting for me," announced Gardiner. "And I asked him to do nothing rash until I arrived."

Cautiously, he stuck his head fully into the open area, revealing himself. The two men stood facing each other, thirty feet apart. They were mirrored opposites, Bösemann holding his gun with his left hand, and Higgins with his right. Both wore a grey suit, although Higgins' was wet and covered with mud, as if he had slipped and fallen. And the clear view gave Gardiner a chance to see how much their host resembled Beethoven, including the cleft chin and untamed hair.

"I should have known," said Bösemann. "You were waiting for aid."

He took his eyes off his adversary momentarily and glanced at Gardiner.

"Sir, we have not formally met. My name is Heinrich Bösemann. And you are?"

"Gardiner."

"Doctor Quentin Gardiner," he said. "Of Miskatonic University?"

"The same."

"Yes. It's not surprising. I've seen the names of Gardiner and Higgins associated more than once. Doctor, I must say that I'm pleased to make your acquaintance. I read your thesis not long ago. Your ideas are more interesting than the rabble who have come before you. Before us both. We are quite ahead of our time. There is much in common between us. Your career is just beginning, but working with Mr. Higgins here is a fast way to end it."

On this point, Gardiner did not necessarily disagree. But he said nothing.

"You have no response to that, Doctor?"

A few seconds passed. When the echoes stopped, Bösemann spoke again. This time, Gardiner thought he heard a note of sadness in his voice.

"Yes, perhaps the time for talking is done."

The final word was masked by gunfire, two nearly simultaneous reports echoing madly off the stones of the chamber. The pair were so close that it was hard for Gardiner to imagine either had missed his target. But he didn't have the luxury of using his imagination. A noise from behind made him confront the reality of the abomination they had been searching for these past weeks.

Its form was deceptively human, disguising itself as a young woman in order to escape detection. When attacking or feeding, however, its true form was revealed, any semblance of a face replaced by a tentacle-wreathed maw.

The unholy creature closed the distance rapidly, but the Doctor managed to present the stone in time. Merely holding it out was enough to instantly paralyze the thing, but its momentum couldn't be arrested. Gardiner threw himself down onto the floor. The creature continued over him, brushing against the wall before tumbling into the chamber. It hadn't hit with much force, but the impact on that particularly weak spot was enough.

He was already crawling forward as the wall fell inward. Though able to avoid being crushed outright, a large stone rolled onto his left leg, pinning him in place. Tons of damp earth poured down on top of him, overwhelming his efforts to clear it away. The massive weight squeezed his chest, emptying his lungs. He took quick, tiny breaths, trying to suck every last bit of life-giving air from the dirt. The panic of being smothered made his thoughts dart around: Higgins, Bösemann, the murdered women, the thing that had killed them, the many maddening puzzles associated with this, his tomb.

So many mysteries here...

Misty mysteries here...

Mystery ministers...

Mini...

4

His mind went grey.
then...
black.

Air!

The crushing weight was lessening. A hand held one of his.

"Gardiner!" Higgins' voice sliced through the fog of oxygen deprivation.

He could tell that the man was vigorously shifting material off of his body. But one hand, soft and warm, still held his, while yet another cleared the dirt from his face.

"I'm all right," coughed Gardiner.

He cracked open his eyes and beheld a vision too precious for words; one of the loveliest women he'd ever met was kneeling in front of him.

"Thank goodness," she said. After giving Gardiner's hand a light squeeze, she released it and got busy digging.

Sybil Hastings was a singular and wonderful combination of intelligence and beauty. With a will as strong as Higgins, Gardiner believed that she was a perfect match for him. The two had hit it off soon after their first meeting, a few weeks previous.

"What were you thinking, Sybil?" demanded Higgins. "Aside from putting yourself in danger by following us, you *banished* the creature?"

"I saved your life, Jebediah!"

"You had time to destroy the thing."

"Why do you always insist on killing?"

"If you had just let me—"

"Must we argue about this right now? While we're digging him out?"

"I can do both."

Gardiner listened to the exchange and grinned. They sounded like an old married couple already.

PART I

ONE

A PACKAGE ARRIVES, 1925

The Divided God.

The phrase echoed ominously in Gardiner's mind. Birthed decades before, the exasperating riddle associated with those three words had secluded itself in the dimly lit corners of his consciousness, feasting upon whatever random musings had wandered by. It had eaten well over those years, emerging from the shadows as a fully mature obsession. Other, more mundane thoughts and concerns made half-hearted attempts to quash it, but to no avail. It was no contest, really.

The Divided God.

He liked to think he was master of his own mind. As a practical man of science, he had earned the respect of his colleagues at Miskatonic University, enough to be named head of the Department of Archaeology. As an active leader of the community, he had also earned the respect of his neighbors in the town of Arkham, Massachusetts. It was plain to anyone who knew him that the scientific and civic accomplishments for which he was lauded could only have been achieved through dedication and self-control. Balance was key: determining how to best portion out the precious minutes available on any given day when pursuing multiple goals. Fixating on any one thought for an extended length of time could stall, or even doom, the rest. He knew that it was better to push distractions away, out to the periphery of his mind, in order to think and act more efficiently.

The Divided God.

It certainly hadn't been Gardiner's choice to breathe life back into an enigma that had lain dormant for so long. No, it was the telegram he'd received at dawn—and still held in his hand—that had done it:

```
Quentin:
Please retrieve bed. package for you from Arkham
telegraph office.
Rainer Donau
```

As a young man at the beginning of his career, he had worked with the much older Doctor Donau just once, but each had left a lasting, positive impression on the other. Their first meeting was undeniably unique, the older man claiming repeatedly that the two had met before, both plainly acknowledging that they couldn't have. Despite the oddness, or because of it, the ice had been broken, and they grew to like each other from that very moment.

Circumstances had permitted them to cross paths rarely during the subsequent decades, but they had corresponded frequently for both business and personal reasons. As a result, Gardiner had latched onto his mentor's use of "bed." as shorthand for the German bedeutend—significant. Appearing in such an unexpected communiqué, he had wondered only briefly what it might mean.

The Divided God.

Once the thought had popped in, there had been no escaping it.

He had dashed out of the house after throwing on whatever clothes he could find, only barely restraining the urge to run the mile to the telegraph office. His automobile would have gotten him there faster, but as an archaeologist, the need to hike to remote sites had kept him in good health, and over the years he had developed a strong preference to walk whenever possible—even with the most exciting news of his career likely awaiting him at the other end. Unencumbered by equipment, and with solid pavement underfoot, he kept up a pace that would have put many of his younger colleagues to shame.

By the time he reached his destination, the fierce anticipation lent a tremor to his hand as he signed for the package: a bulky thing, thickly wrapped in paper and tied up with twine. It was heavy, but not overly so. The clerk smiled uneasily as he handed it over. In fact, the young man had looked uncomfortable ever since he'd arrived. The cause was made clear when he came from behind the counter to help with the door.

"Would you like to borrow a hat, Doctor Gardiner?" His voice was low, even though it was just the two of them in the lobby.

Gardiner caught a ghostly reflection of himself in the glass of the door: an ordinary man of average height, weight, and build. Rounded features made him naturally suited to smile, matching his easygoing personality. The image showed that all seemed to be in order…except for his uncovered brown hair, greying around the edges. It stuck out, still disheveled from sleep. He had taken the time to put on a tie, but had neglected a hat.

"Thank you, but it's not far." He pulled a quarter out of his pocket and pressed it into the clerk's palm. "Just please don't tell anyone you saw me in this state."

"Yes, sir."

The trip home passed in a euphoric fugue, his brain bereft of all thought. His eyes saw the landmarks, told his body where to go. Ten elms, evenly spaced, then a left onto Linden Street. At the corner, a Golden Retriever named Minnie was out in the yard. Ordinarily, he'd stop to pet her. Today, he only waved at her playful barking as he went past. At the end of that block, a right onto Wigglesworth. All that remained was a straight shot to his own house.

Broad oaks—both great and small—were favored by the residents along this stretch. None of his neighbors were outside as he marched by, but the squirrels were active in the branches above, taking care of their bushy-tailed business at a pace that nearly matched Gardiner's rhythm. Occasionally, when one darted across his path, he'd take notice of the scurrying, but really, his only concern was the precious package tucked under his arm.

Home.

He tried to find his key.

No!

The metallic jingling in his pocket had only been a few coins. The key he needed was likely upstairs on the dresser, where he kept it during the night. He admonished himself for his foolish behavior: forgetting both hat and key, two items in plain view that he had merely needed to pick up on the way out. It would be at least an hour before his housekeeper arrived with the spare.

Damn!

Though years in the past, memories of the encounter under Copp's Hill flooded in whenever his heart raced with stress such as he felt now: that abhorrent creature, the silent, the smothering weight of damp earth. But also, the indescribable delight of being able to breathe again.

Sybil…

He'd wondered more than once about the fortuitous chance that had caused him to notice Sybil Hastings that first time in the University library. She had been at the front desk, having a disagreement with one of the employees—who, it must be said, seemed to have a knack of attracting disagreement. But what if Gardiner hadn't seen her? What if he hadn't walked over to investigate, and Millicent Brody's stubbornness had outlasted Sybil's? That day at Copp's Hill, Sybil had put herself very much at risk by defying Jebediah and following them into the catacomb. By doing so, she had saved two lives. Except for that one fateful glance over at the desk on his way out the door of the library, Quentin Gardiner could very well be dead right now.

Stop that!

Though he was well aware that the most miniscule of details could have the greatest impact, he had to remind himself that he had only forgotten a key. There should be no dramatic consequences from such an innocent act. And, regardless, there was definitely no immediate, earthshaking need to get inside right now. Patience was called for. Simple patience. He needed to wait one hour. That was all.

The Divided God!

He grabbed the knob and turned it out of desperation.

The door opened.

By happy accident he'd forgotten to lock it. He laughed silently at his own stupidity as he closed the door behind him and locked it. Before allowing himself to move away, the knob was checked, not once, but twice, needing the extra sensory confirmation of his fingertips. Reassured by both sight and touch, he moved through the foyer toward the small library off to the right.

The house was far larger than necessary for one man, but Gardiner had made the commitment to it long ago, shortly after finishing his doctoral thesis. In those days, he still had thoughts of finding a wife, settling down, and raising a small family. This four-bedroom house would have been the place for it... Would have been, could have been. But reality had intervened. Not the reality of typical day to day problems: finances, health, social pressures. No, it had been the reality of the horrors hidden behind the veil covering everyone's eyes. Or, most everyone's. Gardiner was one of the few who'd peeked behind that veil. He had learned too much. And with that learning came a responsibility that couldn't be shirked. Given that commitment, any hope for a normal life—a family—had evaporated as the years went by.

And so, even though his home was a near-constant reminder of lost dreams, he still liked its familiar creaks and groans, the oak trees front and back, the relative warmth through the bitter New England winters. He had grown comfortable in it. And the extra bedrooms did occasionally get some use: James Dunlevy and Patrick MacNulty had both stayed with him a few times. Dunlevy would never stay under the same roof as Higgins, even though Jebediah's house was far better suited for putting up guests.

Once inside his library, now more mindful of details, he locked that door as well. And checked it. Twice.

The central table was mostly clear of clutter. He set down the package and grabbed a letter opener. After slicing through the strings, he found a letter addressed to him under the first layer of paper:

My friend Quentin:

I must apologize for this surprise, and for the assumption that you would be willing to drop everything and depart without hesitation to South America, but I believe that you will do just that after seeing the item in this package. Great pains have been taken to ensure the secrecy of this trip, so do be careful with whom you speak.

When Herr Koch-Grunberg died this past year, I nominated you to succeed him as the director of our researches there, but was voted down by the committee. Another opportunity presented itself recently, when a landslide revealed a temple along with the enclosed item, and at nearly the same time, the new expedition leader tragically died. I again suggested you, and this time you were accepted when a young man added his voice to mine in championing you.

So, yes—I well realize that, as your first and only experience with this matter occurred in the Mesopotamian region, this will seem an odd request. But you must go to Guyana. My health remains good, but this endeavor is better left to someone younger than I. Tickets for the eight a.m. train to Boston are waiting for you at the Arkham depot. From Boston, the cruise ship Wachsam will deliver you to Miami. The young man I mentioned, Jonathan Harris, will meet you there and accompany you the rest of the way. You will be able to learn everything you need from him.

I also do realize that this will interfere with your scheduled lectures in Europe this Summer, and do regret that I will not be able to meet up with you as we had planned. It would have been very nice to see you again after such a long time. But, as things go, this is much more important.

Please have safe and speedy travels, and do me the favor of solving this mystery that has preyed upon my mind for as long as it has yours.

Rainer Donau

The job of getting through the numerous wrappings frustrated Gardiner's first view of the object for a while, but finally, a piece of precisely cut marble emerged from the package. It was about an inch thick, and about eighteen inches square. It had two flat and two curved sides opposite each other, suggesting that it had been part of a circular structure or decoration. The first real shock he received was seeing the clearly legible phrase chiseled into the rock in cuneiform, a phrase he knew well, having found a match for it, years before at a site near Mosul. It read, when translated:

All praise

to the one

who is two.

The original tablet from Mosul, which had been made of clay, was currently in London. But he had carefully made and preserved a rubbing of it soon after finding it, years ago. He rushed over to the shelf where the paper was stored, brought it back, placed it over the stone.

The two were perfectly and completely identical.

For an unknown time, he could only stare at the impossibility sitting on the table before him. When the numbness wore off, he worked with a bright light to try to find a flaw or mismatch between the rubbing and the stone, but couldn't. It was as if they had been cut by machine from the same pattern. Because the paper was known to represent an item over four thousand years old, and from an entirely different continent, that idea was not worthy of consideration.

He pulled out a powerful magnifying glass and examined the wedge-shaped characters. Oddly, there were no scratches at all within the cuts, subtle or otherwise, as would have been left behind by a chisel. The surfaces were so smooth that the impressions seemed to have been made as was typically done with wet clay: by smoothly pressing a writing tool into the surface. But doing so would have required an application of heat in the thousands of degrees Fahrenheit in order to soften the material sufficiently. And that type of unnatural heating would have left telltale discolorations. But once again, there was no sign of anything of the sort.

Added to the clearly quantifiable details was a less scientific one: an eerie feeling of familiarity. As he handled it, a gut instinct told him that the material both felt and looked like a type of marble well known to Iraq, though he'd need to perform a painstaking inspection to be certain. There were locations in the Americas that could supply stone very much like it, but his decades of experience in the field led him to believe it had originated in the Middle East, near Mosul.

How can this be genuine?

Despite the fact that the artifact had come from Doctor Donau, neither of them had been present for its discovery and retrieval. There was a very real probability that it was a hoax created by recent technology.

He turned it over again—and had the answer: The outer face and edges were marble, but the underside was composed of a thin layer of sandstone that had seemingly been fused onto the more durable material. Determining how that had been done would need to be left for another time, but unlike the polished obverse, the reverse was covered with bumps and gullies. A match of the rough sandstone against its origin on the temple mentioned in the letter would establish provenience, and leave no doubt in his mind as to its authenticity. He'd be able to see for himself once he reached the site.

His mind overflowing with theories, it took several rings of the telephone before the noise intruded enough to be recognized. Reluctantly, he left his prize and crossed the room. In his agitated state, it took a few seconds to register that it was quite strange—rude, even—for someone to call so early, and wondered who it could be. Even as the thought formed, however, he felt that he knew the answer.

"Hello?"

"I knew you'd be awake by now," came the voice of Jebediah Higgins. "I need you to get rid of those infernal books."

As usual, Higgins had gotten directly to the point without any preamble. And though his request was ambiguous, Gardiner knew exactly to which books Higgins was referring.

"What? Why? Jebediah, it's still very early. Why are we having this conversation now?"

"You're right. Talk isn't necessary. You should have no trouble handling that pipsqueak in charge."

Gardiner frowned.

"I can advise Doctor Trautmann, but you know I have no authority over him."

"Advise him, then. Public access to those volumes needs to be removed. Now."

Gardiner sighed. Even after working with Higgins for decades, it was still difficult at times to think of him as a friend. He did act in everyone's best interests, but the onerous man often neglected to explain his rationale. It was as if everyone else was obliged to interpret any given set of data the same as he, and—of course—reach the same conclusion. Very often, yes: Everyone involved would ultimately bear witness to the truth that Jebediah Higgins had made the right choice, or performed the correct action. But at a time like this, with a demand made out of the blue, his brusqueness was simply annoying. A glimpse of the mystifying artifact sitting just a few feet away on the table further diminished any willingness to deal with this situation.

"Jebediah, I can't do that. You'll have to talk to him yourself if you want it done."

"Fine, then. Set a meeting for half-past nine."

"Today? Must it be today?"

"Yes."

Gardiner clenched his jaw, aware too late of what he'd suggested, and knowing that only he had the clout to set up a meeting with the director of the library on such short notice. He also reminded himself that each of the members of their tiny cabal had responsibilities to the others; blocking anyone's progress wasn't conducive to a healthy working relationship. If such a thing was even possible with Higgins.

TWO

FRIENDS AND COLLEAGUES

Although the list of tasks in his head grew larger with almost every step, the obsessive mantra stayed firmly in the front of Gardiner's mind as he crossed the campus. He could have—should have—banished the distraction, but the words provided a comforting source of energy upon which to draw, and based on previous experiences he knew that he would need energy in the days ahead. He had every right to lead from behind a desk as head of the department, but his zest for field work had not diminished, even at the age of fifty-two. This case, of course, went far beyond professional zeal. If needed, he could disguise it as such to even his closest friends, but inside burned a giddy excitement he could scarcely contain. He would have left that same day if needed, but was grateful for the extra time to let him wrap up some loose ends.

His first destination was Beaumont Hall, and therein the second-floor office of Professor of Mathematics, Samuel Josephson. It was hours earlier than the lunch they had planned for that day, but Gardiner was fairly sure that he'd be in his office between classes. He knocked lightly on the closed door, then entered.

Seated at his desk, Josephson put down the papers he was holding.

"Sam," said Gardiner. "I'm glad I caught you."

"Quentin. Is something wrong?" He stood up, forehead wrinkling with concern. Well over six feet tall, he towered over most everyone, which helped immensely when dealing with the random unruly student.

"Yes, I'm sorry, but I'll to have to postpone our lunch indefinitely. I have an opportunity to travel to a newly discovered site. I leave first thing tomorrow. I'll need every bit of the time between now and then to prepare."

"No need to apologize. Where are you going, if I may ask?"

"I received a telegram from— I'm off to—"

He wanted to tell his friend everything he knew: the clay tablet he'd stumbled across thirty years previously, the marble one he'd just received, the perplexing fact that the two matched. Josephson could be trusted to treat the matter as confidential, but Gardiner couldn't figure out how to summarize it all coherently.

Josephson put his hand up when he observed the tongue-tied man.

"Ah, I see. Never mind, then. I retract the question."

"I'm going to South Ameri—"

"Tut! No need to say anything. The nature of your work necessitates a bit more flexibility and secrecy than mine. It's rare when I've needed to excavate a differential equation, must less sneak away to Egypt to do so."

Josephson's eyes twinkled in the way that Gardiner had come to associate with his friend's sense of humor.

"I'm glad you understand," he said. "It's very sensitive. I don't even want to tell Jebediah. Speaking of which…"

His voice trailed off when it dawned on him that he truly did not want to tell his colleague. Was there some amount of jealousy involved? Higgins was younger, stronger, wealthier, had more influence in desirable social circles—but it was honestly none of those. What gnawed at Gardiner was that, even though it was *he* who had been appointed as the public face of their small group for the occasions when their exploits were less than covert, it was still Higgins who somehow received credit for their successes. Even among the intelligentsia, the plebeian barometer of wealth held the greatest sway.

"Speaking of which," he repeated when he noted his longish pause, "I think our meeting the other night with your young Mister

Adderly has disturbed him more than he let on at the time. We'll be meeting with Edward Trautmann shortly. Higgins wants to lock up those ancient tomes and throw away the key. But I need to persuade Edward to leave them be."

"So, despite his protestations, Higgins does believe there is a connection between the Ancient Ones and the inexplicable death of young Elizabeth?"

"If asked, I'm sure he wouldn't admit it," Gardiner said. "But it seems so."

"What about you?"

"I can't say. Jebediah convinced me that it wasn't related, and so I hadn't given it any further thought. But now he's acting as if he has reversed his position. If I had more time, I would look into it, but this new development is far too important for me to ignore." Gardiner checked the grandfather clock next to the door. "Sam, time is running short on me. I have to leave."

"And my class is about to start."

"Freshmen?"

"Thankfully, no. Some of these have actually demonstrated to me the ability to make use of the three pounds of grey matter wedged between their unwashed ears."

Josephson's eyes twinkled again as Gardiner chuckled.

The Library was adjacent to Beaumont Hall, and there were still a few minutes before the hastily arranged meeting, so Gardiner thought he would have some time to speak with Doctor Trautmann privately. His eyesight still excellent, Gardiner scanned the grounds before entering the building, but was not able to spot the purposeful stride of Higgins anywhere.

But the plan for a private conference was derailed as soon as he arrived. Doctor Trautmann's secretary was hovering outside of the ornate double doors that led into the Director's office, wringing her hands.

"Doctor Gardiner, I'm just— He just—"

She displayed equal measures of anger, embarrassment and confusion. He was familiar enough with the woman's usual demeanor to know that something truly vexing must have occurred.

"Is it safe to assume that Mr. Higgins has arrived?"

She nodded.

"Then, I apologize for him. As his keeper, that is one of my duties."

He smiled in an effort to soothe her.

She did her best to return it. After pausing to regain her composure she opened the doors to the cavernous office.

"Gentlemen," Gardiner said, entering quickly. "You started without me?"

His entrance had the desired effect of interrupting Higgins, who had apparently been flogging the poor Doctor Trautmann with his reasoning. Though slight of build and with his thin face obscured by thick lenses, Edward Trautmann was deceptively powerful, adept in wielding the twin weapons of politics and bureaucracy. At the moment, that power was not evident; the man looked at Gardiner with genuine relief, mouth agape.

"And no, Jebediah," Gardiner added. "I'm not late. You're early." He seated himself in the remaining chair.

"Gardiner. Yes, I overestimated the amount of time I'd need to get here. I was clarifying my position to Doctor Trautmann."

"And because you chose to start without me, you'll need to do so again."

Higgins' brow wrinkled. "This morning you told me that Doctor Trautmann has sole power to make decisions regarding the volumes here."

Gardiner focused on Trautmann, and, almost telepathically, an unvoiced message passed between them. Normally, the disposition of any book on the shelves was unquestionably under Trautmann's control, but there were some that fell into a grey area. Most definitely, all were books, but a few could also be loosely labeled as archaeological artifacts. As head of that department, Doctor Gardiner could theoretically remove them from the Library, do with them as he saw fit, and render this meeting moot. The Archaeology Department, however, had neither the space to store them, nor the manpower to handle the tedious administrative work of scheduling requests and ensuring that the delicate items were handled correctly. He wanted them to stay where they were, and was fairly sure that the Director enjoyed the notoriety of having them there, one in particular above all others.

"That is correct," said Gardiner. "I also said that I have the ability to advise him, and that's what I want to do. I need data in order to advise him properly."

Higgins sighed loudly.

"I was pointing out to the good Doctor Trautmann here that the evil knowledge contained in the more esoteric texts is often put to ill use."

Gardiner mentally flinched upon hearing the phrase *evil knowledge*; Higgins had likely chosen the words on purpose in an attempt to rile him.

"Jebediah, we use those volumes as well."

He paused to consider how explicit he wanted to be. Trautmann likely had a rough idea of how many hours Gardiner had spent poring over the *Necronomicon*, but there had never been a need to go into detail until now.

"The copies here aren't the only ones available. Removing access in Arkham may necessitate a trip to London, or Buenos Aires, or somewhere else. That doesn't solve the problem; it merely shifts it to a different location. And books are not the only source of such knowledge. I don't want to burden Doctor Trautmann with the ghoulish details, but you know of what I speak. It's simply not possible to police the entire globe. Until a good strategy is determined, we should leave the information available. Censorship is never a solution. And some of those people with access may benefit us. You know very well that *she* did."

Higgins stiffened. Gardiner knew that the man's relationship with Sybil Hastings hadn't ended well. The subject was almost taboo. But he needed to play that trump to get an edge, and it had been done correctly: Her name had not been mentioned.

"Getting aid is a rarity! You know that as well as I. Far more often, that evil knowledge has put us on the defensive, where we need to hurriedly react to a situation that has already escalated."

"There is neither good nor evil knowledge! Knowledge is quintessentially just that: knowledge!"

Gardiner strongly disliked raising his voice, instead preferring to punctuate with precisely chosen words, but conversations like this with Higgins often transformed into debates, then arguments. Staying calm was difficult. He closed his eyes for a heartbeat, opened them, and finished, "We cannot edit facts for our own convenience."

"As I have said repeatedly, I am not suggesting edits," said Higgins. With his ire up, the words were spoken singly, an exclamation point implicitly appended to each. "I want total suppression. Remove all access."

And as was often the case, Higgins' desire had been stated as a command, leaving no room for compromise.

"Suppressing them, removing them, hiding them," said Gardiner sadly. "Call it what you like. Those acts create a void where something was once known to have existed. Voids fill. You know the measures desperate men will take when something coveted has been unequivocally denied them. Five years ago, that man in Barcelona nearly killed Patrick MacNulty—"

"How did I know you would bring that up yet again?" It may have been the timbre of his voice or his position in the room, but of the three, Higgins' words in particular reverberated throughout that space. "No one died. We succeeded in stopping him."

"Only barely, and due to the lucky happenstance of a rat—a rat!—distracting him."

Higgins glowered at the reminder.

"I spoke to the man, Caballero, afterwards, while he was in the custody of the police. His intentions were not...*purposely* evil. Yes, I know: It was a gray area. Patrick wanted to take time to gather more information, but I agreed with your assessment that action was better. However you must see in hindsight that we acted rashly in dealing with him. If we had proceeded more slowly—"

"We would have risked another Copp's Hill incident," said Higgins bluntly. "We had no way of knowing how he would use the knowledge he was gathering. Going too slowly could have been a fatal mistake."

That quieted Gardiner. It was true. MacNulty had seen some pattern, had some intuition regarding the truth of the matter. James Dunlevy had stayed out of that argument, as he often did, letting Gardiner cast the deciding vote. Inwardly, he had preferred Mac-Nulty's approach, but, fearful of a repeat of those grisly Boston murders, he had sided with Higgins. Had his decision been the tipping point, causing events to avalanche nearly out of control? It was a sobering thought.

"Edward, we shouldn't act rashly in this case," said Gardiner. "Do you understand the implications of the opposing sides to this matter?"

He put a barely noticeable stress on *implications*, hoping that it would be picked up. Having an inaccessible copy of the *Necronomicon* would be equivalent to not having it at all, impacting Doctor Trautmann's reputation.

"Mr. Higgins," began Doctor Trautmann, his voice wavering slightly. "I must begin by saying that I agree with you on general principles. As you made reference earlier, people are at the root of the problem—that is, the information to which people have access, and how it is applied. Gunpowder can be used to make a bullet. That bullet can be used by a man to kill a deer, and so feed his family. It can also be used to kill his neighbor. Two vastly different results."

"But?" snapped Higgins with a glare.

"Yes, I—exactly," stammered Trautmann. "There is a *but*. Doctor Gardiner has a valid point. Making the books unreachable could have undesirable consequences. I believe it is in our best interest to leave them available in some manner. Is there a compromise?"

Gardiner smiled to himself; he had gauged the man correctly.

"No," snipped Higgins.

"I used the term *police* earlier," proposed Gardiner.

Trautmann picked up on the suggestion and ran with it.

"Yes. We could be the policemen, only permitting access by written approval of either Doctor Gardiner or me. Additionally, the whole set could be moved to a more secure room in the basement. That would seem to be a good solution."

"What say you, Jebediah?"

Higgins stood abruptly. His muscular frame was impressive by itself, but an intrinsic charisma made him seem larger and more intimidating when in a mood like this. Gardiner was accustomed to the man after knowing him for so many years, but Trautmann had met him for the first time just minutes before, and reacted with a start, even seated safely behind his desk.

"Obviously, I have no say," he said. "You're going to do what you like. We can only hope that there are no unfortunate repercussions."

He stared at both men briefly, indignation smoldering, before stalking off.

Gardiner waited until the doors slammed shut before speaking again.

"I'm sorry for dragging you into this with so little warning, Edward. Early this morning I learned of an opportunity in South America that I can't ignore, and I needed to be sure that you and I were of the same opinion before I left. Higgins has a rather...forceful personality."

"Yes, I see that," he said shakily.

"Now, I want to be clear: Jebediah Higgins has put his own life on the line numerous times. He's saved mine at least twice. It is a fact that his intentions are beyond reproach. His wealth and influence are also invaluable. Bear that in mind if you have a need to deal with him again."

"Certainly," said Trautmann, making some notes on a sheet of paper with an ornate fountain pen. "You make it sound as if you'll be gone a while," he added without looking up.

"I may be. It's hard to say at this point."

Gardiner stood up, thought about shaking the man's hand, then discarded the idea: The size of the desk between them would make such an exercise clumsy, a factor that Edward Trautmann may have taken into account when choosing the furniture.

"Have a safe trip then," said Trautmann dismissively, continuing to write. With the threat of Higgins gone from the room, his aloof persona had reemerged.

Knowing that there'd be no further discussion, Gardiner left quietly. It was true that his relationship with Jebediah Higgins was frequently challenging and volatile, and could only marginally be described as friendship, but it was refreshingly warm compared to the cool and distant Trautmann. Given the option, he'd take fire over ice every time.

THREE

THE ADVENTURE BEGINS

The tickets were awaiting him at the train station and his destination was a fully equipped dig, so really all that Gardiner had to do was show up on time with clothing. But he still took the time to pack an extra bag of tools and supplies. The small rock hammer and trowel he included, for example, were personal favorites, light and comfortable in his hands, yet sturdy and dependable. For other reasons he wasn't able to put into words, he felt compelled to add an assortment of chisels; various knives; some litmus paper; a highly accurate compass; some candles and a supply of strike-anywhere matches, as well as a flint; a new flashlight with powerful batteries; an excessive amount of paper and ink; and a collapsible measuring device that could be unfolded to twelve feet. That valise was abnormally heavy and caused some consternation from the baggage handlers who were unfortunate enough to help him, but he tipped them well for their efforts.

The train to Boston was the last bit of familiarity he could indulge in. With the short taxicab ride from the depot to the waiting ship serving as a prelude, his adventure officially began when he boarded the vessel, although with days of unexciting ocean travel ahead. He wished for some way to prepare further, but he had nothing to study aside from the artifact and its accompanying letter. Settled in safely on the ship, he removed the stone from his briefcase. When another examination of it revealed nothing new, he came to the conclusion that it would be better to stop wasting energy and just relax for a few days.

It wasn't something that came naturally, but he did, playing the part of a wealthy, world-weary traveler—though minus the wealth. There were some pleasant distractions to pass the time: conversing and playing cards with other passengers, and relishing the sun and increasing warmth as the ship headed south. The strategy worked for the most part. But the five syllables of his mantra never strayed far from his conscious mind.

The ship arrived in Miami mid-morning. With the vessel no longer moving, there was no breeze to drive away the steamy heat. And the crush of bodies on the dock made it worse. As Gardiner pushed his way through the crowd, he heard his name being called.

"Doctor Gardiner!"

Shielding his eyes from the sun, he found the source: A man in his mid-twenties, taller than much of the surrounding throng, waving to him. He was protectively shielding a pretty young woman at his side.

Gardiner found an open spot, pointed at it, and began moving toward it.

"Hello, Doctor," said the younger man as they met. "I'm Jonathan Harris, and this is my sister, Frances."

Gardiner exchanged handshakes with both. Although Harris was by any standard a handsome man with the trim build of an Olympic athlete, of the pair, it was Frances who stood out. She was well along in her pregnancy, the billowy maternity clothing doing little to disguise it. Gardiner estimated she was past seven months, possibly into the eighth. A delicately small nose and mouth served as accents on a round face, which was softened even further by the extra weight she was carrying.

"It's very nice to meet you both. My dear, this heat and humidity must be especially taxing for you. I confess I'm having a time of it."

"Yes, Doctor. I do find myself getting more easily fatigued lately, but I was born and raised in the Mediterranean. The atmosphere here is heavier, but I've adapted."

27

Her accent became evident after a few words: British, but mixed with Italian or Spanish. And the complexion of her skin *was* slightly darker compared to her brother.

Gardiner looked back. The flow of bodies down the ramp was dwindling.

"I suppose we can retrieve my bags then get onto the next ship."

"Yes, but we have five hours before it departs," said Frances. "The upcoming days will be wearisome. A little extravagance before boarding is called for. I made reservations for lunch. How does that sound?"

"Excellent," said Gardiner. "I'd like to keep going, but I think a few hours on a solid surface will do me well. And a leisurely meal will give the two of you a better chance to say good-bye."

He then noticed her wedding ring.

"Will your husband also be joining us?"

Harris looked at Frances, who nodded.

"Doctor Gardiner," began Harris. "Frances is coming with us. She is fully qualified as an archaeologist, although her specialization is anthropology."

Gardiner was dumbfounded. He had learned long ago to not underestimate the strength of the so-called *weaker* sex; working closely with Sybil Hastings had taught him that lesson. She had contributed just as much as Higgins and himself in their defeat of the madman who had unleashed that blasphemous horror on Boston.

No, it wasn't an effrontery of his sensibilities, but rather concern over her health. He knew that an expedition like this could drag on for months.

"Ummm. Of course. But..." was all that came out. He gestured feebly to indicate her condition.

Frances patted Gardiner's arm reassuringly.

"I thank you for your thoughtfulness, Doctor, but the promise of what we'll find has lent me the strength to see it through. When Jonathan told me of the temple and all that it implied, I couldn't resist the chance to see it for myself."

Gardiner still found himself at a loss for words.

"And as for my husband…" she said, looking down at her hand. "I've kept my ring on purely for social purposes in my current state. He died not long ago, a victim of one of the more loathsome tropical diseases."

"Oh, that's terrible."

"Yes, it was ill-timed; the child will never know its father. But once we reach our destination, I'll help with a survey of the site, then head to a spot of civilization for the delivery. I've made no plans beyond that."

"I see."

"And if something goes awry and the baby decides to arrive early, I can be comforted with the fact that the savages there have success-fully been giving birth in remote jungles for thousands of years. Surely it wouldn't be an issue for me."

He only nodded in response.

Although Frances' casual attitude toward her pregnancy fell some-where between curious and alarming, she projected a natural charm and kept the conversation flowing until lunch was served. Officially, their pre-meal interactions could be categorized as conversation: Gardiner did speak occasionally, and Harris did nod a few times. But Frances was firmly in control. He desperately wanted to learn more from the young man about the artifact he'd received, the temple that had been found, the route they would take, … But he simply wasn't given an opportunity to broach any of those subjects.

With the meal concluded, they relaxed with drinks. Gardiner chose Irish Coffee, Harris a dessert port, and Frances a glass of cham-pagne. They toasted the success of their forthcoming trip. Each sa-vored their first sips, and that relative silence presented Gardiner the break he needed. He dove on it.

"Can you say how long it'll take to get to the site?" he asked. His tone was very casual, but the hurriedness of the words defeated his attempt at innocence.

Frances studied him briefly before speaking, a half-formed smile dancing on her lips.

"Please, Doctor," she chided him. "It's best we keep that under wraps for right now." More quietly, she added, "You never know who may be listening. In the days ahead you'll find out everything."

She was right, he had to admit. Jebediah always took the same type of precaution when in a public setting.

"You were born on Ischia, you said earlier?" he asked, changing the subject to something safer.

"Yes. My mother was native to the island. She died shortly after I was born. My father—our father—was German. An anthropologist. I remember his face well, though I never saw him much. He was always away for months at a time, off exploring. One day when I was twelve, he removed himself from my life for good. For years I wasn't sure if he'd died, or simply left. It turned out to be the latter." There was a curiously cold glance at Jonathan before she continued. "Foster parents raised me. Life on the island was…pleasant. But the inhabitants were ridiculously superstitious. Their system of beliefs was on display for my entire youth, a strange mixture of the ancient pagan right alongside the more modern and overt Christian. Whether naturally, or due to the little influence my father had had on me, I developed an interest in social behavior and anthropology. And much like Frazer's exploration into the myths regarding Diana at Lake Nemi, I started down a path. And kept going."

"I hope you trod one a tad more narrow than James Frazer," Gardiner remarked. "Where did your path lead?"

"Starting only with curiosity about why people touch iron for luck, or are afraid of the evil eye, I wondered about the social pressures that cause such behavior to propagate down through the centuries, all the way to our present time. That line of inquiry led me to take an especial interest in the religious ceremonies used to placate gods or ask favors of them. Taking into consideration everything I had learned, I connected the dots and reached a conclusion most would find shocking."

"What would that be?"

"I've determined that the influences behind these superstitions were external: Gods are real, and humanity is not alone in the universe."

Gardiner had accepted that truth long ago. His perusal of those haunted tomes had opened his mind, so much so that actually witnessing the alien things with his own eyes was almost anticlimactic when it had happened. But it was so very rare to hear someone outside of his tiny circle of colleagues speak that opinion.

"You really think so? That's quite a different conclusion than what's been reached by the dusty old men in charge."

"Proving it is an entirely different matter, but yes. I do. The patterns of cause and effect I've found present more than enough proof in my mind." She shrugged. "It's a different thing, being a woman. I think I have a different perspective than those dusty old men."

"Indeed. And, to reassure you, I'm not shocked by your theory. Surprised, but not shocked."

Gardiner turned to Harris, utterly quiet to that point, his attention focused on his sister.

"What do you think, Jonathan?"

"He's heard my theories countless times," said Frances. "In fact, we were in agreement right from the start, when we met for the first time in Germany."

Jonathan's mouth twitched, and he used his left hand to smooth down his hair with a well-practiced stroke.

"By the way," said Gardiner, "I do find that fascinating: the fact that you were raised in different countries, and yet managed to locate each other after being separated by an ocean."

"I suppose it could be seen as extraordinary, but really, we were both converging on a shared past, so to speak. Following the same path, it would only make sense that we would meet one day. Personally, I had an incentive to track down my father when I learned that he had been at Heidelberg University. He was in America by that point, but I stayed at the University to study. A coeducational school with a liberal-minded administration allowed me to progress farther than most women these days. Dear Jonathan joined me a few years later, and we've been together ever since."

"Yes," acknowledged Harris, left hand in his hair again.

Gardiner waited, giving him a chance to add some further syllable or two of explanation, but there was nothing. The man was definitely the younger of the pair, although seemingly not by the amount of time in which the father had supposedly been in Italy for Frances' childhood. Gardiner surmised that he must have met Harris' mother during the period in which he was still in Europe. Abandoning the girl to the care of others, in order to presumably marry a second wife and raise another child, struck the Doctor as vulgar and contemptuous, but he didn't voice that opinion.

"You never married, did you Doctor?" asked Frances.

Gardiner was caught slightly off guard by the question.

"Uh, no. No, my work keeps me too busy."

"I can imagine. The reputation of Quentin Gardiner is starting to become world famous."

"I find that hard to believe."

"What about your upcoming lectures in Europe?"

"Doctor Donau had more than a little influence getting that arranged, I have to say. And unfortunately, those plans are likely to be cancelled now. I can't believe we'd wrap up this…*trip* in time."

"But the end result of this *trip* will make up for that. Don't you think?"

The Divided God.

"To be sure. But I have to temper my expectations. We may only discover more questions instead of getting real answers. We won't be able to publish anything with too many unknowns hanging. Or the answers may prove to be too sensitive to reveal."

"Of course." She leaned forward. "But, in your experience, how often does a situation like that occur? Discovering the details, but not being able to publish them?"

"There are always details that aren't published. With both of your careers just beginning, you'll come to learn what should or should not be made public. As you may have guessed, it's largely the most dramatic bits that are made known. Drama brings interest, and money follows. It's always money at the root of the matter."

He didn't try to mask his feelings, the last words tinged with cynicism.

"And yet regarding your most recent expedition to Egypt," Frances said, "nothing was printed. Was there nothing noteworthy? Surely the trip was worth even a small article in a second-rate journal—something to generate interest? The University likely would have preferred *something* to nothing."

This was a delicate topic. As far as the public was concerned, they had unearthed a quite-normal mummy. But the truth was far different. It was a lich, still alive, after a fashion, but dormant. Trapped for thousands of years, it had awoken when the stars had been right. Far more dangerous than expected, they'd beheaded it, then dissolved the body in acid. It had been problematic to justify the additional expenses involved with that trip, although Higgins had helped with much of the financing. Total secrecy had not been possible, but they had covered up as much as they could with a believable story, and Gardiner saw no need to alter it now.

"Yes, I'm sure the University would have preferred *something*. Unfortunately, a combination of carelessness and miscommunication resulted in damage so extensive that the expedition was written off."

"And so, all the work was for naught?"

"It may seem strange from an outside perspective, but yes. There was a graduate student involved whose family had some degree of influence. While not entirely his fault, making the episode known would have cast him in an undesirable light and overshadowed his career."

He tried to smile in a way that implied he did not like the reality of political maneuvering—which was true enough—though it was actually the lie he was telling that troubled him.

"It was a learning experience," he finished.

"The wealthy must be treated with a special deference at times," Frances said. "But hopefully you see the good as well as the bad. The school must have a sizeable group of contributors."

"Indeed."

"Would I know any of the names?"

"Oh, yes. Rockefeller, Durant, Carnegie, Peabody, Higgins."

Some internal alarm sounded as soon as he mentioned his colleague's name. In an attempt at diversion, he quickly continued.

"Even some rich eccentric from Austria has been sending an annual contribution for decades."

Gardiner chuckled, as the thought really did amuse him, and the others joined. But the mirth did not color Jonathan Harris' eyes. He noticed the disconnect and made another attempt to get Harris to speak.

"Jonathan, did I hear a New England accent in your voice? Are you from that area?"

"Boston."

"In my experience, there's a bit of one-upmanship, between anthropologists and archaeologists. Does your father approve of your career?"

"I can't say. He died when I was young."

"Oh? I'm sorry to hear that."

Harris nodded and looked down.

"He was killed. I saw it."

He continued to hang his head for a while, Gardiner growing uncomfortable with the silence, then words suddenly poured out of him.

"My mother also died, when I was six. I can remember curly, chestnut-colored hair, and a button nose, but that's all. The Harris family took me in after I was orphaned, but they were all killed in a house fire after a few years. I decided to track my father's path backward, to Germany."

"That's enough talk of the dead," said Frances dismissively. "They're buried, and should remain so."

Harris said nothing and smoothed down his hair.

FOUR

THE DEATH OF QUENTIN GARDINER

As Frances had warned, the days that followed grew progressively wearisome. The ship from Miami to Puerto Rico was a much smaller vessel, and so more easily influenced by ocean swells. But Gardiner's constitution was up to the task, and he did not succumb to seasickness. After a short layover, the same vessel departed for Georgetown, with that final thousand ocean miles being a copy of the previous. During the trip, the seas were truly neither rough nor calm; it just took a certain amount of time to become accustomed to such a moving platform for a sound sleep. Gardiner felt that a few more days on the water would allow him to adjust, but was also grateful that he wouldn't get a chance to prove himself right.

The rainy season was underway by the time they arrived in Georgetown. In fact, it was an exceptionally heavy start to the rains that had led to the serendipitous discovery of the temple toward which they were headed. Two men were waiting for them at the dock, apparently entrusted to get the luggage off the ship. Frances exchanged only a few words with them before leading Harris and Gardiner through the dark and stormy night to a taxicab.

"We'll be leaving before dawn, Doctor," said Frances, when the cab had gotten underway. "Do get a good night's sleep."

"That shouldn't be an issue, with the floor no longer moving. And I like listening to rain while falling asleep." Lightning flashed, thunder boomed. "That's not as relaxing, however."

"The rooms will be dry, at least," said Frances. "It's not the best hotel in the area, but they recently replaced the roof, and the staff are quite proud of it."

And indeed, they were. Gardiner's knowledge of Spanish hadn't previously included the word for roof, but he learned *techo* over the course of the next ten minutes, as it was repeated numerous times by three different people. As promised, the room remained wonderfully dry through the abbreviated night of rest.

As the sun gleamed red on the horizon, they were already on the water again, moving west along the coast to the immense delta at the mouth of the Essequibo River. Above, patches of blue were visible through the broken cloud cover, but there was no doubt the sky would turn fully grey—or even black—before long, and so the motors were pushed to their maximum in order to make as much progress as possible. The pair of boats were of the same design— twenty feet long with a canopy high enough to allow standing—and each manned by two hired hands. Frances rode in one, along with the greater portion of their luggage and supplies, while the other held the two archaeologists and the remaining bags.

Some effort had been made to give the pregnant woman a fair amount of comfort: the seat was padded with towels, and the luggage had been stacked to give her a backrest. She was Queen of the Amazon, seated upon a moving throne, the two men in that boat her devoted subjects—quite devoted, seemingly. They were the ones who had met them at the dock the evening before. In the rear, the driver, Pai, checked on her at least every minute. The spotter in the bow, Forte, would likely have also been doing the same had his job not required his full attention. Gardiner knew nothing of those two except that they were from Brazil. The Portuguese they spoke was similar to Spanish, but their dialect was nearly unfathomable for the Doctor; he understood not even a tenth of what they said.

Jonathan Harris had no throne, but he refused to permit the unyielding wood of the bench seat to diminish him in any way, sitting erect at all times. Gardiner recalled the interactions he'd observed between the siblings, and the man's oddly subservient attitude toward his sister. He thought it possible that she had commanded her brother to maintain that posture, though it could just as easily have been an act of defiance on his part. Or neither. The Doctor was well-educated in a few areas, but didn't count psychology among them. One thing he did notice, though: With the speed of the boats making it pointless to keep a hat on, the wind tossed the young man's hair constantly. And never once did he reach up to smooth it down.

Gardiner managed to learn a little about the other men in his own boat. They were Pemon, from Guyana, and defaulted to their native tongue when talking with each other, but spoke enough Spanish to allow the American to ask simple questions or make his wishes known. The spotter was an affable teen nicknamed Chico, and the driver was his older cousin, Velo. These two were hired the day before by Pai. They knew very little about their route—up-river—but were pleased with the wages they'd been promised.

The initial leg of their voyage had been choppy, the ocean stained a color typical of any coastal region near a river. All of that changed when they got onto the Essequibo. The going was smoother, but the water was a nauseating, murky brown, the detritus of jungle decay having been funneled into it via countless overflowing streams. Though any bumps were magnified by the speed of their passage, it was still calm enough for Gardiner to begin sketching a crude map. After making a reasonable guess of their speed, he used his compass and pocket watch to determine direction and distance. Annotations about notable landmarks were added as well.

He made a few attempts to strike up a conversation with Harris, but the other man seemed to be lost in thought, never saying more than a few words. So, aside from updating the map at regular intervals, Gardiner watched the water and the myriad objects bobbing along in it. Mainly, logs and branches floated by. Occasionally, it was something else, but it was often impossible to focus on the thing long enough to determine what it was he'd seen. Until once, when he did. And regretted it.

"A man!"

Gardiner was sure of it. He pointed at the lifeless man just as the forces within the current turned the body over, transforming it back into another ambiguous, dark shape. Harris saw him motion, gazed at the spot, and shrugged.

"That was a dead man!" shouted Gardiner, trying to raise his voice above the noise of the engines and the rush of the wind.

"What?"

"A dead man!"

Harris nodded an acknowledgement, but only shrugged again, eliciting a frown from Gardiner.

"He's already dead," explained Harris, lifting his voice above the noise.

No other boats were visible ahead of them. Some were scattered closer to the shores, but the unlucky man couldn't have come from any of them. He must have fallen in a while ago.

"I suppose that's life on the river," muttered Gardiner. "Commonplace here. I'm not ignorant of death, but...not comfortable with it, either. We're in an untamed, dangerous part of the world."

Despite the ambient noise, Harris acted like he'd heard.

"Dangerous," he said.

"How was your previous trip to the site? Were there any deaths?"

"There's always death." The man seemed content to stop there, but he added more. "Elias was a strong man. Frances' husband. We were saddened when he succumbed."

There seemed to be some pain in those words, making the Doctor regret that he'd induced him to speak of something he was probably trying to forget.

Chico pointed to the right just then, and Velo acted on it, veering slightly to avoid the floating obstacle. Gardiner idly wondered if the young man had seen the body, and carefully made his way to the front of the boat. He got Chico's attention by tapping him on the arm, but fumbled with the translation into Spanish. The spotter spent too much precious time trying to understand what the older man was asking.

They hit something.

Though crouched down, Gardiner had little chance to maintain his balance. Spinning almost completely around, he did manage to stay upright—until his knee rapped against the gunwale. With the boat continuing to move, his feet went out from underneath him. He grabbed at a supporting strut for the canopy, but missed. Instead, his forehead clipped it and he toppled out of the boat awkwardly.

Even before Chico could react, Harris dove into the repellent water. Velo slowed the boat and circled back while Harris kept the Doctor expertly afloat. When close enough, Chico reached down and tried to pull Gardiner up by the armpits, but the dead weight of the stunned man was far too much for him.

"Wait," coughed Gardiner, shaking his head. "I need a moment."

As he gasped and blinked, Velo shouted something. Harris responded by swimming to the front of the boat. After a brief inspection, he dove under, then surfaced and made his way back.

"Sin daños," he reported up to Velo. As the other boat came close, he turned to the Doctor. "Good now?"

Gardiner closed his eyes tightly, opened them, blinked. "Yes." Grabbing the side of the boat with both hands, he drew himself up slightly, and kicked his right leg out. After hooking it over the side, Chico was able to help, pulling him in. A similar maneuver was repeated for Harris.

"What happened?" asked Frances when her boat had drawn in. Concern and annoyance fought for control of her voice.

"My fault," admitted Gardiner. "Not only did I distract Chico, I was standing when we hit something—due, of course, to my first mistake."

The two boats side-by-side, she handed him a towel. The guides held them together, engines idling.

"Thank you."

"My brother should have cautioned you," she said pointedly.

"We all live and learn," replied Gardiner, trying to deflect blame from Harris. "Consider the lesson learned. I was curious if Chico had seen the dead man. Did you?"

"A dead man? No. Are you sure it wasn't a river dolphin?"

His senses not yet entirely restored, Gardiner tried to recall what he'd seen, but couldn't.

"Perhaps," he allowed.

Very gently, he probed the bruise on his head with a fingertip. It had swollen a bit already, but that wasn't surprising given the force of the blow.

"Jonathan, I can't thank you enough. I can get around in the water fine, but you swim like a fish."

Harris shrugged.

"I've spent a fair amount of time in the ocean," he said, pulling up a pant leg. Something small and black clung to his calf. As he removed it and tossed it into the water, blood began to seep from the spot.

"You'd better check for leeches," he added.

The trip resumed at only a slightly slower pace, all on board making sure to grasp a piece of the boat at all times. For the first few hours within the massive estuary of the Essequibo, it had sometimes been hard to find any land at all. At Bartica, the last city of any size in the area, they switched onto the Mazaruni. It was a more average-sized river, although its character shifted continuously in the lower reaches. When the sluggish water pooled between distant banks, it appeared to be a lake. At other times it would be more swamp-like, with a tangle of tributaries taking varied paths through untamed jungle. And when the channel narrowed and the water sped up, it was clearly a river, and one beset with obstacles.

They made it all of the way to the first of those, Marshal Falls, before the daily deluge hit. Patience was taxed as they were forced to pass nearly an hour moored to some trees on the riverbank below the waterfall. When the rain slowed, the manual portage was accomplished efficiently, the higher water level making the operation less challenging than in the dryer parts of the year. The extra volume of water also helped with several sets of rapids that normally weren't navigable. In those cases, however, *navigable* did not equate to *easy* or *safe*. Gardiner's knuckles were white as they bounced their way up through the mercilessly swift flow.

Villages dotted the riverbanks as the boats headed south and west, and they passed a notably large outpost—Issano—after the sun had sunk below the tops of the trees. Though all day their speed had only varied between fast and reckless, they made it to their destination for the night with some light to spare. The accommodations were primitive compared to the bed in Georgetown, but a cot with mosquito netting was luxurious as far as the exhausted Gardiner was concerned, and he slept straight through until dawn.

In the morning, the bruise was still sore to the touch and there was only a slight headache. Upon emerging from his tent, he was pleased to see how large the encampment was, not having noticed much of anything in the twilight when they'd arrived. A dozen other tents had been set up within a crude perimeter of stick fencing, likely to keep the caiman out, or at least deter them. The thick foliage had been cleared, and dedicated fire pits and latrines had also been established. Shovels, picks, baskets, and other tools were also visible, nicely arrayed. In short, he was certain that a dig site was nearby.

Harris stepped out of his tent just as the Doctor's excitement grew.

"Are we here?" he asked Harris. "Is this it?"

"No."

Gardiner's face fell.

"But there is something up the hill that you must see."

"Lead on then."

They walked a good ways up a zigzag trail freshly cut with machetes, passing no one. He hadn't seen any natives in the camp either, which was odd. For any type of work in equatorial climes, there was always a bustle of activity beginning even before sunrise in order to take advantage of the cooler part of the day.

41

When the path leveled off, the pair met Frances, Pai, and Forte in a clearing that provided a nice view of the surrounding region.

"Doctor Gardiner," said Frances. "Good morning."

"Good morning."

He looked around. The hillside fell off below them, covered in resplendent shades of green, but there was nothing he judged as being different or noteworthy.

"Jonathan said that there's something here to see. What is it? It's all the same to me."

"Here?" she asked, waving her hand at the area in which they stood. "There is nothing here."

She then pointed at an area off in the distance, indicating a small opening in the trees.

"Now, that is a slightly more interesting place, however. That is the dig site that was set up over the past few weeks using the equipment you likely noticed this morning. But below that—" Her hand lowered. "That is the most interesting of all."

He picked out some landmarks, retraced his route.

"How so? Isn't that the encampment where we spent the night?"

"It is. It's also the place of your death."

FIVE

ONWARD AND ONWARD

"Excuse me?"

Frances smiled and held up a finger. Nothing happened for a few seconds, but then there was a loud *whoomp* that caused the ground to shake. As if being melted by a great flame, the area they'd been looking at dissolved in an avalanche of green and brown. Saturated by the recent rains, and given an incentive by explosives, tons of vegetation and mud swept down, leaving behind bare earth as it continued all of the way to the river. And just like that, the encampment at which they had slept no longer existed.

"There you have it, Doctor. You died there—as did we all."

"What? But why?"

"Secrecy," Frances said, smiling again. "Doctor Donau made it very clear that we must take all necessary precautions to keep the true reason for this trip hidden for as long as possible. Everyone will be searching for us here while we continue onward. He knows the truth and will ensure that we are listed as missing instead of dead."

"But you just obliterated one archaeological site for the purpose of concealing another."

He fought to keep his voice level; the mere thought rankled him to the core.

"No." She shook her head emphatically. "It was faked. A few bits of pottery were planted—just enough to merit an encampment. Most of the workers left two days ago, after setting everything up. Only a small staff was left behind—"

43

Gardiner's eyes lit up as he heard that, and again scoured the devastation.

"—but they're currently conducting a native ceremony of some kind." She pointed off into the distance. "No one was there when that mass swept through."

He took a deep breath and tried to absorb the situation. It was still early, and to start the day with something like this was unnerving. He looked at the others. The two guides gazed back blankly. Her brother was also silent, but nodded as if to confirm her words. Yet despite this almost unbelievable turn of events, he found his thoughts turning to The Divided God, and the promise of learning heretofore forgotten knowledge. The thought helped to calm him.

"This is unorthodox to say the least," he said at last. "It is difficult to accept."

"If you had left a family behind, some other plan would have been formulated. Considering all of the factors, it seemed as if this scenario would work to everyone's advantage. Shall we go?"

He nodded numbly and fell in line. His legs moved mechanically as thoughts of friends and colleagues filled his mind. How would they react to the news of his death? Even if Doctor Donau could legally have them declared as missing, for any who heard the news, *missing in the jungles of Guyana* effectively meant the same as *dead*. He wondered how long he would have to remain here. Six months? A year? He had made preparations to be away for that long, but it was the deception that bothered him. What would happen when he returned? He would be forced to either admit the truth, or continue the lie somehow. Trying to think through the repercussions of each tactic, and the impacts upon the people he knew, was too taxing. There were too many variables in too many scenarios. Frustrated over trying to guess how dozens of people might react, he dismissed the tangle of what-ifs. His mind emptied of thoughts, one returned. These days, it always did.

The Divided God.

He imagined himself famous, another Hiram Bingham, discovering a previously unknown civilization hidden in the jungles of the

New World. Any future decisions would have to wait, he decided. He was here, now. He had a job to do. He may as well do it.

It was only after the group had reached the very bottom that Gardiner was afforded a good view of the destruction. And his heart nearly stopped. The artifact—the one he had received from Doctor Donau—had been in a sturdy briefcase and continually by his side up until he had left it in his tent to hike up the hillside. Now, he could no longer point to the place where his tent had been. If he'd had some warning, he wouldn't have left it behind to be buried under the mud.

He was still trying to find the right words to describe the turn of events when their group met up with the remaining guides. Velo was sweating heavily and taking deep breaths, as if recovering from a great exertion. He handed over some very expensive-looking binoculars to Jonathan Harris. Chico also held something in his hands—a bag with handles, roughly woven from leaves. He gave it to Gardiner. It was heavy, and the Doctor received one of the more pleasant shocks of his life when he looked inside and saw the piece of marble.

"How did you know?" he asked Chico eagerly. "Como supiste?"

The young man pointed at Frances.

"No, Doctor, we did not forget about that priceless item," she said. "I told him to check through your tent for anything particularly valuable, but specifically for the stone. Your empty briefcase and some personal effects of ours were left behind on purpose to provide some evidence that we had spent the night. One boat was moved out of the way before the mudslide hit, and the other was left in place to be swamped by the floe. Rescuers should spend plenty of time searching the area between here and Issano. No one should go upriver."

They set off upstream along the riverbank with Pai and Forte in the lead, Chico and Velo in the rear covering their trail. It was a fifteen-minute walk, but at no point did Chico stop talking. Without the drone of the engine and twenty feet of boat separating him from the only family member within dozens of miles, he seemed to feel the need to catch up on all of the conversation he missed out on the day before. But it was a one-sided affair. Velo was much like Jonathan Harris, largely just listening, and would either grunt or nod in response, although he would speak up when needed to direct or correct his younger cousin.

When the group came upon a pair of boats moored to the shore, it answered Gardiner's unasked question of how they were going to continue if only one had been saved. The boat in which Frances had ridden, with the bulk of their supplies and luggage, was there. The new one was a few feet longer and held an assortment of baskets, screens and tools thrown haphazardly into it. It also looked as if the luggage from the other boat was there as well, underneath the equipment. Based on Velo's tone and gestures, he was very unhappy with Chico for not loading the boat in a more orderly fashion. They argued intermittently while taking time to organize the gear, after which Harris and Gardiner climbed in.

Both boats were on their way as the rain started. It was unrelenting. Everyone on the boats, including Frances, took turns bailing. After a full day, they stopped for a rest at a temporary camp their guides created from nothing more than branches and leaves.

That night was easily the most miserable that Gardiner could ever recall out of many spent in the forgotten realms through which he'd travelled. They slept in hammocks, in itself a tolerable activity, but blustery winds kept rearranging the awning of leaves he was positioned beneath. No sooner would he fall asleep than he would subsequently be awakened by dripping water.

Or by a nightmare.

Even on less stressful nights the experience beneath Copp's Hill would sometimes play through his mind, but with the twisted surreality of dreams enhancing the original terror. Waking him every time, the panic it induced was usually short-lived, costing only a few minutes of sleep, until his heart slowed and a warm bed negated the ugly memory of damp earth squeezing the life out of him. The suffocation had never been real before—until this time. The waking world collided with the stuff of nightmare when a handful of water drained down directly onto his nose. He woke, terrified and cough-ing.

Air!

He spat and hacked until he was finally able to breathe normally again. The rest of the group seemed to have slept through the out-burst.

While repairing the awning, he glumly questioned the decision to follow through with the elaborate deception. His few available options were reviewed, the merits of each weighed. In the end, there was but one answer: He could not possibly back out now. Changing his mind would mean that one of the boats would be needed to transport him back down the river. That in itself would slow the research effort. Also, his presence without Jonathan and Frances would lead to troublesome inquiries. It wouldn't be long before any web of lies dissolved, making public the highly sensitive nature of their excursion, inevitably luring others. In the end, he'd probably learn the truth behind his obsession, but wouldn't share the glory. On the contrary, he might be ostracized, especially by his elderly mentor, a man who had thought highly enough of him to hand him this very special opportunity. No, Gardiner decided that he'd have to bear it out to the bitter end.

SIX

THE TEMPLE

The steady rain continued past dawn, testing Gardiner's resolve. But his patience was rewarded when the clouds broke mid-morning. Despite the stifling heat and humidity, the high equatorial sun helped to dispel the dampness in their clothing and lift their spirits. They had travelled mainly northwest for all of the previous day and most of the morning, but then the river's course had turned sharply south. A few more hours of travel brought them within view of another waterfall, off in the distance.

"Which are those?" Gardiner asked Harris, pointing at the thundering water.

"Peaima Falls."

"Are we headed up there?"

The falls weren't overly impressive or very tall, but the river gorge turned alarmingly rocky ahead. Maneuvering the larger of the two boats through the churning water and up the steep cliffs looked to be a daunting task.

Harris shook his head, and pointed off to the left. As usual, the jungle was a blanket of green, but a few miles beyond the edge of the river a distinctive feature poked up through. As was not uncommon with the geography in the region, the higher ground was a *tepui*—a plateau set high above the surrounding land on nearly vertical sandstone walls. The top of this formation was only about two thousand feet above the jungle floor, relatively low for a typical tepui, and looked to have about the same diameter as height.

Hugging the left side of the river, the boats slowed. From his spotter position Forte searched within the thick bushes. After untangling some vines and branches, he jumped onto the bank and tugged on one side of the mass to reveal the mouth of a smaller stream, cleverly camouflaged. When both boats were through the opening, he knotted everything back together and made an effort to remove signs of their passage.

The higher water once again worked to their advantage, letting them penetrate upstream for nearly a mile, a course typically impassable for most of the year. The way narrowed until the larger boat could go no farther. They moored at a spot where Frances could easily climb out.

With each of the men carrying as much as they could handle, they set out on foot. The vegetation was very thick initially, but opened up a little as they went. Through small holes in the canopy, Gardiner spied a bare streak slicing through the green. Based on the note from Doctor Donau, he felt sure that the temple was located somewhere near it.

"The smaller boats used on the previous trips were able to penetrate farther up the creek," Frances explained, "though the jungle is now reclaiming the trail."

She stopped and listened, then looked up at the clouding sky through a gap in the leaves. Gardiner glanced up in time to see a shape cross the sky. It was large enough to briefly cover the sun.

"Pai," she said. "Chuva?"

In the lead, the two Brazilians stopped, sniffed the air, and conferred before nodding to her.

"More rain is imminent," she said. "We should make haste."

By increasing their pace, they were able to make it to the camp before the first drops fell. It was crude compared to the one destroyed by the landslide downriver, but it was plain that effort had been expended in setting up the shelters: lean-tos and covered hammocks for sleeping, and a solidly constructed central meeting area that could serve as kitchen, dining room, and research facility. In the middle of that last one sat a table of light-colored wood, clearly of

European or North American manufacture. An islet of civilization within the expanse of chaotic jungle, its presence was jarring, but still gave comfort to the eyes. It must have been an effort to haul it all the way from Georgetown, but Gardiner was pleased to know that there would be a nice, flat surface upon which to work when needed. In contrast, surrounding the table was a hodgepodge collection of chairs and stools constructed of tree limbs, each lashed together with vines.

"May we talk about the site now?" asked Gardiner, making an effort to use a humorous tone. "I think it's safe to say that no one is eavesdropping on us."

He took a seat on one of the stools.

Frances looked at the Doctor, then glanced up toward the roof of the shelter.

"That depends," she said, signaling Forte with a finger. He also looked up and began to move toward Gardiner.

"On what?"

Forte drew his knife, causing Gardiner to react with a jerk. That movement was enough to trigger a strike from the anaconda that had been lowering itself from the rafters. It nearly connected, but Forte drove his blade up through its lower jaw, changing its trajectory. Velo was close enough to get a good grip right behind the head, holding it still. Pai delivered the death strike with two hands, his own blade penetrating the skull to the hilt. The serpent went limp.

"On how you define eavesdropping," said Frances with a playful smile, but Gardiner saw as much fear in her features as he felt.

With the body of the snake repeatedly wrapped back upon itself, there was no way to tell how long it truly was. Chico got into the rafters with a boost from his cousin and began to disentangle it.

"Snake for dinner, Frances," said Harris. "It's been a while."

It was a rare occasion, Harris actually speaking up without being prompted. Brother and sister looked at each other, sharing a memory.

"Sierra Leone," she laughed. "I really hated that man. A pity we don't have his wine cellar to pick from for this meal. You paired the python with a Chardonnay, I recall."

"There was more oak in it than I would have preferred, but still it went well with the wild garlic."

When they grinned at each other, Gardiner felt that he understood Jonathan Harris a little better. His sister obviously cared deeply for him. The recent death of her husband, added to the combined stresses of her pregnancy and the expedition, simply made her much more demanding at the moment. He was tolerating her abusive personality because he knew that, in a few months, she would be a much different person—back to normal.

"Have you ever tasted snake, Doctor?" asked Frances.

"Frankly," admitted Gardiner, "I can't say for sure. I've had my share of stews and the like over the years, never sure of what was in them. Often, I just eat whatever is handed me. Most times, it's very good. Only once did I get sick."

"Pai knows best how to prepare the local fauna, so he'll do most of the cooking, but Jonathan excels at it. He knows how to coax the flavors out." She looked at her brother. "I believe that ostrich was the best you've ever done. I can still taste it."

"I was very happy with that, myself," said Harris.

"Ostrich? Is it like chicken or duck?" asked Gardiner.

"Far from it," said Harris, his face lighting up with the recollection. "It's more like beef. We had a Merlot. The wine was nothing special by itself, and too sweet, actually—"

THUD!

Freed by Chico, the greater bulk of snake fell to the ground behind them, narrowly missing Gardiner's head. Frances' eyes flashed.

Chico jumped down.

"Lo siento, lo siento," he apologized to Gardiner.

Before the Doctor could respond, Velo tore into his cousin with some choice words in their familial language. The young man's face turned red. Gardiner was embarrassed to witness the disciplining. He tried to divert attention by asking the men to straighten out the snake as much as possible. He then measured the thing using the device he'd brought along.

"Seventeen feet," he said to no one in particular.

It wasn't long afterward that the downpour slowed to a drizzle. Three of the guides went back to the boats to haul back more of the supplies. Pai stayed behind, displaying a protective interest in Frances, as if he were her personal bodyguard. Gardiner continued to feel the vibration of the boat motor in his body, and he tried to work it out by alternately pacing and stretching, but knew that a more vigorous exercise was needed after sitting still for the larger part of the past few days. When the men returned with the first load of supplies and set out again for another trip, he was quick to volunteer.

"Jonathan, we're running out of daylight. One more trip should do it if we both go along."

The younger man stood up to leave, but paused.

"Frances, we're both going to help get the last of the supplies. Will you be all right?"

He smoothed his hair. Only after she looked over and showed her approval did he move. The tension between the two had returned already.

After hustling to catch up to the others, they walked along the jungle path in silence. Upon reaching the creek, Forte got into the boat and began handing out bags to Velo. While waiting his turn, Gardiner decided to try once more to get Harris to interact.

"You seem to truly enjoy a good meal, Jonathan. Is there any particular flavor you're partial to?"

"I—"

Gardiner saw what looked like irritation on Harris, but so very brief, immediately replaced with a wide smile. His body also relaxed.

"Food preparation is akin to a symphony. The flavors should be subtle. All the players need to be in tune, the score designed so as to let each shine their brightest. When one is too strong, the rest are cancelled out."

"I concur, but my palate isn't particularly sensitive. I know what I like, but often can't say what I taste."

"It's just a matter of training," insisted Harris. "Any palate can be educated, given enough time."

Chico moved off with his load, following Velo down the path, and Gardiner stepped forward.

"Well, I'm past fifty," he said as he was handed some supplies. "If I haven't learned by now, I may never."

"I'll see what I can do about that," offered Harris.

Even the drizzle stopped as they finished that final trip. With the clouds dispersing as the sun set, the stars prominent points of light in the darkening sky, a much better night for sleeping seemed to be in store than the previous. The dinner of anaconda was delicious, though there were plenty of bones to either eat around or crunch through. Harris described many subtle flavors to Gardiner, who tried his best, but really identified less than half.

Based on his past experiences in the wild, Gardiner assumed that the four natives would rotate watch through the night to be on the lookout for jaguar, but Frances said that it would not be necessary. Speaking at length about the cleansing effect of the rain to negate their scents, as well as geographic obstacles, hunting ranges and the relative amount of food available at that time of year, she convinced him that no such precautions were needed.

Only Chico was as apprehensive as Gardiner, and the young man added a new fear to the American's list: Mapinguari. Velo laughed when he overheard Chico describing the legendary bipedal creature of South America. But the ribbing sounded hollow, as if the man harbored some belief in its existence.

With some effort, Gardiner was able to rid himself of his fears, both old and new, but that left an empty spot in his mind that rapidly filled with speculations of what the following day would bring.

The Divided God.

The mantra, once introduced, played over and over for entirely too long, but exhaustion from the previous night caught up. The last thought he had before sleep overtook him was how unusually quiet the jungle seemed to have become.

Gardiner would have been content to start the day with just a cup of crude, native coffee, but Frances forced him to slow down and eat: some fruit and nuts, plus leftover anaconda.

"We must all keep our strength up in this heat," she insisted. After she judged that everyone had eaten their fill did she allow the group to set out for the site.

Seen from a distance, tepuis seem to rise straight out ground, but they are surrounded by foothills at the bottom, rising at relatively shallow angles from the jungle floor to meet the vertical walls a few dozens or hundreds of feet up.

The bare streak Gardiner had noticed on their way to the camp the day before was on such a hillside. Approaching from the east, their sight of it was blocked by a wall of antediluvian stone. As they came around the corner of that obscuring wall, Gardiner got a good look at the denuded landscape. Thousands of feet above, tree roots and vines dangled over an edge of freshly exposed rock at the very top. It seemed obvious that a section had splintered off and fallen, causing a slide similar to the one that had been artificially created downriver with explosives.

"There it is, Doctor," said Frances.

Part of the way up the slope, expertly cut blocks poked out of the earth, an incongruous, angular creation imposed upon the natural background. Frances stayed back, with Pai at her side. It was filthy work for the others, wending their way through piles of debris, then clambering up and over slippery rocks and mud, but they eventually found themselves standing before it. Or, part of it, anyway.

Only a section of wall and the top of a curved arch to the left were exposed, the arch protruding out from the wall about two feet. All else was buried under mud. With the top of the arch at chest level, it was likely that they were standing atop at least six feet of compacted mud, stones, and vegetable matter.

54

"The greater part of it is underground, isn't it?" asked Gardiner. "We're not going to uncover a complete temple here, just a doorway."

"That seems to be the case," agreed Harris. He pointed behind the arch. "We should only need to excavate some of that material to be sure."

From a knapsack on Forte's back he removed the artifact that had been mailed to Gardiner.

"But see for yourself, Doctor. There's only one place where this could have come from."

Hands trembling, Gardiner accepted the stone. Two pieces of marble facing had been knocked off an underlying sandstone base: a central piece at the top of the arch, and the one to its right. What he held in his hands was undoubtedly the former, and as he moved it closer it was plain that the piece would fit precisely—and it did. The bumps and dips on the back of the stone matched up with complimentary dips and bumps on the exposed sandstone, as if part of a three-dimensional jigsaw puzzle. It stayed firmly in place even after he released his grip.

"Indeed," was his only, breathless comment.

The five men spent most of the first day testing the stability of the area by digging small test holes for quite a distance up the hillside. Having been buried alive once, Gardiner wanted no part of that again. Once he felt confident with the results of their probes, he and Harris began to focus on the temple itself, while the remaining men undertook the back-breaking task of creating a path through the compacted rubble of the landslide. Aside from the goal of making travel safer, emphasis was placed upon drainage of the ever-present rainwater.

Spending the second day digging into the area above and behind the arch, the two archaeologists were able to confirm their theory about the structure being embedded underground. Below the newly-fallen material was a layer of accumulated jungle decay, but under that was undisturbed earth, then stone. As there was no need

55

to spend more time there, they shifted attention to the area in front of the archway. The other missing piece of marble facing was located before long, and after cleaning it off, Gardiner placed that one in its slot as well. The central stone was the only one with any marks on it.

Before heading back to the camp at the end of that day, Gardiner walked a good distance further west to get a different perspective on the site. One detail stood out to him right away: About sixty degrees further around the circumference, an escarpment rose at an unnatural angle up from the jungle floor to within about two hundred feet of the rim. The sight bedeviled the geologist in him because it was inconsistent with what he knew of tepuis. With it being too far away to easily reach, and Frances considering it to have no bearing on the business at hand, he was forced to file it away as another oddity to be resolved later.

And so began days of the less exciting side of archaeology: the pure drudgery of digging, moving and sifting. The men were diligent in their study of the excavated material, but found nothing. The environment of South America wasn't conducive to the preservation of organic matter, but there weren't even any bits of cookware or the like. It wasn't totally unexpected, as the front of a temple wasn't an appropriate place for a midden, but there was nothing that looked remotely like a decoration that might have fallen off the exterior. What was slowly exposed was utilitarian and featureless, with the single exception of that cuneiform inscription in the one stone.

Once a safe path was cleared, Frances joined the men in front of the temple and took charge of the sifting. She also directed the work of the native guides in fluent Portuguese and Spanish. Actually, Gardiner had to admit to himself, she took over *everything*. He was supposed to be leading the expedition, and initially she phrased her guidance in such a way as to let him counter or override it, but he never did. Before long, she had them working efficiently and bore the mantle of responsibility well. For that, Gardiner was grateful and let her have at it. Not having been in the field for a dig of this type in several years, he was enjoying himself and wanted to concentrate on the minutiae of what was being uncovered.

Unable to know what the young woman was going through, Gardiner reflected on the difficulties inherent with just the pain of an occasionally creaky back, and he marveled at her willpower. Never once did she groan or complain, although Pai was ever at her beck and call to handle any lifting, or guide her through patches that remained slippery despite their efforts. And Frances' presence right there with them meant that Pai was able to contribute as well. With all seven working at the site, progress was swift.

Aiding the group, the temple faced west—exactly west, as far as Gardiner could tell with the compass he'd brought along. With the mass of the tepui blocking the morning sun, and a thick jungle canopy to screen them in the afternoon, there were a couple of hours in mid-day with the sun directly overhead when work slowed or even stopped. Frances did not hide the fact that she expected hard efforts from every one of them, even Doctor Gardiner. But she was also a realist, and made it clear she knew that weakened, sick, and dead men get far less done than those who are healthy.

In a little over a week, the years of accumulated filth were removed from in front of the arch, revealing a pair of massive stone doors beneath it. The arch was a perfect semicircle and the tops of the doors were curved to fit snugly against its contour. Each door was a slab of the native sandstone. The workmanship was extraordinary, with nearly invisible gaps between the doors themselves, and also between the doors and frame. A flagstone patio—roughly twenty feet wide by ten deep—was also revealed in front of the door, the workmanship still skillful, but more *normal* in appearance. That is, it truly looked as if it was thousands of years old, with some stones having cracked or settled unevenly over the course of what was guessed to be millennia. In contrast, the vertical elements—arch, doors, and walls—were all in staggeringly good condition, seemingly immune to the weathering and decay-inducing effects of unceasing moisture.

Frances hadn't allowed any attempt to open the doors until every last bit of dirt was removed. But, finally, the cleared area fairly glistened. It was time. Anticipation was high as lots were drawn to see who would be the one to open the doors. Chico won. With no knobs or handles, the only option was to push. He tried, at first casually, then with all his might. Nothing happened. The other men also tried, in singles and pairs, until all were struggling with their combined might to increase the size of the infinitesimal crack between the two slabs. Despite the many attempts, there wasn't so much as a quiver. They may as well have been pushing against a solid wall, thought Gardiner sourly. No hinges were visible, either; they were assuming that the large blocks beneath the arch were doors, meant to somehow be moved.

After those failures some effort was made to excavate beyond the outer edge of the patio, but nothing of note was found. For Gardiner the roadblock was a normal part of the job—another riddle to be solved—but Frances had a different view of the matter. Getting inside the temple seemed to be a necessity for her, and she made no effort to disguise her mounting irritation at their lack of progress. When Harris stepped backwards and accidentally knocked a few trowels down the hillside, he watched them tumble and slide, but made no move. That inaction was something she seemed to have been waiting for.

"You fucking imbecile! Go get them!"

His shoulders tensed for one second. Two. Then relaxed. Then slumped. As Gardiner had come to expect, Harris' hand shot up to his scalp reflexively. But this time, the unwashed palm, moist with sweat, stained his forehead with a muddy streak. He started down to retrieve the tools.

For Gardiner, the woman's obstinate need to solve this conundrum had gotten out of hand.

"Frances," he probed, gently.

Part of the way down the slope, Harris froze.

Frances turned toward Gardiner.

"This…mystery…of the doors is vexing us all. I certainly don't want to spend any more time in the jungle than needed, but these kinds of things happen. I assume you've made plans for the birth. Do you think it time to put this work aside? Your health, and your child's health, are far more important than what is waiting on the other side of that slab."

"Tell me, *Doctor* Gardiner," said Frances. "Does your formal training include obstetrics, or even general medicine?"

"It does not."

"Then I would like to think that I—after having lived a lifetime in it so far—may perhaps know my own body better than you."

When she whirled and strode away, Gardiner absently removed his hat and began to reach up—but caught himself in time.

No! She'll not have me doing that, too.

SEVEN

DECIPHERING THE MYSTERY

"What are we missing?" asked Gardiner for at least the tenth time. He stared at the smooth, blank stones before him.

Harris, seated on the ground, only shrugged and looked down.

The Doctor didn't bother enumerating once again the various attempts they had made over the past days to open the doors, or the areas they had searched for hidden levers. No markings or grooves were evident, even after going over every square inch of the exposed area with a magnifying glass. At Frances' *suggestion*, they had even repeated that wearisome task.

Thankfully, she had left for the day with the four guides, and the two men had a rare opportunity to relax without her demanding presence.

"Are you in any hurry to get back to camp for dinner?" Gardiner asked.

Harris responded with a single shake of the head. He seemed to have fallen into a semi-comatose state: alive, but evidently so miserable as to be nearly lifeless.

The evening was cooler than average, and dry, unlike many recent days. The refreshing breeze was welcome, even relaxing. Gardiner joined the other man on the ground and regarded the structure. Problem solving of this sort had rarely been required of him through his career. Fitting together pieces of the puzzle was fine when the pieces were there to see on a table. In this case, the puzzle had already been built; the picture just needed to be transformed somehow—twisted or rotated—in order to make sense.

"We need something different," he muttered. "Something out of the ordinary."

The only option he knew they hadn't tried was to apply some form of magic, but that was admittedly the weakest part of his background. In his study of the *Necronomicon*, he'd come across many ceremonies, but he knew they were nothing for a novice to play with, and so wisely hadn't. Both Sybil Hastings and Patrick Mac-Nulty had tried to teach him simpler spells, but it never worked for him. His mind was too grounded in the more *conventional* sciences. Suggesting the use of magic to another scientist was usually a fast way to ridicule, but the question needed to be asked.

"Are you…familiar with…the concept of…magic…as a real, scientific phenomenon?" he asked, then held his breath.

Harris nodded.

"Good. As am I. But I have no real experience in its use. I've come across mentions—as every archaeologist must—but I've never—"

"What comparisons can you make between this site and the one in Mosul?"

Gardiner was stunned. He looked over at Harris, who continued to hang his head. That sentence was easily the longest that the man had uttered all day, if not longer.

"Where you found the other plaque with the same message," he added, still looking down.

"Oh. Yes. That. I'm afraid that…no comparison can be made." He hesitated before continuing, "I've rarely told anyone aside from Doctor Donau the truth before, but withholding any information now may prevent us from finding the answer."

That pronouncement stirred some life in Harris. He looked over at the older man and waited.

"I didn't find that plaque. A tomb robber did. When my research team crossed his path, he had a sack full of treasures. One of the guides in my party was so outraged that he killed him before we could learn anything. The man did leave behind enough of a trail that we were able to ascertain where he'd been, though. We followed his tracks to the base of an outcropping we had already searched. It took a large effort to even locate the door: a well-balanced stone that could be tipped to the right, revealing a hole large enough for a man to crawl through.

"Inside, there were dozens of burial chambers hewn into the walls of a catacomb. The thief must have been systematically raiding it for a long time, removing a few items on each trip, as it was nearly empty of everything except mummified bodies. Although it was fairly simple to infer the original owners and placement of nearly all of the stolen items, that piece was the one for which we could not. Or rather, we did deduce where it had been, based on the evidence."

Gardiner hated speaking of this detail most of all.

"But in my opinion, that item didn't belong within that group of tombs. Yet it could not have come from anywhere else. Even if I had been the one to find it in there, I'd have doubted my sanity."

Both men watched the stars emerge from the dark blue velvet overhead.

"Have you heard of *Das Halbierte Kind*?" asked Harris after a few minutes.

"I have." It took Gardiner some effort to remember where he'd come across the term, and he nearly shuddered when he did. "*Unaussprechlichen Kulten*. You're familiar with that terrible book?"

There was a grunt and a nod.

"There were two mentions in there, as I recall. Why d–? You think there's a connection to *The Divided God*? How long have you thought this?"

Harris didn't answer for such a long time that Gardiner almost asked again. At length he said simply: "Today."

Gardiner quoted as best he could a passage from that haunted tome that seemed to be relevant:

"Is it better to show more respect to the parent who is absent, or the child who is present? Favor from the parent is paramount. The parent will know—even in absentia—of your respect for the Halved

Child; that, in turn, yields favor. I say again: Worship the child, and the parent will know of your devotion to them."

It was oddly worded, as the final plural *them* implied a reference back to the singular *child*. However, if the child were *halved*, as *Halbierte* implied, then the plural form of the word would make sense—in a macabre way. Of course, a more conventional interpretation would be that the word *them* referred to the pair consisting of parent plus child. However, conventional—or sane—thought processes were never a hallmark of the cultists. But to be fair, it took intelligence to record such observations. Though not a guarantee, intelligence implied some kind of internal consistency, given the correct perspective. As he had come to know all too well, truths were indeed hidden in those forbidden tomes. Recognizing—or understanding—the truths was the hard part.

"That was a keen insight, Jonathan. Do you think it will help us open the door?"

"No."

The moon shone above the treetops, nearly full, illuminating the polished stone of the arch. The lettering on the central piece glimmered slightly with the moonlight striking at a unique angle, something more easily noticed from where they sat in the semidarkness.

When the Doctor's stomach growled loudly enough to be heard even above the incessant insect chatter, he stood and patted his belly.

"We'd better go and eat. Your sister will want us to keep our strength up." He smiled wryly and added, "We may need to concoct a story to explain our tardiness. Perhaps some aspect of the arch looked peculiar in the fading light."

"There is a *slight* glow," said Harris as he also stood up and began turning down toward the path.

"Did you notice that too? I couldn't decide if it was a glow or a reflection of the moonlight."

The Divided God.

Gardiner started to follow Harris, but on a whim, went back and stopped in front of the doors. Eyes closed, bowing slightly, and in the most solemn tone he could manage, he said, "All praise to the one who is two."

Smiling at his silliness, he turned away and started down the path again, but stopped after taking just one step. Harris was pointing at the temple.

Gardiner looked.

The doors had silently opened, revealing an interior choked with inky shadow.

"Stay here," said Harris. "I'll get them."

He ran off.

Gardiner studied what he could see of the interior, but all that was visible was a hallway made of the same smooth, unblemished stone. The doors were not there. If hinges had been used, the edges would still be evident, implying that they had either retracted into the walls, or had somehow been completely removed. Some bizarre trick of light was also in play, as impenetrable darkness began a short distance beyond the opening; he could see only about six feet in, if that.

Despite the relief of getting past the doors, the wait for the others was maddening. He had an awful feeling that they would close again. Obviously, if it did happen, the first thing to try would be to repeat that same phrase. But how had that even worked? It was an innocuous action, spontaneously birthed from a combination of the dark of the night, an empty stomach, a restful breeze, and general exhaustion. Could a different set of factors have caused him to make the same attempt? Possibly. MacNulty had once told him, 'Results come not from thinking you've tried everything, but actually trying everything.' Once again, the adage had been proven true.

When the group showed up, he was pleased to see that dinner had been brought along for him. The soup had cooled, so he was able to gulp it down while brother and sister studied the opening. The four guides were also invited to look closely, being warned to keep their bodies entirely outside. Multiple torches were placed around to ensure the maximum amount of light could penetrate, but they were unable to see beyond six feet deep no matter what was done. Afterward, they compared notes: No one had noticed anything the others had missed.

Gardiner fully expected Frances to make the decision about what to do next, but it seemed she was waiting for him to make the first move. So, he did.

"Let's try this first," he said, reaching down for a rock about the size of a golf ball. With a flourish, he directed everyone away from the opening, and lightly tossed it through.

It vanished.

From the trajectory, it should have landed about a foot inside, within the lit area, then clattered along the stone floor as it rolled into shadow. Instead, the rock had been gone from sight as soon as it broke the plane of the opening. And despite the chatter of the nighttime jungle, they should have heard *something*.

The incongruity between expected and actual unsettled the scientist, but his mind found an answer that made sense.

"Illusion," said Gardiner. "Look."

Getting a torch from Velo, he knelt down low and held his left arm out, the torch behind it. The shadow was visible on the temple wall, but cut off right at the doorway. It should have continued through to be seen inside the entrance, but no manipulation of the torch or his arm would produce any bit of shadow past the edge.

"And so, it comes to this. One of us must enter the temple blindly." He looked from one sibling to the other, recalling the conversation with Harris. "You wouldn't happen to know of any…nonstandard…way to detect a trap, would you?"

Frances raised her eyebrows, seemingly surprised by the question.

"I do not. Neither does Jonathan."

Harris clenched his jaw and smoothed his hair.

Gardiner nodded. He hadn't expected any sort of useful response, but, as per MacNulty's *Rule of Trying Everything*, the question had needed to be asked. And so, barring anything magical or miraculous, there were few options. He mulled them over, made a decision.

"I'm not looking forward to discovering how painfully fatal a five thousand year old booby trap can be," he said, "but I'll volunteer to go in. You two have full lives and careers ahead of you."

"Nonsense," said Frances. "One of the guides can do it."

Gardiner bit down on his lip to hold in the first words that came to mind.

"I'm not exactly *comfortable* with telling one of these men to possibly doom himself for our betterment."

"There is no reason why he cannot also be bettered. They are being paid a good wage, but it is a pittance compared to our total expenses. We can easily afford ten times the amount to whichever one volunteers."

Gardiner considered the suggestion.

"Agreed," he said reluctantly. "But if no one volunteers, I'll go."

Frances detailed the offer to the four natives. Three of them shook their heads. Chico scratched at his chin and thought, weighing the potential small fortune against the dark unknown.

"Lo peligroso?" he asked Gardiner.

How dangerous?

Gardiner knew of one occasion when a trap mechanism had survived the centuries and someone had been impaled in the leg. The resulting wound wasn't grievous, but the poisoned tip had been covered in a protective layer of oil, preventing full evaporation. The poor man had suffered for two days before succumbing. Even if they'd been able to transport him to a decent facility in time, the nature of the poison would have been anyone's guess; there would have been no way to treat him effectively. Other traps he had found during his career were less lethal, having been deactivated by the passage of time, or only resulting in smaller injuries, such as a broken wrist or sprained ankle.

"I don't know," he shrugged. "Ah, sorry. No lo sé."

The young man studied the arch.

"Yo voy."

"Okay," sighed Gardiner, not liking the response, but accepting it.

Velo also made it clear to Chico that he didn't approve, but the younger man refused to listen. Gardiner interpreted Chico's pointed rebuttal as: *I'm a man! It's my decision!* Velo stopped trying, threw his hands up in the air, and backed away.

The six of them stepped to the edges of the patio to allow Chico a clear path to enter, and potentially exit if that option presented itself. He took a deep breath, walked straight in…and disappeared. It seemed to Gardiner as if the transition had been natural and even, but in the flickering light of the torches, he couldn't be sure.

Tense seconds ticked by. Then Chico's disembodied hand waved in the air at about shoulder level, eliciting a chorus of screams. A moment later he stepped wholly back out.

"Que no me escuchas?" he asked.

"No, we didn't hear you," responded Gardiner, shaking his head. Relieved at the young man's safety, he added, "No sólo el diez. Veinte!"

The young man's eyes flew open wide.

"Viente!"

Frances pursed her lips at the Doctor's unilateral generosity in doubling the payment, but said nothing.

Gardiner was about to ask who wanted to go next when he noticed the faintest of smiles flicker across Harris' features. Then, it was gone, and he walked boldly through the doorway. His disappearance wasn't a surprise, but his unannounced action caught everyone off guard. Frances scowled.

Suddenly, the rock Gardiner had thrown in earlier came rolling out, stopping near her feet, followed by Harris.

"Amazing!" he exclaimed. "It's more than just an illusion. It must also block all sound, as Chico indicated. I shouted very loudly, but you didn't react at all."

"No," said Gardiner. "We neither heard nor saw anything."

"There is no hallway at all. It immediately opens up into a much larger space. We'll need some torches to explore it thoroughly. And like a one-way mirror, images from out here go through, though nothing from inside is visible out here."

"Should the rest of us try then?" asked Frances.

"Yes," said Gardiner. "Please do—one at a time. I'll go last. I was the one who opened it. I fear my entry may cause it to close."

Frances went next, then the three remaining guides, each entering, pausing briefly, and coming back out. Finally, Gardiner entered. The doorway remained open behind him.

The interior was just as Harris had described: a largish room, spotlessly clean, with walls he judged to be ten feet high. In fact, the stonework looked as if it had been cut and laid into place only days before. He paused to relish the cooler temperature. Looking around, he was able to pick out an altar in the center of the floor. There was absolutely nothing to hear, but the faintest of breezes from somewhere farther inside carried a subtle and vaguely familiar vapor past his nose. He tried to identify it, but, try as he might, couldn't. At least, not without a slow, deep inhale.

"There's an odor of seawater inside," he said right after rejoining the others.

"The ocean is over a hundred miles away," noted Frances. "Any water we find in there must be fresh."

"Did you not smell it?"

"I smelled *something*," she said. "Perhaps some jungle decomposition that has a profile reminiscent of sea water."

"That could be a possibility," he said. "Or even a source of fresh water running over a salt deposit, creating a saline pool."

"Surely there'll be many odd things to figure out. We've all entered and exited without incident. It seems to be safe enough. Shall we explore?"

"Yes, but I'm going to suggest one precaution: One of the three of us should remain outside at all times, along with at least one of the guides. If the door closes, that person should theoretically be able to open it again by uttering the phrase chiseled into the arch."

And thus began the investigation, by torchlight. Frances took the first shift outside, reexamining the doorway, while Gardiner and Harris went in. The first sweep of the interior revealed an inscription, again in cuneiform, on the east wall. Gardiner spent his time studying the altar, that lone decoration breaking up the otherwise empty room, while Harris concentrated on the western wall. After only an hour, the already long day began to have an effect on the Doctor. He knew, even without Frances' speaking up, how vital rest was. It was he who proposed that they stop for the night.

Although it was blessedly cool inside, it got to be too much after a while. Gardiner guessed it to be about sixty degrees, maybe lower. The fact that the temperature remained a constant, even right next to the opening, confused him utterly, as there should have been some degree of heat transfer between the two radically different climes. But Frances stated that she had never felt the least bit of a breeze while at the doorway.

Harris had been quiet, as usual, during their researches and the trek back to the encampment, but there was no indication of sullenness. On the contrary, he seemed to be subtly excited.

"Did you notice something, Jonathan?"

"A new mystery."

"Only one?" It was a small joke after a long day, and it did elicit a twitch of the mouth from the younger man. "Do you want to discuss it now?"

But Jonathan shook his head and went off to bed without a word, leaving Gardiner to ponder what the next day might bring.

EIGHT

INTO THE VOID

The exhilaration of being able to gain entrance was soon overcome by Gardiner's professionalism: It was thrilling, but really no more so than any other ancient structure. Strangeness did abound, though, and he began to compile a list. Aside from the temperature difference, the interior was spotless, despite the passage of likely thousands of years. He never expected to find the grit and dust of Egypt, but the dampness of the environment was ideal for mold or moss. Puddling from leaks should have been present. Even the remains of stray animals or insects should have been found. But there was nothing.

They flung themselves fully into the work even after a night of broken sleep. Gardiner recalled Harris' mention of a new mystery, but there was plenty to keep him occupied, so he waited for the younger man to speak up.

The job of transcribing and translating the cuneiform inscription on the east-facing wall fell to Frances, as it allowed her to sit in place for the most part. The flashlight Doctor Gardiner had thought to bring along was well suited to the task. To conserve battery power, she turned on the light for brief periods to memorize what she saw, then turned it off again and worked by candlelight to copy it into a notebook. As a result, flashes of light illuminated the interior at odd intervals.

Harris had volunteered to stay outside for the morning. With the help of Velo, Gardiner measured the southern part of the room, as the younger archaeologist had been working on the other half the previous evening. It soon became plain that, unfortunately, there was very little to discover. In fact, it contained only two points of any interest: the unmarked podium in the center of the room, and the cuneiform that Frances was studying. Gardiner had worked his way around the west and south walls to meet her at the midway point of the east, when Chico came in and asked everyone to join Jonathan outside.

The shift of nearly forty degrees was shocking to Gardiner, but he welcomed the warmth. And that caused him to wonder about Frances. She was having a more difficult time getting around lately, leaning on Pai almost constantly. Would such drastic temperature changes impact her health, or that of the baby? As per usual, she seemed to have an ability to detect the concern, and speak or act so as to stifle it. Before he could put voice to the question, she called out to her brother.

"Jonathan, what have you found?"

"Something," responded Harris. He looked at Gardiner. "Inside, how long is the front wall from the entrance to the point where it touches the southern wall?"

"Fifty feet, three inches."

"I measured the same on the opposite side, and so the entrance is placed in the middle of the western-facing wall."

"Symmetry and convention are hardly interesting," she pointed out, voice dripping with exasperation.

"True. But look more closely." He pointed at the archway, and then to either side of it.

On the right, there was nothing to see for nearly a hundred feet except for a barely perceptible undulation. On the left, however… Gardiner's brow furrowed as he estimated the distance. The hillside took a sharp right turn about forty feet over, bending back about thirty feet toward the bulk of the mountain before again continuing to the left. "How far is that?"

"Forty-two feet, six inches. We checked it three times."

Frances looked suitably awed.

"The interior space is larger than the exterior," she said.

"Yes."

71

All seven quietly regarded the rock and dirt and plants. This time, there was no illusion. A stake had been set into the ground at the point where the hillside jogged back, the top of it marked with a knotted bit of red cloth. That contrasting splash of color was forty-two and a half feet from the doorway, Harris had said. Gardiner saw no need to question that measurement, nor the one inside. There had to be a way to explain this conflict. Normally, the simplest explanation should be correct.

What if...

"I have an idea," suggested Gardiner. "A bit radical, perhaps... But what if that interior space,"—he tried to frame it with his hands—"isn't...*there*? What if it's elsewhere, further in? Or down? Deep down. That would also account for the much cooler temperature. If it's far underground."

"So that archway is a portal to somewhere else," summarized Frances.

"Yes. Exactly that."

She considered it, then nodded. "It makes the most sense. But I wouldn't have imagined a thing like that to be possible. Magic is traditionally applied for more subtle effects."

Gardiner was relieved to hear her say that. It had seemed likely that brother and sister both had an open mind regarding the concept of magic, but he had never been sure until now. Oddly enough, he actually suspected another, different force in play.

"Quite right," he said. "In my experience, magic is almost always human-centric and interactive. Something along these lines, continuing indefinitely, and without the need for a human mind to provide guidance, that smacks of something else."

"You're suggesting an engineered solution?" she asked.

"Yes. Physics holds some interest for me. I've read a little about the great strides made recently. I would say this is some very advanced type of science."

"So advanced that we have no hope of understanding it."

"That goes without saying, I believe."

"What I am saying," clarified Frances, "is that there is then no need for further discussion on the topic. We don't know how it works, and will not be able to determine how, given the time and resources available to us. Because the mechanics involved will not impact the discoveries we hope to make in our own fields, we need to turn our attention back to problems we *can* solve. We are wasting time."

Her voice took on a slight edge as she spoke, the final sentence clearly indicating her opinion. That bewilderment she'd displayed was already gone; the taskmistress had returned. Gardiner only nodded, taken aback, as she moved toward the arch.

"Frances," he said before she went inside.

She stopped, but did not turn to face him.

"How are you coming with the transcription?"

"I'll need another hour."

"Can Jonathan or I help at all?

"No."

Then she vanished through the archway. After she had gone, Gardiner let out an unsteady breath.

"She seems to be testier than usual. Is it the pregnancy? I imagine she'd be more pleasant under different circumstances."

Harris said nothing, smoothing his hair with the flat of his hand.

"I'm done with the survey around the southern half of the room, Jonathan. Would you like to finish what you started last night while she completes her work?"

Shoulders slumped, he went inside.

Gardiner felt sorry for him. At times there would be a glimpse of a polite and engaging Frances—but always in control of her brother. Those glimpses had been nonexistent recently. Since starting the dig, she had shown him progressively less respect, treating the hired hand Pai better than her own flesh and blood.

Then again, maybe not.

Frances also dominated that man, but on his part, there was an unmistakable amount of willing servitude. At least, it seemed to be willing.

While waiting for the siblings to wrap up their work, Gardiner decided to try a small experiment. To the left of the arch, around the corner marked with the stake, he found what looked to be a stable section of hillside, and had Chico slowly and carefully dig into it at about waist height. The hole was two feet deep before it started to fall in on itself. After another foot it became too difficult to go any further—and pointless. There were some loose rocks in the soil, but no sign of the type of stone that made up the chamber.

That room is definitely not here. It cannot be.

He told Chico to fill up the hole as best he could. Having Frances think they'd been wasting time might unnecessarily incur her wrath.

Oh my. Am I starting to fear her as much as Jonathan?

Assuredly, it wasn't fear—yet. But he did recognize that it was better to act in accordance with her wishes.

Foolish old man. Afraid of a pregnant woman.

It was far less than an hour later that Frances emerged, her dejected brother in tow. She handed Gardiner two pieces of paper: a cuneiform transcription of the writing on the back wall, and a translation of it in English.

"We both verified that I copied the message correctly, but it would be best to have you confirm it as well, just to be sure."

Gardiner read the English version:

All seeking power, die.
All seeking fortune, die.
The ones who are worthy shall live.
The ones who are worthy shall know.
Enter, and discover your intent.
Enter, and discover your fate.

A comparison with the cuneiform copy showed her work to be accurate enough, but the words it contained were troubling.

"Here is your trap, Doctor," she said, echoing his thoughts.

"Yes. The word *worthy* is the one most concerning to me. How are we to know what constituted worthiness to those who were here four or five thousand years ago?" He looked at the translation a second time, realizing exactly what he had read. "Wait—it says *enter.* Enter where?"

"I was careful to not touch the wall at all, but I found another doorway concealed by illusion. After sitting there for so long, it became obvious that a faint draft was coming through the wall, along with that strange odor of saltwater. The etching is above head-height, implying to me that the faithful should walk forward, below the words. I tossed several pebbles through; they didn't hit anything, but I heard them land on the stone floor, so at least there is only visual trickery involved. It seems likely that the worthy ones would pass through in hopes of meeting their god, while the unworthy would perish."

"A safe assumption for the time being," said Gardiner, "bringing us back to the definition of worthiness."

"*Intent* also seems to be key," offered Harris.

Frances glared at him, as if annoyed that he dared speak up.

This time, unexpectedly, he didn't wilt under his sister's gaze. They locked eyes, each seeming to challenge the other to cross some unspoken line.

Gardiner acted swiftly to try to defuse the tension. They were too close to getting answers to let rivalries and egos interfere.

"Yes, quite right," he said. "But that implies command of the awesome technology—or magic—of being able to read a man's mind."

It was Frances who ended the staring contest.

"Perhaps," she acknowledged. "Or perhaps they simply spied on the populace. Anyone approaching would have already been vetted: Has this person paid the tithe, acted in accordance with the laws, et cetera? If so, that one would be permitted to live. The unworthy could be disposed of merely by having soldiers stationed beyond the illusion to deal with them in an appropriate manner. For anyone within earshot, their deaths at the hands of an unseen assailant would reinforce the need to be worthy."

"A tidy thesis," he said, smiling uncertainly. "But if I may remind you of the point you made earlier, we have no way of knowing what method was used. The mechanism to open the doors still worked after thousands of years, and so a technological trap could still be active."

"I'll grant you that. Which is why I've convinced Forte to volunteer to go through first."

"You did what?"

"He'll earn a bonus, of course."

"Bonus be damned! You've persuaded the man to put himself at risk."

"My simple theory of human guards is at least as valid as your mechanism that reads minds, if not more so. In my case, there is absolutely no danger, as there is no possibility of guards. In yours, of course, there is danger, assuming that the trap is still functioning, and additionally, that Forte thinks unworthy thoughts. Considering everything, I believe that he has a greater than fifty percent chance of safety."

She gave him time to respond, but he said nothing.

"Given the variables, if you can think of a way to better the odds, speak up now. With a volunteer, we avoid the distasteful task of drawing lots, and so possibly condemning one of us to death—which, I would like to stress again, seems extremely unlikely to me."

Gardiner thought about it, but only long enough to concede that she was right.

"I would like, as you suggested, to verify your work. If I find no errors, and Forte is still willing, I will not protest further."

She nodded.

He moved past everyone and entered the chamber alone. Near the crate upon which Frances had been sitting and working, he found the flashlight and turned it on. Ignoring the message on the wall, he walked slowly around the perimeter of the room, looking for any details he may have missed, his lonely footsteps echoing.

There was nothing to see, absolutely nothing. This was, without a doubt, the blandest, most unexciting archaeological site he had ever seen or read about. Its very featurelessness was actually the most interesting aspect, as it violated all human presumptions of what a temple should be. Constructed of perfectly smooth, flat stone, there were no alcoves, no statues, no decorations or carvings—save the one verse—to relieve the monotonous emptiness. Not even any paint residue could be seen. Only the podium broke up the interior, its plainness matching the rest of the room.

Returning to the back wall, it didn't take long for him to verify the accuracy of Frances' work. She had made no mistakes with the copying, meaning that her translation was correct. The only difference he could sense from the last time he'd been inside was a stronger smell of seawater. He was ready to go outside and get the others when she entered with Forte, Pai and Velo.

"Your work is faultless, as I expected it would be," admitted Gardiner.

"Thank you. Forte is ready."

"I just wish that—ah!"

The flashlight he held was rectangular, with the battery on the bottom and a carrying handle mounted on top. The construction left the bottom flat and stable when set down on the floor. He placed it in front of the illusory wall and gave it a shove. It slid through and they could hear it come to a stop after a few feet.

"I've at least proven to my satisfaction that a solid floor exists beyond the illusion. And even if the light from this room penetrates it, he'll now have more to see by, perhaps helping to avoid a trap."

"Very good, Doctor."

"Now, tell him that he must clear his mind of—"

"There is no need for special instructions," she said curtly. "He is an ignorant savage, oblivious of what may lie beyond, so power is not a motivation. He is already being paid a small fortune, and so greed is not a motivation. There is likely fear, but there is no man who would not have had fear walking through that hidden doorway into the unknown, either now or thousands of years ago. Just let him go."

Again, unable to formulate an opposing argument, Gardiner moved aside. It was incredible how much she reminded him in that moment of Jebediah Higgins: both were volatile, both strong in their convictions. But even from the start of his relationship with Higgins, he found it easy to disagree with the man without considering reprisal. Frances' ruthless attitude, betrayed by the occasional disconcerting comment, actually instilled an amount of trepidation in him. He prayed that his acquiescence had not doomed the hired man.

She waved to Forte, who hesitated almost imperceptibly before striding up to the wall, and passing through. After fully disappearing, Gardiner thought he heard a gasp, but it was quickly followed by a single word.

"Seguro."

Safe. Thank God.

Forte wore a strange look on his face when he came back out.

"What did you see?" asked Gardiner eagerly.

Frances relayed the question in Portuguese.

"Maravilhas."

"Wonders," she translated.

The Divided God? Right there?

Gardiner could feel his heart rate rising. Concern for Forte had turned to relief, but it now was unbridled excitement that gripped him.

"Would you like to see for yourself, Doctor? You were last to enter the outer doorway. You should go next here."

Hardly hearing her words, his numb feet shuffled forward. He looked at the wall, blank and smooth, and took a deep breath.

He exhaled and stepped through.

On the floor at his feet, the flashlight still had enough life to show...nothing. It was just another empty room.

"Frances, there's nothing in here."

He reached down to pick up the light, splashed the beam around the walls of the chamber.

It revealed…horrors.
He was surrounded.
He screamed.

Nine

THE FATEFUL TRUTH

The string of nightmarish events that followed was nearly impossible for Gardiner to unravel. A torrent of terrible sights and sounds and smells flooded in too rapidly, piling up into an unprocessed, confused muddle. But eventually, the world slowed. Eventually, he retook control of his mind. And looking at the disturbing reality around him, he began to sort it out. A bit at a time, he put things into the proper sequence.

By far the largest portion of his disbelief still stood all around him. Even if he refused to accept what he *saw*, he could not deny the tactile proof, as his arms were firmly held by two of *them*: amphibious creatures, very man-like, but with a stature and firmness hinting at the strength needed to live in the remote depths of the ocean. Most held spears; the rest had knives of some dark metal.

He had seen things such as these only once before, and from a distance: five years in the past and thousands of miles away on the seacoast near Innsmouth, Massachusetts. And yet here they stood, or beings very much like them. Although their heads strongly resembled fish, with large, unblinking eyes and pronounced gill slits in the neck, he thought of them more akin to frogs, with four limbs, light-colored belly, and amphibious nature fully revealed by their presence on land. A stench of ocean death and rot clung to them.

The next image in his mind was the death of Velo, his body still where he had fallen. Gardiner's scream had alerted the poor man, drawing him in, the illusion on the doorway preventing him from seeing what lie in wait. With his arms restrained by the creatures,

Gardiner could only watch as Velo rushed forward, two of the creatures readying their spears. They struck the man fatally as soon as he was through: one in the chest, the other in the neck. He may not have even seen what had hit him, crumpling to the ground like he did, and hopefully dying quickly.

The most egregious blow to Gardiner's sanity, however, was the image that followed: Frances striding through the doorway triumphantly, accompanied by Pai and Forte. As ever, Pai acted as if he regarded her to be holy. Fixated on her, it did not matter to him in the least that he was in the midst of a dozen of the blasphemous, batrachian creatures. Forte, on the other hand, trembled visibly. Even while Gardiner was struggling to cope with the surreal scene, the man's fearful shaking was evident.

"Doctor?"

He focused on the source of the voice: Frances. The small flame from the candle she held lent her face a ghastly, skeletal caste.

"You seem to have recovered nicely from what must be quite an unexpected turn of events."

He made no attempt to suppress the enmity that rose up from within, and tried an experimental lunge at her. The alien hands that held him tightened their grip. Saying nothing, he waited for her to continue. She liked to talk, he had come to learn over the preceding days.

"You've been judged unworthy."

"I've surmised as much. These past days you've had many opportunities to kill me. Why go to such elaborate lengths?"

She paused as if weighing her options. "I see no need to lie any further. We needed you to open the temple."

"That's absurd. Anyone would have tried what I did, out of sheer desperation. In retrospect, it is obvious what needed to be done."

"You *are* right. It *is* obvious, and—" She bent over and clutched at her midsection, caught up in the pain of a contraction. "Finally," she panted after it had stopped, then stood straight. "I don't know why, but only *you* could open the temple. And frankly, I don't care to know why."

81

"This makes no sense. Why me bring me along at all? I did open the door, but you had no way of knowing that I'd be successful. You could've undertaken this entire quest without me. My inclusion—"

Chico stumbled through the illusionary wall just then. Off balance, he hit the floor. Terror of the unnatural abominations surrounding him was wiped out when he saw the body of his cousin. Sobbing, he fell on it and went limp.

As the creatures pulled Chico up and forced him to stand, Jonathan Harris strode in, standing taller and more confident than he had in weeks.

"Vengeance," he said, the word dripping with triumph. The expression on his face didn't match, though. Instead, there was undisguised irritation.

"Jonathan witnessed—"

"No! YOU be quiet for once! You and your damned drama. We could have been done with this last night."

Pai and Forte both tensed at the outburst, but Frances made a barely noticeable hand gesture that calmed them. She disguised the movement by bringing a finger to her lips, as if to indicate some thought. She was clearly still in control of the situation, but had chosen to feign…weakness, or magnanimity. Gardiner wasn't sure which.

A revolt is brewing.

"Very well, brother," she conceded. Her hideous sneer wouldn't have fooled even the smallest child.

Harris glared at her a while longer before facing Gardiner. "I was in the tunnel that night. I saw everything."

Caught completely off guard by the remark, Gardiner blinked. "And…which tunnel would that be?"

"The one beneath Copp's Hill Burying Ground."

It struck him then, his stomach flipping as he tried to come to terms with the awful truth.

"Your father…"

Gardiner could see the resemblance now. The jawline and mouth, the wave in his hair, … But the eyes, especially. The eyes matched perfectly between the two men. And Harris' were fully open, revealing the madness of the mind behind them.

"My father—*our* father—was Heinrich Bösemann, and he was teaching me at the time. It was I who controlled the creature that preyed on Boston. I commanded it to attack you, and watched the tunnel collapse on you. You should have died that night. But Higgins shot my father through the heart, and Hastings sent my creature away. I'll get them as well, one day. Today, it's you." He had closed the distance as he spoke, and now stood directly in front of Gardiner. "We knew that evidence of this temple would lure you here. And now, at the moment you imagined might be your greatest triumph, you'll finally die."

Outnumbered so severely, Gardiner harbored no real hope of survival, but he saw an opportunity to stoke some fires, knowing how emotions can induce mistakes.

"Why not right now, you coward? Be a man for once."

The words were hardly out his mouth before Harris began choking him, thumbs pressed into his windpipe.

"No!" shouted Frances. Pai and Forte each latched onto a wrist and pried his hands off. "You idiot! He's baiting you!"

Gardiner wheezed, wishing he could rub his throat, but the creatures had held his arms during the encounter and continued to do so. In fact, aside from the four who were restraining the prisoners, all of them had stood silently—until now.

"K'thnug b'nguit."

Quentin Gardiner knew of the language, had heard many attempts to pronounce the words by humans, beings whose vocal apparatus were ill-equipped for such an act. Hearing just a few syllables croaked from a *native* speaker chilled him. It was a language only suitable for evil.

"Doctor, it's time we were going," said Frances, tossing the candle aside. "It'll be raining soon. Did you bring your bumbershoot?"

Throat still sore from the attack, he frowned at her.

The troop of amphibious things led the way, followed by their conspirators, with the two prisoners still held in the grip of their captors bringing up the rear. It only took a few steps before the dying glow of the flashlight was left behind. Based on the echoes, it sounded as if they were in a corridor he guessed as twenty feet wide, about half that in height. Chico kept murmuring to himself, but Gardiner had no idea what he was saying until he spoke it in Spanish.

"Que esta pasando?"

What is happening?

"No lo se'," whispered Gardiner.

There were no turns; their route took them straight through an impenetrable darkness. The going was slow, perhaps due to the inability of the humans to see, perhaps because of the creatures' difficulty moving on land, or perhaps even out of a respect for Frances' condition. In any case, the visual deprivation made the passage of time immeasurable.

After a while, there were noticeable changes, as the intensity in the ocean smell increased, and the temperature rose. Bits of brightness were visible from up ahead. Even as Gardiner realized that their footfalls were not echoing the same way they had been, it became plain that they had emerged from the tunnel into open air. With the stars and moon covered by thick clouds, the light was provided by flashes of lightning.

"Welcome, Doctor Gardiner, to the Inner Sanctum of the temple of The Divided God."

Without the ability to defend himself, goading the brother further would be too risky. He decided it was time to try irritating the sister.

"*Inner* implies inside, my dear girl," Gardiner said as condescendingly as he was able to. "We are clearly *outside*."

"Look again, old man."

A bold stroke of lightning gave Gardiner a chance to pick out details. They stood on a stone causeway that poked out into a body of water, a shoreline hundreds of feet ahead. The walkway terminated at a circular platform about thirty feet wide at the center of the pool. Were it fresh, it might be described as a sinkhole or cenote, but the scent was unmistakably that of seawater. There were no waves visible, but the fishlike heads of many dozens of those creatures poked out of the surface, silently watching.

Clearly, escape by water is out of the question.

A succession of bolts lit the area long enough to confirm the glimpse of ground level he'd just had, as well as get a good understanding of what was above: Walls rose up to the sky, surrounding them in stone. This was no natural chine within which they stood; it was not believable that any erosive or geologic process could have produced such sheer, perfectly vertical effects. A swirling breeze pushed aside the salty aroma from time to time, carrying the faint but familiar aromas of the jungle up and over those walls.

"This is—"

"We are within the tepui, at the bottom," said Gardiner, interrupting her. "Or somewhat below. The walls around us seem to be higher than the top of the tepui above the surrounding land."

With lightning occurring more frequently, he was able to see that his strategy may have worked; she stared daggers at him.

"There's no need to delay this any longer. Pai!"

Her servant was at her side right away, holding out a wad of leaves, which she put in her mouth and began to chew. She grimaced at the taste, but did not stop.

At last, the rain began to fall, huge drops exploding on the stone as they hit. This seemed to be a signal to the creatures, as both Gardiner and Chico were released. All of the things dove into the water, leaving the six humans on the causeway. But looking back along its length, Gardiner could see, at the point where it met the shore, four of the creatures had climbed back out, blocking the path.

Escape by land is also out.

Frances began shuffling toward the circular area, leaning on Pai.

"Follow them," instructed Harris, pointing ahead. Forte came back to help him guard the rear.

Gardiner could see no other choices at present. He started forward, noticed that Chico was not moving, grabbed him and pulled. The young man was looking everywhere, measuring distance, steeling himself for what would likely be a failed and fatal flight.

"Not now," said Gardiner, just loud enough to be heard above the rain. Getting no reaction, he said, "Ahora no."

Some sanity seemed to seep back into Chico as he nodded and began to walk forward. They didn't have far to go in order to reach the circular terminus. Harris pointed them to the right side, with Frances and Pai positioned on the left. Harris and Forte stayed behind, standing at the point where the causeway met the platform. There was a dark patch at the very center—a circle about six feet in diameter—that was visible even in the dark.

If Frances had been holding it in, she could contain it no longer, and screamed as the pain of childbirth began to wrack her body. She squatted down. Acting as midwife, Pai was already seated on the stone before her. The storm, meanwhile, had worked itself into a frenzy, with tremendous arcs of lightning etching luminous spider webs across the sky. Her wails were synchronized with the blasts of electricity and simultaneous thunderous claps, with the maelstrom now centered right above them.

Frances ultimately emitted a shriek nearly inhuman in its intensity. The bolt that accompanied her ululation was blinding. Gardiner braced himself for the crash of thunder, but instead—

Silence.

Darkness.

It was the silence of unreality, a state that simply could not exist but in the vacuum of space. It was as if the world had ceased to exist, yet it was plain that it still did. He could smell the ocean water all around, and feel the rain pelting down, and the ground beneath his feet. With his eyes already taxed to function between flashes of lightning, the visual deprivation was as nothing compared to the profound lack of any aural input. How long did it last? A microsecond? A millennium?

Light!

Sound!

The reintroduction of lightning and—especially—thunder hit like a hammer. All four of the men who had been standing dropped to their knees, stunned as if struck. They covered their ears from noises that were nothing at all out of the ordinary. But as they recovered, another sound intruded: the cry of a newborn.

Gardiner watched as Pai carefully cut and tied the umbilical cord, the afterbirth already having been ejected. With one arm cradling the child, he pushed the placenta into the water. His proud smile glowed as a bizarre beacon in the shadows.

Frances covered herself and rolled over to get on hands and knees.

She uttered a short phrase in the language of the creatures, something that Gardiner had no hope of understanding, and turned to her left.

Quentin Gardiner looked where she did. A man stood where no one had been, at the edge of the circular platform, directly across from the end of the long causeway.

Who?

Wearing a simple, dark robe, he was easily seven feet tall and projected a royal, even pharaonic, attitude. The lines of his face were sharply defined, dark hair cut short, and eyes—

No!

Gardiner stopped himself in time, but a glance to his left during a lightning flash showed Chico, Forte and Harris all mesmerized, staring up at the *man*. Gardiner continued to think of *it* that way, though he knew full well that the thing that stood only a few feet away was not human, but rather a puissant being dressed in the shape of a man.

Pai and Frances were not paralyzed like the others. He handed the infant to her and helped her up. They shuffled forward slowly, Frances demonstrating a remarkable strength to move about so soon after her ordeal. They were both within arms' length of the dark being when they knelt down in a show of religious obeisance.

Pai put a name to the thing. "O Escuro," he said, adoration evident.

The Portuguese was close enough to the Spanish for an easy translation: Dark One.

Nyarlathotep.

TEN

BLOOD IS THICKER

The lightning struck at steady intervals, illuminating the scene often enough to allow Gardiner to keep track of where everyone was.

Wait. Think.

He had to count himself lucky. Many of Nyarlathotep's reputed thousand-and-one forms were too grotesque to even glimpse and remain sane. Others were categorically lethal. While in human form, it at least acted as one, but there was no way to know what powers it still commanded. Gardiner convinced himself there was still a chance to get out of this, but he would need to wait until that entity was gone. At least he had one ally: Chico was a prisoner as well. He tried to forget the fact that the water around them was swarming with those abominations, making escape impossible.

Think.

To his right, still kneeling, Frances held the baby up above her head.

What?

She was offering it to *Him*! Gardiner's soul went numb. He did not think such an act was conceivable by even the most corrupt imagination.

The dark man reached out and touched it on the forehead with just the merest tap of a finger.

The crying ceased instantly, leaving a void in the noisy chaos.

She drew it back down to her bosom. Hope shown in her face and grew, but then twisted into a scowl when the tiny form began to convulse.

"No!" screamed Frances.

She practically threw the baby at Pai. He snatched it out of the air and cradled it against his chest as she began to berate him mercilessly in Portuguese. The man took an appalling amount of abuse without protest. He stroked the child, trying to comfort it, as the poor thing continued to shake. Finally, it was still. Even over the sound of the rain Gardiner thought he heard the man sob.

But Frances had still not exhausted her anger. She stood and shakily walked over to her brother.

"Even weaker than yours! This entire plan was a failure from the start!" She looked off into the distance for a while, then declared, "I will *not* try again."

Whatever spell The Dark Man had cast was now broken; it was Harris' turn for apoplexy.

"That's not an option! *He* is here! The plan must continue!"

Forte stirred with that outburst. He looked at Frances expectantly.

"Then we switch to an alternate."

"There is no alternate."

"You know very well that there is."

Gardiner could not detect it, but there must have been some sign from Frances—a gesture or a word—to cause Forte to seize Harris by the arms, and take him down hard onto the stone. Harris tried pleading with the man in Portuguese, but since the very beginning, it had been clear to Gardiner that Pai and Forte owed their allegiance to Frances. Harris was himself a very strong man, and taller, but Forte was more powerful and had the advantage of leverage.

"Pai!" shouted Frances.

The man did not respond, still cradling the dead infant.

She marched over.

Ripped it from his hands.

Hurled it to the ground.

The dull thud against the stone made Gardiner's stomach turn. He closed his eyes and took a deep breath, staggered by her callousness.

The act jolted Pai out of his daze. He moved over to assist Forte. Together, they held Harris' arms behind his back and maneuvered him forward to stand before his sister.

"You've always been the backup plan," she explained to her brother. "I only went along with your suggestion because it appealed to me. Being the mother would have granted certain privileges."

"It can still work!"

"Dear brother, I do agree with you. It *can*. But I suggest that *you* try giving birth three times. Let us see how patient *you* are afterwards."

Harris struggled to break free, but could not. They kicked at the backs of his legs, forcing him down to his knees. Chico became more animated, looking around, brushing Gardiner with a finger to get his attention. Even with Harris restrained by the two Brazilians, as far as the Doctor was concerned, nothing had changed. The water still contained an unknowable number of enemies, and the presence of the tall, dark entity required supreme caution. He shook his head at Chico.

"No," he whispered.

"Unfortunately," continued Frances, "in this case, a small, symbolic sacrifice must be made. You know that as well as I. It needn't be anything important, of course. Something unused. A finger, an ear."

She studied her brother.

"Língua," she said.

Harris roared, then spat in her face and clamped his mouth tightly shut.

"E cabeleira," she added, wiping the spittle away.

Leaving Pai to hold Harris, Forte swung around to the front, and threw the full force of his weight into a blow to the man's jaw. Coming at a quiet point between the claps of thunder, the *crack* of breaking bone was sickeningly clear. Harris was clearly dazed, as well. He stopped struggling, then groaned, as his mouth was forced apart. Gardiner watched helplessly as Forte pulled out his knife. Rudely gripping Harris' tongue between his finger and thumb, he sliced it off in one quick motion, and discarded the ounce of flesh into the water without a second thought.

The lightning illuminated the scene enough to show the blood pouring from the man's mouth, hitting the stones before being diluted by rain. Gardiner also noticed that they were all currently standing on the central dark spot.

Inner sanctum. Why mark that spot?

The butchery wasn't done yet. Forte used the blade to trace a groove entirely around Harris' scalp. After prying up a starting finger hold, he was able to rip it off with a sound not unlike the tearing of cloth—that is, when it could be heard above Harris' agony. Once removed, that trophy was also tossed into the water.

The work finished, both Forte and Pai moved away, leaving Harris to fall with a splash, blood flowing so heavily that the rain no longer diluted it. With an inhuman effort, he dragged himself forward, a bit at a time, toward the tall, silent being. Arriving at the thing's feet, he tried to stand. And failed.

"Buscá-lo!" said Frances impatiently.

Pai moved forward as soon as she spoke, but Forte stayed put until she gestured violently at him. One on each side of Harris, they hauled him up onto his feet and stepped aside, but stayed ready to catch him.

Gardiner was astonished to see that the man still had the coordination to remain upright. On wobbly legs, he raised his mutilated head to the entity shaped as a man before him.

As had been done with the newborn, the dark man reached out and touched Harris on the forehead. His body spasmed as if shocked by a current, and his legs gave way.

Frances didn't even wait for him to hit.

Gardiner was able to hear her say something that sounded like, "Kuk'wm sh'gth!" Those previous gore-filled minutes would be etched in his memory forever, but what happened next was equally distressing.

It came out of the water from all around them, a viscous, oily black nightmare, and flowed over the stone. Numerous eyes coalesced, then dissolved, as it moved.

Shoggoth!

Gardiner froze, recalling what he'd read about such creatures, but was dumbstruck to see that it went between all legs and feet, avoiding contact with everyone except Jonathan Harris. After a particularly fearsome blast of thunder, he glanced to his right.

Nyarlathotep was gone!

This was the time to act.

Frances was still standing on the black area at the center of the platform. Pai and Forte were farther away, next to Harris—who was now wholly enveloped by the shoggoth. All three were entranced by what they were witnessing. If that thing was going to kill or devour him, it would be very soon.

But the shoggoth… wasn't attacking him at all. It was healing him! Harris' scalp had partially knitted up already, healthy skin evident, but devoid of hair.

What can I do? How can we—

Inspiration flashed. It was desperate to be sure, but he imagined that even Higgins would attempt it given the same situation.

It was plain to Gardiner that he had unlocked the outer door, with Frances having confirmed that. Somehow, this temple had been keyed to him. And that dark circle on the stone was the perfect shape to attract his curiosity, not to mention its conspicuous placement, and its very inclusion as a decoration in an otherwise featureless structure. In short, he was willing to bet his life that it was another doorway of some sort.

Gardiner raised his arms and intoned in a loud voice, "All praise to the one who is two."

Frances did not vanish as hoped, and worse, his outburst had attracted the wrong attention. The time for sheer desperation had come.

"Agarrarla! Grab her!" he told Chico, then shoved him toward Frances and followed right behind. They had the angle on Pai and Forte, who were blocked just enough by Harris and the shoggoth to buy precious time. However, the movements of the two prisoners had incited a flurry of splashing: the creatures were already climbing out of the water.

Frances was slow to react, and as she had likely anticipated, the amphibious things were rushing to her defense. Chico held her easily by the arm as Gardiner had told him to, and she wasn't struggling.

As Gardiner neared the dark spot, he was able to see: Pai and Forte closing on him; over a dozen of the things approaching from all sides; and Jonathan Harris lying on the ground, bald scalp completely healed—and no sign of the shoggoth.

What!?

There was no time to make sense of that final image. He reached out, grabbing Frances and Chico at the same time, and stepped forward.

"All praise—"

But he stopped himself. There wasn't any need to finish. As soon as he'd set foot in the circle, everything around them had changed.

Eleven

THE DOORWAY

There was no rain, no light whatsoever. Wherever they were now, it appeared to be underground. And the temperature had fallen possibly thirty degrees. Their soaked clothing would likely have them shivering before long.

It worked!

Frances recovered her composure quickly.

"Congratulations, Doctor. You've found an escape I did not predict. Do you know where we are?"

With the '*are*' she struggled violently to pull away from the two men, who were still holding her. Chico lost his grip, but not Gardiner. He firmed his handhold, and managed to blindly latch onto her other arm long enough for Chico to find it again.

"You've displayed an absolute lack of anything resembling humanity, and so I feel no need to treat you with the courtesy I would normally afford a woman. Do you understand?"

Those last words came out with a ferocious intensity. In all his life, he couldn't remember feeling as much disgust for anyone.

She forced out a resentful grunt. He waited for his fury to dissipate, counting to ten, then twenty.

"I can't say for sure," he continued, "but I firmly believe we're in the chamber where the faithful would meet their god."

"No. We *were* there," she said. "I told you. This is someplace else."

"So you say."

Frances tittered, and the sound echoed evilly.

"You *still* don't know the identity of that god, do you?"

Gardiner could hear her smirking, felt his face turning red with both embarrassment and outrage. She was obviously trying the same tactic he'd used on her earlier. He made an effort to remain calm, but the baiting had the intended effect. The anger he'd just dismissed came roaring back, crowding out good judgement and allowing barbarian urges to fill the void.

Should I kill her?

Could I?

Under less stressful circumstances, he would be ashamed of the notions.

Would Chico stop me, or help me?

Standing in the cool, silent darkness, he forced himself to *think*. In truth, her only triable offense to this point was commanding the reprehensible attack on her brother, though Gardiner's last view of the man showed him to have been healed somehow. Velo had been killed by the creatures, not her. And she had given birth to a live child, which had died shortly afterward, and not by her hand.

Would even Jebediah do such a thing?

He couldn't know. That man had an uncanny knack for processing data and making connections that others couldn't. If he had that special certainty about her that made her too much of a threat to remain alive, he *might*. But Gardiner wasn't Higgins. He didn't have that man's detached way of making decisions—and on top of it all, he'd never known Jebediah to kill a woman.

I refuse to be like you.

"Luces," said Chico, voice wavering.

Gardiner looked around, then up. It was as the young man had said: points of light moving around in the air above them. He first thought that they were insects, but while insects flitted about randomly, these stayed together in an eerily coordinated way. And besides, the luminescence of a firefly would cycle off and on. These lights stayed constant.

A second group flicked on, to the right of the first, and moved to position themselves on the opposite side of the trio. A whimper escaped Chico, but Frances remained still, giving no indication of any nervousness.

Surrounded!

Both sets moved lower and closer, each group staying in a line, or nearly so. The only sounds to be heard were their own fear-filled breaths. Gardiner decided on a defensive posture, their backs to each other. He transferred Frances' wrist to Chico, then spun her around to get a hold of the other. By the time they stood in a triangle, the lights had descended to shoulder height, and were mere feet away. The luminescence they provided was enough to discern the details of the horror they faced.

Each of the lights was a lidless, staring eye, glowing sickly yellow. They were set at irregular intervals along the length of the tentacles, which writhed to some degree almost constantly. All of those eyes were focused on the three of them.

Frances began to laugh. It was very loud. Her body shook.

"Be quiet!" cautioned Gardiner, trying to hold his voice low.

"Do you think it hasn't seen us yet, Doctor?"

"Laughter can be interpreted as a sign of disrespect!"

"You poor man. This is my way out of here. Now let me go, or I'll give the command to rip your arms off!"

The confidence in her voice was indisputable; she had a far better understanding of the situation than he. Gardiner let her go, then reached over and tapped Chico on the arm. The young man did not respond. Gardiner used both of his hands to try to pry his fingers from Frances' wrist, but if anything, the grip tightened.

Frances cried out in pain, then shouted a string of harsh, nonsensical syllables.

With unimaginable swiftness, one of the tentacles wrapped around Chico's torso and the other around his arm. There was a forceful pull. After a tearing of flesh, Chico screamed, and Gardiner was left holding the limb. A tattered artery spurted wildly before Chico clutched at the empty socket with his remaining hand, then collapsed.

Stunned, Gardiner released the gruesome trophy. It landed on his left foot, a dead, terrible weight. The flow of blood was simply too great to stanch, oozing between the young man's fingers with each of his heartbeats. As Gardiner considered how he might comfort the dying man, Frances spoke again. A tentacle encircled Chico's head and twisted violently, breaking the neck with a crack. Any evidence of life, any tension in the body that had remained at that point, was gone. The appendages silently returned to their relaxed position, floating in the air about five feet off the ground.

"Mercy," said Frances, massaging her wrist. "You saw for yourself. I have the ability to grant mercy."

"Mercy?" asked Gardiner absently, studying the smears of Chico's blood on his shoe. Outrage wanted to boil up again, but he was numb from death.

Deaths.

"He suffered little," she insisted. "He was hurting me. If you recall, I just gave birth. I've had quite enough of pain for today."

She scrutinized his grisly remains.

"A pity," she said. "He was very attractive."

"And so, what now, exactly?"

"Exactly? I can't say. I *can* tell you that I'm leaving shortly. You'll remain here, to die of starvation, or thirst, or the deadly cold that will slowly settle into your bones. Or perhaps you'll offend the resident in some way and be killed."

This prospect caused a spike in Gardiner's heart rate.

"I should thank you," she continued. "Bringing me here has aided me immensely. I should show you some mercy and grant you a quick death as well, but you annoy me only slightly less than my brother. I'd prefer you wither and die over the course of time. Would you like to see what it is you will share this space with?"

She didn't wait for a response, making another demand of whatever unknown thing was under her command. Spots of light blinked on all at once. Gardiner saw the patterns as the lights undulated in groups. Hundreds of lights—all eyes!—attached to dozens of writing arms. Slowly, he lowered his gaze, tracing them back to the source.

There was enough light to see…it.

Not far away at all, fifty feet or so, was a massive, chaotic pool of something that should not exist in Nature. It was alive, in constant, fluid motion, and yet constrained. The tentacles erupted straight from the surface, some staying aloft, some retracting and being replaced. All swayed back and forth, influenced by eddies and swirls in the pool. Or causing them. It was hard to say which.

A single word from Frances in the alien tongue was enough to cause the greater portion of lights to go out again, leaving only the original glowing sets.

Gardiner steeled himself for an attack, having no reason to trust her. Trying to readapt to the sudden change in light, he listened for movement. But all he heard was, "Good-bye, Doctor. Lng'yr ph'n-glui Gh't'n Tho'h hfl'rop'hs!"

An oblong shape, its edge well-defined even in the darkness, appeared in front of Frances. She stepped into the blackness and was…gone.

A doorway!

But before he could react, it also vanished.

Gardiner took stock, trying his best to think logically. The thing had still not attacked him, so it seemed safe to trust Frances' words and believe that it would leave him alone unless he did something rash. He tried shuffling a few feet to the left, then back to the right; the eyes tracked him all the while. Frances had commanded the thing. It listened and acted. Therefore, it was intelligent.

Could it work again?

He raised his arms above his head, bowed slightly.

"All praise to the one who is two."

Nothing.

He did not return from whence he had come. No mysterious portal materialized. There was no reaction from the creature, no indication that it understood what he was saying. He knew a bare few words of the alien tongue, so true communication was out of the question.

And saying the wrong thing might be fatal.

The cool temperature was beginning to give him a chill. He had to try *something*. Looking at the lifeless body of Chico, he gathered his thoughts and his courage.

"My name is Quentin Gardiner. I am on a quest for knowledge. For years—"

HELLO, QUENTIN GARDINER.

The fantastic intensity of the words reverberated with a force so great it knocked the breath out of him. He paused to listen for echoes, but heard none. Upon reflection, he was sure that the communication had been soundless, the words popping into his mind—but more than that: They had *filled* his mind, blotting out all else.

"I am Quentin Gardiner," he said cautiously, preparing himself for the next message.

YOU HAVE BEEN AWAITED.

The inflection, if such a term could be applied to thought transfer, gave off a *feminine* energy. Sharp even under pressure, he put together the bits and pieces of lore he had collected over the years: the unearthly appearance, the feminine aspect, the location seemingly deep underground.

"You are Shub-Niggurath."

THAT NAME IS BEFITTING.

The confirmation was mind-boggling. Given the association between the cultists he fought against and the very same *Black Goat of the Woods with a Thousand Young* whom they worshipped, he firmly believed that he should be dead by now. The fact that he was actually speaking with the entity conflicted with everything he knew. It was imperative that he survive this encounter and get back to tell the group about this. Especially Higgins.

"What should I do now?"

A MISTAKE, TO BE CORRECTED, MUST FIRST BE MADE.

Gardiner nodded, hoping that he wasn't missing some crucial detail with the cryptic comment.

SPEAK YOUR FATED DESIRE.

Fated desire?

Time ticked by as he reviewed the small amount of communication with *her*, and tried to piece things together. He, specifically, had been awaited. Somehow, *she* knew that he would be here at this time. This exchange seemed to be a scripted formality.

Awaited. Fated desire.

And not only scripted, it also was at an end.

Go home? Follow Frances?

Both options were strongly appealing, but he settled on the desire that had set him on the path to get to that very place.

"I wish to learn of The Divided God."

Similar to what had happened with Frances, an infinitely black shape appeared before him, hanging in the air. Peeking around it, he saw it had no thickness whatsoever, and was also not visible from the other side. It was effectively a one-way hole in the universe, leading somewhere.

Steeling himself, Gardiner walked into an ebon unknown.

PART 2

TWELVE

TAMAR

The sharp rise in temperature was the first thing that Gardiner noticed. The only thing, really. With no eye-encrusted tentacles to provide light, it was even dimmer than the place he had just left. Despite that, he could tell that he was still underground, though now in a tunnel of some sort. Both walls were less than an arm-length away, and the ceiling was inches above his head. Checking all around, he judged that the way he faced was definitely the way to go: It was the only direction with any light at all, a dim aura off in the distance.

He shuffled forward, slowly, blindly. An accidental brush against the unevenly hewn wall filled the air with dust, causing a coughing fit. After getting himself back under control, and carefully sniffing the dry, flinty atmosphere, he realized how familiar the scent was. Too many months of his life were spent in the deserts of the Middle East to not recognize that environment. The shock of travelling thousands of miles by striding forward one step awed him, briefly.

Creeping forward more carefully, he reached the end of the current passage, but was forced to choose between branches to the left and right. The steady glow from the right indicated that the source was more likely the sun rather than a torch or candle, and a careful look around the corner confirmed that daylight was not far off. Sounds echoed down that tunnel as well: dull pings of metal against stone, and muffled voices.

Gardiner's experiences with the peoples in this part of the world had varied wildly. He'd largely been treated neutrally, as simply a stranger, but there had also been a few occasions when he had been welcomed enthusiastically into villages and homes with open arms. And once just the opposite, when shots had been fired from a hostile band of Bedouins, wounding two of his group.

He watched for a few minutes. No one passed by. There didn't seem to be a point in waiting any longer.

Exercising caution, he forced himself to walk forward as quietly as he was able. The grinding of sand on stone beneath his shoes made more noise than he would have liked, but felt that the coughing had been prolonged enough to defeat any true attempt at stealth.

At the exit point he poked his head out. To the left was an expanse of open sand running to the horizon. To the right was the source of the metallic noises. He counted eight masons busy at work in the shaded area at the base of a cliff. No one moved about in the sun except for some young apprentices making trips to get any needed supplies—mainly water, from what he observed. Everyone was dressed in robes and sandals, all but the youngest sporting thick beards.

I need those people for water, food, information.

He couldn't see anyone acting as guard. There were no weapons in sight, no guns, not even a sword. It seemed safe to step out and reveal himself.

Be as friendly as you always are, Quentin.

But all coherent thought was wiped from his mind the moment he emerged from the cave. Further to the right, he was able to see what the masons were working on. The clean perfection and lack of adornment was unforgettable. He had memorized the dimensions, and even from a distance, knew that the measurements would be the same.

Before him stood an exact replica of the archway of the temple of The Divided God—the marble facing of it, anyway.

Like the version in Guyana, this one abutted a hill. The structure was nearing completion, the masons finished with the sides and beginning to work on the curved portion at the top.

Mesmerized by the vision he beheld, he tried to walk right up to it. But the men put their tools down when he got near enough, and

105

stood in his way. His progress blocked, some semblance of thought returned.

"Hello," he said, trying to sound as friendly as possible. Smiling, he looked around.

A man enormous in both girth and height, and with the bearing of a foreman, approached slowly, incredulity etched into his features. He studied Gardiner's clothing before rattling off a question in an unrecognizable tongue.

"Sorry, I don't understand. I don't suppose anyone here speaks English?"

There was no response, all faces displaying pure bafflement. He reached into his memory and fished out something appropriate.

"Hal tatahaddath alearabia?"

This time, the lack of any feedback was concerning. He would have been the first to admit that his pronunciation was on the poor side, having relied almost exclusively on translators and guides when in this area, but the words and intent should have been intelligible.

"Hablas espanol?" he tried out of desperation.

Confusion was replaced by apprehension, the whispers increasing. The entire group also seemed to be fascinated by his clothing, with some pointing at his trousers and shoes.

The only other language with which he had any familiarity at all was German. Stone masons are entrusted to do fine work, and need to be more intelligent than the average worker. It seemed entirely plausible that someone here could have picked up a small amount of German—if exposed to it. Flustered, he tried to remember where von Bissing had concentrated his explorations—

"No, no," he muttered to himself. "He was in Egypt. Friedrich Delitzsch came through here. Yes."

Having gained some confidence, he asked the crowd: "Sprechen Sie Deutsch?"

The foreman had apparently gotten tired of listening to his gibberish. He began again, this time reprimanding him, exuberantly pointing first at the open desert, then up at the sun, and finally at his own head. One of the words—*Assur*—was spoken a few times, reminding Gardiner of...something familiar.

His tirade complete, the man waited for a response.

Crazy. He thinks I'm crazy. For dressing like this, for...for walking across the desert in the middle of the day...from Assur!

It hit him then, as he looked around and the myriad details clicked into place. The workers themselves gave no indication of anything out of the ordinary, with their clothing falling within the norm for desert dwellers. But their reaction to him was definitely not normal. And over there, left behind on the ground, were *bronze* tools. And clay tablets were scattered around here and there, covered in cuneiform writing, but not dusty and decaying from the passage of centuries. They were freshly made!

But in truth, it was the mention of Assur that hit him hardest. Recently excavated, the ancient city hadn't been inhabited in over five hundred years. And yet the foreman seemed to be talking about it as one would Boston or New York. As a trained archaeologist, he was ashamed it had had taken him so long to see. Judging from the style of cuneiform, Gardiner estimated he was currently standing somewhere in the third millennium B.C.

Not only thousands of miles, but thousands of years.

With the foreman's expression changing from aggravation to disgust, Gardiner knew he needed to make sense, somehow convince the man that he wasn't a lunatic.

"Assur!" he said loudly, pointing at his chest then at the desert. "I need to go to Assur."

He waved a few times in what he assumed was the correct direction.

Perhaps it was something in Gardiner's bearing or the conviction with which he spoke, but one of the workers seemed to have an epiphany. He approached the big man and the two had an animated conversation. The foreman began by repeatedly shaking his head, refusing to believe whatever was being suggested, but stopped as doubt seemed to creep in. He motioned the other to silence, examined the peculiarly-garbed stranger, sighed, and nodded. He then waved his arms and yelled at the group. Everyone scurried back to their stations—except for the one with whom he'd been conferring. That man motioned for Gardiner to follow him. He fell into line behind his guide, and they moved off to the edge of the camp together.

When they reached the side of the cliff, far out of the way, the man pointed at himself.

"Tamar," he said, taking care to enunciate.

Gardiner did the same.

"Quentin."

They exchanged smiles.

Tamar pointed up at the sky, then toward the sun, which was behind the wall of rock, and lowered his arm slowly to a horizontal position.

"Yes, it would be better to wait for the sun to go down," agreed Gardiner. He looked around for a comfortable rock.

"Tamar!" A constant throughout much of civilization, the voice of the foreman carried the same threat as it did in the twentieth century. After a long look at Gardiner and a few ambiguous nods, Tamar ran back to work.

It wasn't long before a feeling of pure elation rose up from within the archaeologist, as he realized that he was witnessing history, not guessing at it. He watched the men carefully as they worked, looking for habits, mannerisms, gestures—anything that might differ from men of his own age. In the end, all that Gardiner learned was that—as he saw with the foreman—men were simply men, regardless of the millennium in which they lived. The basic characteristics hadn't changed much over the past few thousand years. Gardiner stood and paced from time to time, itching to get nearer the temple, or even just the masons. The foreman kept a wary eye on him though, and became visibly tense if he wandered too far from his rock.

The shadows grew longer as the hours wore on. A few times a small boy came by with a water skin from which Gardiner cautiously drank. It was gritty and had a chalky taste, but smelled fine.

Eventually, the foreman signaled that the workday was at an end. The men put their tools down, stretched, and stood in line for food. Tamar motioned for him to stay where he was, and the man soon joined him with a hot meal for each of them, plus a water skin. Gardiner's stomach grumbled; he would have welcomed nearly anything, but was pleased with what had been brought: a piece of some kind of bird, cooked plainly over a fire, plus a chunk of coarse bread. The meat was burned in places, and there was a gamy, wild taste to it, but he savored the greasy fattiness. The bread, unevenly torn from a larger loaf, helped fill him up. Whenever Gardiner slowed his intake, the other man urged him on. When both only had a few bites of bread left, Tamar gestured that they should get moving. As they walked into the desert, the sun minutes from setting, the foreman shouted something. Tamar turned and waved, then led Gardiner away.

They walked and walked beneath an ocean of stars. One hour turned into two. Gardiner was proud of the condition he was in for a man of his years, but his legs became fatigued. Trudging through the shifting sands was not an easy task, and Tamar's brisk pace didn't help matters. Knowing that some urgency was in play, Gardiner was reluctant to ask for a rest, despite the mounting pain. At the top of a rise he was finally rewarded for his patience: the walls of a town were not that far off, not even a quarter mile, he estimated. The lights of a few fires and the faint but comforting bark of dogs carried across the distance.

"Assur," confirmed Tamar.

The distance was a little farther than he'd thought, but the path was well-worn, and the compacted sand made for much easier going. The two men were soon at the closed gate. Tamar was either known by the guards or had a password, allowing access to the town, although not before answering a series of questions from the bemused men. They looked at Gardiner suspiciously as the native man pleaded his case, but let the pair pass.

Tamar led him through a maze of narrow, dark streets, arriving after a few wrong turns at a house that seemed to be no different than any of the others. He rapped on the door and waited.

It opened, a crack at first, then more fully. A man came forward and bowed slightly, looking confused. Tamar whispered rapidly, sounding apologetic, but plowed on breathlessly. When the narrative was done, he motioned for Gardiner to speak.

"Hello," Gardiner began, unsure what to say, or whether it even mattered—as if anyone here could understand him. "My name is Doctor Quentin Gardiner and—"

Even in the darkness he could see the stranger's shock, his eyes briefly flaring wide. He hushed Gardiner, and then spoke to Tamar, possibly thanking him. After a wave good-bye to Gardiner, the mason trotted off.

The man opened the door wide and motioned for Gardiner to enter. When closed behind him, the room was very dark, only the dim orange embers of a cooking fire glowing from the other end of the room. A minute of coaxing, plus a small stick of fresh wood produced a flare of light, and the man motioned to a pair of roughly hewn stools.

They both sat down. The obviously troubled man some took time to collect his thoughts, and while he did so, Gardiner relished the chance to rest. Tamar had obviously led him to someone who could help. Or, was this instead an expert in dealing with gibberish-speaking men, someone who would assess his sanity and make a recommendation? Would Gardiner end up being worshipped as a god, or banished into the desert, or just killed outright?

Enough of that.

His host studied him. At times, the confused expression was replaced by what seemed to be anger, or at least irritation. Twice, he almost spoke, but remained silent.

Gardiner smiled and tried to appear as disarming as possible. By fire light, he looked around at the small hut. It was minimalistic, undecorated. The wall with the door had a small window, as did the one to its right. It was likely that they were the east- and south-facing walls to maximize the amount of light let in during the day, though now both windows were covered by curtains. Wooden shelves were scattered around, anchored into the crude walls in some undetermined way, holding all of the necessities for life: a few dishes and bowls; some utensils; and either clothing, or towels, or both. Much of the shelf space was unused, however. Two beds occupied most of the floor space. The place really was larger than necessary for one man, more suited for a small family.

The man cleared his throat to attract Gardiner's attention.

"My name is Jakop," he said, voice low. The words were accented, but unmistakably English.

Doctor Quentin Allan Gardiner, Ph.D., man of science, never at a loss for words, tried to speak. He tried. His mouth moved, but nothing intelligible came out.

"Shhh. We have much to discuss. But it must wait until morning."

"But—"

"Sounds travel too easily. We *must* wait."

As exhausted as he was, Gardiner's body welcomed the opportunity to lie down. But his mind—that was another matter. It darted back and forth restlessly, fueled by traumatic energy. When sleep did come, it was more akin to a coma. Or oblivion.

Thirteen

JAKOP

A hand grabbed Gardiner by the shoulder, shook him. The improbable sequence of events the previous day left him unsure of what had happened and exactly where he was. Being awakened was jarring, almost terrifying. He vaguely recalled a stranger speaking English.

"What?" he mumbled. "Where am I?"

"Shhh," came the voice, right next to Gardiner's ear. "We must leave now."

More English. No dream. Jakop, did he say?

Gardiner cracked open his eyes, but in the pre-dawn darkness he saw only the vague outline of a man. A robe and sandals were placed into his hands.

"Leave? Where?"

"No questions!" snapped Jakop, voice still constrained to a whisper. "Not yet. Get dressed."

He stripped off his clothes quickly, but was mystified by the design of the unfamiliar robe. A few wasted moments were enough to elicit a growl of disgust, and reluctant aid, from the other man. Oriented correctly, it slipped on easily. The material was coarse, but it fit comfortably. The sandals were a little small for him, though not anywhere near as much of a challenge in the dark as the robe had been.

Jakop hid his old clothes, and they were about to leave when Gardiner realized that his compass was still in the pocket of his trousers.

"Wait," he said softly. "My compass."

The pressure to get moving was nearly palpable, but he needed that item, that one remaining, precious connection to the twentieth century. In a few seconds he felt its comforting shape in his hand and they were out the door. After a stop at a nearby well to fill a pair of water skins, they went through the gates, and before long were well away from the town, Jakop setting a pace that rivaled Tamar's. Even with no one around, every attempt to ask a question was reprimanded. The repeated shushing became irritating.

The sun rose during their walk, lending some light, casting long shadows. The harder-packed path outside the town was easy to walk, but before long they were forced to veer off, and spent many minutes slogging through uneven footing. A few times, Gardiner found himself tripping on smaller rocks. Jakop, on the other hand, seemed to have no trouble, and so Gardiner fell into step behind him. Together they snaked through an area filled with boulders eroded by the dust of countless sand storms. The spacing between the boulders shrank to nothing, becoming walls, growing taller on both sides as they went down a slight grade.

"Here," announced Jakop, coming to a stop. The path dead-ended not much farther off, the rock walls on either side nearly vertical. "Now you may speak."

"Oh? May I?" fumed Gardiner, stepping up closer. Bitterness threatened to override his self-control. "Well, thank you. I am in the Middle East—is that much correct? Will you at least tell me that?"

"Yes."

"Good. Now. Is that town truly the Assur I know from—"

From having read about it and seen pictures of artifacts from it? Insanity!

"From history?" finished Gardiner. It was difficult to speak the words. The short time here hadn't been enough for the truth to completely sink in. But the proof he'd witnessed was incontrovertible.

"It is."

"As you've undoubtedly noticed, I don't belong—"

113

"Indeed," snapped Jakop. "You do not. I need to know how you arrived here."

"And I need to know how a Bronze Age man can become fluent in a language that does not yet exist."

Jakop didn't respond.

"I'm from the United States of America," said Gardiner. "The early twentieth century. 1925. Assur has been dead for centuries. Being able to speak English, you must be familiar with that dating system."

"I am."

"Then what year is this?"

Jakop frowned at Gardiner from beneath thick eyebrows.

"You do understand the question?"

"I do."

"My background is archaeology. I'm very familiar with this area. Give me something. Anything. A name I may know."

"Ur-Nanshe has been the ruler in Lagash, to the south, for three years now."

"That's good enough."

Gardiner silently calculated. He swallowed. The full impact of forty-four centuries produced a strange calm. Or numbness.

"Your presence here is alarming," said Jakop.

"I imagine it would be," replied Gardiner. "I'm a bit alarmed myself—though admittedly a bit elated as well."

"Do not treat this lightly," warned Jakop. "I know how an event like this can occur, but there are frightening implications. Only few of the Great Ones can effect such a transport."

Great Ones?

Enough sunlight washed over the edge of the cliffs above to make Jakop's face clearly visible for the first time. A largish, flat nose poised above a full mustache and beard. The man was younger than Gardiner, with a smaller and much thinner frame. Aside from being a little older than the average worker, he looked very similar to any of the natives at the temple site the previous day, with the exception of one detail: the eyes. Something lurked behind them—an unnatural

wisdom, as if he had looked upon the face of God and been enlight-
ened with the knowledge of the ages.

There was a flash of movement.

What?

Smoothly and swiftly, Jakop had stepped to his right, blocking
the exit. At the same time, he'd also pulled a knife out of his robe.
Sharp or dull, the threat was very real.

"I need to know how you came to be here," he said evenly.
"Do not lie. I will know if you are telling the truth. If you say the
wrong thing, I will kill you. Do you understand?"

Gardiner nodded, eyes on the blade.

"Who sent you?"

Jakop moved a half-step nearer and tensed, ready to attack.

"I wasn't—I was in a temple. In South America. My companions
turned on me, and—"

"Who sent you?" demanded Jakop. "Which entity?"

Gardiner paused, tried to think, but could only focus on the
blade. The small measure of calmness he'd had was gone. He desperately sifted through the twisted wreckage of his mind for the
words needed to save his life.

The man stepped forward.

The crude knife drew closer.

The metal touched his throat.

A memory solidified for Gardiner: A voice. No, not a voice.

A mistake, to be corrected, must first be made.

"Shub-Niggurath," he blurted out. "I was in the presence of
Shub-Niggurath. Do you know that name?"

Jakop studied Gardiner for several tense heartbeats. He withdrew
the blade, relaxed.

"I do."

He moved away and motioned toward a nearby rock. "And that
name may well keep you alive. But I must know everything before
departing this place."

He waited for the Doctor to take a seat before sitting down himself in a position to block any escape.

"Please begin."

Please?

After collecting his thoughts, Gardiner began with the information he'd recently related to Jonathan Harris: how he had first learned of The Divided God through the interception of the tomb robber. He followed that with a description of all of the events from the point when he'd received the inscribed stone, supposedly from Doctor Donau, up until he'd been delivered to Jakop's door in Assur the previous night. Twice during the narrative, it looked very much like the man wanted to interrupt with questions, but didn't. One was the first mention of The Divided God; the other was the first mention of Frances. The name of Nyarlathotep also caused a reaction: a grim nod.

Jakop sat, unmoving and expressionless, after the story ended. Gardiner took the opportunity to sip some water and stretch his legs. He thought that walking around as he did might have been enough to invoke a verbal warning, if not explicit knife waving, but there was no reaction from Jakop, who continued to stare off into space. His knife hand hung so limply that Gardiner thought he might be able to wrest it away, or knock it loose.

"Do you believe what I've told you?"

Jakop looked down at his weapon before slowly putting it away.

"I do," he said. "And I apologize for my behavior. I needed to be sure of your allegiance. The descriptions you gave eerily match my own current situation. That woman, Frances, is truly a devil."

"Yes, I've never known anyone—" Something in the way that Jakop spoke the final sentence turned Gardiner's insides frigid. "She's…here. In this time."

"For at least a year, from what I can determine."

"But how did we both— I didn't even—"

"The reasons are likely unknowable. But your presence here, and hers, must be…necessary."

"We left minutes apart."

Jakop shook his head.

"That, I can definitely say, has no bearing. The portals through which you came here were separate events. They had separate destinations."

"Separate in both space and time?"

Jakop nodded.

Gardiner digested that, wondered what evils Frances might have wrought given a year.

"What do you know of her?"

"Her exact plans are unknown to me, but her actions betray her allegiance. Your memory of what she uttered was good enough to match what I know. Did any of the words she spoke in the cavern register as being more significant than the others?"

Gardiner knew from experience that the degenerate worshipers of the Ancient Ones often distorted the words they spoke, with few knowing what they meant, learning through blind repetition. The language seemed to encourage a seamless string of sounds, barely a pause between them. Frances' pronunciation was very clear, but he couldn't pick out anything in particular that seemed to have had more significance. He shook his head.

"My own knowledge of that language is limited," said Jakop. "Normally, I wouldn't have been able to identify it from your narrative, but, as I said before, recent events here coincide with your descriptions. She spoke the name Gh't'n Tho'h."

Laid bare of surrounding gibberish, and pronounced as clearly as it was, the twisted jumble of letters was recognizable by Gardiner, though only as a string of syllables he'd heard a few times previously.

"I've heard that, or something like it, but know no details."

"I will spare you the details," Jakop said soberly. "Little has ever been recorded about the thing—a legend here or there. But a certain...effect...is reputed to be associated with that entity. I had doubted it myself, but found proof of it. And that is what caused me to become involved. I did not intend to—"

He stopped himself and restarted.

"I discovered this Frances of yours to be at the root, somehow. The fact that she comes from the future...everything now makes more sense. Her knowledge gives her a fearsome edge."

"She is extremely intelligent; I'll give her that. And strategizes well." He grinned broadly. "*But* she is not infallible. I did surprise her by activating that portal to transport us to the underground chamber."

"You did," acknowledged Jakop. "That is encouraging. But I must ask: What did you expect to happen?"

"To that point, Frances had displayed a habit of telling the truth when it was clear she had the upper hand. She said we were in the Inner Sanctum of The Divided God, but there was no god evident. It seemed to me that her amphibious allies were not meant to be there. To me, their presence indicated that a vulnerability in the cavern had been exploited. If the god wasn't there, in that Inner Sanctum, it had to be nearby. The dark spot was out of place, a flaw in an otherwise pristine environment. Based on the other oddities I'd seen, I gambled that it was a doorway."

"As it happens, the Divided God *was* meant to be right there," said Jakop, "but I can tell you more about that later. So, you didn't see The Divided God there, but hoped to find it on the other side of the doorway?"

"No. I thought that such a thing, if ever there, would be long gone."

"And you still have not spoken a name. You still do not know the identity?"

"That's what I had hoped to learn. I've been trying for decades, but haven't yet. There are many gaps in the knowledge that has survived the centuries, either accidentally or purposefully; this is one of them."

Jakop studied Gardiner, as if considering whether or not to answer what had obviously been a plea.

"We must go," he said, standing up and gesturing to the area around them. "Pay attention to the path. I will point out landmarks along the way. One day I may need you to return here without me."

They began retracing their steps through the rocks and sand, heading back in the general direction from which he had come the night before.

"Where are we going?" asked Gardiner.

"To my place of work. We can use your appearance to our advantage. You will be a priest, overseeing me. This English we speak will be a holy language to everyone, as incomprehensible as that used by the Ancient Ones. Just never say more than a few words when anyone is near, and assume that I will never reply, as I'll need to act subservient to you."

"What is it that you do?"

"I am an *architect*, of sorts. I designed the temple from which you came. It is currently being built."

Gardiner stopped.

"You? The arch that Tamar is working on? That's not a copy?"

"No, not a copy. It will be part of the temple very soon."

"But how will you get it there?"

"You'll see for yourself before too long," said Jakop simply. He waved to get Gardiner moving again.

They walked quietly for a while, mainly due north, the walls of the city in the distance off to their left. After mounting a small hill, they turned right and walked into the rising run, toward a site already bustling with activity.

"Tamar," said Gardiner. "How did he know to bring me to you?"

"Some few know that when the temple is complete, strangers will appear. He showed an impressive amount of initiative by thinking you may be one of those."

"What would cause strangers to appear, if I may ask?"

Jakop didn't answer right away. They continued to trudge along, the rising sun working to dispel the coolness of the desert night.

"As you likely know," Jakop finally began, "there is much more to the universe than what we can be seen. Innumerable facets. Many thinking beings, including humans, believe that they are trapped within this common facet. But that is not the case. The mind is the key. What you may know as magic is another tool, a science, for the mind to use."

"I am familiar with magic. I've never been able to get the hang of it, though."

Jakop ignored the comment and continued.

"You also likely realize that the Ancient Ones are not gods. They are composed of a type of matter that breaches dimensional barriers and makes them immensely powerful and unimaginably long-lived. But they are not gods. They are, however, god-like enough to warrant worship among those peoples and cultures too primitive to understand the processes involved. And with a few exceptions, those entities are not actively evil—merely selfish or indifferent to the ways of humans. But *men* will always seek to impose human ideals, even where they are not applicable."

The word *men* was stressed in a very odd way. Disgust perhaps? It was so unexpected that Gardiner's attention lapsed before he refocused on Jakop's voice.

"...harbors no active malice. It is simply a fact that its very essence is incompatible with most forms of life. The inclination of its priests to make sacrifices to it is yet another failure of human society, another example of the stronger exploiting the weaker. If Frances seeks to gain from this somehow, we can only hope that she cannot actively communicate with it. Her patron, the one you know as Nyarlathotep, is among the worst enemies of mankind, however. Though it is reputed to carry out the will of a higher power, it has become plain to those who have studied it that there is another, separate, selfish agenda involved. It revels in chaos and anguish, and furthers its own goals whenever they do not *actively* conflict with those of its master. Honestly, what I fear most out of all of this is unknown motivations of Nyarlathotep."

Jakop quieted while a small group of men crossed their path.

"But one of those few beings that does show actual compassion toward mankind is the Great Mother," he said when they were alone again.

"I beg your pardon. Who?"

Jakop seemed to be embarrassed. "I am sorry. That was— The one you know as Shub-Niggurath. The motivation for this is unclear, but she will help when needed. As will her offspring."

Offspring!

"*She* is the parent of the Halved Child?"

"Yes. Child, or children. Tradition holds that one became divided into two—normally a fatal experience, but we are not dealing with normal entities. Your *Divided God*, Doctor Gardiner, is Nug and Yeb. The children of Shub-Niggurath."

FOURTEEN

MISDIRECTION

Jakop spent their last few minutes of privacy coaching the archaeologist on how to be a priest. For the most part, it required disdainful aloofness, a relatively simple task, though it contrasted with Gardiner's natural personality. But it was stressed repeatedly that he keep his face concealed: No one was to get a good look at him. Jakop made sure of that by wrapping a cloth securely around his head, leaving it loose enough to be comfortable, but leaving just his eyes exposed.

The twentieth-century man spent much of the day in a giddy daze, the relief of finally getting to the bottom of his decades-old mystery tempered by the arrival of more questions about the barely-known Nug and Yeb. This was no *gap* of knowledge as he'd stated earlier; it was a chasm! It was becoming more commonly accepted that the ancients knew more than what was generally believed, but the data had been hidden behind a veil of myth, obfuscated with riddles, or sometimes erased outright. Having the vaguest reference to the twins within that terrible text preserved the information, but only in the most fundamental sense. It was a pencil sketch, a cartoon outline of a picture. The verification from Jakop had colored it in.

Gardiner was under the impression that he'd spend the whole day standing around by himself, looking stern—and it did begin that way. But it wasn't long before Jakop approached him.

"Your arrival is well-timed," he said. "I can use your help."

"Certainly," replied Gardiner. "What can I do?"

"First, I need you to criticize me. Loudly. Act as if you're disappointed."

"In what?"

"It doesn't matter. The blocks. The quality of the quarried blocks."

Gardiner let loose with as much mock anger as he could muster.

"Oh, these blocks are wretched. Do your men have the least bit of common sense? The porosity of the stone is unsuitable for a temple dedicated to the great Nug." The small amount of interest he'd attracted from those nearby increased dramatically at the mention of that name. He looked around and singled out one stone in particular. "There! That one. There are far too many striations in it. Were I a real priest, I suppose I might be truly disappointed. And I might also go on for quite a while more, but seeing as I'm not really angry, it's very hard to keep this up."

Jakop had dropped his head at the start of the outburst, and he kept it lowered.

"That was...sufficient. The tone was good. Say nothing else, but grunt as I speak."

Gardiner grunted.

"Good. Some of the sandstone has veins of magnetite which can be used to our advantage. The first job is to identify and sort the blocks. We need to find the ones with the largest amount of magnetite impurities. Your compass will make that easy. Please follow me."

Another grunt.

Jacob led him away then, head still down. Pairs of eyes followed the men, observed the bizarre new dynamic: their leader cowed into submission by the new priest. The silence of their passage wasn't broken by even one whisper.

They stopped in a storage area empty of other people at the rear edge of the compound. Blocks of fairly uniform sizes were stacked in chest-high piles. All of them looked to be too heavy for Gardiner to handle safely by himself, though he judged that stronger men should be able to move them without much trouble. An open area would allow closer examination of about a score of stones at a time.

"These are left over from my original temple design," explained Jakop. "I am glad I did not dispose of them." He considered what to next say. "You know from your own experience that a spatial displacement portal was, or will be, installed in the temple. And you conjectured that an advanced technology was in play. I can confirm that. The actual implementation also includes a projector to cast an illusion—again, something with which you are personally familiar. The addition of magnetite lowers the power requirements of those devices. A typical installation would tap into the thermal energy of the planet's interior, but the magnetite, combined with the equatorial locations of the temples, will let us use the power of the sun instead—something much more easily engineered.

The scientist in Gardiner latched onto the near-magical concepts he'd come across: teleportation, visual illusions, some method of carving perfect grooves in the stone, a way to treat materials to resist the passage of time. And added one more: now, the ability to harness the power of the sun. The knowledge was too exciting.

"Teach me!"

The words had leapt out of Gardiner's mouth, surprising both men.

"Please," he added.

"I fully intend to," said Jakop. "I'm not an expert in every field, but you need proper instruction to be able to work effectively. I will do the best I can."

Jakop left, and Gardiner got to work with a visual inspection of the stones. Many on the right side of the area seemed to be the most promising, based upon his geological experience. With no one around, a surreptitious check with his compass gave him the reassurance—a twitch of the needle—he needed.

The compass went back into his robe the instant he heard some noise. Jakop was back, a group of large men in tow. He motioned for the men to stop, then approached Gardiner, still acting subservient.

Gardiner pointed at the blocks he estimated were most promising. It was an uncomfortable thing to do, but he kept his tone sharp as he spoke.

"I'll need those men to start breaking down those piles so that I can check each stone more closely. And make sure they understand to stay far enough away so as to not get a good look at my compass."

"Be assured, they are aware."

Jakop bowed, backed away, gave the men their instructions, then left. The four men teamed up in pairs when needed, but they were all very muscular and handled most of the work singly, slowly breaking down the first few piles. The stones were placed in a grid with enough spacing between them to allow access to all sides. For the most part, great care was taken. But one stone was mishandled and dropped.

All four cringed and glanced at Gardiner. Not relishing the role of stern taskmaster, he ignored the opportunity to curse, instead pretending to be meditating. Before long, the first batch was done, and the men returned to the perimeter. They watched with fascination as Gardiner passed judgment on the stones, either blessing or cursing them with enigmatic movements of his cupped hands. When finished with his analysis, he waved the men back over and guided them by just pointing. Two piles—good and bad—were created.

Then the process was repeated, over and over.

When the sun was an hour from setting, Jakop dismissed the men and led Gardiner back in the direction from which they'd come in the morning. They went far enough to ensure that they weren't being followed, then ducked behind some large rocks for privacy. Gardiner waited while an inner turmoil seemed to wrack the man: a matter of deciding exactly what to say, or whether to say anything at all? He finally spoke.

"Let me begin by admitting that, like you, I am also a time traveler. Of sorts. You had probably surmised as much."

Gardiner nodded. "It explains the English we're speaking." Then he asked, "Of sorts?"

Jakop paused before replying.

"It is only my mind that travels. I once visited England of the twenty-third century."

"Does it involve the use of magic?"

There was another pause.

"I'll say that it is not magic, but I don't wish to elaborate. Now, even though it is possible for me to travel through time mentally, it is not possible to do so physically."

"And yet you believed the tale of how I came to be here."

"Yes. It is a unique solution to the problem. The Great Mother commanded a multi-dimensional creature to create the hole in space and time through which you walked."

Jakop waited for Gardiner to give some indication that he understood what he'd been told.

"You're saying that I travelled outside of our normal three dimensions in order to get to here?"

"You must include time as well. So, four."

"But I appeared inside a cave, and a narrow one at that. It—*She*—placed me there. What would have happened had I materialized a few feet to the left? Or right? I would have been in solid stone. I would have been killed!"

"Incredible, yes?"

Jakop gave the shaken man a moment to collect himself before asking, "Did you spend any time *Outside*?"

"Outside of our world? I don't think so. The transfer was accomplished with a single step forward."

"You were shielded from it then. Good. It can have detrimental effects. The mind attempts to adapt, and often does, but it can leave a person changed."

"But how did it...she know to do this? To send me here? How did she know I would find what I was looking for? Was there magic involved? Mind reading? Prescience?"

"Something much more mundane, I would think," said Jakop. "She remembered. She knew."

"But that was the first time we ever met. How could she know?"

"From your perspective, it was the first. Based on your description of the encounter, I have the impression that she had met you already. The two of you will meet again for *her* first time, and it will likely be soon. It just hasn't occurred for you *yet*."

Gardiner's mind churned, then settled, as he reflected on the chain of events—a chain with a loop in it—starting with his strange meeting in the cavern.

"*A mistake, to be corrected, must first be made*," he said. "What was the mistake?"

"I too have been wondering about that," said Jakop. "My only thought is that it refers to Frances somehow."

"She travelled into the past in order to change the future? And I'm here to correct it?"

Jakop said nothing, giving Gardiner an opportunity to think it through.

"So, she's the one who made the mistake. No, wait. That statement was addressed to me. I made the mistake? No, not yet. But I will?"

The fact of his presence in the past complicated any normal sequence of cause and effect. Internally, he understood what had happened. The multi-dimensional concepts all made sense. But speaking about it was another matter. The addition of words seemed to subtract a dimension, and any fingerhold on comprehension went flying right out the window.

Forcing himself to be quiet, the pieces coalesced again in his mind, fitting neatly back together. He studied the problem from a different angle and discovered that he had missed one other possibility.

"Wait! The mistake. What if it was Shub—"

"Frances," declared Jakop, seemingly weary of the other's guessing. "It was Frances who made, or makes, or will make, the mistake."

His explanation had such finality that Gardiner accepted it without question. "You sound as if you have some insight as to her plans," he said. "She's been here for a year. Have you learned anything?"

"Little, but enough," said Jakop. "Frances' location is unknown to me. Or perhaps it keeps changing. But I discovered a trail of bodies—though *trail* is the wrong word. There is little connection from one death to the next, though there is a definite link. There are also indications that an army is being amassed. In the history of your planet—"

my planet?

"—it is a relatively small one, but it is large enough." He paused. "I would very much like to be able to prove to you without a doubt that the army and Frances are tied together, but cannot. I only have a...*feeling.*"

Jakop had shown a tendency to place unusual stresses on some words, as if finding them distasteful to speak, or disappointed that there wasn't a more appropriate term.

"It's enough of a *feeling*"—Gardiner tried to say it the same way— "to have convinced you, though."

"It is. And I'm fearful of the implications. Or possibilities. An army controlled by Frances is a disturbing idea." There was a sincere heaviness to the words, and Jakop paused before continuing. "My original purpose for visiting this place and time was simply to learn. A passive act, learning. However, in the face of a threat of this nature, action is required."

"The temple?"

"Yes, but temples. One for each child. With them, and given enough time, I hope to raise an army of my own to counteract that of Frances'. Shub-Niggurath would help protect us if we could contact her, but the children are more accessible and will provide a similar service after they are called down from the heavens and reside here on Earth, within their respective temples."

Gardiner allowed a snort of laughter to escape, then quickly wished he hadn't. Jakop was being perfectly serious. "You believe that can actually be done."

"I do. But even with the combined presence of Nug and Yeb, numbers of men are still needed. But not just any men. A certain resilience of the mind is needed when these types of entities are involved."

"Without a doubt," said Gardiner. "But why South America? Why not build the temples here?"

"There are several reasons, but the most important is belief. The people of this region have had more than their fair share of gods. The large variety has jaded them. A nascent science has taken hold in some areas as well, contributing to a lack of faith. Or maybe it can be better described as an increase of doubt. There are exceptions of course, but too many have grown cynical, now only giving lip service to once-crucial concepts. And without faith there can be no zealotry. The natives of South America, on the other hand, are still primitive enough to be swayed. I've been able to convince them that Nug is the true head of their traditional hierarchy, a deity who has been guiding them all from behind the scenes for generations, and who has now chosen to reveal himself. Being able to actually see the god… That is a powerful incentive when recruiting soldiers based on faith."

"And Yeb?"

"It is a matter of symmetry. Aside from the aesthetics, there is a…scientific necessity for balance: two protectors spaced equally apart. The temple of Yeb will be at very nearly the opposite point on the Earth from that of Nug. And that location allows us to take advantage of a unique historical detail. The natives of the Pacific Ocean have a culture that extends further back in time than many know. It includes stories passed down through the generations, vague remembrances of a civilization on a now-sunken continent, and the human sacrifices that had been exacted from them. The opportunity for revenge, combined with the fact of seeing Yeb, will be more than enough to fill out the army."

"Then, if it's not too late, we find Frances and defeat her."

"I am glad to hear you include yourself in this struggle."

Gardiner shrugged. "She came here because of me. Even knowing how accidental it was, I have to admit a certain level of responsibility for her presence."

A silence fell between the two men then. Jakop seemed to be struggling to decide what to say next. Gardiner was sobered by the immensity of the project before them, but recovered his voice first when a seemingly-obvious truth popped into his head.

"But…why are you even involving yourself in this? If you're just visiting this period as you say, you can leave at any time."

"You are correct. That is within my power."

"It seems to me that you're taking an unnecessary risk." On a whim, he added, "This isn't even your planet."

That final comment evoked a start, then a squint from Jakop, barely visible in the fading light.

"Yes, I must admit to having said that," he sighed. "Speaking of my true nature is a difficult thing. Because it is a criminal act in my society, it is rarely done. But it would likely have been necessary eventually. It is true that I am not originally from this world, but my race has…adopted it. We have an interest in protecting it. I have lived far longer than you can imagine, on multiple worlds. It seems to be a universal custom to reckon time by counting revolutions around stars. I have known a countless number of those cycles."

He paused before continuing awkwardly.

"For your kind…constrained to a relatively short lifespan…time is fleeting. You can experience only so much. There is seldom a chance for boredom. My…excursions…through time are the only thing that keep…life…interesting for me. They are my only chances to learn something new. Do something different. You see?"

Gardiner would be the first to admit that he was overly trusting. A good lie, or good acting, would be enough to convince him of nearly anything. To that point, Jakop had spoken with confidence, or not spoken at all. It had been consistent. This time, he labored to find the right words—though he had also mentioned *learning* earlier. That much, at least, was consistent. And true as well?

True enough for now.

"This is a chance for some excitement?" asked Gardiner, playing along.

"As you say. Also, you were deposited here by a being that knows the facts of history. Your placement here cannot be accidental, and must be related to Frances' presence. In this place and time, with a year of experience less than she, you need help from someone to defeat her. That person must be me. If I leave, you will likely fail. And so, I cannot leave."

And that makes perfect sense.

"A bit of both selfishness and altruism?"

"Is there ever a circumstance in which that is not the case?"

"Never," barked Gardiner.

Jakop looked at the horizon, the setting sun painting the sky in shades of red and orange.

"Come. We need to get back, eat, rest. Many of the days to come will be much like this one."

They started moving back toward the town.

Gardiner chuckled, trying to relieve some of the stress he felt.

"Assuming we survive this, it'll make quite a story when I return."

Jakop stopped.

"Doctor Gardiner…" And for the first time since meeting him, Gardiner heard something akin to sympathy in Jakop's voice. "I was hoping that you would have understood by now."

"Understood what?" But even before Gardiner had finished uttering the words, he realized that he did, in fact, understand.

"I know of no way to send you back."

FIFTEEN

CONSIDERATIONS

For Quentin Gardiner, the novelty of living in the very same past he had studied all of his life had been too intriguing to consider much else. To be sure, life was harsher than what he was used to, but civilized *enough*. So many theories of that period—*this period*—were constantly being either confirmed or broken as he observed. The sights, sounds and smells—many, many smells—had simply delighted him from one minute to the next since the moment he'd arrived.

But the revelation of being trapped there soured his attitude. The stink of sweat and excrement became constant irritants. The smoke from cooking fires seemed to never dissipate, nearly choking him at times. Hunger and thirst were annoyances. The days were too hot, the nights too cool. The coarse fabric of his clothing itched.

With that sharp change of attitude, the following day began poorly, but he forced himself to stay busy with a continuation of the task from the previous day. This time, he traced the veins of magnetite impurities within the blocks from the "good" pile using a device that Jakop had given him. It looked to be an ordinary clay tablet engraved with a cuneiform prayer, but hidden within it, he was told, was circuitry that would cause the characters to glow in different ways based upon the concentration of the mineral. To reinforce his priestly ruse, he was to mumble the prayer on the tablet from time to time as he studied the stones and marked them with chalk. Initially, he was careful to prevent the men helping him from seeing

132

the red glow of the tablet, but as the day wore on, he grew careless. A few times it lit up with a surprising intensity.

It was during one of those occurrences when he noticed that one of the workers seemed to be more fixated on his actions than the others. A heavily muscled brute, he preferred to sit apart from the others, exchanging words with them only periodically. The man's left arm and hand were scarred, as if healed from a burn, along with a portion of the neck and head. The scalp on that side was the worst, with all the hair burned off and angry red flesh visible. Gardiner was amazed that he had survived such an injury in this place and time. Every glimpse of that scarring reminded him of the butchery of Jonathan Harris in the pouring rain—and the cause of it. Even if he couldn't leave this era of history, he knew that stopping Frances was vitally important, a goal to work toward regardless of his attitude, or the time and effort needed.

His focus renewed, it was easier to concentrate on the work at hand—though a lapse in another area crept in. Wearying of the cloth over his face, he loosened it. At some point—exactly when he couldn't say—it fell open completely.

And he never noticed.

It was during the period when his face was fully exposed that Jakop came by. He wore a great frown, but said nothing. Gardiner fixed his mask.

Near the end of the day, Jakop pulled the doctor aside. Prepared to be admonished for his earlier mistake, he was instead puzzled when discretely handed a small tablet inscribed with English. It was gibberish to be sure, but definitely English.

"Please memorize this then destroy it," whispered Jakop quietly. "I've written it out phonetically for you. It means, 'Excellent work today. As a reward, you may all leave early.' I want to dismiss everyone and show you something."

Gardiner practiced mouthing the words, eventually repeating them back as quietly as possible. After some corrections, Jakop picked up a large hand drum and smacked it several times with his palm. When all eyes were upon him, he bowed his head. Only two short days of treating Gardiner as the ultimate authority on the site demonstrated how well he had played his role. As soon as he bowed, everyone shifted their attention to the archaeologist and did the same.

Gardiner calmed himself, then spoke the words as loudly as he could. Satisfaction with his performance dissolved into a mild panic as he sensed complete bewilderment from everyone.

But Jakop was ready to reinforce the message. He said something that caused everyone to speak in unison. "Thank you very much," is how Gardiner interpreted it. The confusion turned to mild delight, and everyone began putting tools away.

When most had left, Jakop led him to a large, upright slab into which a rectangular depression had been hewn. A very fine-grained sandstone, it was decorated with well-crafted lintel, jambs, and sill to make it look as if it was a doorway. But it led nowhere, reminding Gardiner of the Winchester Mystery House.

"Would you like to see the progress on the temple for yourself, Doctor?"

Its seeming nowhere-ness now made sense.

"Very much so! This is a doorway directly to South America?"

"A portal, yes. I've had natives working there for six months," said Jakop. "Now, watch where I touch." He looked around to be sure that no one was nearby then pressed his index finger just once to the right of the door. "There is a security feature in place," he added. "You must take one step through, stop, then immediately go to the left."

He shifted his body for emphasis.

"Anyone not knowing that will die. And the change of scene can be described as…shocking. Prepare yourself."

Gardiner nodded.

"This portal is currently configured to permit passage of one person at a time, so no one will be able to follow us. I'll go through first and be ready to grab you if needed. Remember to touch the jamb again after I go."

He walked through the doorway and vanished.

Gardiner wasn't sure which was more dramatic: Jakop walking—seemingly—into solid sandstone, or Frances disappearing through the black oval, or personally using the illusionary doorway at the temple. For all, the effect had been equally impressive.

Okay.

He touched the jamb, took a deep breath, walked forward.

A verdant blanket of jungle stretched off into the distance, only interrupted by the muddy, brown scar of a river. He heard the cry of a raptor from somewhere *below* him. Cotton puff clouds floated seemingly just out of reach. His breath caught as the full impact of the vista hit, then he sidled to the left. Jakop grabbed him gently by the arm and pulled him backward a step.

"Very good, Doctor."

Gardiner exhaled.

"Over the years, I've learned that an even temper often helps when dealing with the unexpected."

He looked to his right, craning his neck around to see where he had come through. Where his feet had been, there couldn't have been more than eight inches between his toes and the vertiginous edge. To the right was a flat area much larger than where they now stood. The vertical wall that served as the doorway on this side was an unadorned, perfectly flat, clean section of sandstone. That same material was all around them, as well as under foot.

"This can only be the top of the tepui," said Gardiner, studying the coloration of the stone.

"Yes, and take note of that pad." Jakop pointed at the wide, inviting area to the right of the landing area. "That slab is loosely balanced. Any weight at all upon it will cause it to tip."

"Has anyone fallen yet?"

"As far as I can tell, one native at the very beginning. And not due to this trap."

Gardiner inched forward to the edge and looked down, tried to imagine what the speck of a spattered man two thousand feet below might look like.

"This way," said Jakop.

In the Middle East it had been late afternoon, but here it was morning, the sun still climbing. Despite that, a rock ledge directly above them kept the area cloaked in shadow, obscuring a set of steps up which Jakop led him. The stairs were in mint condition, with sharp, square edges.

They emerged from a hole onto the roof of the world. The view of the jungle was no different from fifteen feet higher, but the expansive vista felt more commanding, with the top of the tepui having been cleared of vegetation to expose the stone. The area upon which they stood—a thick rim—seemed to be wide enough to contain a standard pitch from the only sport Gardiner had ever played in his youth: association football.

I would hate to go out-of-bounds, though.

But below that rim, the feat of engineering currently underway was nothing less than spellbinding.

Many hypotheses—some quite preposterous—were continually being introduced to explain how many ancient structures could have been built, but no man of science from Gardiner's time had ever conjectured anything remotely like what he was witnessing with his own eyes. The natives held poles six to eight feet long with a bronze-colored hoop attached at one end. As they swung the tools with slow, easy strokes, the hoops contacted the stone—and the material disappeared! They were digging through solid rock more easily than swinging a scythe through grass.

As he watched in fascination, he saw how men with larger hoops were roughing out the basic shape of the hole, while others with smaller ones performed finishing work, smoothing the surface with flattened or squared-off hoops. Multiple ramps wound down in curves along the inside of the hollowed area, like the rifling in a gun, allowing the workers access to the top. A plume of dust coming from the left drew Gardiner's notice, and he gawked at the most marvelous sight of all.

Ingenious.

Torrents of rock and dust were spewing from hoops mounted at the top of the tepui. He smiled with some satisfaction as he put two and two together.

"They wield your portals in their hands! The material is transported to those matching exit points, where it falls down the side of the mountain, building that artificial hillside in the process."

"Just so," said Jakop.

This was a rare event for Gardiner. So often in his career, he could form a hypothesis from the evidence at hand, provide some amount of proof, convince himself and others. But not actually having firsthand knowledge left a residue of doubt. This was a far different case, far more satisfying.

Mystery solved!

"Disintegrating rock," said Jakop, "requires much more energy than taking advantage of the edge effect of the field to disrupt matter and transport it. Some safeguards can also be built in. To be effective, the carving tools cannot be moved too quickly, and so the men cannot do much harm to each other if they lash out in anger. Also, they need to be held in both hands for the displacement field to be activated."

"And they've done all this in only six months?" He walked towards the edge and looked down into the massive hole. "They're nearly at ground level, it seems."

"Nearly."

Gardiner stared into the depths, replaying the images of his harrowing escape from the future.

"This is a solid mass of sandstone, isn't it?"

"It is. And below that is granite. Also solid."

"And so, as you dig below the local ground level, you may encounter a natural aquifer, but that will yield fresh water."

"Correct, but I was able to verify that there is none."

"In the twentieth century, the cavern is flooded with seawater."

"Yes."

"Regardless of how it gets there—likely due to Frances—simple physics requires that the hole be deep enough to allow a flow from the sea. That is, it must be below sea level."

Jakop pursed his lips and nodded.

"How deep had you originally planned to dig?"

"Ground level, roughly. Down to the granite."

"And now that I'm here, and I've told you of the future, your plans have changed, haven't they?"

"Now…I think…several dozen feet below ground level would be a better depth."

"And so my presence here changes history?"

"No," said Jakop. "Time is a closed system. The totality of events must be evaluated from outside the flow for it to make sense. From that perspective, there are no paradoxes."

"You're saying that my presence changes nothing? I was meant to be here, and I was meant to give you information that causes you to change your plans, even though that change is not a sound decision."

"But it *is* sound when viewed in its entirety. It is just not the choice we would prefer to make."

"But you are arranging events to give an advantage to the enemy."

"That cannot be a consideration. It doesn't matter."

"How can it not matter?" asked Gardiner, perplexed.

"All events throughout time have already occurred."

"The future cannot be changed?"

"Correct."

"Then what is the point of my being here?"

Jakop shrugged.

"There is no point other than you were meant to be here, at this moment in time, asking me that question. Whatever you consciously choose to do, or not do, will make no difference to the outcome that has been predestined."

"No. I cannot accept that all of history is already written. I thought that I was put here in the past to correct a mistake. How do I do that? Where is free will?"

"It does not actually exist. It is an illusion due to the fact that we all—with very few exceptions—are forced to perceive time in a linear fashion."

Shaking his head, Gardiner studied the workers as they carved into the rock. Some buried notion was trying to dig its way out of the depths of his mind. There was something different about his presence here... He swiped his foot at a loose piece of debris left behind. It rolled and hit another, then ricocheted off a third before coming to a stop.

That's it!

"Jakop, I see a difference where you do not."

He reached down to pick up a pair of pebbles, tossed them into a shallow puddle of rainwater nearby. Ripples spread out from two points, crashing quietly into each other, overlapping. Gardiner pointed at the water.

"The difference is that I am here. Physically. You, your people, only cast your minds through time."

The other man's eyes narrowed. He opened his mouth to speak, closed it again.

"You told me when I first arrived that my physical transport through time was unprecedented. Could that have an unforeseen effect? And bear in mind, of course, that Frances did the same. I posit that our arrival in the past, and our actions in this time period, *can* affect the future."

"No," declared Jakop. "The system cannot be perturbed."

"Drips of water, given enough time, can erode a hole in solid rock. Over the course of thousands of years, can two pebbles such as Frances and myself not create change?"

There was a long delay from the troubled man. Gardiner waited for his response, but after minutes had passed, still none had come.

Sixteen

KANNIT

After they returned through the portal to the Middle East, Jakop quizzed Gardiner about the dimensions of the temple: exact measurements when known, best guesses when not. Lacking paper and pen, clay and stylus were used to make some rough drawings. Jakop nodded with each answer he was given, but still appeared unsatisfied. They made their way back to Assur in silence, both thinking deeply.

Ignorant of the mechanics of his dislocation in time, Gardiner couldn't bring himself to worry over any metaphysical implications. There was no way to undo the effect from the cause. Instead, his own thoughts had turned to the concept of free will. Jakop's championing of predestination bothered him terribly. Given that model of the universe, what would be the point of life—of any life—except to occupy a specific portion of space during a certain segment of time?

I don't know.

What would be the point?

I don't know.

The dispiriting cycle dragged him lower and lower.

What would be the point?

I don't know.

What would be the point?

I don't know.

Going round and round, getting nowhere, he was spiraling down the drain toward true despair when the physical world intruded: His stomach rumbled. That gnawing sensation drew him back, kept him afloat. He latched onto his last thought and realized the simple truthfulness of it.

I don't know!

And that was it. No person existing within the framework of four-dimensional space and time would ever be able to know, so there was no point in worrying about it. Free will, the illusion of free will... Whichever it was, the best he could do going forward would be to tread as carefully as possible and make no glaring mistakes.

Jakop, however, still hadn't escaped his own mental trap by the time they arrived in Assur. If anything, his stupor had gotten worse. He was unable, or unwilling, to answer even simple questions. The condition reminded Gardiner of the *shell shock* suffered by soldiers from the Great War.

The suggestion from Gardiner that he get supplies for dinner was enough to instill some life in Jakop—but only briefly. He wasn't gone long before returning with a few loaves of bread and the gutted carcass of a medium-sized bird. That was the extent of his animation, though. Gardiner handled the cooking. Jakop ate mechanically. Further attempts to coax some life out of the man after dinner were ineffective, so Gardiner went to bed. He turned his back on the flickering, final remnants of the cooking fire and let his host sit, staring into the flames.

In the morning, Jakop was gone. After a breakfast of leftover bread, Gardiner scraped his teeth with a makeshift toothbrush he'd fashioned, then chewed some spearmint that grew wild in the area. As he washed off his face, he felt his thickening beard and longed for a razor. Even afield in the jungle or desert he normally stayed clean-shaven. He wondered if he would ever be able to do that again.

His morning toilet complete, Gardiner headed to the work site. Jakop wasn't there, which was slightly worrisome, given the state of the man's mind. He told himself that there was no need to panic yet however, and continued tracing the magnetite and marking the blocks

Jakop showed up mid-morning, bleary-eyed, but better—though, applied to him, the term came nowhere close to meaning anything like normal. His eyes still held that haunting implication of hidden wisdom. He dismissed the workmen, then turned to Gardiner.

"I've done much thinking about your speculation," he announced.

"The entire night?"

"Very nearly. I have come to the conclusion that there is no way for me to know for sure if your presence changes history or not. My people know very little of this era. I have nothing to compare the current situation against. Therefore, my only course of action is to continue as planned."

"And trust in free will, perhaps?"

A small but genuine smile splashed across his face.

"I will not go so far as to say that."

"And what of the depth of the excavation?"

"There is an interesting turn of events associated with that," said Jakop. "I was wrong. We must go fifty feet below ground level."

"Oh?"

"In order to contain the being, Nug, an enormous container must be fashioned. We will be calling it down from a place of much lower gravity. When it arrives, it will not initially have the strength to hold itself together. That was the reason for the work being done in the first place."

Gardiner recalled what he had seen in that underground cavern, made a rough calculation of the eventual size of the hole, and imagined it filled with a horrific, pulsing mass of alien protoplasm.

"The child—children—will be similar to the parent then?"

"Yes, but a more important detail is the mistake I discovered and corrected. I admit that—"

Gardiner stopped listening. His mind already back in that cavern, those cryptic words came echoing back easily. Was this the *mistake* that Gardiner's presence was meant to correct? Jakop might not even entertain that as a possibility, and it seemed unwise to mention it. The man had just crawled out of one hole; there was no need to push him into another.

Or drag him. Gardiner had fallen back in himself, fixated on trying to unravel the knot in his thread of time. Was his aberrant appearance in ancient Assur actually necessary? Or, would the astute Jakop have discovered his error in time. Was Gardiner's presence in the past needed? Was it making a difference? Did it matter?

Stop it, Quentin.

Gardiner banished the thoughts with a shake. What mattered, what was most important, was that the mistake had been corrected. He refocused and caught the tail end of Jakop's explanation.

"—in contact with the roots of this world. That is, the granite. This requirement could be likened to a flow of electricity. Being completely in contact with the granite allows for a better *flow* of power, a stronger *field* of protection. Those terms aren't entirely appropriate, but close enough."

"So, Frances spoke truly when she described the excavation as the Inner Sanctum," said Gardiner. "I find myself questioning anything she ever told me."

"I can imagine. But yes, we will proceed as planned for both temples, call down the entities, and…"

Gardiner waited.

"…*hope*…that all turns out well," finished Jakop, nearly choking on the one word. "Either the events remain true, and at some point, the bowl is breached and flooded with sea water, or history is changed and Nug actually remains in place to protect this world. At this point I believe that either of those choices will be satisfactory. There are, of course, less satisfactory ones, and our job will be to minimize the odds of any of those outcomes."

"You seemed to have been satisfied yesterday with respect to the dimensions of the temple," said Gardiner, trying to reassure him.

"Yes," said Jakop. "I can show you."

He pulled something from a pocket within his robe. it looked like a plain piece of aluminum, less than a foot square with all edges rounded, not even a quarter-inch thick.

"The particulars you related match against my original plans to the inch. Those details kept me grounded." His look turned very serious. "I gave much consideration to departing this period, returning to my own time." His features lightened. "Obviously, I did not. Staying here was the better choice."

He either waved his hands over the device, or touched it; Gardiner couldn't tell which. As if by magic, a design for the temple appeared on the surface, fine black lines against the silvery background. Jakop's hand motions manipulated the image in various ways, rotating, magnifying, switching between annotated drawings and full color pictures of the South American site. He paused to describe some of them. As Gardiner had been told earlier, the plans matched up exactly with the measurements he'd taken with Jonathan Harris.

After a general review of the construction plans, Jakop let Gardiner get better acquainted with the device. He was captivated by the thing, but mystified at how the display could be manipulated by just waving his fingers and hands above it. But it wasn't long before a hubbub came from around the corner. Jakop snatched it away and concealed it within his robe.

"Stand tall," he whispered. "Look angry and be silent."

No sooner than the words had left his lips, a very important-looking man came around the corner, surrounded by an entourage of guards. Jakop bowed deeply at the waist and held that position. Except for an evident belly that indicated that he ate very well, and a robe made of a fine, silky fabric, the stranger looked much the same as anyone else from this era, with a full beard, deeply tanned skin, and dark eyes.

Gardiner did as he was told and did not waver, even when a guard separated from the group and headed over to him. Before the burly man had a chance to touch him, Jakop shouted a few words, only one of which was obvious: Nug. The guard stopped and looked back at his boss, whose displeasure slowly dissipated. He called the guard back and waved Jakop upright, then commenced to grill him. Jakop's answers were consistently brief, with a few gestures directed at Gardiner. Finally, he bowed and backed away.

"This man, Kannit," he said to Gardiner, "is singlehandedly financing the creation of the temples. I've told him that you are only permitted to speak a holy language, and that I must translate. Say a few sentences about anything, but angrily, and mention Nug one time."

The sentence ended on a rising note, as if a question was being asked.

"I am head of the Archaeology Department at Miskatonic University, and I have been fighting the scourge of the Ancient Ones for years! It is wonderful indeed to learn that the beings Nug, Yeb, and Shub-Niggurath are allies, willing to help mankind!"

"Excellent."

Jakop returned to Kannit and spoke to the man for quite a while.

When he finished, the benefactor gave a contented nod and said one word that Gardiner knew.

"Tamar!"

The mason from Gardiner's first day had been hidden behind the mass of guards, but upon hearing his name, shot out into the open and bowed.

Kannit then pointed at Tamar and said something to Jakop, who hesitated for a heartbeat before replying affirmatively. After a few more words to Jakop, Kannit and his guards departed. As soon as the group was out of sight, Jakop gave a set of instructions to Tamar, who nodded as each command was given. The younger man left wordlessly.

"I have made another mistake," bemoaned Jakop when the man was out of earshot. "And now it is likely too late to correct."

"What is it?" Gardiner asked, concern in his voice.

"Kannit has taken a liking to Tamar, and has ordered me to place him in charge of the construction of the temple of Nug."

"Why is that bad? What is the mistake?"

"I neglected to have him killed."

Astounded, Gardiner blinked.

"Why would you even consider that?" The words came out very loudly.

"Keep your voice down," Jakop said sternly. "He led you to me! He saw you."

"Yes, but my face is concealed now."

"He also heard you. How much English did you speak that day in his presence?"

Gardiner conceded the other man's point.

"He is an excellent stone mason," continued Jakop. "And very ambitious. And has a reasoning ability far above average. If he did not react to your voice then, he will likely deduce your identity before too long. A mysterious priest is here with me, just days after delivering another mysterious man to my door? If I had known he was near, I would not have had you speak at all."

"Why must you assume the worst? Can he not be another ally?"

"We cannot trust anyone. And I forbid you to try. This situation may yet be salvageable as long as you stay aloof. Removing Tamar from here to the South American site will help. If absolutely necessary, I can still eliminate him, but only with great care. Kannit would need to be positively convinced that such an event was an accident."

Gardiner took a step forward and uncovered his face for emphasis.

"It damned well better be an accident! I will refuse to work further with you if Tamar dies purely based upon your overly-paranoid suspicions." Right after speaking the words, he wondered if he could carry through with that threat.

Does this alien know of poker?

They locked gazes for a long moment, measuring each other. Jakop broke the stalemate.

"Your position is noted."

"As is yours," said Gardiner grudgingly. "I will refrain from any contact with Tamar. If he makes the connection and determines who I am…I am open to discussing options at that point."

"As I said, I am not eager to eliminate him. Kannit is a powerful man who makes a good ally, but would be a worse enemy. He is under the impression that the army we recruit will be under his control."

"Was it wise to promise him that?"

"I spoke truthfully to him. Every man who lives after the coming events will be his to command."

SEVENTEEN

TRUST ISSUES

With Gardiner's sensibilities pushed to the limit, it took a while for him to fully calm down. But, left alone and able to concentrate on his task of marking the blocks, he finally did. Jakop showed up at the very end of the day. He waited until the workers left before approaching.

"It's not completely unexpected that Tamar showed up today," began Jakop. There was a note of resignation in his voice, an unvoiced apology. "Tamar had previously sent word that the marble facing had been completed and would arrive soon."

"And Kannit?" asked Gardiner.

"Also, not unexpected. He's not averse to making a trip here in order to get a personal update on the progress. And the timing of his visits follows no pattern. He was here not long ago, but the frequency has been increasing of late."

"He doesn't trust you?"

"He trusts no one. He is very odd."

Odder than you? thought Gardiner. Being tactful, he said nothing.

"But what *is* unexpected," continued Jakop, "is their appearance together today. I don't recall ever mentioning Tamar's name to Kannit. It would seem to be out of character for the mason, but I can only surmise that he personally told Kannit the news of the marble work. And Kannit must have decided to promote him."

"And their appearance together was meant as a point of emphasis."

"Yes, I had no choice in the matter. But there is some good news here. With Tamar overseeing the temple in South America, much less of my time will be needed there. Work on the temple of Yeb is far behind. I'll be able to shift my attention there. And being busy, and far removed from you, Tamar may forget about the strange priest. Still… His unknown motivations make me nervous."

"I've sensed nothing untoward from that man," said Gardiner. "He was very helpful that first day when he led me to you." But as he spoke the words, he knew that he hadn't sensed evil intent from either Frances or Jonathan. And he knew that Jakop knew that.

Jakop, perhaps learning a measure of tact, said nothing.

They headed home, walking quietly for a long while. A strong breeze, heralding rain by the smell of it, refreshed them both, flapping their robes. Jakop stopped as the walls of the town came into sight.

"I have somewhat of an awkward request, Doctor Gardiner," he said. "But I'm certain you will understand my reasoning."

"Go on."

"We have an advantage," said Jakop, "one which I am loath to give up: Frances does not know that you are here, in this place and time. You spoke of her ability to plan and prepare, but also mentioned that she can be surprised. If she discovers that you are here, we lose that."

"Yes, we definitely need to minimize my exposure. I can't say I like keeping my face covered, but I'll manage. Isn't that enough?"

"I don't believe it is. It's too easy to slip up, to forget. Even a strong enough wind, such as what we have now, may dislodge the cloth at the wrong time. I propose that the best solution is to alter you. Surgically."

"It's not possible."

"It is," Jakop insisted. "The tools for it are available. It was not common in the culture from which you came, but in later years, there will be a powerful social trend toward surgical manipulation of one's features."

"It sounds painful."

149

"In that future time, it is not. Here and now… I will not lie to you and say otherwise."

Gardiner understood the reason for the request, but thought it excessive. Silly, even. But he granted Jakop enough respect to treat the suggestion seriously. Wishing for a mirror, he settled on recalling a memory of the last time he'd shaved, back at the camp in Guyana.

"What would you suggest?"

Jakop stood to the side and studied him.

"Obviously, without proper, biologically inert materials, only subtraction is possible. Your chin is very strong; we can safely re-move some bone there, perhaps create a cleft. The nose could be made sharper, a subtle change, but one that contributes much in terms of identity. I can also alter your hair color permanently, a pro-cedure much less painful than the surgery. And I would suggest add-ing a small scar somewhere on the cheek."

"Is that all?" Gardiner asked sarcastically.

"It's enough." Either the sarcasm was lost on Jakop or he ignored it. "You'll be losing weight due to lower food and water intake. I would also encourage you to expose your face to the sun after the surgery has healed in order to darken your skin. With all of that, you shouldn't be recognizable by Frances if she happens to see you. Speech would be a different matter. Talking would shatter the illu-sion."

Gardiner felt his chin and nose while reviewing the list. Had he some hope of returning to 1925, he would have rejected Jakop's suggestion outright. But aside from continuing to hide his face, no other alternatives presented themselves. Reminded again of being trapped in the past, he couldn't summon any desire to think crea-tively. Besides, defeating Frances was paramount. Surgery was an extreme option, but foolproof.

"Do you concur?" asked Jakop.

Gardiner paused, but nodded. It wasn't an agreement so much as a refusal to resist.

Jakop led the way to the dead-end in which they had had their confrontation on the first morning, frequently looking behind them as they went. Once there, he pressed his fingertips upon an area of the rock in a spiraling pattern, then walked boldly through the solid wall. Once he had completely disappeared, he stuck his arm back out and motioned for Gardiner to enter.

They stood in a man-made cavern, probably twenty feet high, right angles everywhere. There were no windows, illumination coming from strategically placed lighting fixtures along the walls. A stark lack of decorations was reminiscent of the temple in Guyana. The cool temperature also felt familiar.

"This is a storehouse of technology," explained Jakop. "There a few caches like this around the globe, placed in carefully chosen spots, places that have been researched to remain undisturbed through the course of history."

"We're underground again," Gardiner said. "I know that you'd want to hide a room like this, but who would find a door disguised by one of your illusions? Why go to the extra trouble of also placing it under the surface?"

"In that, you are correct. The doorway itself is the primary concern, but for a place like this to be useful, it must remain both intact and accessible. However, you are ignorant of the scale of time involved. This room was created over seventy million years ago. Over a span like that, the drifting of continents and other geologic processes become valid concerns."

As Jakop started forward Gardiner's mind boggled at the figure.

Nearly as old as the dinosaurs…

"Doctor?"

Gardiner's senses returned and he followed. Six wide corridors shot off to the right from the main cavern in which they walked. They passed the first two and went down the third. Lights came on as soon as they stepped into it, revealing a perfectly smooth walls, floor and ceiling. Compact lighting fixtures and the outlines of ceiling-height doors, fully ten feet wide, were the only details he could pick out. The fixed pattern of their layout only served to emphasize the monotony.

"This is where you got the digging hoops? And the device I've been using?"

"Yes. I constructed them here."

Jakop examined each door as they passed it. Gardiner looked closely, but could not detect any kind of label to distinguish them.

About halfway down, Jakop stopped next to a door on his left.

"Take a deep breath and hold it," he cautioned, then pressed his fingers on the wall in a specific pattern.

The door opened so swiftly that it seemed to have simply disappeared. With its absence, an avalanche of what looked like sand began to pour out of the enormous cavity. Gardiner flinched at the obvious danger, but the other man did not move a bit. Even as the *sand* flowed, it dissolved into nothing, never reaching more than a few inches through the open doorway. Not even a minute later, it was all gone, even the granules at the bottom that would have stayed entirely inside the chamber. Jakop held his hand up, indicating that it was not yet safe to breath. A wispy odor of ozone tickled Gardiner's nose as he began to struggle with the effort.

"Now," hissed Jakop, taking in a large gulp of air.

"What was that?" asked Gardiner between breaths, waving his hands where the sand-like substance had been.

"It is best described as a preservative, greatly reducing the effects of entropy and decay. My people engineer well, but lubricants evaporate, and some delicate apparatuses cannot last forever. There is no way to halt the flow of time, but it can be minimized. At a ratio of a million to one, the contents of this room have aged approximately seventy years."

"But how is that possible?"

"I cannot describe the physics behind that material. Your own people are only beginning to explore that area of science. You would not comprehend it." The final comment was spoken dismissively, bordering on insulting. But before Gardiner could say anything, Jakop continued. "Perhaps I will go over it in more detail one day. Now is not the time, and there are many, far more useful skills for you to master first. Come. We should get done with this."

As Jakop led the way into the opened vault, Gardiner watched as he searched for, and found, the equipment he would need. The walls were lined with shelving units organized to optimize storage space by allowing one unit at a time to be accessed through a movable gap. Again, even though there was no visible sign or labels, Jakop was able to locate what he needed. A few taps of his fingertips would cause the shelves to move, opening the gap where he needed it to be. A kind of continuous belt within each unit must have also been in play, bringing the desired shelf up or down for easy access to it.

He placed what he needed on a central table and motioned Gardiner over. The objects looked as if they had melted. Very light in weight, they still felt to be solidly built. Everything clicked.

"This is a machine shop, not an operating theater."

"A fabrication facility," Jakop confirmed. "The tools in this room are meant to shape harder substances such as stone and metal."

"And you're going to use them to drill into my face?"

"There will be no drilling. This one, for example, uses a very fine beam of highly concentrated energy. It cuts through flesh so easily and painlessly that it is actually quite dangerous to use. Carelessness can result in death."

"You said that the procedure would be painful."

"It's the healing that is painful. Emergency first-aid has been included with the equipment, and so minor wounds can be numbed, but bone is another matter. Your chin will be in great pain for a few days. But I see no alternative. If an effort is made to disguise you, we should not take partial measures."

Gardiner closed his eyes and tried to draw upon all of the courage at his disposal.

Could this be any worse than the time I broke my arm?

It could, he conceded. The greenstick fracture of his arm was a memory, forty years in the past—actually still thousands of years in the future, but in his own, personal past—and the ache of knitting bone had never been forgotten.

"Shall we begin?" prompted Jakop.

There was no turning back from such a change, but, as he was told, without a way to return to the future, this shouldn't be a concern. And besides, it's not as if this man would be butchering the face of Rudolph Valentino.

But he's not a man, is he? He's some kind of mind or spirit dressed in the body of a man. He has questionable values, unknowable motivations, an unguessable agenda. And just because he doesn't— That's it!

Gardiner looked at Jakop.

And shook his head.

The other man frowned. "Please explain."

"The surgery is simply unnecessary. I don't like keeping my face covered—Lord knows I don't—but I can continue to do so as long as needed. And I promise to be more vigilant."

The frown deepened.

"But more importantly, just because you know of no way to return me to the future *right now*, that doesn't mean that I remain here. We may yet discover how, or you may not be involved in the solution at all. And I grant that it seems nearly impossible, but someone I know may come to rescue me. Anything could happen."

His arguments had sounded fine at the start, but Gardiner wished he hadn't concluded them the way he had. His conviction had dropped off at the end. Audibly.

"You don't trust me," said Jakop.

Gardiner cringed.

"Please don't take offense. My inclination is to trust everyone. Over the course of my entire life I've always considered that to be a strength. With recent events however, it seems as if I need to cultivate suspicion. And you admitted to not being human. That is an unanticipated variable. How am I supposed to react to that? Can you understand this from my perspective?"

He held his breath, hoping that he hadn't completely alienated the only person in this ancient world he could talk to.

"I can," said Jakop. "We can skip this for now. Be assured, I will remind you of this decision if events require it. Or if there is an ill-timed issue with your disguise."

EIGHTEEN

MAMMUT

Jakop said little the rest of that evening. Gardiner couldn't sense disappointment or bitterness, but his imagination helped to create it,
inviting introspection and again allowing despair a foot in the door.
He second-guessed all of his recent decisions: continuing with the
expedition after his faked death with the landslide, opting to come
to this place and time in order to learn about The Divided God,
agreeing to the surgery in the first place, then changing his mind
about it. He even bemoaned the fact that he had let himself be lured
to South America in the first place, but reason overcame emotion at
that point. There was no doubt that the artifact he'd received was
real, and the involvement of Doctor Donau—the letter likely forged,
he now admitted to himself—was the clincher. He would never
have ignored an invitation like that and had to accept the fact that
his enemies had set their trap too well.

The final bit of regretful truth was that he had kept the trip hidden from Jebediah due purely to selfishness. For once, he had wanted
the glory.

"Too many mistakes," he whispered to himself.

He shook his head, looked over at Jakop, but the other gave no
indication that he'd heard.

*That's enough of that, Quentin. I must remain in control of my
faculties. I can't display any weakness to this man.*

Gardiner zeroed in on that key word.

No, not a man.

Despite the ease of being able to communicate in English, he must never forget that he was currently dealing with a being that professed to not be human, and the alien mind had given clear indications that a basic human empathy was lacking—or at least being held at arm's length.

Like Jebediah, he's willing to burn the trees to save the forest.

The thought of an encounter between Higgins and Jakop made him smile; he wondered if either would survive.

Patrick would have a challenge there.

Of all the people he'd met in his life, Patrick MacNulty was the most soft-spoken and gentle man he'd ever known, able to transform enemies into friends almost instantly. His self-deprecating personality and innate humor acted as a kind of damper that kept emotional personalities under control. And it was put to use almost constantly when his two friends, Jebediah Higgins and James Dunlevy, were together. Where the former was stubbornly and passionately opinionated, the latter was fearless. Dunlevy never blinked in the face of danger, be it lion, or bear, or some unnatural abomination, and was unwilling to suffer fools. Unfortunately, Dunlevy often felt that Higgins was a fool.

But somehow, the four of them had met over a decade ago and had been together ever since. And Patrick was the glue. Most recently, they had added a fifth member—Sam Josephson—something that Gardiner had had mixed feelings about. Sam's request to end his involvement in their risky and arcane adventures had come as no surprise.

The thought of that canceled lunch filled him with regret. His lunchtime chats with Sam were simple and unexciting, but still very gratifying. He swore that he'd make up that missed lunch a hundred times over—if he was ever able to get back. But was that still something to hope for? Would Jebediah follow him here? Despite their last meeting not being on the best of terms, he was convinced the man would come if he could—if there was an actual trail to be followed. Frances and Jonathan had done an excellent job of covering their tracks.

He fell asleep wondering what his friends were doing—would be doing—forty-four centuries hence.

In the morning, Gardiner was prepared for a long, tense day, but his host acted as if nothing untoward had happened. Right from the very start, Jakop outlined plans for the twentieth century man to begin learning more about the advanced sciences employed by his race. The word *nanotechnology* was used to describe the microscopic, but highly potent, circuitry that would be embedded into the marble and sandstone. The plan was to fully construct both the outer archway with the portal, and the inner doorway which simply cast the illusion of a solid wall. They would then be broken back down, transported to Guyana, and rebuilt in the proper places.

The pair visited the work site first, but only long enough to ensure that the supervisors left in charge would continue with the necessary tasks. The rest of the day was spent at the underground alien storehouse. Jakop began with a crash course in electrical engineering and the tools that would be used to construct the needed mechanisms. Gardiner had a rough idea of the concepts underlying electrical circuits and so built upon that base. What was most befuddling for him at first was the ability of the tiny wires to handle the tremendous power flow. He knew that ordinary copper wiring would never be up to the task at the infinitesimal scale of the circuitry. The solution was to make use of a *superconducting* matrix within a multi-layer coating. The superconducting effect, where the electrical resistance of a metal was lowered to zero, was known to Gardiner, but as a curiosity requiring abnormally cold temperatures. The materials employed in this case did not need an external source to lower the temperature, instead depending upon some kind of feedback mechanism within the coating on the impossibly thin wires to create the refrigerant effect that was needed.

Learning to use the tools was easier for Gardiner than learning the esoteric science behind them. The main instrument was about the same size, and worked about the same way, as a fountain pen. With his years of experience as an archaeologist, he already had a steady hand and light touch, as well as a superb attention to detail. By the end of the day, Jakop had him practicing on small blocks of lower quality than those to be used in the temple's construction. Judging that his student had learned enough, he declared the day a success. The necessary supplies were gathered up and taken along, everything small enough to be easily concealed within their robes.

At the work site the following day, Jakop monitored Gardiner closely at first, but left him alone before long. More days passed with Gardiner working unsupervised, his skill and knowledge increasing steadily as he made changes to the stones that were invisible to the naked eye. Jakop spent more and more time traveling to the temples on one side of the earth or the other, only inspecting Gardiner's work at the end of each day.

But Gardiner was never completely alone. He would often need to have the heavy stones shifted one way or another, and the same group of four men were ever on standby to attend to his needs. Seeing them as often as he did, he came to learn their personality quirks. One was clearly unmotivated, always doing the bare minimum, never volunteering unless the work required the strength of all four. Two others were so similar-looking that they seemed to be brothers, that impression furthered by the fact that they spoke to each other very often. But there was something about their heavy brows that made Gardiner nervous.

The fourth man—the one with the burns on his left side—was most worrisome, however. As the days passed, he seemed to hover closer and closer to Gardiner. There was never an overt sense of being threatened, but the sheer size of the man, the power within those massive arms, was intimidating.

One day, when Jakop had finished with his business earlier than usual, Gardiner took the opportunity to ask about them while they were all occupied with a heavy piece that required a combined effort.

"How much do you trust these men?" asked Gardiner.

"I will say that I have not hired anyone whom I distrust. This small group I trust more than the rest."

"What about that large man with the burns?"

"Those are the result of a recent accident. His name is Mammut. He is immensely strong and does the work of any three men. I disliked the thought of losing him when he was injured, and so, contrary to my instincts, I intervened to minimize the chance of infection. The recovery was a painful ordeal for him, but I was able to keep him alive."

"He watches my every move."

Jakop observed Mammut unobtrusively while Gardiner pretended to be busy with some sort of ceremony.

"You're right," said Jakop when the chanting was finished. "Go over to him, wave your hands as if blessing him, and say: Fahat arotta."

Gardiner did just that, and the reaction was immediate, with Mammut falling to his knees and weeping. He was grateful for the cloth hiding his very unpriestly astonishment at what was undeniable religious fervor. "Up," he said in English, hoping that it would be enough.

It was. Mammut stood, and looked at him expectantly. When Gardiner dismissed him, he backed away. The other three men followed quietly, awed by merely being on the periphery.

When all were gone Gardiner asked Jakop, "What did I say to him?"

"It was a harmless, ambiguous blessing: *He smiles upon you.* I've come to know some men of that type in this era. For whatever reason, he is much more easily motivated than others by religion and the promises of the gods. Your presence here, as a priest, provides a focal point for his fervor. With those simple words, you have created a zealot who will fight and die for Nug."

Gardiner likened the man to a puppy dog: trusting, eager to please, and hungry for the smallest bit of praise.

"I'm not certain if I'm comfortable with that. In fact, I know I'm not."

Jakop shrugged.

"We do what we must," he said. "Those who lead are ever presented with difficult choices. If the two of us die, will anyone else have the knowledge and ability to confront this demoness, Frances?"

The Doctor sighed, knowing that he was right.

"And so, others must die so that we may live. Ideally, no one dies. But reality is never ideal."

He speaks so easily of death. With war looming, there is no denying it.

"And never address Mammut by name," added Jakop, "because—"

"Because I must remain mysterious," spat Gardiner. "Yes, I know. You've stressed it often enough."

"It's imperative. You may need to order these men to their deaths one day, and such a thing must be done without a second thought. Soldiers are expendable resources."

Gardiner didn't respond. Having seen Mammut's reaction to the blessing, he felt that words wouldn't even be needed; barely a gesture would suffice for the man to throw his life away.

When the sandstone blocks of the outer arch were assembled, the marble facing was bonded to them with a type of glue that could be easily dissolved so that the structure could later be broken down again. Only the topmost, central piece of marble would have any circuitry built into it, but before adding that, the cuneiform would first have to be engraved. An artisan with an exemplary reputation had been employed to help with this step, and Gardiner's legs grew wobbly when he saw for the first time what the man had produced, The tablet revealed to him was the very same one stolen by the tomb robber, and which he would, one day in the future, again hold in his hands. Now, with the clay freshly dry, it was a thing of beauty.

In order to carve the inscription into the marble, another trip to Jakop's workshop was needed. Aside from the clay tablet, they took the actual stone to be inscribed, and another scrap of marble of about the same size. The two men worked together to set up a pivoting arm that would allow precise carving of the marble as the original was manually traced in the clay. The tool used to cut into the marble was some kind of disintegrator powerful enough to disrupt the atoms in any material at its tip, even diamond. It was potentially very deadly, but worked slowly. A side-effect of it was to leave behind a surface so smooth that the erosive effects of time were greatly reduced, something that would be crucial in the steamy environment of South America.

They prepared the clay tablet by spraying it with a hardening agent to better resist any scraping from the tracing pen. After a few test runs on the scrap marble to get the feel of the tool, they put the real piece into the jig and began carving. Jakop could have built an automated device to perform the work, but didn't think it worth the extra effort. It took a couple of hours, with the two alternating shifts and taking the utmost care. Gardiner was delighted to see each wedge-shaped letter emerge from the blank, and in the process, solve the very first of those riddles from 1925.

Another item on their list was to record Gardiner's voice so that the outermost doors would be keyed to open when he spoke the very phrase that he did in the twentieth century. Jakop actually clarified that the words *open* and *close* were inaccurate, as there were no hinges involved. The *doors* would simply be transported into place if ever needed in an emergency, summoned via portal from a storage area, closing off the archway with perfectly fitted blocks. Once the archway was blocked off, a match of the voice recording would be the only way to open it afterward, thus preventing any entry into the temple until the appropriate time. The technology to handle all of this was, once again, miniscule, fitting into a hole in the back of the marble facing that was the diameter of a hair.

Although the doctor very much championed the idea of free will, the voice recording complicated his philosophy: He seemed to have no choice in the matter. Repeating the phrase exactly as he'd spoken it the first time would allow for the events of 1925 to proceed as they had happened, but if he chose to do anything else—and there were a multitude of options—what would happen then? It was impossible to say for sure, but using free will in this case seemed to

162

invite the possibility of a temporal paradox. He wanted to broach the subject with Jakop in a purely speculative manner, but was afraid that his curiosity might be interpreted as some sort of rebellion. If Jakop thought that Gardiner was trying to see what might happen by exercising his *human right* of free will, Jakop may interpret it as sabotage and flee back to his own time. And Gardiner would be left to fend for himself.

Wait. What if...?

Standing in front of the arch in 1925, he had chosen freely to speak those words. That had been a spontaneous action, a spontaneous utterance. That was his moment of free will. *That* was the key.

Key! Lock and key!

The terms described the situation perfectly, and it made even more sense. He wasn't trapped into repeating the phrase. He had simply created—or was about to create—the lock, here in the past. In the future, the corresponding action was the key to fit the lock. It was simple cause and effect again, just twisted around in his own personal timeline.

The events that led to his presence in the past needed to happen somehow. Did it matter if he was the one to actually carry out the work? It didn't. In fact, it was very gratifying.

It took only a small amount of time the next morning to fit the central piece of marble into place before testing could begin. They tuned the exit point to face back towards them, about six feet to the right of the entrance.

But this new portal would still just be a slab of stone, like the ones that allowed travel to South America and entrance into the underground storehouse. A side effect of the spatial disturbance did allow for a picture to be projected within the transport area, however. Jakop handed Gardiner the thin, metallic device from the day of Kannit's visit and had him look through images of shadowy doorways. It took little time for him to find the right one and he smiled when he saw it, again satisfied that it was he doing the choosing. Jakop somehow transferred the picture over, and soon their portal was disguised with the illusion of a hallway choked in darkness about six feet in.

Either the technology was foolproof to begin with, or the alien mind within Jakop did an excellent job with the engineering, because it was obvious from the first attempt that it worked flawlessly. They began by tossing pebbles through, then larger objects. A long piece of wood was held within the portal and moved around while they closely watched the far end moving freely in space off to their right.

With the device working for inanimate objects, the next step was a living thing. A caged bird was pushed through. Jakop examined it closely when it emerged, testing its responses several ways.

"It is unscathed," he said. "We need a human subject."

Gardiner's stomach turned when he thought of the things that could go wrong. He tried to invent a reason to delay, but couldn't.

"When he enters," said Jakop, "point at the arch and speak these words: Toth etta hatosh. It means: Enter and be rewarded."

After Gardiner nodded reluctant approval, Jakop sent for Mammut. The large man entered the room and approached them, looking from one to the other. Somehow Gardiner was able to maintain his priestly attitude as he pointed at the arch and commanded the man as Jakop had instructed. He then turned and walked toward the invisible exit point, to set himself up as the first thing Mammut would see if all went well.

It was thankfully over too quickly to even hold his breath. He heard the man stride forward, and instantly saw him. Mammut cried out as he focused on Gardiner, then fell to his knees. Jakop rushed over and performed a more comprehensive series of tests than he did with the bird. Eventually he stood up, and silently indicated that Mammut had suffered no ill effects.

Gardiner waved a fake blessing, then moved within arm's length, and held his hand out. The awestruck man took it and stood, then bowed, and shakily departed.

"You should not have done that," chided Jakop when they were alone again. "That is not how a priest behaves."

"But that's how *I* behave. Besides, we need that man. You yourself admitted that you saw his value and helped to heal his injuries."

"And I regret doing that. We need no one specifically. Within an army, all men are all the same. A single man cannot make a difference."

"I don't agree," said Gardiner. "I am one man. And I cannot believe that I am not making a difference."

Nineteen

SUSPICIONS

With the outer portal finished, it was much easier to do practically the same thing for the emergency doors that would be used to block off the archway. Because this second copy of the circuitry would only be used to transport the large slabs, it didn't need to be tuned as finely. With periodic inspections, Jakop let Gardiner handle the larger portion of the work by himself.

The final large-scale item was the inner doorway, the one masked by the illusion of a solid wall, and through which Gardiner had stepped to find himself surrounded. The same man who created the inscription above the outer arch was brought in to help again. Because the writing would be located deep underground and not be exposed to any weathering, there was no need to repeat the previous copying effort. Instead, Jakop instructed the man to chisel the characters directly into sandstone that would be fitted into place. Clay tablets with the wording were handed over, along with the required dimensions. They spoke for a few minutes, each exchanging questions and answers. As the artisan turned to leave, Gardiner—silent to that point—called out for the man to wait.

Gardiner reached into his robe, pulled out a cloth-wrapped package that clinked slightly, and handed it to Jakop. As they had rehearsed beforehand, the Doctor said in English: "Tell him to use these blessed tools on this holy work, and to allow no one else to see them."

After a respectful bow to Gardiner, Jakop turned to the craftsman and unrolled the cloth to reveal a set of silver chisels made of an alloy much harder than anything available in that time—or for that matter, thought Gardiner, anything from his own.

The man's eyes lit up as he saw the polished metal. They grew even wider when he picked one up and felt the extraordinarily light weight. After the piece was replaced, Jakop rewrapped the tools and passed along Gardiner's message before handing them over. They were accepted reverentially.

"That seemed to go well," said Jakop when they were alone again.

"It may be hard to get them back from him when he's done," said Gardiner. "Although, we can threaten him with the wrath of the gods." He frowned and added, "Or just kill him."

"We have options," said Jakop, not reacting to Gardiner's jab. "As for the technical aspect of this project, I want you to handle that on your own."

Embarrassed over his verbal attack, Gardiner didn't know how to respond.

"I... Are you..."

"Is there anything wrong?"

"No, no. I'm grateful you'd entrust me with the responsibility, but the fact is that I know nothing about this."

"But you do," said Jakop. "The device to project the illusion will be different, but the techniques for working with the circuitry match what you've already mastered. You need but a small amount of additional instruction."

"Is there any reason why we can't work on it together, as we did with the portals? I learned as we went along."

"You did, and in a short amount of time. That's why I am confident you can handle this. I'll be away frequently from this point onward. There are too many details I need to personally inspect. At both temples."

"I thought Tamar was overseeing the construction in Guyana."

"He is, but he doesn't know everything. The decisions are mine."

"With what I know of that temple, and your experience with the technology behind the illusion device, doesn't it make more sense if we swap these tasks?"

"It is too dangerous for you to be spending time around Tamar."

Tired of hearing that yet again, Gardiner took a deep breath before trying a new tack.

"What about the other temple then?" he asked. "No one there knows me."

"Language would be a barrier—which, yes, could be overcome. But I prefer that it be built as per my design with no input at all from the future."

"I have no desire to change your design," said Gardiner.

"I appreciate that, and I do believe that you would consciously avoid it. But this free will you so espouse… Could it not come into play? Perhaps even unconsciously?"

"I have no answer for that."

"Nor do I. Any small change may have undesirable effects. In the stream of time, your fate is already intertwined with the temple of Nug, but not the other. I prefer the temple of Yeb remain uncontaminated."

Gardiner juggled the information in his mind, still not fully comfortable with this new view of causes and effects. A longing to visit Asia wasn't worth the possibility of adversely influencing future events. He told himself he'd have time for sightseeing once both temples were done.

Resigned to follow Jakop's lead, he threw his hands up.

"Then let's get started. Teach me what I need to know."

They left for the storehouse, Jakop explaining as they walked. Using a preselected image for the illusion—as was done with the outer portal—wasn't an option because there was almost no chance of finding something appropriate that would blend in well. Instead, the device to be built would use tiny cameras and projectors to overlay multiple images of the same small section of stone, overlapping them slightly to completely blanket the archway. A very careful study would reveal the fakery, but the dimness of the room would prevent that. Power would come from the outer portal itself: Aside from transporting objects, that gateway through space allowed energy to flow through as well. Tiny wires would be laid down from the portal to the illusion projector during the final phase of construction.

In the workshop, Jakop located the fabrication machine Gardiner would need. It took the strength of both men to carry the bulky thing from the storage shelving over to a workbench. As they were setting it down, Gardiner noticed that something on the tabletop seemed to catch Jakop's eye, but Gardiner saw nothing there.

"Shift it to the right slightly," Jakop suggested, and they did so. "I have an instruction manual, and a translation of it that you can set up on the left."

After a short bit of hunting around, he returned to the table with a set of metal leaves covered with alien symbology, and the same type of thin, aluminum-like plate Gardiner had previously used. Having the two items sitting side by side next to the machine made it easy see that the latter displayed a translation of the alien text in cuneiform writing. English would have been better, but with Gardiner's background, it was enough to go on. The pictographic style of the alien script, similar to cuneiform, made it easier to learn, but there were many technical terms for which there was no equivalent in the ancient Sumerian. A few hours of tutoring by Jakop, however, and Gardiner had a base on which to build.

The machine produced objects atom by atom, creating materials to suit almost any conceivable need. Because Jakop's race could potentially control the bodies of many diverse races, some non-human, the interface was simplified to the extreme, with no moving parts. Along the same lines as the other examples of engineering from that race, it took only light touches and hand movements to activate the functions.

Along with the microengineering, he also learned about power supplies and power transmission. The harnessing of solar energy was much more efficient than anything he knew of, and the energy storage technology was phenomenally more powerful, and more compact, than anything available in the twentieth century.

The machine was pre-programmed to make thousands of useful items, one of which Gardiner had already learned something about: the preservative substance that slowed the effects of time. For that one, as well as many others, he found a common theme—a *container* of microscopically small size that could be packed with a tiny amount of any substance. The composition of these structures was strong and stable, but certain disturbances could cause it to break. Tuning the point at which the containers broke, and so releasing the contents, seemed to be key to getting desired effects.

Initially, just the thought of learning an entirely new field of science at his age was discouraging. Gardiner was versed in basic physics and electronics, but some of the concepts in metallurgy and engineering didn't make sense at first. After some initial frustration, the challenge of that new, non-human symbology was what hooked him and kept him going. As he picked up more and more of the language, any desire to think about a more comfortable subject, such as archaeology, was displaced by a hunger to soak up as much knowledge as he could.

He spent days at the fabrication machine, practicing and slowly getting better. The need to learn how to construct the illusion-projector, as well as actually doing so, necessitated a large investment of time. Jakop didn't seem to care, though. As he'd indicated, he was only around in the mornings and evenings, leaving Gardiner to fend for himself during the days. But they exchanged regular progress reports, and in that time, set a date for the ceremony to call down Nug. There seemed to be some leeway, as the star of primary importance—unnamed in the twentieth century—was often in a favorable position at the current time of year. Jakop did mention one day in particular as a goal to meet, but given the amount of work remaining, Gardiner didn't think it possible.

After much effort, he had a set of tiny components that did what was needed. He even made a couple of extra sets in case there were unanticipated snags, as well as a number of tiny batteries needed to provide power for his tests. With that done, it was back to the work site, where he began experimenting to find the best coverage pattern for a convincing illusion.

He often had Mammut help with the simpler tasks and began speaking casually with the man. The small vocabulary Gardiner had accumulated in the local language was adequate for the work on the temple, and for procuring food and water, but it wasn't enough to get very far with meaningful communication. When Mammut began responding to some of Gardiner's mutterings in English, it became clear that the large, brutish man had an ear for languages. At that point, Gardiner began to teach him the *holy tongue* of English. For Mammut, it was an honor; for Gardiner, it was a relief to be able to speak with someone aside from Jakop—from whom he kept the tutoring a secret.

One morning, Gardiner gave a demonstration of the illusion projector to his teacher. Jakop studied the unreal stone wall from various angles and distances.

"Very good, Doctor. I am impressed with your skill. This came out very well."

"Thank you," said Gardiner appreciatively. "This tested my artistic abilities, something that's rarely exercised. I'm more squares and circles…"

Circles.

"…than…"

Circle!

"Jakop! The other portal! We forgot about the portal in the inner chamber—the black circle I stepped onto."

"I did consider it, but we do not know how to set the destination. We have no choice but to wait until Nug is summoned, then communicate with it to learn what is needed."

"But how will the device be powered? Don't we need to account for that? It'll be more work to add in the power connection later."

Jakop glowered, a harsh expression on his normally placid face.

"We have four millennia to finish the temple! Time is not an issue." He continued more calmly. "As you described it, that feature was a way to escape, and likely to be used only once. In that case, powerful batteries can easily be hidden within the stone. Even over the course of thousands of years there will be little energy loss. There is a solution for this."

"All right," said Gardiner, taken aback slightly. "That does make sense. We can put that aside for the time being. Tomorrow I can help you with this device."

Jakop shook his head.

"No. Tamar has demonstrated an adequate ability to help me. He doesn't understand the science as you do, viewing it as magic. But he is very perceptive, and follows directions well."

"But—"

"No."

"I really cannot fathom your excessive reluctance to let the two of us meet."

"Each day that goes by without seeing you allows his memory to fade a little more, especially because I have given him an enormous workload and much to think about."

When Gardiner opened his mouth to protest again, Jakop continued.

"Have no fear: You will definitely be present at the ceremony. That point has never been in doubt."

Gardiner had no idea if Jakop would keep his word, but had no choice but to wait a few more days while the projector he had worked so hard to build was installed without him. Determined to not be upset, he directed his energies toward more learning.

Back at the storehouse, he browsed through the list of materials preprogrammed into the fabrication machine. Reading through description after description, not looking for anything specific, sparked some creativity in him. He saw different ways of combining and using the materials. In particular, two stood out: tiny particles that could transform infrared and ultraviolet radiations into visible light.

He would just need to coat a piece of glass with them to make them useful.

He had already begun the process of making a batch of the powder before it dawned on him that he had no glass. Stopping the machine, he wasn't sure what to do with the stuff that had been created. It was such a tiny quantity of harmless, grey dust. He blew on it, dispersing it.

As he wiped the tray clean with a corner of his robe, he saw an even, light red glow through the particles suspended in the air—but there was a pronounced difference when he looked at the tabletop. Near the base of the machine was a blurry, blue smear. He cleared away the smaller items and carefully looked at the bare surface from various angles through the settling dust. The heat signature was a uniform red—except for a blue splotch near one end of the table.

When he rubbed at the smear, a spot of blue transferred to his fingertip. There was a memory of Jakop wanting to shift the heavy machine down to the end in order to give him more space at the other, and it had made sense at the time…

But what could be underneath?

There was no way for him to handle the thing by himself, and he mulled over the idea of bringing Mammut there, but ruled it out as being too risky.

Curiosity driving him, he set to work programming the machine to make a piece of glass with a layer of the infrared detecting dust embedded within. It wasn't long before a disc about two inches in diameter was ready.

He quickly put his new toy to good use by examining the blue patch on the tabletop. Now, with a dense, even coating of that material to peer through, the nature of it was plain: smeared versions of the alien pictograms with which he had recently become acquainted. Some of the writing was clearly exposed, but most was covered by the machine. Of what he could see, only one character was both familiar and intact enough to discern: the one for *total*.

When further scrutiny of the tabletop yielded nothing, he held the piece of glass up to the light to ensure that it was clear of fingerprints—and was flabbergasted at what he saw. There were symbols *everywhere*: labeling corridors, shelves, doorways…everything. The markings were effectively printed with a permanent, invisible ink. Showing up as blue, he theorized that it absorbed heat somehow. Even as he began to explore, the heat from his own hand neutralized the efficacy of the small glass, turning it an opaque red.

"I need a bigger piece with an insulated border," he said aloud as he pictured the new design. "And I need Mammut."

Less than an hour later, he and Mammut approached the rocky area in which the workshop was concealed.

"Close your eyes," Gardiner said when they reached the doorway wall. He unlocked it after Mammut obeyed, then tugged on the man to position him squarely.

"Walk straight ahead."

Slowly, Mammut walked through the illusion of the stone wall. Gardiner followed. When they were both well inside, Gardiner cautioned Mammut.

"You may look now, but be prepared for a surprise."

It was an awe-inspiring sight for a man of that era. Perfect ninety-degree angles and utterly flat, clean surfaces were everywhere he looked. But what he fixated on the most were the lights: steady sources of illumination without the flickering of a flame. Gardiner gave him time to adjust, then led him to the workroom.

A soft beeping from the machine greeted them as they entered, indicating that it was finished making the updated glass he had designed before he left. Gardiner turned off the alarm and pulled out the new item. The small handle and frame around it were made of a porous ceramic that conducted heat very poorly, so there was no longer a limit on the amount of time that it could be held and used.

"Please pick this up and move it to here," he told Mammut, pointing first at the machine, then the opposite end of the table. "Be very careful."

Even as he spoke the final words, he knew they were unnecessary. The man was handling what he believed to be a holy object; he would treat it more gently than he would a baby.

For Mammut, getting a handhold on the bulky object was more of an obstacle than the weight, but he wrapped his arms around it, got a good grip, and lifted it straight up. He shuffled over a few feet and set it back down.

"Thank you, Mammut. Now let's see what is there."

The native man looked at the empty spot where the machine had been.

"I see nothing," he said.

Gardiner took a peek through the glass to confirm his suspicion, then held it out so that the other man had a view of the table top through it. "But now there is something. Yes?"

"Yes! I see!"

"Mammut, I need to study this. You may walk around and look at things. Or sit. Please do whatever you want." He emphasized his words with hand movements to reinforce the meanings, a technique that had helped the other man learn the language at an incredible rate.

Mammut looked around for a short time, then pointed at the ground.

"I sit."

Gardiner saw right away that the blue figures revealed through his looking glass were, for the most part, mathematical symbols instead of text, which made sense. These calculations were likely made the night that Gardiner posited that the future could perhaps be changed. Some of the numerical operations, such as simple addition or multiplication, were clear when translated into decimal values. But many others were indecipherable. Little of it was connected, leaving too many holes in the interpretation and making the overall translation vague.

The few scattered symbols he saw that weren't numbers reminded him of similar situations when he was the author of scribbled notes and calculations. The English language lent itself to the use of abbreviations, and they were so ubiquitous that many were commonly understood. Why bother to write out the word *abbreviation*, when *abbrev*, or even *abbr*, could be used? Gardiner often depended on such shortcuts, but there was no equivalent in this pictographic language. Each needed to be completely written in order to retain its meaning. Due to this, he was able to pick out *split* (or halved or divided), and next to it the one for *child*, but also identified the one for *mother*. Based on the ordering and other clues within the body of writing, it actually seemed as if the bulk of the calculations referred to *mother*.

"But in this context, *mother* could mean only one thing. Why would he bother to make calculations about Shub-Niggurath?"

His rhetorical mumble had been spoken in the general direction of Mammut, who reacted by jumping to his feet.

"The Great Mother." He inclined his head.

"Yes, your people would know more of her than her offspring."

"Offspring?"

"Her sons."

"Ah, yes. You said me that. Nug and Yeb."

Gardiner grinned at the small mistake, then became aware that his expression couldn't be seen. The small opportunity to connect with another human being had been lost in his hood.

This man deserved to know the truth.

"No more lies," he declared, uncovering himself. "Mammut, I am not a priest."

"Not priest?" Confusion danced across his face.

"No. I'm from…far, far away. But I'm just a man."

He looked at his handheld glass. The edge on the bottom of the handle was probably sharp enough. Applying enough pressure, he scraped some skin from a knuckle on his left hand.

"See? Just a man. I bleed."

Mammut looked down at his own hand, but said nothing. Gardiner hoped he hadn't made a mistake.

"When I arrived here by the power of Shub-Niggurath I was a fish out of water. I didn't fit in, didn't know the language. Jakop suggested a disguise would be best and I agreed. Being secretive would allow me to stay out of social interactions that might be dangerous. He spoke my language, due to an exceptional circumstance that is difficult for even me to grasp. He's helped me. He's also helped you, or so he said, although you may not know it. The point is this: I am here is to defeat a woman more evil than any person I've ever known. The temples we have all been working on are related to this struggle. They are intended to be used to recruit an army to fight against her. My problem right now is that, even though Jakop has been the primary force in designing and creating the temples, in light of this new evidence, scant as it may be, I do not know where he stands. He has acted oddly at times ever since I told him…something that caused him to write these symbols."

Gardiner pointed at the table.

"Although, it must be said that he is very odd to begin with."

Mammut remained silent and looked at the blood on Gardiner's hand.

"I'm sorry. I should have spoken more slowly and used words in your vocabulary. But this woman must be brought to justice, and I cannot do it alone. I need your help. Will you help me?"

He held out his right hand, trying to keep his cool after confessing to a man who could break him in two that he'd been lying to him for weeks.

Mammut nodded, slightly at first, then more vigorously, and finally shifted his gaze up to look Gardiner in the eyes.

"I help you," he said, reaching out to shake hands.

Gardiner smiled, relieved.

"Thank you very much, Mammut. My name is Quentin."

TWENTY

PREPARATIONS

Gardiner had no idea on how long it would take Jakop and Tamar to finish the work at the temple, but he felt he could risk one more day of having Mammut at his side in the storehouse. And although he was now willing to trust the man with his life, he couldn't bring himself to show him how to open the door. There were too many variables associated with this venture. If the smallest error was made, the influence of nearly magical advanced technology on this society—and on his own future—could be disastrous.

While looking through the lists of materials in the machine, he kept up a dialog with the native man, teaching him English. Each took turns choosing random subjects: childhood, food, the weather. New words were introduced a bit at a time so as to not overwhelm the student, and syntax errors were gently corrected whenever they were too glaring.

Of all of the ideas that popped into his head, two seemed to be both easy to make and potentially useful. The first was a "bag of air." Knowing that the temple would somehow be flooded, and hoping that it wouldn't be while he was there, he nevertheless thought the ability to breathe underwater would be valuable. He set up the machine to stuff pure oxygen into those tiny containers, and filled a small, malleable bag with them. The membrane of the bag was tuned to be selectively permeable: it would let nothing in, but let the oxygen flow out.

He tested it by emptying his lungs, putting one in his mouth and biting down on it. His lungs filled with air, and he counted ninety seconds before needing to take a breath. It seemed possible to go even longer, but he dismissed the thought. In a real emergency his heart rate would be elevated, increasing the body's oxygen demands. One minute per bag, though: that could be enough to make a difference.

The other idea was for a weapon, although one of last resort: a bomb with separate pockets of potassium and water. Because the outer container was the same type of flexible bag, it wouldn't produce a concussive force or have any shrapnel. The violent, sustained reaction caused when the ingredients mixed would create a fantastically deadly heat, however. The bombs and the oxygen supplies looked nearly identical, with a rough texture on the side of one being the only way to tell the difference between them.

When the machine had produced four of the bombs, he took two of them and set up the fabricator to work on the oxygen supply bags. Outside, they walked for almost an hour, heading away from known civilization to a valley with abandoned and decaying brick houses surrounding a pool of stagnant water a few inches deep—a dead oasis. It was a place that Mammut had known even before it had been abandoned, and he assured Gardiner that they would not be discovered there. Hiding behind the corner of one structure, Gardiner tried tossing the first bomb onto packed earth.

Nothing happened.

"That's good. We at least know that accidentally dropping one won't set it off."

After retrieving it, Gardiner noticed the remains of a wall about a short way off, and across from it another house that would provide protection. Thinking that the upright target would let him use more force, he threw it as hard as he could, then darted over, behind his cover.

But it bounced off the wall and landed unspectacularly on the ground.

"Throw harder," suggested Mammut.

"That's as hard as I can. You try."

179

The larger man put more energy into it than Gardiner was capable of, and that did the trick. He got out of the way as the flames exploded outward in a terrifying display. Gardiner held a hand out, but yanked it back.

"My god, we can't be anywhere near that when it goes off." He looked down at the other bomb. "I don't know how useful these will be. Only you can set them off, and you may cook yourself doing so."

Mammut looked around, forehead etched in thought.

"A stick," he said.

Scanning the area, he spotted a bush with long, straight stems and headed over to it. "Stay here."

With his dagger, he cut off a four-foot branch and stripped it clean of leaves. He made sure that he had Gardiner's attention and threw the rudimentary spear expertly. It flew in a lazy parabola and planted itself in the ground a few feet to Gardiner's left. "Throw it," shouted Mammut, pointing to his right. "Here."

The Doctor pulled it out of the ground, got a feel for the weight, and launched it. For never having done anything of the sort, it was a good first attempt, but landed a few feet short and skidded when it hit.

Mammut threw it back.

"Again."

Gardiner had the hang of it before long, and when he had made three consecutive good throws, Mammut cut a piece of cloth from the edge of his robe and used it to tie the bomb to the end of the spear. Gardiner winced as the final knot was cinched tight, knowing that too much force would doom the man to a painful incineration, but after Mammut returned and handed it over, he saw how the greater portion of the tension was on the wood. The deadly bag of chemicals was taut, but not under much pressure. Thrown correctly, the weight of the stick would be enough to puncture the bag and allow the contents to mix.

The extra mass changed the center of balance slightly, but Gardiner felt confident in being able to compensate. "I was hoping to see how much stronger the reaction would be in water." He pointed at the pool, fifty feet away, measured the weight against the distance, then again.

"I do it," offered Mammut.

Gardiner shook him off.

"Just a little closer, I think."

He walked forward a few steps and took aim. The pool was plenty large enough, roughly eight feet across, and he had proven to himself that he could throw it straight; it was the distance that was in question. After taking a deep breath and releasing it, he reared back and launched the spear. It was a beautiful arc, nearly too long, but it hit the farther edge of the water.

A fiery maelstrom blossomed, sprouting orange petals of flame.

Gardiner dropped to the ground just before the wave of heat washed over him. The bare skin of his exposed hands got very hot, but did not burn. When it was safe, Mammut ran over and helped him up.

"Very good!"

"It would be a true bombshell if we ever use it, that's for sure."

After he dusted himself off, they went over to the pool. It was much smaller, the shoreline dried and cracked, but water was already slowly creeping out toward the edges again.

"Water must be seeping up—"

"Look," said Mammut, pointing at the cloud of steam and smoke they had created, drifting away on the wind. "Someone see that. We go."

They hurried out of the area, taking a circuitous route in order to stay out of sight of any trails that led to the valley. Mammut also made an effort to erase their tracks for a while, but stopped when their footprints began overlapping with those of other travelers.

By the time they reached the storehouse, without incident, the machine had produced four of the oxygen supply bags, a quantity Gardiner thought would be plenty. Two of those, and one potassium bomb for each of them, could all be hidden within pockets in their robes. Trying to carry any more would be cumbersome. As he handed the bomb to Mammut, he made certain the man could feel the difference between the two types.

After Mammut muscled the machine back to its original position on the table, Gardiner cleaned the place as best he could to remove any evidence of the other man's presence. When they were ready to leave, he handed the small, original infrared-detecting glass to Mammut, and showed him that it worked the same way as the larger piece.

"Keep it as a souvenir," said Gardiner.

"Souvenir?"

"A thing that has a memory attached to it. I don't know what the future will bring…for either of us. When you see this piece of glass, you can think of me and this place."

"Thank you."

He handled it gently, and tucked it into his robe.

"No, thank you for all your help."

Gardiner couldn't leave the larger glass there either, but he didn't want to destroy it, so he took it along. Outside, he spotted exactly what he needed: a vertical gap between two stones, wide enough to slide the glass in without scratching it. The color of the frame was a fairly close match to the surrounding rock, and actually made it appear, when viewed edge-on, as if it was a splinter of stone. He was confident that only a dedicated search would find it.

The following day was the one that Jakop had set as a goal for the completion of the temple of Nug, and so Gardiner thought it best to remain at the work site—just in case. He continued English lessons with Mammut, but by late afternoon was kicking himself for not spending the day at the storehouse—when Jakop finally returned, at which point Gardiner congratulated himself for his superb estimation.

Mammut was in a position to spot him first, and abruptly stood and turned over a heavy rock—the pre-arranged signal. Gardiner covered his face right before Jakop could see him, then, resuming the priestly role-play, dismissed Mammut with a holy gesture.

Jakop neared as Mammut left, and Gardiner pretended to study the rock.

"Is there something interesting there?" asked Jakop.

"For you, perhaps not," said Gardiner, looking up. "I studied geology as well as archaeology. Mineral veins and rock fabrics are interesting to me—to a point, anyway. I'm just trying to keep myself occupied while I wait."

It was easy to add a note of real exasperation to those words.

"Your wait is over."

"Good. Tomorrow, then? It's late."

Jakop shook his head.

"Now. There, it's early."

"Right now?" Gardiner wanted Mammut to accompany him, but couldn't invent an excuse to take him along.

"Yes. There is about one hour before an optimal astronomical alignment."

Jakop led him to the portal, then stopped and turned to Gardiner.

"The exit point has been moved. There is no longer a danger of falling, but there is no light on the other side. Step to your right after going through."

"The right?"

"Yes."

He's had plenty of chances to kill me.

Holding his breath, Gardiner walked forward into a cool blackness. As precaution, he raised both arms outward. The knuckles of his left hand encountered rock; with his right hand he felt nothing.

Right it is then.

After taking that step, he detected a dim light on the edge of his peripheral vision. He turned toward it, but wound up spinning one hundred eighty degrees before he saw the source. He could tell that he stood in a tunnel about ten feet high and twenty feet wide. In the distance, the rectangular end of the tunnel was clearly illumined by what, in this part of the world, must have been the morning sun.

"Do you know where you are, Doctor Gardiner?" came Jakop's voice from behind him.

"I have a very good idea."

"You may want to count your steps as you go. The portal we came through is hidden in a small niche that has been disguised by some of the extra illusion projectors you created. I personally carved out the recess and installed all the devices myself, so only the two of us know where it is."

As both men walked toward the light, Gardiner recalled his previous experience in this place: shuffling forward slowly, at night, arms restrained. This time, walking freely, it was much more pleasant—especially the sight that greeted them as they emerged into the daylight. Sheer, smooth walls rose up two thousand feet all around them, framing the sky in a circle of dark gold sandstone. Created by the hands of many men—albeit with the help of advanced technology—it was as awe inducing as the view of the jungle from its top.

Standing on the edge of the walkway, Gardiner looked down at the bottom of the manmade crater fifty feet below. He was able to easily pick out the dividing line between sandstone and granite, and imagined the seawater that would fill it right up to the level of the ledge and the attached causeway that jutted out into the center.

Or would it? Will the water be here or not?

He chuckled softly to himself as he reconsidered the looping series of causes and effects.

"Are you ready?" asked Jakop.

"I'm truly not sure."

TWENTY-ONE

THE CEREMONY

With all of the preparations complete and the ceremony under way, there was nothing to do but wait. Tamar had been sent to supervise work on the other temple, so Jakop let Gardiner know that he was free to take off his hood and go wherever he liked—with the exception of the central platform in the middle of the crater, where six natives were seated around an incense-filled censor. Positioned at the center of the cavity, their chanting filled the air with echoes, a light, swirling breeze carrying their words. Among the nonsensical, guttural syllables, Gardiner was able to pick out one oft-repeated word: Nug.

At first, he thought it curious that Jakop wasn't involved with the ceremony, but then it made sense if the mental harmony associated with unquestioning belief was a requirement for success. Jakop only wanted to use the entity Nug as inspiration—a rallying force to build an army of faithful—so perhaps it was better to have his potentially corrupting cynicism removed from the focal point of positive energy.

Because there was enough time for a visit to the outer temple, Gardiner walked back the way they had just come, enjoying the invigorating underground temperature. As he trekked along the tunnel, he used the small bit of sunlight leaking in through the outer portal as a guide. Adjusted to the dimness by the time he reached it, the plain walls of the undecorated room were eerily familiar. He almost expected to see Jonathan taking measurements, or Frances

185

copying the inscription. Turning around, he closely scrutinized the illusion of the solid wall he'd walked through.

Very nice work, Quentin.

It was after tiptoeing over to the outer archway that he remembered that sounds didn't carry through. The patio, which he'd previously seen after having been subjected to thousands of years of jungle moisture, was pristine and beautiful. A burly native stood guard on either side of the arch, each armed with spear, shield, and dagger. Other groups were gathered at a distance, keeping a watch on the temple. With a final glance at the words etched into the wall above the illusion, he strode through the fake wall and back to the Inner Sanctum.

As he neared the other end, he could tell that the light was dimmer than it had been. If it were a cloud doing that, there would be a frightening storm shortly. His pulse quickened at the memory of the last storm he'd seen there. His attitude changed greatly when he glimpsed upward, found the sun, and understood the actual reason for the darkening.

He met Jakop on the ledge that ran around the inside the entire cavity.

"An eclipse!" he whispered excitedly.

The only chance he'd ever had to see one was a disappointingly overcast day in Portland, Maine, in his youth. That day went from dim to dark, and back to dim, and there was never any evidence of the actual phenomenon.

Jakop smiled thinly at Gardiner's childlike eagerness.

"Typically, evocations such as what we will perform are done at night, as it is easier to see the alignments of the stars, but that is simply convention carried forward from even more primitive eras than this. The stars are either aligned, or they are not; it's not essential to see them. For our purpose they will remain in the proper alignment until after sunset today, and so we could wait until this evening—but we would not be able to take advantage of this spectacle. Having a god appear on such a day will make a strong impression on these people."

He pointed at the chanting men.

"We must be quiet now."

Gardiner could feel a static charge building. The hair on his arms stood up, and his skin crawled. The breeze became a wind, carrying a perfumed scent across the gap, but the increasing susurrus made the chants indecipherable. With the moon devouring the sun and the sky growing darker, a subtle glow from the censer became visible. He glanced up and estimated another minute until totality, but caught something moving swiftly through his field of vision, a shadow scarcely noticeable against the wall of sandstone. A second later it hit the bottom of the hollowed-out bowl and exploded in a spray.

The event was so odd that he felt compelled to ask Jakop if he had also seen it, but was afraid to speak aloud at this, the very climax of the ceremony. It was soon evident that the other man had seen it, though his reaction was unexpected. He began waving his arms, jumping, and shouting to attract the attention of the chanting men. With the noise of the wind and the dimming light, there was no indication that they had noticed his efforts. An instant later, Gardiner was blinded as a brilliant light flared on the ground just a few feet away.

"I am sorry for that," said Jakop, clutching Gardiner's shoulder. That hand began to shake, and the grip tightened.

"Why did you do that?" asked Gardiner. Spots danced everywhere, even through closed eyelids. The itching sensation on his skin from the static electricity was gone, and the wind was dissipating. He listened for the chanting, but that too had stopped.

"I had to stop them before it was too late. That was very close." He seemed to become conscious of his pressure on the other man's shoulder and relaxed it, then removed his hand. "That was a person who fell."

"What? Did you have guards up there on the rim?"

"No. There should be no one there. The top had been cleared of all debris and workers."

"An overly enthusiastic spectator then?"

"There's no way to get there. The portal has been moved."

"Can the outside wall be climbed?"

"Not with the tools and materials available at this time."

As the moon continued its transit and the sun reasserted its power, Gardiner's bespotted eyes began to function again. He saw Jakop staring at nothing, petrified with fear, his body visibly trembling.

He's practically in shock.

"Jakop," said Gardiner gently, "you said it was almost too late. What did you mean?"

Jakop blinked a few times, then took a deep breath and released it. Gardiner waited, giving him a chance to recover from whatever trauma he'd suffered.

"Accidental or not," he finally said, "a death during the ceremony would have effectively *poisoned* the result. Nug would have arrived, but in no mood to help us. Just the opposite, there would have been an insatiable need to taste human flesh. It would have been a…disaster."

"What do we do now?" prompted Gardiner.

"Clean up the remains and wait. It will be three days before another attempt can be made. It will not be an optimal alignment at that point, but the stars will not be actively set against us." He gritted his teeth. "And we get answers. There is only one person who could have gotten onto the rim without my aid."

"Tamar."

"Yes. If he can shift the portal based upon the few glimpses he's had of me doing it, he is far more clever than I suspected."

It was an agonizing wait for Gardiner while Jakop traveled to the other side of the world and confronted Tamar. The thought of a traitor in their midst was so sickening that Gardiner assumed Jakop would kill him as soon as he had any proof, and prepared himself for that news.

With that mindset, he truly didn't know how to react when Jakop returned and declared that Tamar was innocent. The man was currently laid up with a delirium, and had been since shortly after he had made the trip to Asia. The symptoms were akin to a fever, but without an elevated temperature. After getting a consistent story from a half-dozen witnesses, Jakop had left him to rest and hopefully recover.

The news was both good and bad. Gardiner's faith in Tamar had been proven correct, but with their sole suspect eliminated, the mystery of how that person had gotten onto the rim had to be revisited. It became even stranger when the remains were examined and found to be a woman, and a pregnant one at that. Mummified, desiccated bodies had always been easy for Gardiner to deal with, and he could even stomach the ghastly corruptions of Nature he had encountered through the years, but the freshly dead were another matter. Even if the bodies were whole to begin with, autopsies could reduce them to a pile of tissue not unlike this one. With no desire to look closely, he accepted the report from Jakop without comment.

Even with the body removed, Jakop was nervous about any residue leaving behind an aura of ill intent. As a precaution, he had a group of the native workers remove a half-inch of material from the stone floor wherever any blood had stained the rock. Gardiner climbed down on a rope of woven vine along with the native workers in order to supervise the operation. He monitored them to ensure that, not only were all remnants of the body removed, but also that the renovated area was smooth and without gouges.

It was during the final inspection that the sound began. Devoting his full concentration to every detail of what he saw, he couldn't pinpoint exactly when he became aware of it. Deep and rhythmic, at first he mistook it to be his own heartbeat. The men doing the work had been standing off to the side, talking amongst themselves, but he noticed them quiet down and also listen to the odd, hypnotizing sound.

He scanned the area all around, looking for anything out of the ordinary. There was nothing to see. And the phenomenon was of such a low frequency that it was truly directionless. Being so far down in that man-made cavity, it was simply not possible for any sounds from the jungle to penetrate. He had the feeling that he was in danger, but couldn't pinpoint why. Whatever it was seemed to be nearby.

And when his curiosity had transformed to anxiety, then crossed the line to fear, the noise stopped. With everyone standing still, the resulting silence was profound. Now, it truly was his own heartbeat that he heard—and felt. His body shook. The other men laughed off the occurrence and began to liven up again. A few pointed at his terror-stricken appearance.

After composing himself, Gardiner wrapped up his sweep. He joined the workers and signaled that they could go. One of the men, larger and more brutish than the rest, held the others back. As muscular as Mammut, this one didn't have the other's sensitivity, and instead relished in bullying. In a mock display of courtesy, he handed over the vine.

Knowing that the intent was to ridicule the *old, weak stranger* as he made the tricky ascent, Gardiner didn't give him the opportunity. Snatching the vine, he ascended quickly, if not elegantly, aided by the adrenaline still in his system. At the top, he grabbed a proffered hand, climbed over the edge and did not look back.

"We may have a new problem," he confided to Jakop as soon as he'd located the other man.

"With the cleanup?"

"No, something else. After we finished, I heard a strange sound that lasted for about a minute."

"When?"

"Not long ago. You heard nothing up here?"

"No. What kind of noise was it?"

Gardiner shook his head. "It was such a low thumping that I couldn't tell if I was hearing it or feeling it. Really, it gave me the impression I was being watched."

Jakop closed his eyes tightly.

"If it truly was as you describe, then yes: You *were* being watched."

"How? What was it?"

"It was very likely a Servitor of Q'yoth. It is a highly dangerous extradimensional creature, but one that can be commanded to do many things. Traveling from place to place is one of the more mundane uses. Using it to travel from one *time* to another is also possible."

"One of those things is how I got here?"

"To me, it is the only solution that makes sense."

"The creature was there, but hidden within a dimension we cannot perceive?"

"Yes, *Outside*. And the person who called it forth was there with it."

"Frances?"

"I can see no other explanation. And having gained control of one of those creatures, it now also makes sense that she was the one on the rim. But, having the chance to kill you just now, wouldn't she have done so?"

"Given what I know about her, she should have." He thought for a moment. "But when her brother attacked me, she mentioned that it wasn't the right time to kill me."

"You think she is reserving your death for a special occasion?"

Gardiner sniggered, able to find a small amount of humor.

"Yes. A birthday present. Or Christmas—wait! No. She doesn't know I'm here." He reviewed the list of changes he'd undergone since she'd last seen him: full beard, a loss of weight that may make his face thinner, the robe… "Would she have recognized me?"

"A very good question."

Twenty-Two

CHANGE OF PLANS

Though everyone involved would have preferred the ceremony have gone off without a hitch, the eclipse itself turned out to be enough to inspire the first wave of volunteers. Man after man approached the temple; the guards did their best to keep them away. And though Jakop would have liked to take advantage of their enthusiasm, two things stood in his way. The first was logistical: The temple had no facilities, the immediate area only able to feed and house just a few priests and guards, not nearly enough to care for this many people. The other was more of a critical distinction. The goal wasn't merely to recruit a large number of men. The main prerequisite, aside from bravery and skill, was having the ability to cope with the monstrously unnatural things they would undoubtedly encounter. The sight of Nug, which Gardiner had been led to believe was much the same as Shub-Niggurath, would be a test of sanity for their soldiers.

Bearing all that in mind, the decision was easy. Jakop had the priests announce that the men should go home, then return in three days. The volunteers would be offered no reason, but they would at least not be milling about and growing restless. With no need to remain in South America any longer, Gardiner and Jakop left for home.

The next day, Gardiner stayed at the work site while Jakop travelled to the temple in Asia to check on Tamar. When Jakop had been gone a while, the Doctor decided to make use of the time by giving Mammut another English lesson in a storage yard on the periphery of the work site. While speaking of different stones and minerals, Gardiner used simple, common terms to help expand the other man's vocabulary. To reciprocate, Mammut was able to show off the masonry knowledge he had picked up over the years. He explained why certain features in the stones made them unsuitable for structural use. More than once, the older man learned something from the younger.

After a few hours, Gardiner thought it better to return and wait for Jakop. To bolster the lie he'd use to justify why they had been gone together, he picked out a piece of marble with a striking, multi-colored foliation, far too heavy for him to carry, and had Mammut bring it along. As they got near, he could see a knot of men standing protectively around someone—someone in a fine robe decorated with glints of gold.

"Kannit is here," he cautioned Mammut.

Gardiner led the way, and found Jakop speaking with his bene-factor. While Kannit was pleased with Gardiner's visit, Jakop dis-played annoyance, clenching his jaw and saying nothing. His eyes narrowed when he noticed Mammut carrying the heavy stone.

The guards must have remembered that the priest was beyond their power to intimidate, but Mammut was not. They made him put down his burden and bow before their boss.

Jakop excused himself to Kannit, then bowed to Gardiner.

"Another interesting rock?"

"You were gone a long time. I'm trying to keep my mind stim-ulated."

Jakop focused on Mammut briefly before looking back to Gardi-ner.

"I see that. I will speak at length now. Act as if you are bored. First, I must tell you that my trip to the other temple to check on the condition of the sick man did not go as anticipated. He is no-where to be found. No one saw him leave, though he was not being watched constantly. I have many men at the other temple searching for him. My technology cannot help in such an endeavor. We can do nothing but trust the natives and wait. Now look irritated and interrupt me. You were not—"

"What does he want?" interjected Gardiner.

"You were not here when I returned. I looked for you for a while, but then came back here to wait. He showed up very shortly afterward. Somehow, he has learned that the temple is complete, and wants to see it in person. I don't want to use any names in front of our friend here, but we both know the most obvious source of that intelligence is the one who is missing. In a few more days we theoretically could have had enough men to resist or fight him, but as of right now, we have no force at all, and I can see no other option. I told him that it wouldn't be possible to go there without your permission, but that argument evaporated when you showed up. I believe it would be best to simply get this done. Pretend to think it over, but agree."

Gardiner paused, looked at Kannit, and nodded.

"He will see how the portal works. Can you change the settings on it after this? Rekey the lock, as it were?"

"I can," said Jakop. "And will."

He went over to Kannit, spoke, and gestured as if ready to give the tour. Kannit pointed at Gardiner and said something.

"He wants you to come along," translated Jakop. He shook his head almost imperceptibly. "It is strange that he has grown impatient after these many months. I'm not comfortable with this situation, but a refusal would be awkward, possibly dangerous."

His eyes flicked between Mammut and Gardiner.

"There are too many unknowns all around," added Jakop suspiciously.

Well, I don't trust you either.

"We must all be careful," said Gardiner pointedly. He added, "Tell him that Mammut must also go along. He is needed to carry that holy stone for me."

Jakop had a clear view of the stone, but he still moved his head around oddly to look at it from slightly different angles. He finally shrugged and relayed the request, which was granted.

Walking over to the rock, Gardiner waved his hands over it and recited the first thing that came to mind: a stanza of a poem by Longfellow. Mammut understood most of the words, but his forehead was etched with confusion as he listened.

Gardiner whispered at Mammut—"We must be careful"—and gestured for him to pick it up.

Three of Kannit's six guards accompanied the group as they went over to the portal. Gardiner watched Jakop activate it, and saw that he tripled the sequence of touches needed to activate the doorway, with errors in the first two passes. He described what would happen, then walked through what had been solid stone moments before. The guards reacted, tensed muscles betraying their astonishment. Through it all, Kannit remained calm, even when Jakop materialized from thin air again shortly afterward.

Without a word, Kannit pointed out the order and directed the men through: one of the guards, then Jakop, followed by Kannit and a second guard, then Mammut, Gardiner, and the last guard. By the time Gardiner came through and spun himself around to face the sunlit end of the tunnel, the others had already started moving. He was only a step behind, but the man behind him gave him a push. Had there been more light, he would have glared in a manner befitting a priest, but that was useless in the darkness.

Upon emerging into the sunlight, the group stopped. Even after seeing it several times, Gardiner was still awed by the smoothly sculpted sandstone walls rising into the sky. Mammut and the guards were also fascinated as they tried to absorb the reality of it. Jakop and Kannit, however, ignored everything and looked at each other. Gardiner noticed the staring contest and wondered what silent communication was going on between them.

A noise from behind them broke the tension: the steps of someone running.

No, not just one.

Breaking eye contact with Jakop, Kannit barked a command. The guards drew their swords and backed Gardiner, Mammut and Jakop against the wall near the mouth of the tunnel. They forced

Mammut to put the heavy stone down. Gardiner looked to his left, and was startled to see three more guards approaching at a trot—the ones who were supposed to have remained behind.

"What's going on?" asked Gardiner.

"Kannit has other plans, it seems. I would prefer to observe his actions for a—" He listened. "Is that the sound you heard yesterday?"

The powerful pulsing soon became too loud to ignore, the vibrations amplified by the surrounding rock. The intensity leveled off at a point that nearly rattled their teeth.

"Yes," said Gardiner, mouth dry.

Suddenly, a woman appeared from thin air near the other side of the cave mouth. Haggard and filthy, gagged, hands bound… Despite all that, her identity was still obvious.

"Frances," hissed Gardiner. It was a challenge to feel pity and revulsion at the same time, but both were present. Some awe was also mixed in, a conscious appreciation that Kannit apparently commanded a fearsome power. Frances had a dazed, unfocused look. Just two steps forward were enough to display a drunken unsteadiness.

Is she drugged?

Another person emerged: Tamar. Physically in better shape than Frances, something about him was still clearly not right. His eyes were wild, darting things, blinking constantly. His mouth spasmed as if trying to speak, but no sound emerged. Each of his movements was cautious, the foot placement of supreme importance, as if trying to avoid stepping on things that weren't there.

As Tamar made his way over to Kannit, nudging Frances when needed to keep her moving, the thudding beat decreased in volume enough to be tolerable. The few inquiries Kannit directed at Tamar were audible, but the echoes defeated Gardiner's ability to understand more than a bare few words. Tamar's responses were all very brief, mainly yeses. With Jakop and Mammut both listening intently to the exchange, the Doctor decided to wait for a better time to ask for a translation. And hoped that there would *be* a better time.

At length, Kannit walked over to Jakop, leaving Tamar and Frances. The two men exchanged some words, Kannit supplying answers to only some of Jakop's questions. Mammut followed the dialog for a while, but then boldly shouted to get attention. He held his hands up and attempted to disassociate himself from the other two prisoners. The nearest guard held a sword to his neck, but he continued to speak, gesturing at Jakop and Gardiner. Jakop shook his head and cursed in the local language as he listened.

The Doctor listened closely. Taken in context with the emotional plea, he realized what was happening: Mammut was begging for his life.

"Your *friend* is abandoning us," spat Jakop.

Mammut's head shook right then, a sharp twitch not relevant to what he was saying.

When Gardiner saw the movement, he turned to look squarely at Jakop and mouthed, "No, he's not."

Expression unchanged, Jakop flicked his eyes at Gardiner and gave the tiniest of nods.

Mammut ended his plea and waited, bowing respectfully. After some consideration, Kannit told the guard to lower his sword, and gestured for Mammut to step away from the other two, off to the side. Another guard patted him down and discovered a small dagger. He pulled it out and held it out for Kannit. After a gesture of approval, it was handed back to Mammut.

Kannit then turned and spoke a few words to Tamar, who led Frances over to the left of Gardiner. She showed no sign of recognizing him, but she barely showed any signs of life at all. Tamar guided her down to the ground and sat her against the wall. With a gesture from Kannit, Jakop also took a seat, as did Gardiner, sitting between Frances and Jakop. Two guards remained behind as all the others left.

"We have to depend on him," said Gardiner, watching Mammut walk away with the group.

"Shhh!" chided Jakop.

Gardiner looked over.

197

"What?"

Jakop pointed at Frances.

Gardiner looked at her and shivered. She was emaciated, the gag in her mouth was disgusting, and an odor emanated from her that was worse than what he'd noticed from anyone in this era. Bruises were evident on her cheeks and her wrists were raw from being endlessly chafed by the crude rope.

The enemy of my enemy...

He sighed deeply.

"Frances."

Jakop cursed using one of the words Gardiner knew.

"Frances, can you hear me? I have a beard now, but it's Quentin Gardiner. My presence here is probably quite a surprise, with you having left me as you did."

He paused.

"I know that neither of us holds any love for the other, but it is in our best interest to work together to get out of this situation."

He waited, but there was nothing from her, even after he touched her gently on the arm.

"She's not there," said Gardiner as he turned back to Jakop, right then hearing the faintest of whimpers. At the same time, he noticed how interested one of the guards had become in his attempt to talk to her, but was able to control his reaction. "Rather, she *is* there, but I think it will be very bad for her if anyone discovers that."

"Understood," said Jakop. He pointed toward Mammut, off in the distance. "You taught him English."

"Yes. He learned very quickly."

"Can we trust him?"

Gardiner thought about how best to answer that.

"Despite the fact that he is from an entirely different culture, he is wholly human, and because of that I believe so."

"I see."

"I'm sorry for being blunt," Gardiner added, "but your reactions are difficult for me to interpret, your methods are often distasteful, and your motivations are impossible to understand."

"I cannot refute any of that." Jakop seemed to deliberate for a while. "I have been thinking about my role in...all of this." His hands indicated the tunnel, the temple, the hollowed-out mountain. "We are clearly different, you and I, but we are both trapped within this web of events, and neither of us can know exactly what the future will bring. Despite the obvious lack of prescience, I feel that my involvement here is nearing an end, in one way or another. I swear that you will be able to trust me right up to that end."

"You have never given me explicit cause to distrust you," admitted Gardiner.

"As you told her, we must work together."

"Agreed."

"She is wholly human, and from your own time and culture. What is your assessment? Can *we* trust *her*?"

Gardiner looked at the broken woman on his left.

"I can't say."

Frances only sat still, staring and silent.

TWENTY-THREE

THE INSANITY OF KANNIT

Whatever Kannit had planned, he was in no especial hurry. He strolled around the circumference of the bowl, inspecting the structure. By the time he finished his circumlocution, a pair of the guards had returned with the priests from the outer temple—the same men who had come so very close to success in the ceremony to call down Nug. The two groups converged near where the prisoners were sitting.

One of the guards forced Jakop to stand up and pushed him closer to the priests. Kannit spoke to Jakop, having him pass a message along to the priests. It was short, and Gardiner could make out the words "Not Nug" near the beginning. The words that followed were incomprehensible, but Jakop physically started upon hearing one in particular. That same word triggered a reaction from Frances: a low whine. Of anger or fear or despair, it was hard to tell.

"Apparently, you and Jakop both know something I don't," he whispered. "Something that will inspire you to cooperate with us, I would hope."

She made no acknowledgement, but he didn't expect one.

Perplexed over the change of plans, the priests debated among themselves, pointed at Kannit and the guards. Jakop was plied with questions, but he did not respond. One man wearing a defiant scowl marched toward Kannit and addressed him directly, declaring that the temple had been dedicated to Nug—or at least that's how it sounded to Gardiner.

Kannit put on a good show for a short while, pretending to think over a message he didn't understand, then signaled the nearest guard. His sword flashed, the tip slicing an inch-deep gash in the priest's throat. A geyser erupted outward as the artery was breached. The other priests lunged forward to try to help him, but were blocked. He fell to the ground, moaning and holding a hand to his neck.

More blood.

The butchery reminded Gardiner of the horrible scene with Frances' brother. Unable to look away from the suffering of the priest, he found himself holding his breath, triggering a memory of the oxygen bags in a pocket within his robe. At that point a burst of inspiration connected needs and knowledge into a workable solution. He should have seen the answer days before, but everything only melded together right then.

"I know how to get us back to nineteen twenty-five," he blurted out.

The exclamation was loud enough to attract everyone's attention. Jakop glanced over.

Gardiner reacted quickly, gesturing toward the dying man, pretending to pray. His words were meant for Frances, but he faced the man and spoke in a singsong rhythm that reinforced the illusion of prayer, raising his voice to ensure that all of the English-speakers could hear his plan.

"You're going to have to trust me. There is a way, but we need your help. You know as well as I that ocean water is needed to flood this place, and you're the only one who might possibly do it. If your gag is removed, can you command the extradimensional creature nearby to create a hole through the earth from here to the ocean?"

He put his hands together and his head down, waiting for the priest to breathe his last, and keeping his concentration focused on Frances. With everyone silent, the only sound being the powerful thumping beat of the invisible creature, it was plainly too quiet for her to respond. But as the man's movements ended, some muttering and shuffling from the remaining priests created enough noise to cover her muffled "Mmm hmm."

Gardiner raised his head and looked at Jakop, who nodded. With Mammut facing Jakop, able to see that, Gardiner hoped his friend was aware that *something* was about to happen.

It wasn't long before the priests seemed to reach a consensus: Being living worshipers of a different entity was better than remaining faithful to Nug. There was no need for Jakop to relay a translation.

Kannit, prepared for their acquiescence, removed something from within his robe. It was smooth and supple, likely a piece of animal hide scraped clean of hair. Gardiner was too far away to see it clearly, but he could tell that the few short phrases written on it were in the familiar cuneiform wedges. Kannit handed it to Jakop, who read it over. Near the end he started visibly.

While looking at the priests, Jakop said in English, "His plan is insanity. It is more terrible than I could have imagined." He then switched seamlessly to the language of the natives and began to explain the ceremony to them.

Gardiner had no choice but to wait and wonder what that plan may be. He had become acquainted with many forms of madness over the years. Frances, for example, despite being in deplorable shape, appeared to be perfectly sane. And yet she had chosen a course that seemed to be inconceivable, allying herself with a being whose agenda was at odds with human civilization. At the other extreme was Tamar, who not long ago was a perfectly normal person. But exposure to the Outside—a view of reality the human mind was not meant to handle—had transformed him into a quivering mess.

And Kannit was apparently a third type, willing to attempt something unthinkable even to Frances.

The priests were excellent students. It didn't take long before they were repeating the words back to Jakop for verification, Kannit listening closely and nodding his approval. He then directed them to move out to the central platform and begin. A guard used the point of his sword to back Jakop against the wall, where he reseated himself.

Gardiner patiently waited what he thought was long enough, but when the fellow prisoner remained silent, he was forced to ask, "What's going to happen?"

"We will all die," said Jakop, hanging his head.

"Please. I need you to tell me what you know."

Jakop shook his head glumly for a while, but then seemed to locate some store of inner strength. Looking up, he said, "Your people have never made mention of—"

He did a very odd thing then, snapping his right thumb and index finger together twice.

"I'm sorry. The name doesn't translate well. It is best pronounced as Kh'kh'rng. The entity is a spirit, or ghost, a formless and invisible collection of energy. It only manifests physically when it makes contact with a planet, using stone to form a body. But the energies cannot be fully contained, and the material liquefies. Imagine an immense worm, perhaps two hundred feet long, made of molten rock."

"Can a thing like that be harmed at all?"

"Not with anything we have available." He rubbed at his forehead. "And if too much pain is inflicted without killing it, it retreats, burrowing down toward the core. It's a death sentence at that point. Within days, the planet explodes. Then the entity dissociates itself from the rubble and drifts off into space, ready to be called down somewhere else. My people have recorded more than a few instances of this."

"What does Kannit hope to gain?"

"Somehow, he believes that he has discovered the proper formulae to control the thing."

Jakop looked at Frances.

"Somehow," he repeated, with a heavy frown. "In any case," he continued, "if he succeeds here, we dare not attack him. If he is killed after that point, the entity will be loosed on the Earth."

"And if Kannit is not killed, he will exact an insane vengeance," finished Gardiner. "We must stop him now." As the priests sat down and began to chant, he asked, "How much time will the ceremony take?"

"As little as an hour. Kannit seems to think that the stars are favorably aligned, and the remaining men have been spurred on by the death of the priest. It more depends on how well they can concentrate."

"She"—he twitched his head toward Frances—"can do what is needed, but I don't have a complete escape plan. I see two ways out of here: the portal we came through, and the creature."

"The creature *cannot* be an option," stressed Jakop. "As long as it has access to this world, through Tamar, we are at its mercy. We live at the whim of Kannit—though he has kept *her* alive for some reason."

"In that case the creature must be commanded to create the tunnel to the sea and depart afterwards. Is that possible?" The question was again directed to Frances, and he turned his head toward her just enough to be able to detect her response.

With the guards watching the priests, she turned and dipped her head ever so slightly toward Gardiner.

"We need some kind of diversion in order to get a head start to the portal," said Jakop.

Gardiner felt in his robe for the chemical bags and looked at the congealing blood around the dead man. It wasn't a nice open pool of water like at the oasis, but there was probably enough extra moisture spilled on the ground and within the body to enhance the potassium bomb.

"Ask that guard to let me go over to the dead priest."

Jakop did so, but the man shook his head.

"What do you want to do?" Jakop asked Gardiner.

Gardiner removed his robe, leaving him dressed in only a loincloth and sandals.

"Tell him it is the custom of my religion to cover the dead man with the robe of a priest," he said, then paused to think. "To allow his soul to be guided in the afterlife. Or invent some fiction you think may appeal to him."

Jakop spoke for a while, using his hands for emphasis occasionally. The guard, surprisingly, listened to the spiel, and at one point even recoiled in what seemed to be horror. Ultimately, he gave in, speaking one of the few words in that language Gardiner knew: "Quick!"

In order to keep up the guise of a harmless priest, he scrambled over, staying low. After straightening out the dead man's limbs, he arranged the robe so that the hidden bomb was sitting squarely on the sternum. Had the thought occurred a few minutes beforehand, he may have been able to discretely remove one or both of the oxygen bags, but it was too late for that now.

"Oh, faithful priest, may your lifeless body provide a flaming distraction for us to escape," he said loudly as a final blessing before crawling back to the wall. Mammut had watched, and Gardiner hoped that his student had remembered what the word *flaming* meant.

Seated again, he put on another show of prayer while describing what he had just done.

"There is a quantity of pure potassium on that man's chest. If the creature crushes it into his body there will be a violent reaction." He measured the distance and recalled the previous experiments. "We're actually too close right now."

Jakop looked down at the back of his hands.

"The priests seem to be concentrating very well. Do you feel that?"

Gardiner felt the static charge building, all the hairs on his body beginning to stick out.

"I do."

"We must act soon."

Mammut rubbed his arms and looked over at Gardiner.

"I'm going to yell at our large friend," Gardiner said. "Translate for me."

Jakop nodded.

Gardiner stood up, pointed at Mammut.

"You," he said. "Come here! You are less important than I. By our customs you must give me your robe!"

The commotion got everyone's attention. Mammut stared back, but made no move until Jakop spoke it in the native language. He took a step toward the Doctor and shook his head.

"If you do not give me your robe, I will curse you!" added Gardiner, and he began waving his arms in a way that seemed to be appropriate for magical cursing.

When Jakop relayed that message, Mammut showed a fearsome amount of rage. He pointed and shouted something back, then pulled out his knife and ran towards Gardiner. The guards let him pass, one even laughing.

"Cut the rope on her mouth!" Gardiner said as he drew near.

Mammut grabbed Gardiner by the right shoulder and shoved him down so violently that he fell on top of Frances, his head landing in her lap. As Mammut stooped over and drew back the weapon, Gardiner wondered for a fleeting second if he had erred in his assessment of whom to trust. But at the last moment the blade changed course, coming down deftly next to Frances' cheek and slicing through the rope.

From his position, Gardiner saw vitality flood back into the broken woman. She stretched her mouth wide then spat out a string of alien syllables. His head cracked on the ground as she vanished from beneath him.

Twenty-four

Rising Tides

The impact wasn't enough to daze him, but some pain blurred the voices into a jumble. By the time Gardiner rolled over onto his hands and knees, the guards had converged on Mammut and a semblance of order was restored. The big man made no attempt at resistance, dropped his knife and knelt down next to Gardiner with his hands up.

Chaos flared again when Frances rematerialized, tumbling out of thin air. With her hands still bound, she couldn't break her fall, but was able to twist around and land mainly on her right arm. The side of her head still smacked the ground, though.

"Five minutes," she gasped to Gardiner, closing her eyes tightly. "Keep him occu—"

The guards were on her quickly, tying another gag in place, the rope yanked tight. She groaned as it bit in, once again abrading flesh that had been similarly mistreated for so long.

Five minutes? Where's the hole? Ahh!

Gardiner hadn't noticed that Tamar was also missing until he blinked back into existence nearby. Kannit walked over with the rest of the guards, conferred briefly with Tamar, and watched the priests for a time. Satisfied that the ceremony had not been interrupted, he said something to Jakop and waved toward Gardiner and Frances.

"Kannit says that was stupid," said Jakop. Kannit continued to speak, with Jakop translating.

"Tamar has protected us from the creature. It can do us no harm. That dog of a woman is less trustworthy than the worst thief I have ever known. She could have used that time to escape, and yet she did not. I confess that I find her to be very strange and do not understand her, but she has proven to be of great value. This man Jakop is also strange, but has a command of many languages and so too is valuable. You, old priest: Are you of value? Do you have knowledge that I can use?"

Gardiner delayed for as long as he dared. While Frances had manipulated the creature to accomplish something almost beyond imagining, the water rushing toward them over a hundred miles through bedrock still had to obey the laws of physics.

"Did you hear what she said about keeping him occupied?" Gardiner asked Jakop.

"I did. I am keeping track of the time."

"Tell him I have knowledge that will benefit him, but I also have questions."

Even as Jakop passed that message along, the amount of static electricity around them went up a notch. Kannit looked over toward the priests. Smiling widely, he magnanimously gestured towards Gardiner, urging him to continue.

"Was that you who threw that woman to her death during the invocation of Nug?"

"I was there," said Kannit through Jakop. "One of my wives slipped. My least favorite one, fortunately."

"She was pregnant."

He considered the news, shrugged.

"I have six sons and four daughters. Plenty enough for now."

"When this entity arrives, those priests will surely die."

"There are always sacrifices in every venture."

"Will we also die?"

"I will protect everyone here who serves me. I may even save your large, scarred friend if you ask me nicely. And provide me with this knowledge you spoke of."

Gardiner nodded. He waited as long as he dared before asking his next question.

"Your change of plan strikes me as being risky. Why not stay with Nug?"

"The army you were on the verge of assembling was, of course, very appealing—but it would have been made of men. And generals are the worst. I hate generals; none can ever be trusted. They are too close to the seat of power and it is too tempting for them. Instead of using generals, I will command Kh'kh'rng to dispose of my enemies. The mountains will explode and emit their lava, and the oceans will boil. This world will burn, or not, at my whim. My empire is at hand." The tone of his voice turned threatening. "Are you with me or against me?"

After what must have been too long of a delay, the sword of the nearest guard touched Gardiner's jugular.

"I don't think I've used up enough time," he said to Jakop.

The words had hardly left his mouth when a bizarre sound was heard by all: a splintering crack. All heads turned to locate the source. As Gardiner saw the body of the dead priest being crushed by an invisible weight, he batted the weapon away, shoved the guard, and spun around to protect his face.

"Now!" is all that he could think to say.

Flames erupted with a *whoosh!* Three of the guards were immolated immediately, far too close to react. A fourth—the one Gardiner had pushed—turned in time and threw himself to the ground, clothes afire and badly burned, but still alive. The other two had pushed Kannit down and had fallen protectively on top of him. They were singed and likely in pain, but seemed largely unhurt.

Tamar was also still alive, but in dire shape. He had stood through the flash, the left side of his body exposed to the enormous heat. After crumpling to the ground, the blackened half of his body was revealed.

Without the protection of his robe, Gardiner had chanced fatal burns, but the unfortunate guard in front of him had proved to be enough of a shield to save his life. Pain flared in different parts of his body as he stood, the rush of adrenaline dulling some of it. A glance

209

at Mammut showed scorched clothing, but no injuries. Using his body to protect Frances, she seemed no worse than before.

"Help her up," Gardiner told Mammut. "We need to get away."

Kannit was screaming at the two guards who had protected him. That pair would certainly be able to overtake the group if they started pursuit.

As Gardiner tried to start moving his leg buckled, but Jakop came up alongside and steadied him. Much of the right side of Jakop's clothing was black, his arm red, but he was moving easily.

"Don't look at your leg," said Jakop. "It's a bad burn, but will heal."

With Mammut holding onto Frances, and Jakop propping up Gardiner, the group began a limping trot into the shadowy tunnel toward the portal. They could still hear Kannit, but the thumping beat of the Servitor was lessening.

"Are you counting off the distance?" Gardiner asked Jakop.

"I suggested the counting for your benefit. I have it marked in such a way that I can locate it."

"The heat-absorbing ink? How do you see it?"

"Later."

A few steps further down the tunnel, the ominous beating was indeed gone, but it had been replaced with something similar: a rumbling vibration. Jakop stopped to look back.

"Kannit and Tamar are gone," he shouted over the din. "And the guards are closing."

Even into the tunnel, the static electricity could still be felt, a swarm of snakes crawling over Gardiner's skin.

"We must keep moving!" Gardiner said. "The w—"

His words were blotted out by a massive blast as the sea water completed its journey from the coast. Moving at hundreds of miles per hour, it burst up through the rock floor of the cavity. The pressure wave of displaced air slammed into the group, shoving forcefully against every part of their backs and legs at the same time. They flew dozens of feet before landing hard.

For the second time in minutes, Gardiner smacked his head on the ground, and this time stars did dance around him. He was able to roll over and sit up, but couldn't find enough balance to raise himself up any further. A roaring filled his ears as he crawled around. Seeing nothing but blackness, he wasn't even sure if he had his eyes open.

"Where?" he asked as loudly as he could.

A pair of powerful hands pulled him up.

"Here," said Mammut over the noise, as he turned Gardiner around. The light from the end of the tunnel, straight ahead, was much dimmer now. The blast had pushed them past the portal entrance. With Mammut holding him firmly, they backtracked some. He could make out the form of a person slumped on the floor near the wall, but couldn't discern who it was, and couldn't even remember how many were supposed to be in their group.

Is someone missing?

Once next to the wall, Mammut felt along it until his arm dropped into the hidden hole. Gardiner had just enough wits about him to sidle into it. But as disoriented as he was, he took one step then fell headlong through the portal.

A pair of sure hands caught him and guided him a few feet away. He fell to his knees, but couldn't even hold that position and had to lay down. When his back touched the ground a flare of pain forced him to roll onto his side. Everything began to spin, the scene flickering like a silent movie at a cheap cinema. He saw Frances tumble through, but Jakop was there for her and set her down.

Mammut came next.

"Two guards come!" he said in English, then leapt away and began searching.

Ill-timed, Jakop had stood up in front of the portal when one of Kannit's men burst through. The blade slashed down to land a solid blow, biting deeply to the left of his neck. Fortunately, Jakop was close enough to do what he'd wanted. Lunging forward even after being hit, he touched the wall to the right of the portal as the remaining guard came through. About a third of the man—an arm, a leg, most of the head—fell into a pile on the floor, sliced as if by invisible guillotine. Grabbing at his wound, Jakop collapsed beside the pile of human detritus.

Mammut returned in time to save him from a second strike, crushing the head of the guard with a slab of stone. When the man went down, Mammut wrenched his sword away and stabbed him through the heart with it.

As that final blow landed, Jakop called out.

"Gardiner!"

The Doctor worked to focus on the voice, only a few feet away.

"Yes." He could see that Jakop's clothing was soaked with blood already, his face deathly pale.

"I'm—" He stopped and held his breath.

Mammut knelt down and peeked beneath Jakop's robe at the wound. He tore a piece off, wadded it up, and pressed where the bleeding was the worst.

Jakop moaned when the pressure was applied.

"This body won't live much longer," he gasped. "Gardiner!"

"Yes. What do you need?" In his delirium Gardiner imagined he was right next to Jakop, ready to help. In reality, he hadn't moved even an inch, and his mumbled words were barely audible. A collage of images flashed as he blinked repeatedly. The next sight he witnessed was Mammut saying *I do*. A wedding vow made no sense right then, but puzzling out the reason for it was too taxing.

"I need a device," said Jakop. "Up there, hidden."

He pointed at an area above and behind him. Mammut looked up at a bare wall.

"Hidden," coughed Jakop.

Before standing, Mammut guided Jakop's hand to hold the cloth in place. Then with both hands, he started feeling along the stone, and before too long found a niche concealed by illusion. He reached in and carefully extracted something: a delicate-looking, pyramidal mechanism made of metal and glass, with a central convex mirror prominently perched atop.

"Put it here, in front of me," said Jakop. After Mammut placed it on the floor, Jakop leaned forward and touched the base, then fell back. The top of the mechanism started to spin, reflecting light in crazy patterns. With some of the glass pieces being prisms, the colors of the rainbow danced all around them. He squeezed his eyes shut, then opened them and spoke sharply.

"Gardiner! Use the machine. Make an antibiotic solution with silver. Silver!"

The strange lights helped Gardiner's concentration momentarily, the words penetrating into his befuddled state.

Antibiotic. Silver.

The effort of speaking those instructions seemed to drain the last of Jakop's strength. He went silent and concentrated on the spinning thing. A low whine began as it moved even faster, the lights becoming lines as they flashed too rapidly to follow. The whine became more piercing and leveled off. After a while, the device started to smoke, and the spinning slowed.

As soon as the machine stopped moving, Mammut, who had been mesmerized by the spectacle, checked on Jakop, signaling that the wounded man was still breathing.

That was all that Gardiner had the strength to witness. It became too much of an effort to stay awake, and he welcomed the oblivion of unconsciousness.

TWENTY-FIVE

FRANCES

Gardiner awoke on a makeshift bed, covered by a blanket. Lying on his side, the stench of vomit assaulted his nostrils and the taste lingered in his mouth. The darkness was lit by a single candle sitting on the floor nearby; it had burned far down, and would probably go out soon. He sat up slowly, but even so, it was enough to cause his head to pound. There was also a terrific pain in his leg, but that was a good sign. If the flames had burned through the dermis to kill the nerves, he would be in serious trouble. There was a fuzzy memory of Jakop saying something about the burn, but he couldn't latch onto it.

Mammut was beside him instantly.

"Are you good?" he asked quietly.

"Not good, but better. How is Jakop?"

"He died. Too much blood."

"And what of Frances?"

"Awake," she said, her voice coming from right behind him. "And patiently waiting for you to do the same. Mammut was kind enough to remove my gag, and give me bread and water. He even moved my hands around to the front to allow me some comfort, but he would not free me without your permission."

Gardiner tapped his head and nodded at Mammut.

"Good thinking," he whispered. He turned around to face her and saw that she was still recumbent; they had been placed head-to-head, some blankets providing minimal padding against the row of stones upon which they lay. "And now I must decide whether to trust you or not."

"We came to an arrangement earlier," she reminded him. "I commanded the creature to flood the chamber. You are now obligated to take me—both of us—back."

"You needn't doubt that. I intend to keep my word and *attempt* to follow through. You and I will assume the same risk. We will both either be restored to our proper time, or we will both be dead. What was never discussed, however, was any stipulation to free you."

She offered no rebuttal on that point.

Gardiner's mind still recovering, it was difficult to organize his thoughts.

Frances gave him some time, then cleared her throat.

"If you are wondering, I will tell you now: No, I cannot call another of those creatures to my aid. Or rather, I do have the ability, but it could be fatal for us. During our escape, Jakop said that Kannit and Tamar had disappeared. That implies that they were picked up by the creature before it left, and so are currently Outside right now. Calling another Servitor would give Kannit an opportunity to both locate us and exit that space. It is a small chance, but I don't want to give him that option. You may believe that, or think it a lie—whichever you prefer. But it *is* the truth."

Gardiner studied her in the dim candlelight.

She's been held captive for months, probably. Abused, tortured. But she remains unbroken and defiant—and so very dangerous. Kannit even said as much. But she wants to get back as much as I do, and needs me to do so.

"Mammut, please free her."

While she held her hands up, the other man reached over, slipped his knife between her hands and cut through the rope.

"Thank you, Doctor."

She picked at the loops of rope until they dropped away, and lightly rubbed her wrists.

"You were…Outside," he said. "What's it like?"

215

"There are few words that come close to being appropriate, but I can say that it grants one a perspective that is unimaginable unless you go there first. And although a person cannot prepare for it precisely, having foreknowledge of its…differentness…allows the mind to adapt. Without that adaptation, there will be damage."

"Like Tamar?"

"Exactly. Even when he was back on this plane, he couldn't disengage his mind. His perceptions had become blurred. He saw things that were both here and beyond here. Kannit, on the other hand…"

She thought for a long while and shook her head.

"He said that I was strange, but he is exceptional. His mind seemed to work on another level. I knew, in a vague way, what to expect of the Outside, but it still had an impact on me. It did not affect him at all, from what I could tell. And he professed to never having experienced it before."

"Interesting," said Gardiner. "At one point before your arrival, I sensed that Jakop had determined, or at least had a guess about, some aspect of Kannit. I never got the chance to ask him about it. You didn't speak with him before he died, did you?"

"No, he only lived perhaps fifteen minutes after that contraption stopped spinning, and said nothing during that time. Do you know what it was?"

"I don't. He never mentioned it, but there were oblique references."

"And you have a suspicion."

Gardiner smiled. A suspicion was all it was, but to have just the illusion of the upper hand on her was gratifying.

"I'll say that I have a good idea. He was yet another enigmatic individual."

"I see."

The candle flickered wildly and went out.

"I get a candle," said Mammut, moving away.

"Wait," said Gardiner. "How long until the sun comes up? How many hours?"

"One or two."

"Did you sleep at all?"

"Some."

"You sleep. I'm awake now." Gardiner tried to stand, failed. "Can you help me up?"

Frances got up and was next to him.

"I'm right here, Doctor. I'm also awake. Let's go elsewhere and talk. Leave the poor man alone to rest."

"For once, I agree with you."

With her aid, he stood. The pain in his leg flared again, but he was prepared for it, and did not lean too heavily on her. Still dressed in a loincloth, he groped around for the blanket and draped it around himself before hobbling out of the room with her.

The moon would sink out of sight before long, but it lent enough light to let Gardiner lead them to a familiar, wide stone that had been worn smooth from continual use. On a more practical note, he knew that there were no cracks in it for scorpions to hide. The sky was largely free of clouds, allowing for some good stargazing, and he took advantage, identifying many of the myriad points covering the sky.

"Mammut is a good man," began Gardiner after a few minutes of silence. "Loyal. And very intelligent."

"He learned English. He must be."

"He has a much better ear for languages than I, I must say."

"Jakop also spoke English. Another savant?"

"Something like that."

"You seem to be reticent to speak of him," said Frances.

"Seem? Oh, no. It is a fact: I *am* reticent."

"Why is that? Are you afraid of him?"

"Not that. It's a petty reason, really. I finally know something you do not. It gives me a certain, small edge over you—something I've not had before."

"And so, it would be fruitless of me to ply you with questions, even though you accused him of not being *wholly human*?"

217

Gardiner cringed, hoping she didn't see the reaction in the dim light. He'd forgotten using those words in her presence. Holding his breath, he waited to be pressed, but nothing further came.

He stared at the sky again, never tiring of the rich array of stars on clear nights in this era. Some trick of tired eyes or concussed brain made the lowest lights down at the horizon glow with an odd brightness.

"Let's talk about something else then," she suggested. "How will we get back? Do you know the location of Shub-Niggurath?"

"I don't."

The admission triggered a thought of that neglected detail at the temple. The black spot that had transported Chico, Frances and himself to that underground lair—it nagged at him. Did he need to be concerned about it?

"Neither do I. My decision to come *here* was…rash, perhaps. I saw an opportunity to…learn something." Her words were tinged with frustration. Or embarrassment. "Then you must know of an alternate method of traveling through time."

Gardiner sighed mentally. Being able to step through some sort of portal and arrive back in 1925 was a much better alternative than what he had in mind. There was no way to avoid telling her, but if he chose the wrong words, she'd likely put many of the unknowns together.

But she'll find out. I can't hide everything.

"I'll begin by saying that it will be neither quick nor pleasant. Our trip of about four-thousand-five-hundred years will take just that long. We won't notice it, however. There is a substance… Well, I honestly can't say how it works, but I've been told that it slows the effects of time at a ratio of a million to one."

"In that case, for us it will be instantaneous." She sounded satisfied by the prospect. "What is the unpleasant part you referred to?"

When he thought about what was to come, his voice wavered.

"We must be buried in it. I've also been led to believe it's poisonous."

Frances paused before answering.

218

"I see."

"Yes. Trusting in this procedure will be a challenge."

"But you know it works?"

"I am as sure of it as I can be, based upon what I've learned. And the explanation given by Jakop did not conflict with that."

"Jakop?"

Gardiner heard disdain in her voice.

"You don't trust him?" he asked.

"Should I? A mysterious person with motivations that are impossible to understand?"

Hearing his own words repeated back to him a second time induced a frown.

"We have no explicit reason to distrust him," said Gardiner. "And, we have no other options."

"I cannot argue that. When can it be done?"

"Today, later," he said. "Some preparations are needed. Let Mammut get some rest."

When he shifted position slightly, his burned leg brushed the stone. He reached down to rub it, but caught himself in time, and bit at his lip as he waited for the pain to subside.

"Jakop said to make an *antibiotic* solution with silver," said Frances. "I'm not familiar with that word, but I might assume it means antibacterial."

"It makes sense, given the context." As the pain faded, he chuckled. "Maybe he left the recipe."

"Recipe?"

He considered trying to explain, decided against it.

"You can see for yourself later."

They sat quietly again for a while, facing east. A lightening patch, straight ahead and low, revealed where the sun would soon rise, and seemed to amplify the light from the stars in that area. Tinges of red made the sky smolder, reminding Gardiner of Kannit's threat to make the world burn.

"I grew up on a little island almost directly west of Mount Vesuvius," mused Frances. "Ischia. Sometimes I would wake up early

219

just to watch the sun rise. I remember a few mornings when it seemed as if the very air was on fire."

"He certainly came close to doing that. Was the ceremony successful, do you think? We're an ocean away and can't be sure unless we return and take a look."

She said nothing, alarming him slightly. She had opened up a small bit, offering a bit of her past, then had gone silent at a question that needed to be answered. The woman was as annoyingly secretive as Jakop had been.

Ah, but with good reason in this case: We are enemies.

And he must never forget that. But still, she had information about Kh'kh'rng that he did not. Frances was the only resource at hand.

"And I strongly prefer to not return there," he continued. "In this era. Although, in the future, we both will. Rather, we already have… And do you know what else I strongly prefer?"

There was a long pause, but finally she asked, "What is that, Doctor?"

"I prefer to never again travel into the past. Speaking about it is entirely too confusing."

He thought he saw her smile at his attempt at humor.

Did that work?

"To answer your question," she began, "I believe we're safe. Jakop labeled the thing as Kh'kh'rng. That's as good a name as any. I can't confess to much knowledge of it, but I can say that any evocation requires the proper conditions." She laughed and finished with, "And for that one, a gigantic bowl of water is not it!"

Gardiner joined her. The absurdity of the situation seemed to be especially funny. It had been a long time since he'd been relaxed enough to enjoy a laugh like that.

"I have to say," he said after their giggles had subsided, "that I was worried when you reappeared and there was no hole in the bottom of the bowl."

"If a visible hole had been created on our end, Kannit would have seen it, allowing him time to react. He probably would've given the order to kill us all without hesitation."

"I was able to figure that out, and was impressed that you were able to give such detailed commands to the creature in that vile language."

"Given enough time, it's possible to learn anything."

"Yes, but how much time?"

"It's my turn to be reticent."

Gardiner grunted, knowing that the conversation was at an end. He looked at the lights he'd noticed previously. There were more now—closer. And flickering.

"Torches." He pointed. "Kannit's men?"

"It is."

"You sound certain."

"Had his scheme worked," she said, "he wouldn't need it. But I have to think he set up a contingency: 'If you don't hear from me, come in force.' I would have done it."

"I'll trust your instincts in this case."

"There seems to be little time. Where can we go? Fleeing to the Outside is an option, but I caution against it."

"No, no need for anything that drastic. There's a place we can hide."

They went back inside and roused Mammut.

"From here, which direction does Kannit live?" asked Gardiner.

The waking man mumbled something, then more clearly: "East."

"I'm sorry, but we must go. Right now."

Twenty-Six

Rest and Recovery

They had luck on their side. The storehouse lay to the west of their current position. Moving as quickly as possible, they scurried away just in time, staying on lower ground or keeping larger objects between them and the advancing force. Gardiner was concerned that they wouldn't be able to cover their tracks effectively in the darkness of pre-dawn, but they made it without incident.

When they entered, Frances looked around the obviously artificial room, but asked no questions about who or how or why. Gardiner was relieved to be relatively safe, but at the same time knew that they were trapped—and without food or water. Mammut might be able to make a few trips to gather supplies, but the combination of his size and his scars made him stand out. If Kannit's men were trying to find any of them, he would be easiest to spot. Frances was the one person they would most likely be actively seeking and so had to stay completely hidden. Gardiner had rarely been in public without a disguise, but his difficulty with communication would severely restrict his interactions. Not to mention his injuries. They would heal with enough time, but he was hoping to be gone from this era before that happened. At least, he *hoped* they would heal. Now, with enough light to examine the burn on his leg, he cringed at the sight of the blistered, bright red skin. He needed to take action on it soon.

Jakop said to use silver. The silver will be easy…and so will the water!

Aside from the small amount needed for the medical application, there was no reason why they shouldn't be able to use the machine to make enough for drinking as well. Excited by his idea, and thirsty, he led the others back to the open workroom, where they were greeted by a small present. The glass with the handle Gardiner had manufactured was sitting on the bench next to the mechanism.

"He found it," said Gardiner, picking it up.

Mammut grunted.

"What is that?" asked Frances.

Gardiner looked through the glass at the rows of storage units in front of them, and handed it to her after pointing it at a good sample of the alien writing.

"Can you read that language?"

She gasped upon getting her first glimpse of the blue scrawl, and went over to get a closer look.

"No, I've never seen anything like this before." She handed the glass back to him. "You were surprised to find this?"

"To find it here. I left it outside. It seemed there was little I could hide from Jakop. He was always a step ahead."

A recurring theme with me.

"Well," he said aloud. "We need water, and this thing will make it for us."

After searching and prodding the mechanism, he discovered that the area in which the finished items appeared could be manipulated so that the material flowed out the side through a chute. Mammut had given the last of his water to Frances earlier, so Gardiner invited him to drink first. Thinking that the water would be a steady dribble, he had Mammut kneel down below the chute with his mouth open. What looked to be a quart of water splashed all over Mammut's face. He inhaled some, choked, and coughed.

Shock turned into laughter. All three had a nice, virtual dunking before Gardiner took the time to study the machine more closely. Indicators that he had previously paid no attention to showed how much time it would take to perform the requested operation, and how much of the raw materials were at hand. From what he could glean, there was an almost endless supply of water—which would make sense even if the thing was merely stealing water vapor out of the air and condensing it. But the speed with which it created water was amazing. Further investigating gave him an answer that made sense.

"According to these symbols"—he pointed at the display on top—"the machine is pulling from some kind of underground stream or aquifer rich with dissolved minerals."

"How is it linked?" asked Frances, looking at the empty space below the table. "There's no visible—wait. Is it using the same type of doorway that brought us from South America to here?"

"I never thought about it, but yes, very likely."

"There's no magic involved in any of this, is there? Every single bit is some kind of advanced science."

Gardiner sensed something then—some subtle mannerism, a stress in her voice, a flash of her eyes—and he knew he'd made a mistake. She saw how valuable this knowledge could be, and had had a subtle, but uncharacteristic, lapse in self-control. How many hours—or even minutes—would she need to gain as much understanding of the advanced technology as he currently had? He almost regretted not keeping her bound and gagged, even blindfolded as well. He couldn't, though. Human dignity and decency were high on his personal agenda. Everyone, without exception, deserved a certain amount.

After a transformation to remove the chute and restore the machine to the way it had been shortly before, he took a look through the inventory. There was plenty of copper available, so he had the machine create a pair of small bowls with flat bottoms, moving his fingers as quickly as he could, hoping that she wouldn't be able to follow what he was doing.

After some patient waiting the red-orange bowls were ready. He handed them to Mammut, restored the chute, and set he machine to create a fine silver dust. With Mammut holding one of the bowls to catch the powder, he started the process. This time, it wasn't a gush, but a slow and steady trickle. It wasn't long before the bowl held a small fortune. Gardiner picked out a nice spot in a corner and poured the silver into a pile, then returned to the machine. Mammut again held the bowl while he filled it with water. They also filled the second bowl, and reserved that one for drinking.

"Any idea how much to use?" he asked Frances.

"No. In that much water, a few pinches perhaps?"

"That's what I would guess. I just wish I had a clean cloth so that I could—" His thoughts jumped from one possibility to another.

"I have an idea," he announced. "If you'll indulge me."

Gardiner felt that it might not prove to be the best use of their time, but there were enough potential benefits to warrant the effort. All of the necessary items *should* be there in that array of rooms, somewhere. A perusal of the place on another occasion had not revealed any other open bays, but that didn't mean that there weren't any.

All three of them walked up and down the corridors, hands in contact with the walls at all times, feeling for openings shrouded by illusion. It was Mammut that found it.

"Here," he shouted, one of his arms poking into *solid* rock.

Gardiner limped over, stuck his head through the illusory wall, and saw exactly what he was looking for: hoops of various sizes. They entered.

The exit hoops, about four feet in diameter and standing upright on a set of squat legs, were grouped together, but the digging tools themselves were scattered all over. Gardiner picked up one of the medium-sized tools from the floor and studied it. There was no obvious on/off switch, so he gripped it as he had seen the workers holding them. A very faint vibration could be felt in his hands. An experimental swipe at the floor yielded the result he'd been hoping for: an effortless gouge about an inch deep, followed by a clattering a few feet away as the bits of stone were transported to, and through, one of the vertical hoops.

Another swipe allowed them to identify the hoop to which the thing was linked. Mammut found a secluded spot outside, away from the entrance to their hideaway, and positioned the hoop there.

Inside, Gardiner got to work, carving out an elongated hole next to the table with the machine, right below the outlet point for the water. The cavity ended up being about four feet long, two wide, and two deep, with the bottom sloped slightly toward one end.

"A bath!" he exclaimed, delighted with his work. "We can make some lye soap and get clean."

Frances looked at him sharply.

"Doctor Gardiner, this diversion of yours skirts the edges of frivolity. But I approve."

With the two of them putting their heads together, they reasoned out a formula for soap. In a few minutes, an ecru-colored bar was produced that ended up working well enough. It was a little caustic, but tolerable; they would just have to be careful to rinse well.

Frances was the first to use the tub. Gardiner let her undress in private, but once she was immersed in the water he kept her in his sight at all times. He didn't like the idea of sending Mammut out for supplies and so didn't broach the subject, but when his stomach growled noticeably, the other man stood up.

"I get food."

With such a trip likely to become more dangerous as time went by, the Doctor consented and crossed his fingers.

He returned sooner than anticipated with enough bread and meat to feed all three of them, and some blankets as well. Mammut was reluctant to look at Gardiner, acting like a guilty child. The Doctor was about to question him, but noticed fresh blood on the other man's knife when he brought it out to cut up the food. They locked eyes at that point.

"No choice," admitted Mammut.

Gardiner nodded and tried to console him as they ate, setting aside a portion for Frances, still in the tub.

When done with her bath, she made an attempt to scrub some of her clothing, but gave up when it started falling to pieces and saw that blankets were available. She also decided that the incessant itching from lice and fleas was not worth the vanity of maintaining long hair, and so asked Mammut to shave her head the best he could. The man's control of the blade was impressive. When done, an image of her brother, bald scalp newly healed by the shoggoth, flashed through Gardiner's mind.

Hair, clothing and dirty water were all transported outside by waving the carving tool through the bath. After being emptied, it was refilled for Gardiner, and a third time for Mammut. When all were clean the hole was widened and deepened enough for two people to lie down. Mammut then retrieved the exit hoop from outside.

As each had bathed, they had taken stock of their various scrapes and injuries. Aside from Gardiner's leg, Frances' wrists were bad enough to warrant a treatment with the silver solution. An area on Gardiner's back was painful to the touch, but was really no worse than a bad sunburn, and they supposed it would peel, then heal normally.

With Frances and Mammut working together to cut, tie and weave, the blankets were finagled into shapes that would at least stay put as clothing. Gardiner was grateful for that task to keep her occupied. The less she knew about the alien technology, the better.

TWENTY-SEVEN

PREPARING FOR HOME

As Gardiner worked out his designs on the manufacturing machine, yet another unresolved item popped into his mind: the placement of the clay tablet where he'd originally found it—or will find it, one day in the far future. Neither that nor the creation of the black spot at end of the causeway had been taken care of. Did they still need to be? He tried to guess at what Jakop would have thought about the situation, but gave up trying to determine if the events of history were malleable or not.

The first thing he made was easy: a length of wire. The machine produced ten feet of it, thin as a thread. The second needed more thought, but was in essence a simple device. Frances, always vigilant, came closer as the mechanism finished creating a small, rectangular lump of gray metal.

"What is it?" she asked.

Before answering her, he wanted to make sure that Mammut was paying attention. The other man, looking confused, was searching for something, but he came closer when Gardiner called his name.

"It's an alarm clock," said Gardiner. When he touched the top of it, a small red spot appeared and began to blink. "We'll see if it works in one minute."

In exactly that amount of time the blinking spot turned a solid red briefly before fading out.

"That's all that this one does. I'm going to make another one that will be set to go off in four-thousand-four-hundred-and-forty-one years. When it does so, it will interrupt power to the field that maintains the time-slowing effect. In other words, we'll wake up."

"Are you sure of the date?"

"Jakop told me that Ur-Nanshe has been ruler in Lagash for three years."

Gardiner looked at Mammut for confirmation, but the other was still distracted, looking around.

After a pause Frances said, "You're off by five years."

"Maybe, maybe not," responded Gardiner. "This far into the past we can't rely on any of our numbers one hundred percent. Frankly, it seems to me that it would be better to overshoot than to come in low. We don't want to get there before we leave. There's no telling what may happen if we do."

"I see your point. In that case, why bother with trying to be accurate? Why not just set it for twenty-twenty-five? Or even twenty-five-twenty-five? We can experience the future as well as the past. Technology such as this"—Her face lit up as she pointed at the machine—"would be glorious."

"I see *your* point," he conceded, "but I want to return to a life as close as possible to the world we left."

"Whatever you prefer, Doctor. Almost anything is better than this filthy era where a simple bath is the pinnacle of luxury."

She had inched over to stand right behind him, and so was in a very good position to observe how his hands moved over the control panel. He wondered how cautious he needed to be around her at this point; they would be headed back to the future shortly. Unlike Higgins, he had always disdained deception. As far as Gardiner was concerned, it was often a waste of time and effort. Of course, he reminded himself, James Dunlevy had been even worse. Dunlevy's acute paranoia had come close to wrecking so many of their plans that it was a wonder their group had ever had any success at all. But in Frances' case, perhaps paranoia was justified.

"Is something wrong, Doctor?" she asked.

"Just woolgathering, I'm afraid," he said offhandedly. "Plenty of time for that later."

As he started the process of creating the second clock, Gardiner looked at Mammut. The man was still searching for something…and had been ever since he and Frances had finished making their clothing. An internal alarm went off in Gardiner's head.

"Mammut, can you please come here?" he asked, then immediately spun around and snared Frances by the arms. In her current state they were like twigs in his hands. She struggled and cursed, and tried to kick at his bad leg, but Gardiner kept it away from her. When Mammut arrived a moment later she was already tiring.

"I wasn't doing anything!" she protested.

"Mammut, where is your knife?"

"I cannot find it."

"Does Frances know?"

When she said nothing, Gardiner carefully patted her down. The blade was easy to find within her crude robe; he handed it back to Mammut.

"What did you hope to accomplish?" He waved his hand before giving her a chance to say even a syllable. "Never mind. Even if you're willing to tell me, I don't want to know. Mammut, please turn her around so she can't see what I do."

Once she was facing away, Gardiner finished entering the proper commands, and soon the second timing device was complete. He switched the output area to be a chute again, found the baffling time-slowing particles in the catalog, and set up the machine to produce what he thought would be enough of the stuff to fill the hole. The press of a single button was now all that was needed to get the machine running.

"Mammut, you can turn her around again." After she was facing him, Gardiner addressed her directly. "Would you like to say anything, ask any questions?"

She glared at him.

"Good. I wasn't truly wanting to answer them."

Among the scraps of cloth was a strip long enough for what he needed. Tying her injured wrists would be cruel, so he tied an end to one of her arms, just above the elbow, brought the cloth around her back, and tied the other end in a similar manner, leaving some play. It was inadequate as a true restraint, but with her lying on her back, her arm movements would be restricted, providing the margin of safety he wanted.

The final detail was to cut the wire up into three lengths and hook up the alarm clock, using the miniature factory as the power source: one piece connected the power to the clock, with another length running from the clock into the open hole. A third dangled from the machine on the table right into the empty hole.

"When the dusty material fills the hole, the electric circuit will…" he started to explain to Mammut, who was mystified at what Gardiner was doing. "Never mind. There's no point in getting into that. When every bit of us is covered by the dust, the only thing you need to do is to touch it here, like I did with the first one."

He pointed at the alarm.

"Do you still have the breathing bags?" he asked.

Mammut pulled two of them out of his robe.

Gardiner took them, subtly ran his thumbs over them to ensure they were both oxygen, put one in his mouth and looked at Frances. He held it there for a while then took it out and dried it off. "A demonstration to show that it's safe." He held the other one out for Frances. She took it and put it in her mouth.

Gardiner looked around, but could think of nothing else that needed to be done. "Mammut, this is the time to say good-bye."

"Now?"

"Yes, I'm afraid so. I have to thank you for everything. I would never have been able to do any of this without your help." While looking at Frances, he added, "We *both* owe you our lives." Her lips pursed slightly, a begrudging acknowledgement.

When he held out his hand, Mammut shook it, but then gently grabbed him in a bear hug. When the big man let go, he was near tears.

Trying to control himself as well, Gardiner turned away. After pressing the button to get the machine working, he watched the dust as it poured out of the chute. When a pile had accumulated, he hopped down into the hole and started spreading it around. When it got to be about four inches deep, he held his hand out for Frances to join him. She jumped in. He helped her to lie down farther from the machine.

"After we are covered you can leave. We will…go to sleep…and wake up in a few thousand years. Home. Or nearly so."

"Home?"

"Yes, we will be home. And I'm sorry, but your home, Assur, may not be safe for you any longer. Go to another land. Live a full and happy life."

The cavity had continued to fill at a steady rate, so Gardiner sat down and started to spread it all around, covering their legs first. It didn't act like a typical dust, hanging in the air and choking them, but instead tended to want to fall to earth and stick to other particles of its kind.

He leaned over toward Frances.

"Listen very carefully. When you feel this dust start to dissolve, exhale, then bite down on the bag. Your lungs will fill with air, and you should have at least a one-minute supply while we wait for it to melt away. For an amount of this size it should take far less than that, but a poisonous gas will be released and may settle down into our hole. Do not breathe it in. Don't even open your eyes. I'll help you sit up and let you know when it's safe. Do you understand?"

"Mmm-hmm."

When the flow of dust out of the machine stopped, Mammut moved the material around them and smoothed it out. He heaped a large pile right next to each of their heads.

As the grains tickled his cheek Gardiner eyed the mound, knowing that it would be covering his face shortly.

For only forty-four centuries. A very short time!

"Goodbye, Mammut. Thank you again for everything."

He put the breathing bag in his mouth and worked his hand and arm under the dust.

"You have my welcome."

Hearing that, Gardiner had to suppress a smile.

"Ready?"

They both took deep breaths and grunted.

As his face was covered, the terror of that feeling returned and made his heart race. It was three inches of dust, not hundreds of pounds of damp earth. Intellectually, he knew that traumatic event in his past was far different from this one, knew that he could simply sit up to escape, knew that the bulky thing filling his mouth would help him breath.

But the smothering was there again, just the same.

PART 3

TWENTY-EIGHT

DÉJÀ VU

Gardiner felt the dust dissolving.

Too soon? Did something go wrong?

Wrong or not, there was only one course of action. As he had told Frances, he emptied his lungs and bit into the bag. After waiting twenty seconds, he sat up. Eyes still closed, he twisted around, reached over, and helped Frances up.

A sting, as if from a hornet, burned in the back of his neck. Frances reacted at the same time with a muffled moan. He felt the spot, able to stifle his reaction. The dust was fully gone, as far as he could tell, so he helped her up as he stood. Safely above the level of any gas, he opened his eyes, spit out the empty bag.

"Safe," he said, and Frances spit hers out as well.

"Untie me!" she yelled.

As he did so, he called out, "Mammut! Where are you?"

"I believe he died several thousand years ago, Doctor Gardiner."

The voice, from behind them, was calm, reassuring, and so very familiar...but totally out of place. He turned to see something inconceivable: a man he both knew and also had never seen before. It took some time to sink in, but it was Doctor Donau standing a few feet away. They had met for the first time when his mentor had been fifty-five. This man was thirty-five? Forty? But it could be no other, with that elongated face and pointed chin. His sparse beard was still very brown, strands of grey woven in.

"What year is it?" Gardiner asked hesitantly.

"1871."

"And you are Doctor Rainer Donau?"

"I am, but you also know me by another name." The voice spoke English with a German accent, but with a bit of something else woven in as well.

"Jakop?"

"Can it be any other?"

Tense silence became silent bewilderment. The man who professed to be Jakop slowly approached them and sat down on the edge of the hollow, legs dangling into the now-empty hole. Gardiner took a seat in a similar manner opposite him. Then Frances sat down as well, the three equidistant from each. Gardiner rubbed at the remnant of a pain on the back of his neck. It had been sharp, but had faded very quickly. There was no swelling at the point where he'd felt it.

Frances was the first to recover her voice.

"You are Jakop?" she asked Donau. "How is that possible?"

Gardiner finished sifting through the facts and spoke up before the other man could answer. "There were only two men who would know of this place, and who we are. If it is 1871, then Mammut is dead. And so, even though you have the body of a young Doctor Donau, you must be Jakop."

"A mind, thousands of years old, transferring between different bodies?" Frances gasped. "If you had the patience to wait forty-four hundred years, why not another fifty? Why did you awaken us early?"

"Why indeed?" the man answered. "First, let me say that I've just arrived in this era myself. I did not wait four thousand years for you, but I *have* been trying to get to this particular location in the desert for almost two years. It has been a delicate dance of politics, negotiations and bribes, first to convince Doctor Donau's University to fund the expedition, then to maneuver through the chaos typical of human societies. All the while, I had to constrain myself to act as your Doctor Donau normally would."

"That wouldn't be too difficult," commented Gardiner. "The man was—is—never at his desk. You were—will be—always off on a dig." He shook his head. "I need to think of you, and refer to you, as Jakop, if you don't mind."

"Not at all. But be careful if others are around."

"But *Jakop* was just another disguise that you used," said Frances. "Who are you, really?"

"She doesn't know?" he asked Gardiner.

"No."

"I'll tell you the truth if needed."

"Then tell us why we're awake now," she snipped.

"Your unique treks through time, your inclusion in past events...it seems unnatural, but has been fully integrated into the natural order of cause and effect. Knowing how much I had revealed to you and how your mind worked, I guessed that you might determine that the preservative dust could be used to return the two of you to your own time. Had you broached the subject with me, I would have told you that substance had deleterious effects on the human mind. I was hoping that you would be content to live the remainder of your lives in the past."

"You had no right to make a decision like that," insisted Frances.

"I have a duty," countered Jakop. "Your presence in the past was necessary for certain events to occur, and it was *safe* for you to remain there—safe for you, safe for history. The action you attempted with the preservative material was *not* safe."

"Why is that?" asked Gardiner. "We were outside of the flow of time. Not having an exact accounting of the date, I did set the mechanism to wake us in 1930, as a precaution."

"That was a reasonable idea, but still not good enough. You were *not* outside of time. It was passing slowly for you, but you were still within the normal stream of time. It is now December of 1871. Are there any events of significance in the next year or two, Doctor Gardiner?"

One seemed to be more relevant to the conversation than anything else. "February 16, 1873. I am born."

"Do you know what happens when two copies of the same person exist at the same time?"

Gardiner shook his head.

"Neither did I, but I do now. It took me years to research and set up an experiment in the far future on a distant world—something that would come close enough to duplicating the predicament we find ourselves in now. I was able to draw a valid conclusion from the result."

"And?"

"True impossibilities collide. It is not the end of things, but a remaking, as the threads of reality are rewoven into a new pattern. I did not witness the event itself, but learned about it afterward from minds I found to inhabit. The event was not actually recorded, as everyone was influenced in the same way. Do you understand? Time itself was reconfigured to allow for a consistent sequence of events. Suffice it to say that your existence would be erased. Now, what if Doctor Quentin Gardiner is never born? How far back is time re-written?"

He bit his lip, exhaled as the realization sank in. "Four thousand, four hundred years."

"Yes. Nearly all of recorded human history would be influenced—how, no one can say. And aside from your race, my people also have a vested interest in it. We have been studying this planet for ages. The stored data in our archives would spontaneously change, our memories would change, decisions would change. My civilization is at risk, as well as yours."

"I have the impression that you're a logical, practical being," said Frances. "It seems to me that the best choice you can make to avert a disaster is to kill us."

Silence.

Frances and Gardiner both looked at him.

"That follows logically, but is not the *best* choice. My preference is to restore you both to a point in time after you left for the past."

"It must be possible," she said. "Otherwise we wouldn't be having this conversation."

"It is," said Jakop. "The two of you must travel forward approximately fifty-four years using the same method you used to go into the past—a hole through time, presumably manipulated by Shub-Niggurath."

"And if this doesn't transpire, you'll kill us." Her voice was flat.

"It will not be by my hand."

"But you just said—" She fingered the back of her neck. "That pain. That was you. What did you stab us with?"

"It is only a last resort," said Jakop. "You must see the need for it."

"For what?"

"A monitor, of sorts." He held out his left hand to show two small, needle-like devices he'd been concealing in his palm. "I've been here about a day, designing and building the sensors and injectors. They are set to detect unusual disturbances in the continuum of space and time. One that is large enough will interrupt your nervous system, killing you instantly. And painlessly, I would think."

"Thank you for that consideration," said Gardiner bitterly. He rubbed his own neck.

"The greatest disturbance would of course be on February 16, 1873. That is a known date, with known effects, but there is an uncertainty involved. What of the point in time nine months before that, when you are conceived? When do paradoxes begin? I don't have that answer, and so all judgments made by any mind, even my own, needed to be removed in favor of impartial measurement."

"So, we have potentially fourteen months, but perhaps as little as five, to find Shub-Niggurath and command her to send us forward to the correct time? Otherwise Doctor Gardiner will die?"

"You will both die."

"Why is that?" she demanded. "My birth is decades from now—and in no way connected to his!"

"In that, you are right. If he dies here, in the 1870's, you could live in this past for years before your own temporal paradox. The simple truth is that I cannot—we cannot—trust you. I have given the both of you an incentive to work together. The two sensors are linked in such a way that the death of either will trigger the death of the other. You may feel free to curse me."

And she did—in four languages, as far as Gardiner could tell. He nearly joined her, but gained control of himself before saying anything. Jakop had acted correctly, he reluctantly conceded. He was still alive, and could remain so as long as they solved one of the most profound mysteries he knew of—the true home of Shub-Niggurath—within the next few months.

He tried to put out of his mind the fact that lifetimes had been spent unsuccessfully in pursuit of that knowledge.

TWENTY-NINE

AN UNEXPECTED ALLY

The surprise of meeting Jakop once again—and in Gardiner's case doubled by seeing Doctor Donau—along with the bitterness over his revelations, were temporarily forgotten when he showed them what he had brought along: clothing and shoes, food, and a small assortment of personal care items—hair brushes, toothbrushes, scissors and nail files. They took the time to eat, dress, and groom, lifting their spirits slightly. Gardiner also wished for a razor, but was willing to wait until they reached civilization before tackling his heavy beard.

Of the two time travelers, Frances proved to have the more resilient mind, quickly displaying her normal, scheming self. A few times when the men were distracted, she was provided with brief opportunities to inspect the fabrication machine. Once, mere seconds of fiddling with it had allowed her to learn some of the functions. On that occasion, Jakop had physically pulled her away, and none too gently.

But Gardiner needed more time to digest everything. He sat down, looked around, and thought. The place looked much the same as they had left it before being buried in—as he'd come to think of the substance—*the sands of time*. The final goodbye to Mammut was right over *there*, minutes ago subjectively, but in reality, thousands of years. He slowly came to terms with the information from Jakop, reviewed what he remembered of all of the events since receiving the telegram, and checked items off a mental list. Again and again he tried to find holes in the chain of causes and

effects that he found himself tangled within, and always he was satisfied to find a consistent framework—as long as a few more details
were attended to.

One was the obvious issue of discovering the lair of Shub-Niggurath so that their escape from the tepui could be set up. The other
was small, but vital, and much easier to deal with: planting the original clay tablet that had been used as the source for the engraving on
the archway. It needed to be in that hidden tomb, to be stolen a few
decades hence and subsequently recovered by Gardiner. Without
that, the entire sequence of events would fall apart.

The tablet was in the same room where the digging equipment
was stored, and Gardiner marveled at it once again as he retrieved it.
The clay had held up well over the centuries, but was starting to
show signs of age. Fortunately, getting to the tomb would not require days of traipsing through the desert. The portals they had used
to cross the globe would provide a wonderful shortcut—if only they
could know exactly where to go. Jakop had a solution for that.

In that same room, near to where the clay tablet had been, an
innocuous-looking object stood against the back wall. It resembled
a scale from a doctor's office more than anything else, with a plain,
upright slab about four feet tall mounted atop a base wide enough
to keep it from tipping over. Jakop described it as portable, and it
was, though two fully healthy men would be needed to move it
easily. With frequent rests and some help from Frances, they managed to wrestle the mechanism into the room with the manufacturing device.

Once in place, Jakop extended some hinged arms that had been
hidden in recesses along the sides of the slab. Unfolded and locked
together, they created a rectangle roughly eight feet tall by four
wide. He then opened up a small door near the top of the slab and
touched an alien symbol. The empty metal frame filled with a very
familiar image.

"That's the desert right outside our front door," said Gardiner,
slightly awed.

"Front door?" asked Frances.

"This will be our home, for the short term."

"This is not a home. I refuse to get comfortable here."

"Instead of comfort, what about safety?"

"Safety implies trust," she said flatly, looking at Jakop.

The unflappable man ignored her.

"It locked onto the signal from the nearest permanent portal as a starting point, but it can be moved easily."

He waved his fingers just above the panel that had been opened. With each movement the scene changed, slowly at first, then more and more rapidly. Sand and rocks flew by at a dizzying speed. Frances alternated between watching Jakop's hands and the displayed scene.

Moving the view was easy, but zeroing in on the location of the tomb turned out to be more tedious. Jakop got them started by positioning the window to the general vicinity of Baghdad. From there, the Doctor attempted to retrace the steps he would take roughly twenty-seven years from their present time. He looked for landmarks; some were easy to find, some not so easy, an aging memory not helping matters. But Jakop's control over the positioning of the portal was exquisite, with Gardiner only needing to point and say, "There." They backtracked frequently, but it was less than an hour later when he saw the stone covering the entrance and recognized it for what it was.

Jakop took the view straight up hundreds of feet and rotated it around. No one was in the area, and there was still enough time before sundown to take care of what needed to be done. Gardiner described how to clear away the obstructing sand and rocks, then Jakop went through the portal—as a young and healthy Doctor Donau—to take care of the manual labor, the only one of the three currently strong enough to do so. After pushing the stone aside to open the entrance, he returned.

Gardiner then went through, cradling his clay treasure. As he crawled into the opened tomb, the light from a portable device provided by Jakop revealed the breathtaking scene of a tomb in pristine condition, all the niches untouched for millennia. He yearned to survey the ancient catacomb, but curbed his professional enthusiasm and got on with the job.

His team had been able to make an educated guess as to where the tablet had originally been, but it had been a guess. Upon arriving at that location, he was glad to see that its placement would be very obvious. A wooden panel, carved and painted with images of the afterlife, had been placed on the chest of the mummy, leaving a flat space of nearly the perfect size. The colors had faded, but the artisanship was still evident. It hadn't been there when they found the tomb, the robber having likely discarded it as trash.

Gardiner's next act was a direct violation of over three decades of training, but he forced himself to place the clay tablet on top of the wooden plaque. He left and didn't look back.

The entrance stone was balanced to be easier to tip back into the covering position, so he was able to handle that task himself. After brushing sand and rocks back into place, he regarded the stone and pondered his transgression, trying to rank it against the sin of tomb robbing. The act was mandatory, but because it was premeditated, did that automatically make it worse?

A small price to pay for preserving all of human history, I suppose.

With a shake of his head, he trudged back through the portal.

"What's the next thing we must do?" he asked.

"Go to London," said Jakop. "Based on what I could learn about this time period, a man named Bertram Hunt seems to play a key role. He recently acquired a Greek edition of an ancient volume known as the *Necronomicon* for the British Library."

"I am quite familiar with that text," said Gardiner, "though not the Greek version." He mentally reviewed the mentions of Shub-Niggurath he could remember, but nothing stood out as being a useful clue to the location of her lair. "And you believe that book or that man has the information we need?"

"Yes. One, the other, or both."

"I actually know a Bertram Hunt from Arkham. He owned a book shop."

"This is that same man."

"Interesting. A colleague of mine was certain that he was hiding esoteric experience." Gardiner recalled a stunt orchestrated by Higgins, where they had tried to trick Hunt into revealing some secret. It had been somewhat successful. "However, he never admitted to anything. And never provided us with more than standard reference materials."

"Yes, I also get the impression this man knows much. Access to such a rare item implies that he has comprehension of it."

"Doctor Donau would have a reason to examine it."

"He would, but the campaign to explore this area of the desert created more publicity for the trip than I wanted. Doctor Donau cannot be seen in London at this time."

"How do you want to proceed then?"

"You must bring him here, by bribery, force, or deceit."

"Through the portal."

"Yes. There's no need to explain the truth behind it. If he assumes that magic is involved, we need not correct him."

"And what of Frances?"

"She will stay here with me."

They both looked at her, expecting angry outrage, but she only smiled enigmatically.

"This past does not interest me. Have a good trip, Doctor."

Wearing a raincoat thoughtfully provided by Jakop, Gardiner walked through the portal into the cool dampness of a wintry London day. The Whitechapel back-alley they had chosen was thankfully empty, and he stood for a moment to gather his bearings. The lung-coating smell of coal dust and the pungent stink of human excrement assaulted his nostrils, each fighting the other for supremacy as most offensive. And not just the odors: all facets of poverty were on display as he limped westward through the filthy streets, his leg not happy with the work being forced on it. He watched the native Londoners and tried to blend in.

In a few more years much of this will be gone.

Gradually, the streets became cleaner. Obvious gutter drains indicated that an underground sewage system was in place, making coal soot the clear winner of the battle in the more civilized part of town—except when a shift of the wind caused the miasma of the Thames to drift over.

He was relieved to reach the Museum without incident. Seeing no need for pretense yet, he went straight to the Reading Room and asked for Mr. Hunt. Outside of the building, Hunt was hardly even known within the antiquarian community, but here he was a genuine hero. Gardiner was asked to wait while the message was passed along. He occupied himself thinking of what he might say, and was lost in thought when a voice startled him out of his reverie.

"I am Bertram Hunt. You wanted to see me?"

Gardiner gasped; he had been practically looking straight through the man and hadn't even noticed him approach. He was of a smaller stature, About five foot four, and very thin, but with a commanding attitude and unexpectedly deep voice. His pale features were accented with wavy auburn hair and hidden behind large mutton chops.

"Another interview?" he asked. "Which newspaper is it this time?"

The Doctor recovered his wits swiftly enough. "No, sir. Not an interview. If you will grant me some of your time and come with me, I can offer you great knowledge."

"I think not. If you're here, asking for me, you already know what I've found. It will take me weeks, at least, to conclude my examination. I can spare no time, and you cannot possibly offer me something greater than what I already have at my fingertips."

"Perhaps not greater, but as great. It's understandable that you don't believe me. As you can tell from the sound of my voice, I hail from New England, the same as you. Born and raised in Providence, I currently reside in Arkham. Would I have traveled across the ocean to pester you, when I could have stayed home and simply waited for your return?"

"I'll admit that makes no sense to me. I'm sorry that you wasted your time and money to come all this distance. I'll be sure to look you up when I get back to the States, if you'll tell me your name."

Gardiner mentally ran through his options. "I don't want to lie to you, so I'll give you no name."

Hunt blinked at the response. "As I said, I am busy. Good-day."

Gardiner wished that he'd prepared for this a little better. Bribery would have involved a lie, as they had nothing of any worth, and he was no good with deceit. Jakop had also suggested force, but he wasn't healthy enough to wrestle the man and drag him a mile. As he turned away, Gardiner said out of desperation, "Your wife is Margaret. Your son's name is Charles."

He froze. There was a tense delay before he turned back.

"I have no son—yet," he said, his voice low. "I should be home for the birth if I can wrap up my work here in time. I've told no one, not even my wife, that I'd settled on the name of Charles for a boy. I have my reasons, but only someone who knows me intimately could have a chance of guessing. And you spoke it confidently, as if a fact. How could you know this? Did you read my mind?"

Gardiner decided to answer as vaguely as he could convincingly manage.

"Given the object you are currently studying…"

Hunt ruminated on the matter for a while before asking, "Is this…clairvoyance you display related to what you want to show me?"

"Obliquely, but yes."

Gardiner held his breath as the other man searched his face for something—some sign of trust to convince, or just the opposite to dissuade. Finally, he sighed.

"Alright, then," the man said. "Lead the way. I can spare *some* time."

The journey was devoid of any chitchat. Gardiner pushed the pace enough for his leg to complain constantly, but he wanted to get this over as quickly as he could. Near their destination, a few small knots of people clustered around the entrance to the alley, but their angle of approach gave them a good view down its length: It was empty.

"We must go down there," said Gardiner, nodding his head toward it.

Hunt's pace slowed. "It's garbage-strewn and filled with muck. What can possibly be down there?"

"You're right. It's not at all obvious, but I can promise you that it will be worth your while."

Without looking directly at anyone, Gardiner scanned the people around them. Some of the men in the area were rough-looking, desperate. He wanted to get past them without showing any weakness.

Instead, Hunt came to a complete stop.

"Please trust me. There's an exit hidden in the alley. We'll be safe."

Hunt began walking normally again, but more slowly, and their hesitation cost them the small amount of inconspicuousness they'd had. Now very close to the alley entrance, they were garnering attention from a half-dozen pairs of eyes. It was obvious they didn't belong there. Even knowing that the portal was open and waiting for them, it was still difficult for Gardiner to turn into the dead-end street.

Partway down, he snagged Hunt gently by the elbow and tried to encourage him to move faster. Hunt resisted, yanked his arm away and turned to run, but stopped when he saw that they were trapped. The end of the alley was now blocked by the men who'd been watching them. The three largest and most intimidating began to advance.

"Gentlemen, please hurry," came Frances' voice from the end of the alley.

Both spun around to see half of her sticking out of the solid wall where the portal entrance was.

"Move!" she shouted, then pulled back through.

Both men dashed toward the portal, nearly tripping while trying to avoid scattered debris. Their pursuers had come to a temporary standstill after seeing a woman partially appear and disappear. It gave the two men the lead they needed.

After they leapt through Jakop closed it, and just in time. Though none of their pursuers were sliced in half by the closing of the portal, they did get badly bruised as they ran face-first into solid brick. The viewing window had remained open, so all four were able to witness the pile-up and its aftermath as confusion and anger became terror. The men streaked out of the alley, crossing themselves as they went.

"We need a nicer neighborhood next time," commented Gardiner. He turned to Hunt. "You see, perfectly safe, as promised."

Hunt knelt on the floor, speechless, staring back into the alley.

"And now," said Gardiner, "you can begin to learn things you never dreamed possible."

Thirty

DESTINATION KNOWN

Hunt was fascinated by the portal, even mesmerized at times, while the view was shifted and he saw different parts of the world from a perspective that no one else in his time was privy to: from the desert right above their heads, to the Alps, the South American rain forest, the Grand Canyon, and on and on. There was no need to put an effort into selling it; it sold itself. Even Frances enjoyed the virtual sightseeing, or made it seem so, anyway. Gardiner believed it more likely that she was studying Jakop's hand and finger movements to learn how to operate the device.

"This is clearly not magic," said Hunt. "It doesn't fit the bill. There's no point in trying to disguise it."

Gardiner glanced at Jakop, raised his eyebrows.

"We were making no attempt to deceive you, Mr. Hunt," said Jakop. "As you have deduced, it is a type of science at work here."

"Yes, something quite a bit beyond steam engines, I would think. Which leads me to wonder how Doctor Rainer Donau could demonstrate such a command of it."

Jakop's head twitched. "You recognize me?"

"Whichever term you wish to use—archaeology or antiquarian-ism—your reputation in that circle is growing and overlaps others, including my own interest of ancient books and esoteric knowledge: magic, in other words. I also like to stay aware of current events, and devour every newspaper I can find, including German ones. So, you know my name, while I know but one of the three of yours—and my confidence in that one is slim."

"I am indeed who I appear to be. I lobbied to mount an expedition to this desolate area because I knew ahead of time what was here."

"The word *expedition* implies a workforce. From what you showed me of the landscape right outside, there are no others around except for these two. Also, based upon the article I read, you cannot have been in this area for more than a week. That is not enough time to learn how to manipulate this mechanism with the skill you display, especially because it is your first visit to this part of the country."

Jakop opened his mouth, but Frances jumped in before he could say a word.

"Enough," she said to Jakop. "No more dancing around." She looked at Hunt. "We need your help. Trust needs to be established, and so we need to start telling you the truth. Our names cannot be revealed, however. I'll clarify that shortly. When needed, call me F." She pointed at Gardiner. "He will be G. Is that sufficient for now?"

"I'll accept that, F."

"Good. The reason you may not know our names is because it may later influence you to make unnatural choices."

"Unnatural? Choices should never be unnatural."

"Normally, they're not."

"Unnatural, abnormal...," said Hunt. He looked at Frances, Jakop, then Gardiner. "You know of my son. You're from the future."

Gardiner's mouth went dry. It felt wrong to speak of it. "Yes."

"That is beyond imagining." He looked around for a place to sit down, meandering at first, then simply plopping right down onto the floor. "If you can travel through time, what can I possibly do for you?"

"Help us get home," said Gardiner. He then tried to explain what had happened to Frances and him. Jakop let him speak, but interrupted frequently. Gardiner finally began concentrating on Jakop for signs of approval or disapproval with nearly every word. In the end, Hunt received a heavily edited version that excluded so many details that his brow was left deeply furrowed. No mention was made of Shub-Niggurath.

When Gardiner finished, Hunt massaged his forehead and sighed. "Please correct me if I'm wrong, but I believe she said a short time ago that you would start telling me the truth."

Gardiner felt himself turning red at the accusation. He tried to analyze what he'd said for any outright lies. "I did omit some items, but bear in mind that there are some things we can't tell you. What would you like to know?"

Hunt stared at the ground, muttering slightly. After a short while he seemed to have reached some sort of internal consensus. "In the interest of brevity, I would like to know what caused this adventure through time. You glossed over exactly *how* the travel was effected. I have a feeling I'll be learning more about that if I'm to help you return. What I want to know is *why* such a journey was made in the first place."

Gardiner had left out a description of his relationship with Frances, but any outsider could read her body language and see how she distanced herself from her two companions. "She—"

"Be careful what you say, G," she interjected. "We are both victims."

"You are most definitely *not* a victim." Gardiner's voice took on an edge of harshness. "You precipitated this mess by trying to raise an army to—"

"No! I was trying no such thing. You assume far too much." She stomped over to stand right in front of Jakop. "Your interference ruined everything. You have no idea of the truth of the matter. And I will not play the part of a verbose dime novel villainess who reveals all."

"But you said that only you and G are from the future," said Hunt. "How could Doctor Donau have influenced any events in the past?"

"He's not Doct—"

Jakop's hand shot out, covering her mouth. "There are some topics we will not speak of." The threat of violence was plain in his tone, but her gaze never wavered. He removed his hand. "Just because the devices are linked does not mean that they cannot be unlinked. I *prefer* to restore the both of you to the proper time, but it is not essential. And *you* are the more expendable. And bear in mind that harming me will guarantee your demise, as future events require Doctor Donau's participation."

No longer able to contain her fury, she turned away and released it with a scream that echoed shrilly in the enclosed space. An instant later she spun back around to face him. "Be on your guard! Given a chance, I'll hunt you down through all the years and have revenge!" She left then, stomping down the corridor.

Hunt and Gardiner looked at each other, listening to Frances' footsteps, and curses that she made no effort to muffle.

"Quite an interesting group dynamic you have here," offered Hunt.

"It *is* complicated," said Gardiner sheepishly.

"One moment," said Jakop. "You did that on purpose. You provoked her."

Hunt grinned crookedly. "I wanted to see what I was getting into. My suspicion proved to be correct." He paused for effect. "But, as I recall, you said something about knowledge—great knowledge, in fact. Is this it?" He waved at the portal, still showing the Pyramids of Giza, the last location on their world tour. "Proof that technology like this will exist one day? That's not a revelation. Given the progress of the past few years, it's inevitable. What of events in the near future? Can you tell me what is to come so th—"

"No," declared Jakop. "Knowledge of the future is not allowed."

Hunt's mouth started and stopped as he seemed to try to find the right words. "Forgive me, but I prefer to speak plainly. If I am here to help you, I expect some sort of recompense."

"The intent has always been to compensate you. Your time is valuable; our time is short. All things considered, a hasty conclusion to this business will benefit everyone."

"Go on."

"Opening a portal through time is a non-trivial task, obviously. How do you think those two were sent back to ancient Sumeria?"

"My only guess is an extremely complex piece of ceremonial magic." He added, pointedly, "*That* part was glossed over."

"That is not far off the truth, but magic and science overlap in places, do they not?"

"They do."

"How many gods have you met in your life?"

"What kind of question is that?" Even as Hunt spoke the words, his eyes widened with insight. He looked down at the ground, shaking his head slightly. "There are many possibilities," he said softly. "But if you need my help, then it must be related to something that only I know."

"It is," confirmed Jakop.

"Things that overlap," he murmured, then went silent.

Gardiner watched him think for a while, then checked on Frances. She was fairly far off, now quiet.

"The Greek and Latin versions of the *Necronomicon* differ in subtle ways," said Hunt. "Just a few words, here and there." He looked up and said, "Shub-Niggurath."

"Incredible," said Gardiner, impressed with the man's quick mind. "How did you arrive at that?"

"A passage I translated from the Greek a few weeks ago seemed to be relevant. The English translation of the more well-known Latin version is:

Know that you may find the Great Mother, near dream, between the moon and the sun.

The older, and more accurate, Greek is:

Know that you may find the Great Mother near Dream, between the moon and the sun.

The word *Dream* denotes a place, not a state of mind."

"Well, yes," said Gardiner, picking up on the difference in the two passages due to Hunt's emphases. "The Earth would lie between the moon and the sun during a lunar eclipse, but the consensus has always been that Shub-Niggurath is somewhere upon the Earth.

We're closer now to an answer, but where is the *Dream* that is mentioned?"

"Knowing this now, the answer is very obvious," came Frances' voice, echoing. She began to walk back. "Have you never dreamed?"

Gardiner waited for her, slightly upset that she had overheard and had again added to the pool of data at her disposal. But the way that sounds carried in this space, they would have needed to consciously whisper everything to prevent her from hearing. She drew near enough to speak easily with the men, but kept her distance.

"I do dream," said Gardiner, "but forget much of it, remembering unconnected bits of imagery when I wake."

"And what of you, *Doctor Donau?*"

"I do not dream," responded Jakop.

"Mr. Hunt?"

"You are alluding to the Dream-world?" he asked. "I do dream, and know of that shared, astral universe, but have never found its entrance. Besides, it's not a valid solution to the problem."

"Why do you say that?" asked Frances.

"In my opinion, there is always information hidden in the utterances of people speaking freely. Conclusions can be drawn from even small pieces of truth. Doctor Donau used the word *met*, and so it seems to me as if you've physically been in the presence of Shub-Niggurath. The Dream-World is a purely mental construct, however, shared among the totality of all human minds, with no physical form. Therefore, you could not have been there."

"I do admire your very clever mind, Mr. Hunt," said Frances, "but there is one error in your logic. Just as science and magic overlap, so do worlds. As the passage indicated, the entity we seek resides *near* the Dream-World, implying a place that is possible to visit. As we obviously have."

"Where worlds overlap?" asked Gardiner. "How do we get there?"

"How do we get to any extradimensional place?" she asked, looking at the three men.

While Gardiner went cold at the thought of the invisible creature and Jakop nodded resignedly, Hunt's face lit up with the eagerness of a child ready to play. "We've all arrived at the same answer," he said. "It's the only one, really. When do we leave?"

His enthusiasm gave Gardiner a jolt. "Are you really sure you want to do that? Do you want to be involved?"

"For an opportunity to be in the presence of Shub-Niggurath? Of course! And for a while now I've been wanting to go Outside. I didn't want to try it alone, though."

"That's only part of it. You've seen the tension between us. We're ..."

"Only reluctantly cooperating, and poorly," finished Frances when the doctor stopped to search for words.

"Exactly," said Gardiner. "You're welcome to join us, but bear in mind that you may get involved in a conflict that isn't yours."

Hunt mulled that over before replying. "I still want to go."

THIRTY-ONE

THE SOUVENIR

As luck would have it, a partial lunar eclipse was due within a week. Jakop theorized that the alignment might somehow weaken the veil between the parallel planes of existence in order to allow passage from one to the other. The stub of a plan they had was for Frances to call the creature, which would then transport them Outside. After that, where to go and what to do was anybody's guess.

Gardiner was nervous about every aspect of the scenario: the thought of dealing with an invisible creature, the need to trust Frances, and knowing that traveling into such a space may affect their sanity as it did Tamar's. Because they had no choice, however, he did his best to accept the situation.

That was still days away, though. In the nearer term they wanted to verify Hunt's work. Having a scientific disposition, Hunt welcomed another, independent confirmation. He worked with Jakop to position the portal in the basement of the Library at the British Museum, then crept through with Gardiner and Frances. Doctor Gardiner regretted that her command of ancient Greek was better than his, but consoled himself with the thought that she likely would not learn anything new. Frances spent about an hour verifying the translation and searching for other clues in the surrounding text. In the end, she was satisfied with Hunt's work. Gardiner was at least grateful for having seen the Greek version. He had been in London twice before, and had not been able to arrange a viewing on either occasion.

With that complete, Hunt declared that he needed to continue with his work. Remaining in London, he arranged with Jakop to use that basement location of the library as a place to exchange messages. For the others, the intervening days were spent resting and healing. Repeated antiseptic treatments and a much higher caloric intake helped Gardiner's leg and France's wrists to both look and feel better. The food that Jakop had brought along was quickly exhausted, but Gardiner was able to replenish their supplies by visiting markets in London.

It was on the first of these trips when he was reminded that Christmas was only days away. On his walk from Whitechapel to the Museum he had seen some holiday decor, but had been too preoccupied that day for the idea to register.

The festive decorations brought back memories of Christmases past—or rather, yet-to-come. Of the people he knew in this current year, the idea of visiting his parents was of course a deplorable, possibly fatal, inspiration. Doctor Donau was right here with him, but at the same time, not. Frances... He distanced himself from her on purpose. They had spoken civilly for a few minutes that one desert night, and had shared a laugh, but he knew something like that would never happen again. And finally, his friend Sam would be about ten years old, living in Connecticut. New London? He couldn't remember now what Sam had once told him about his childhood, and that troubled Gardiner, leaving him feeling even more isolated.

The melancholy of missing a traditional Christmas, combined with the relative inactivity of waiting for the eclipse, was frustrating for both Frances and Gardiner. Jakop was least affected. He seemed to be content to sit and wait, or take an occasional walk. They all walked around a little outside, but never went far. On one of those rambles it dawned on Gardiner that they had a building full of books available, and convinced Hunt to snatch a few volumes from the shelves for them. That helped the time pass more easily; it was much like getting a Christmas present.

Although the desert heat was none too pleasant compared to the cooler temperature inside, Gardiner preferred to sit outside and read. He had found a spot of ground away from the portal doorway, in the shade, where the rocks provided a natural back rest. Being immersed in the book was enough to distract him from the discomfort of the heat, as his experiences in the distant past had acclimated him to it.

The drawback to this setup was the dust and sand that would blow around from time to time. He covered his nose and mouth with a cloth when needed, which was often, but knew it would be difficult to explain how a volume that had not officially been checked out of the library had become so begritted. As a precaution, he made sure to carefully wipe pages clean before turning them.

When a strong, swirling gust deposited a few grains into the gutter, he turned it upside down to dislodge them. But after that maneuver he got a start when he saw a pair of unfamiliar, sandaled feet. Standing in front of him was a man dressed in garb traditional for the area. The dust on his clothes was fresh, as if he had recently spent a good amount of time outside, possibly crossing a great expanse of desert. With his nose and mouth also covered, only his eyes were visible. He was of average height and gave the impression of being thin and stringy.

Gardiner slowly closed the book, pulled the covering from his face and smiled. "Hello," he said cautiously.

The man moved his head around, and studied Gardiner from a few, slightly different angles, but always keeping his right hand on the haft of a sheathed blade. After a while the stranger relaxed a little and reached into his robe with his left hand. He extracted a small piece of cloth, folded up, and handed it over. His voice was heavily accented, but what came out was English. "Tell me what is this."

Gardiner had no idea what the stranger wanted as an answer, but then felt something hard within the cloth. He opened it. Slackjawed, he beheld two pieces of glass which clearly fit together to form a circle about two inches across. The outer edge was rough, some small bits were missing from the break, and the surface was etched with countless, tiny scratches, but there was no doubt in his mind that it was the same piece of infrared-detecting glass that he'd handed over to Mammut. A flood of memories choked him up briefly. "*Souvenir* is probably the word you're looking for. I created that glass long ago and gave it to Mammut as a souvenir."

The stranger nodded. "Gardiner?" he asked.

"I am Quentin Gardiner." He stood up, slowly. "I've been asleep for a long time. How did you get that?" He pointed at the disc for emphasis, not sure how much English the man might know.

"Father give to son. Again, again, again."

"What is your name?"

As Gardiner asked the question he heard, then saw, movement behind the man: Jakop was running in to attack, and the unnamed man was spinning and drawing his weapon. "No! Wait!"

The command came fast enough to prevent the men from striking each other, but to be sure he stepped between them.

"Wait!" Gardiner said again. Both men kept up their wary, offensive postures, ready to attack the other, even though Jakop was armed with a stick. "This man is a descendent of Mammut," he told Jakop.

"How do you know that?"

"Because of this." Gardiner held out the cloth. "This was my first attempt to create something to let me see that invisible writing. The one you found, with the handle, was my second. This first one I gave to Mammut. It can be nothing else."

Jakop studied it, then handed it back to the stranger. "It's safe," he called out. "You can come around."

Frances walked into view, also brandishing a long stick or rod. As she came closer Gardiner was able to identify it as the broken handle of one of the digging hoops.

"Frances," said the man, gazing at her. He lowered the knife and put it away.

"He knows her name as well," Gardiner said to Jakop. "That proves it. I barely spoke to him before you showed up, and did not mention her name to that point."

261

"Why are you here?" Jakop asked the man.

"I look here. You come here. One. They not come here. They come out."

"What is your name?" asked Gardiner again.

"Nergal."

"Like the god?"

"Like god." He then bowed slightly to them. "I go. I look."

And with that, he bowed slightly and walked off into the desert. Jakop followed him for a long while; the man's course was as straight as an arrow.

"I don't know why he is walking that way," Jakop said. "The nearest town is over there." He pointed off to the side.

"Could there be some kind of hidden guard shack? Have Mammut's descendants really been watching this place for all this time? I *did* create a zealot."

"You should stay inside and read. It's not safe to be out here alone."

"On the contrary. We have an extra set of eyes on us. I feel safer now."

"I don't. I have no idea how he got as close as he did without me spotting him. I happened to check on you, and suddenly he was right there, just feet away. We came out as fast as we could."

He turned to look back at Frances, but she wasn't where she'd been. The broken handle she'd been wielding was on the ground.

Nergal should have also still been in sight, roughly fifty yards away. But he too was gone.

Gardiner and Jakop each went around the rocky outcropping in opposite directions, both shouting for her. The Doctor was moving better now, with only a slight limp when walking, but running was still too painful. When they met, it was obvious that neither had seen any sign of her. They didn't expect her to be inside, but checked anyway.

"What...?" asked Gardiner. His voice failed temporarily as he tried to comprehend the events of the past minute.

Jakop was silent, but that in itself said something. Even though the body of Doctor Donau was right there, he did not act the least bit like that man. Instead, the mannerisms of the alien mind known as Jakop always shone through. And after being with him for weeks, it seemed to Gardiner that something was being held back, left unsaid.

"How can she be gone?"

"I have theories, but can prove nothing," replied Jakop.

"But you know something. What are you not telling me?"

"I know that Kannit was not who he appeared to be."

Gardiner's mind did a somersault.

"Kannit? Why mention him now?"

"Do you recall that Kannit and Tamar had vanished while we were fleeing?"

"I do."

"It seems a good guess that the creature had picked them up and taken them Outside before it left the area, which it had been commanded to do by Frances."

"She thought as much," said Gardiner. "And with Tamar burned as badly as he was, it seems likely that he died. Kannit seemed to have depended on Tamar to manipulate the creature. With him dead, Kannit would have been trapped there."

"That's right. He *had been* trapped there."

"And now he's not? That was thousands of years ago and thousands of miles from here."

"You're thinking in too limited a manner. Those creatures exist in a place outside our space and time."

"What?" Gardiner scowled. "Do you actually believe that this Nergal is Kannit? There's a height difference of several inches between the two men. Besides, the odds of Kannit escaping and coming to this place at nearly the same time that you revive us are astronomical."

"As I said, he was not who he appeared to be," Jakop said quietly. "Remember: I am not who I appear to be."

Gardiner shook his head at the improbable suggestion.

"You mean to say that...he is of the same race as you?"

"That is my hypothesis. In our final confrontation in the temple I began to suspect as much, but it was not the right time to speak of such things. That bit of knowledge would have had no impact on the events that transpired. When my mind returned to my own body, I was able to do some research. I identified some candidates, but I can't say for sure who he really is. Perhaps he will reveal himself, subtly or blatantly, perhaps not. It doesn't matter. He is likely a criminal who avoided his fate by sending his mind into the body of Kannit. But this is just conjecture."

"Keep conjecturing, then. How could Kannit defy the odds to be here with us at this same point in time?"

"He didn't escape from the Outside and come here a month ago or a year ago. He could have been here, in this land, for ten years, or a hundred, or a thousand, waiting."

"No amount of technology will keep a man alive for a thousand years."

"With my people, it is only the mind that needs to survive. We are already comfortable with casting our consciousness out, swapping with a host. Normally, all is restored to normal when we depart, but in the case of a criminal, the original body has been killed. He has nowhere to go."

"Magic," said Gardiner, doing his own conjecturing. "Magic involves the mind and will more than anything else. One of your kind has the potential to live forever, possessing body after body."

"And so, we think along the same lines," said Jakop. "It seems that he has been waiting for Frances, as he kidnapped her at the very first opportunity. He needs her still."

"For what?"

"Who can say? But his goal likely remains the same: to summon and control Kh'kh'rng. If that's the case, we can be sure he will not make the same mistake twice. There will be no possibility of water."

"That hollowed-out tepui reminded me very much of a volcano—a stylized one, but a volcano nonetheless."

"A volcano would make an excellent container for such a thing," said Jakop.

"Yes, but which?"

"He would want one that is at least partially active. And his ego would likely require him to make a statement. The sudden appearance of that entity could trigger an eruption, potentially killing thousands."

When another memory darted in, Gardiner shook his head dolefully.

"Millions. Vesuvius."

"Why do you think so?"

"Frances is an expert in deception and scheming. At this point I trust little of what she ever told me, but…" He shrugged, knowing that he was on shaky ground. "She did say that she grew up in Italy, near Vesuvius, and I have a feeling that she was telling the truth about that. Surely, Kannit would put that one near the top of his list anyway. If he can discover that part of her background, would he choose it? It might be a way to emphasize his control over her."

"He would choose it," said Jakop. "This world will burn."

Thirty-two

PLANS AND SCHEMES

Although neither man had actual experience with magic, both had witnessed enough of similar things to understand how Frances could have been taken from right under their noses. Of the pair, Gardiner was more of the specialist, having closely examined such volumes as *Unaussprechlichen Kulten*, the Latin translation of the *Necronomicon*, the Egyptian *Book of the Dead*, the *Lesser Key of Solomon*, and numerous others. It was his opinion that visual deceptions were the easiest of the magics to master. The ability to become invisible would also have explained how Kannit had been able to get so close without anyone having seen him approach.

Gardiner knew that Kannit's best strategy would be to simply wait until the darkness of nightfall before moving. That being the case, the odds were very good that Kannit and Frances were both still nearby. But trying to find an invisible man—one with a sword, and trained to use it—could be a fatal mistake. They moved the portal into the air and scanned the area for tracks or footprints, but found nothing—as might be predicted. With Kannit showing the boldness to make the move he did in broad daylight, it didn't seem likely he would make a simple mistake like that. That night, they did look over the area from above with an infrared filter on the portal viewer, but noticed nothing other than nocturnal animals. They had to concede this round to him.

While waiting for Hunt to begin his day at the Museum, Gardiner dissected Jakop's supposition. In the end, he could find no holes. The evidence they had on hand was consistent. The truth could be far different, but there didn't seem to be a need to invent a new explanation just yet. They did make a point to not presume the proposal to be factual, and stressed to each other the need to take extra precautions at all times.

"We must tell Hunt the truth about you," insisted Gardiner. "He knows that there's something strange going on with Doctor Donau."

"No."

"But with Frances gone, we need his help, and he's already stated that he doesn't trust us."

"Confiding in you was a violation of the laws my people hold dear. And Frances knows, as well. A third would be far too many."

"Can we concoct a believable story?"

"Lie further to gain trust?"

Gardiner looked down, embarrassed.

"Yes, well…"

"Could I be a human time traveler from the far future," asked Jakop, "casting my mind into successive human hosts, and in pursuit of Kannit who is doing the same?"

"Kannit is a criminal and you are a policeman? That could work."

"No." Jakop dejectedly waved his hand at the walls around them. "This storage area, and especially its contents, cannot be justified that way. There's no manufacturing infrastructure in this era to create any of it."

"What if physical time travel was possible for inorganic matter only? The devices could have been sent back from the future." He shook his head. "Never mind. That's far too contrived."

"It seems as if we can't avoid the truth."

At the appropriate time they opened the portal within the Museum. When they caught a glimpse of Hunt moving around, Gardiner went through and got him. He was surprised by the early morning contact, but became intrigued at the turn of events, and satisfied when Jakop finally revealed his secret.

"It now makes sense how Doctor Donau can march for hours across an empty desert and come straight here," observed Hunt. "Do you prefer that I refer to you as Jakop or Donau?"

"Among our small group, Jakop would be less confusing."

"Does this Kannit know who you are? Or rather, that you are both of the same race?"

"That is a key question. When I was building that temple thousands of years ago, he must have known. All of the technologies involved would have been familiar to him; maybe he didn't know the location of this storehouse. Or if he did know, he didn't care to take advantage of it."

"Yes," said Gardiner. "He seems to be relying upon magic instead—which may be the reason for his obsession with F. He could easily have killed her, both then and now. But he hasn't."

"More importantly," said Hunt, "does he know that the same mind he encountered thousands of years ago is here, now, in this body of Doctor Donau?"

"I think we must assume so. In this time, Doctor Donau has started to build a reputation as a superior archaeologist, but in my haste to get to this site, I may have left behind an unscientific trail. Kannit knew, either from Mammut or his descendants, that F and G were here, suspended in time. If Kannit had been watching this area, he would have expected them to emerge one day—when their proper time period had been reached. Before that happened, Doctor Donau showed up, went straight to a hidden doorway that likely only Mammut's descendants knew of, and entered it easily. Shortly afterward, the two of them were spotted, awake. I can see how he could connect me between past and current events."

Hunt rubbed at his chin and stared at the ground.

"Describe the man who called himself Nergal," he said.

"He was of average height, perhaps a little shorter," said Gardiner. "He was entirely covered up, but from how his robes hung on him, and what I could see of his face, he seemed to be quite thin. He said very little, but his English was understandable."

Hearing that, Hunt was silent, seemingly mulling over something. He nodded and cleared his throat.

"In the interest of solving this mystery, I'll now make a confession," he said. "I did not *find* the Greek copy of the Necronomicon for which I am being lauded. It was handed to me for a ridiculously small price by a man matching that description."

"That is too coincidental," said Jakop.

"You're right," said Hunt. "He knows. Somehow, he knows."

"What?" asked Gardiner.

"What will happen," said Hunt. "He knows the future. He still wants F, but also wants you out of here, sent back to where and when you belong. He knew that tome provided the information you'd need to accomplish that, although you'd arrive in a place and time already controlled by him."

"Yes," said Jakop. "This era would be the best time for him to strike, before technology advances enough to defeat him. He wants to rule this planet, possibly for thousands of years. Taking the first steps now will maximize the probability of success."

Gardiner took a deep breath and tried to assimilate the latest ideas. Leaving Frances behind and being done with this business was so tempting. He had done his best for her, hadn't he? They had traveled together over four thousand years through time. Given what he knew of her, it could be argued that his efforts were more than she deserved. On the other hand, giving up now meant that he would be going into a future already enslaved by a madman. Jebediah might execute him for cowardice if he ever discovered such a truth.

And I wouldn't blame him.

The other two men waited for Gardiner to collect his thoughts.

"If he can indeed know the future," he finally said, "how can we have any hope of defeating him?"

"There is a chance," said Jakop. "He and I are of the same race, holding the same beliefs and the same misconceptions. You introduced a theory to me, shortly after we first met, which shook me deeply. My people have always labored under the belief that all events throughout history are permanently set. We explore through

269

time without disrupting the flow because only our minds travel. Your physical presence in the past was an unanticipated variable. To this point, events are still playing out in a manner to prevent perturbations, but because we are taking care to ensure the outcome. Consider what would have happened had you completed your journey back to your correct future time as you had intended: History would have been rewritten in order to prevent two copies of you from existing simultaneously. Kannit is probably not aware of this. I suggest that whatever method he is using to know the future, he is seeing those events that are the *most likely* to occur. But they are not *guaranteed*. Your presence here in this era is something he must have prepared for, but your presence by definition introduces an element of randomness—one that even he cannot predict."

"As a friend of mine might say," said Gardiner, "he has stacked the deck. Providing the tome, and bringing us together has increased the probability that I will abandon F. Kannit wants her far more than the rest of us. His basic and sensible assumption that I would prefer my life over hers *may* be coloring his interpretation of the future." At this, Gardiner looked at Jakop with some disdain. "But," he continued, "you've influenced my decision by providing an incentive to make sure that I don't abandon her."

"Nor she, you," he countered. "And there is no way for him to know of that contingency."

"What's that?" asked Hunt.

"Never mind," said Gardiner sourly. "A few days ago, our plan was for F to call one of those creatures. What do we do now, with her gone?"

"This Kannit of yours took care of that. Before handing the book over, he made a point of showing me a half-dozen passages, including the one describing the method used to invoke a Servitor of Q'yoth. At the time, his purpose seemed to be a way of proving that it was unabridged and authentic, but in light of this news it seems to have been a pretext."

"So, he not only stacks the deck, but has an ace up his sleeve," said Gardiner. "Calling and using a Servitor pushes us further along the path he wants us to follow, increasing the odds of his success."

"I cannot argue that point, but can we afford to miss this opportunity? Lunar eclipses aren't rare, but should you wait weeks or months for the next one?"

Gardiner weighed the risks of proceeding along the path that Kannit desired against the reward to be gained if they were to succeed.

"No," he said dejectedly. "I don't like it, but we should stick with the current plan."

"If you know of another method of traveling Outside, please do mention it," said Hunt.

"A gate could be opened—" Gardiner stopped himself. After some thought he shook his head and quietly said, "No."

"Yes, you see the problem," said Hunt. "A gate *is* an option, but can attract attention from whatever may be on the other side of it, and the amount of time and effort involved in such a complicated process means that we must rule it out. The creature we will use is admittedly ghastly, but has been proven to be dependable."

"You'll be able to command the thing?" asked Jakop.

"My vocabulary isn't large, but I know enough of that infernal language to do what needs to be done."

Gardiner grunted, knowing that the confidence exhibited by Hunt would contribute to their efforts. But would it be enough? All three of them were intelligent, giving them the numerical advantage against the one, but they were being herded along a path where the odds were in the enemy's favor. They needed to make a daring choice, create a fork in that path, somewhere.

But not just yet.

"No more poker, gentlemen," declared Gardiner. "That gives our opponent the edge. We need to begin playing chess."

Thirty-Three

Outside

The evocation to be performed was relatively simple and required little preparation, but as a precaution, Hunt took the time to teach the other two a few simple phrases in the throat-twisting language of the creatures. Jakop was familiar with some of the words, and having an innate skill with languages, picked it up easily. Gardiner had developed the ear for it over the years, and knew what needed to be said, but there was something lacking in his execution. The correct pronunciation seemed to demand a great energy, or intent, that the mild Gardiner did not naturally have in abundance. Hunt told him flat out to speak the words only in a true emergency, cautioning him that a simple mistake could have lethal consequences.

Because the description, "near Dream, between the moon and the sun," was more than a little vague, Gardiner suggested that they travel Outside as early as they dared, before the actual event. He posited that the path they must take would not likely be obvious, and that they may notice a change when the eclipse began. The other two agreed, and after some discussion, they all settled on an amount of time they hoped would be minimally detrimental to their minds. Of the three, the alien intellect of Jakop would be least at risk; Gardiner and Hunt would need to be mindful.

An hour before the start of the eclipse, Hunt got as comfortable as he could on the stone floor, and uttered some sort of incantation to put himself to sleep. Minutes later, deeply under, he chillingly spoke the words of a second spell to birth a nightmare. His voice was lifeless, but the words were clear.

Hunt's terrible dream began shortly afterward. Before too long, his body began to tremble and his legs kicked violently.

As his seizing continued Gardiner grew concerned for the man's safety. He wished he would wake up. But at the same time, he knew that his waking meant the creature would arrive.

Regardless, arrive it did, its presence felt before being heard, the stone around them vibrating with each powerful beat. Hunt's eyes flicked open as it drew near, appearing more exhilarated than fearful.

Gardiner's reaction was just the opposite. He took a deep breath and released it, trying to control his nervousness. With the first pounding beat his already-quickened pulse had shot up even further. To that point, it had all been words. He could analyze the issue, know the dangers, and commit to the path anyway. But now, with that horrendous *thing* once again nearby, potentiality had become actuality and there was no turning back. He most definitely wouldn't resist, but he was grateful that he wasn't the one being depended upon.

After helping Hunt up from the floor, they all looked at each other and nodded their readiness. Hunt commanded the creature to pick them up.

As soon as the words were spoken, it was done. Gardiner could see that he was still in the same location, yet also not there. It was a difficult concept to assimilate. The transition into that other space wasn't physically sensed, but he felt his mind expand like a balloon being inflated—or better, one that was already inflated being thrust into an area of lower air pressure, causing it to grow in size until reaching a new equilibrium. The experience wasn't painful, but it was disorienting, and there was no way to stop it, or even slow it down just a little.

Closing his eyes had the unexpected effect of helping him get a better handle on the situation. Even odder, he could still sense everything around him: the other two men, the walls of the underground vault constructed long ago by Jakop's race, and... the creature.

With more than a little trepidation, he turned his concentration to the thing and found that it wasn't as terrifying as he had imagined it might be. For one, the fearsome pounding that signified its presence was not evident here; and for another, its true shape had a bizarre, but logical, symmetry. Studying it as dispassionately as possible, his newly-expanded thought processes allowed him to imagine how it would project into the normal world: an abhorrent array of thin, ropy tentacles, each tipped with a pincer-like mouth.

"Is everyone all right?" asked Hunt. His voice was clear, unaccompanied by the echoes Gardiner had grown used to hearing in the chamber they'd left behind.

"Yes," said Jakop.

"Yes," seconded Gardiner, "although it is quite something to get used to. Is this what you expected? I feel as if my mind has gotten stretched like taffy."

"I didn't know what to expect, but this is consistent with what I've read." Hunt moved his legs and feet, as if trying to walk, but he stayed in place.

Gardiner and Jakop tried the same thing, and with the same result. After a few moments Jakop visibly shifted position. Then again. Then he began moving around smoothly, gaining speed.

"It's all thought," he said as he slowed to a stop. "Focus on where to want to go, and you will move there. In fact, we should be able to—" And without warning he zoomed into a wall. He then emerged from it, unscathed.

"The wall still exists in three-dimensions, but we are not..." He searched for a word. "*synchronized* with it, and so are not bound by the physical laws that apply to it."

The other two tried and soon became adept at moving around, carefully avoiding the creature, perhaps the only other thing in the area that was solid relative to the three of them. Before trying to travel through the wall, Gardiner stopped next to it and stuck a foot in. He felt no resistance; the wall was truly not there. Screwing up his courage, he plunged in. It was dark, totally so, but he still retained that knowledge of where he was. It was actually easier to be confident in that sense of location. As he had learned right before, dependence on vision hindered adaptation to this place. He knew that he had to learn to think differently here, but was having problems with it.

Satisfied that they had practiced enough, the men converged at their original positions.

"Do we need to actually be able to see the moon?" asked Gardiner.

"It may not be necessary, but it is probably in our best interest to get to the surface, rather than stay where we are."

"Okay," said Hunt. "Go straight up then?"

Jakop nodded and floated through the ceiling.

Before Hunt could move, Gardiner called out to him.

"Wait. What about that thing? He pointed at the quiescent creature. "Is it safe to abandon it?"

"If we'd started out in a more populated area, I'd be hesitant; that incredible thumping would be noticed. But to answer your question: yes. It'll just stay there and wait. If it eases your mind at all, try thinking of it as a dog. Or no—a golem is a better analogue."

Though familiar with such constructs from Jewish tradition, Gardiner had never even known of one being successfully animated except for the reputed Golem of Prague. This Servitor of Q'yoth was not a creation of clay, however; it was a living thing, and had mouths full of teeth for a reason. Although Hunt had called it to them by offering a sacrifice of some kind of dream, and it had eaten, Gardiner had to wonder how long it would remain sated. Would it wait, or would it grow bored and leave, trapping them there? Worse, would it come after them, looking for another meal? Before any of these concerns could be voiced, Hunt left him.

With a final look at the quiescent creature, Gardiner followed. Though he knew he was safe, it took longer to travel blindly through the hundreds of feet of earth than he would have liked. Near the end of the journey, he became aware that he had stopped breathing. Shortly after, there was a burst of mid-afternoon sunlight. It should have been blinding, but wasn't. The heat should have warmed his face, but didn't. And the dry, flinty desert dust couldn't be smelled. As he also discovered that his thirst was gone, a thought struck: With no need to breath, drink, or eat, a person could exist here indefinitely.

"I'm becoming acclimated to this place already," said Gardiner when he joined the others. "It's actually nice, not having to deal with the more mundane requirements of life. Have we passed that point of endangering our minds?"

"We can't be sure," answered Hunt. "Entering this realm can jar the psyche. We were prepared, and so that risk was minimized. The next hurdle will be readapting to the normal three dimensions. It may be hard to unlearn the reactions and behaviors of this place."

"We need to complete our business as quickly as possible," added Jakop. "I cannot stress that often enough."

The moon was visible as a pale disc hanging right above the horizon. They all took note of their general surroundings, then focused on it and waited. Of all the novel sensations bombarding him, Gardiner struggled most with the odd passage of time—while being still, at least. Motion was inherently coupled with time, but a lack of movement allowed the mind to forget about it as a concept. The flow wasn't smooth in that place, but instead was experienced in sputters and spurts.

Eventually, Jakop announced that he could see an edge of the moon darkening. At that point all eyes turned to examine anything and everything *except* the moon and the sun, trying to compare the current scene with what they had been observing. Jakop was silent, but Hunt and Gardiner both uttered curses as the minutes dragged on.

In desperation, Gardiner spun around to look in a different direction. When he locked gazes with Hunt, he was aghast to realize that, once again, he'd fallen into the trap of depending on the three-dimensional, human habit of vision.

"Don't look!" he shouted. "Use your mind!"

He then shut his eyes and tried to sense things around him, shifting his concentration so swiftly that he almost missed what he'd been trying to find. In fact, it wasn't a specific thing at all, but a lack of a thing. The veil between worlds had been torn to shreds at the start of the eclipse. Rips in the invisible fabric were knitting back together, leaving holes that were closing at different speeds. Randomly placed, randomly sized, the overall scene was not unlike Swiss Emmental cheese.

There was no way of knowing where they each may go, or to consider that they might lead to different places—and certainly no time for debate. Without thinking, he grabbed the other two and charged at a nearby hole large enough for all of them to get through. It seemed for a heartbeat as if they were going to make it, but for the first time in this extradimensional space he felt resistance. They were clearly within a hole, but the combined willpower of all three wasn't enough to push through. He could sense the boundary shrinking and knew they didn't have long.

Without warning, Jakop left the men, descending into the ground.

What is he—?

The opening shrank some without him, but the continued presence of Gardiner and Hunt prevented it from closing completely. Soon, only the hole that they occupied remained.

Flustered that Jakop had gone, Gardiner tried to concentrate all of his willpower to push through, but there was still no change. Despair threatened, but was replaced by alarm as he sensed another presence nearby, moving rapidly—far too rapidly to react. His one thought before the collision was that the creature they had left behind had grown hungry after all.

THIRTY-FOUR

ANOTHER DOORWAY

There was no pain associated with the impact, but Gardiner could sense an extreme pressure from both front and rear, as he was forced against the barrier resisting their efforts to penetrate. The membrane was immensely strong, but it flexed in a gelatinous manner, and finally gave way.

The transition from one reality into another was like an electric shock. But even as that feeling registered, it was followed by the pain of hitting the ground, the knowledge that ground was actually there to be touched, and the renewed, inescapable pull of gravity. The most awful of this cascade of experiences however, was the abrupt shrinking of Gardiner's perceptions as the extra dimensions were removed. Once again only able to identify left-right up-down forward-back, he knew that there was more to Creation than what he saw around him, but was unable to grasp onto the missing pieces, or even imagine where they might be hiding.

He wanted to flee, thinking the Servitor was right there with him, but needed time to unjumble his mind. With all the willpower he could muster, he forced himself to stay still, eyes closed, while listening for the frightful thumping. There was nothing to hear.

That wasn't the creature.

Letting himself relax, he reacquainted himself with the physical world once again: the unyielding stone against his back, scrapes on his palms from the fall, mildew in his nostrils, the light of day on the other side of closed eyelids. Raising his head, he looked around slowly. He found just one other man: Jakop, in the shape and clothing of Doctor Donau. Bertram Hunt was not there.

Gravity made the simplest movements seem so awkward, but the effort to roll onto his hands and knees was more mental than physical. He decided to sit for a while before attempting to stand, opting instead to speak.

"What did you do?"

Jakop also rolled over to sit, facing Gardiner.

"I thought that I sensed a weaker spot between the dimensions below ground," Jakop said, "but that wasn't the case. Desperation struck. I thought that a running start—so to speak—could force us through, and it worked. Unfortunately, Hunt was off center of my approach. I missed him."

"He's still Outside? How do we bring him here?"

"We cannot communicate with him, and so the question is moot. We must hope that he determines there is no need for him to remain there, and that he can return to the starting point in the chamber via the creature."

"He…should…do that," said Gardiner, trying to convince himself to not worry. He looked around. The immediate area was mainly exposed rock, granite-like. Patches of dark, fuzzy moss or lichen clung to it here and there, with no other vegetation or animals visible. A feeble sun hung low in the sky behind thick grey clouds, but it seemed there wasn't even enough light to cast a shadow for a sundial. "I wonder where we are. And where we need to go."

"I know exactly where we are," declared Jakop. The words exuded confidence.

"What do you mean?"

"It's hard to describe, but I've developed a sense of…location. It's a certainty of my place within the universe. Do you feel that as well? Do you know what I mean?"

"I do remember *something* along those lines, but whatever I felt is gone now."

"I've retained it. I even know where we are in relation to the Earth. We just can't reach it."

"Do you think that sense is permanent?"

"It's impossible to say."

"Where do we go then?"

Jakop chuckled. It was an alien sound coming from him.

"Anywhere. Pick a direction."

Gardiner looked around. On one side was the base of a mountain that towered above them. Opposing that, a plain of rock ran out to the limit of his vision, bare and flat. Undulations in the ground between the two kept much of the area around them hidden from sight.

"Must I question your sanity?"

"I'm sorry," said Jakop. "If you could visualize the mathematics of it as I do, you might be amused as well. This dimension has a strange geometry, much like a Möbius strip. All roads lead to the same place." When he got a blank look from Gardiner, he pointed at a path that led upward on a slope of about ten degrees, but was free of loose debris and so promised fairly easy going. "There. That route is probably shortest."

It was a strange effort for Gardiner to stand and balance himself on two legs. But after some ambling around on flat ground, the act of walking felt normal again. When he indicated that he was ready, Jakop led the way up.

At the crest it became more obvious where to go: a path led down the other side, at a grade shallower than what they had ascended. They followed it into a cave at the base of the mountain. Within, the path was plenty wide enough for the pair to walk abreast, but it wasn't long before they left the weak sunlight behind.

Straining to make out details in the impenetrable gloom, Gardiner slowed, then came to a stop.

"I can lead us through the darkness," said Jakop. "I still know where to go; no light is necessary."

Gardiner put his hand on the other's shoulder.

"Lead on, then."

A shuffling rhythm developed and they made progress, the path leading down, steadily down. With the way consistently smooth and clear, they garnered the confidence to walk normally.

There was no sign of life—no bats, for example—only the sound of their own footfalls. The grade was easy, but long, and they rested a few times. At each successive stop they noticed that the temperature had decreased just a bit more.

Not long after the third one the path leveled, and Gardiner had his own sense they were nearing their destination. It was confirmed when floating lights became visible in the distance.

"Let's keep moving forward a bit more," he said. "Based on my last experience here, I think we can assume that we won't be attacked. Oh—and prepare yourself for the communication. You may find it…unsettling."

They advanced at a slower pace, with Gardiner concentrating on the insect-like, hovering bits of brightness. It seemed that they were in very nearly the same spot as the previous visit.

"Here," he said.

The lights dropped down to meet them, at close range again resolving into glowing eyes. The small amount of illumination they provided was enough to at least see each other. Jakop didn't react at all to the grotesque sight.

Gardiner launched straight into his prepared speech.

"Hello. I apologize for our intrusion. My name is Quentin Gardiner. This person with me wears the body of a man named Rainer Donau, but you may detect that he is currently being controlled by an alien intelligence whose true identity is unknown to me. This is the first time you have seen either of us, but in my personal timeline this is the second meeting between you and I. I have become lost in time and space, and I am seeking your help."

He braced himself for a reply, but none came, and that made him uneasy. Not getting the conversation he had hoped for, and having already spoken what he'd prepared, more words poured out.

"A woman named Frances who is not with us is also in the same trouble as I am. We've lost track of her. Actually, she was kidnapped by another party. We must find her somehow. Once we do, I need to ask several favors of you. First, we need a way to return to our correct time in the future. I only ask this of you because you are the one who provided us—or rather, in the future, will provide us—with a doorway to the distant past. Frances commanded you to do so, and I followed her, more or less. We also need a way to return to this cavern in about fifty-four years so that we can begin our convoluted excursion. Or rather, I do, with Frances and another, different man. And last, right now, we need to get back to our Earth from this place, which I understand to be some kind of parallel dimension."

He paused again to listen, but there was silence.

"I'm sorry. That came out in a badly. I can go through it all again more slowly if you like."

Again, there was no response, so he turned to Jakop.

"How much of that can you repeat in that language of the devils?" he asked quietly. "I spoke English last time, and there was no—"

YOUR WORDS ARE TRUTH.

Though Gardiner had known what to expect, he was still stunned. Not only did he *hear* those words, there was an extraordinary amount of hidden meaning embedded within that short sentence. He could feel a certain *love*—if that was the right word—for all humanity by the speaker, but at the same time there was also *disappointment* regarding the rare few individuals who had been there previously, always greedy for power or knowledge. Coloring that was a subtle *regret*—about what, Gardiner couldn't tell. And finally, there was a sense that Gardiner had uniquely set himself apart from that crowd by humbly asking for help. This was his nature though, and he was embarrassed that his act should elicit such a reaction.

"Are you all right?" Jakop asked him.

The message was still echoing in Gardiner's mind, further nuances revealed with each reverberation.

"Did you hear all of that?" he asked.

"All?" said Jakop. "There were four words."

"Yes, but there was much, much more. The subtle implications of each word were… She…"

He stopped and shook his head, trying to make sense of it all.

Jakop looked at him oddly, then asked, "Parli italiano?"

"No, I don't speak any Italian."

"Ho freddo."

"Yes, it seems as cool as the last time I was here."

"Do you know what I did?"

"I have no idea. You asked me about Italian, then the temperature."

"I spoke in Italian. Both times."

"You couldn't have. I heard English."

"That is what the Outside did to you. That's why you heard so much more in those four words from the Great Mother than I did. I believe you're now able to understand *any* language." His forehead wrinkled. "We should go now."

"Go?" Gardiner was incredulous. "We just got here."

"And now that we know how to get here, we can come back after Frances has been located. In my opinion we should not disturb the Great Mother unless there is a specific task at hand."

"There are plenty of tasks."

"None which are well-defined."

"Finding Frances is one. Stopping Kannit is another. We have an idea of where they might be, but can use some help."

"The Great Mother is neither omniscient nor omnipotent. This is her first encounter with you. Events are happening just as blindly for her as for us. In the future from which you came, she knew where to send you into the past due to knowledge obtained from her past—from *now*."

"But leaving now? I don't know."

YOU KNOW.

Again, from two tiny words, a cascade of meaning blossomed in Gardiner's mind. *You know* that events must proceed logically, one after the other. *You know* that fate can be trusted even if people

283

cannot. *You know* that, for the future to occur as it should, other opportunities will arise. *You know* that all possible data need to be considered in order to make the best choices. *You know* that leaving now is the best action to take.

"You know?" asked Jakop.

Gardiner looked at him, and a final thought popped in: *You know* that things are not what they seem.

Not what they seem?

He opened his mouth to speak, but stopped. There was a peculiar feeling associated with that last thought: For some reason, he felt it would be bad to speak it aloud. Instead, he latched onto the one before.

"The implication," he said, "is that your suggestion is a good one. We should leave now and return when it's appropriate to do so. How do we manage that though?"

USE THIS.

A black circle, the same size as the one he'd used to get here with Frances and Chico, appeared on the ground. Gardiner had a steely surety that it had been attuned to his mind. He needed only to imagine their destination and they would go directly there.

"Hunt," said Gardiner. "We need to find him first."

Jakop nodded, and without a word, they stepped onto the circle together.

THIRTY-FIVE

SIGHTSEEING

Without any sense of movement at all, the pair found themselves standing in the underground storehouse, as Gardiner had mentally wished.

But there was no sign of Hunt.

"Bertram Hunt," Gardiner called out tentatively.

Both men listened closely. The echo of his name bounced through the stone chamber.

Aside from the absence of Hunt, Gardiner was puzzled to see that the water was gone, and utterly perplexed that the food was dried up and inedible. He took an empty container over to the manufacturing device and tried to create some water. It didn't respond.

"Jakop, what's going on? The water is all gone, the food has rotted, and this machine won't work."

Jakop walked over and tapped on the input panel. When water began flowing, Gardiner put the container underneath to catch it. "With Kannit having shown up, and Frances missing, I took the precaution of locking this mechanism before we left."

"But we were gone for only hours," said Gardiner, thinking back to their descent through the lightless cave. Jakop's face contorted as he riddled it out.

"Time must flow more slowly in that other dimension," he said almost shamefully. "It's not unexpected. That would account for the condition of the food and the evaporation of the water. And Mr. Hunt must have grown tired of waiting for us."

The portal was still set to that deserted corner of the Museum they'd been using. Gardiner poked his head through and listened, but was afraid to go looking for him, as it was mid-day in London and the risk of getting caught was too high. After Jakop moved the portal to a nearby alley they had used on a previous trip, Gardiner went through and restocked their supplies. At one point he had a feeling of being watched, but a scan of the crowd showed nothing out of the ordinary.

It was at the end of his shopping trip when he wondered about the date. Warmer than his previous visit, the grey, drizzly sky and neutral temperature gave no clear indication of what day it might be. As he bought a newspaper from a vendor, he noticed that the trees were greening. The pleasantness of that observation softened the blow a little.

"April 22nd," said Gardiner as soon as he was back in the chamber. Four months. His mind reeled at the thought of the sensor in his neck, the threat of death that much closer.

"That is unfortunate. Does the newspaper mention anything about Vesuvius?"

He riffled through the paper, scanning the headlines as quickly as he could.

"No."

"Then we still have time, although I would think not much. The emphasis must be on gathering information from around that area. He must be there by now. We must make good decisions."

"Good decisions? I think we need to court and marry Lady Luck to have any chance at all. We're guessing at everything. It's futile."

"It will be difficult, but this is the only theory we have and we must persevere," insisted Jakop. "Do you concur?"

There was an undertone of nervousness, as if he were afraid that his ally was ready to throw in the towel.

Gardiner did nod after a bit, knowing deep down that the fight must continue despite the odds against them. He rubbed absently at the back of his neck.

"What do you suggest?" he asked.

"I think you should go there first, and simply look and listen. There's a chance you'll learn something. Although I know the language to a small degree, your new ability makes you much more qualified."

"What will you do?"

"I'll stay here, and use the portal to search the area from above. I may see someone acting suspiciously, or a cleared area or structure where none should be."

"That makes sense, I suppose."

"You can get some rest. It's late afternoon there now, and you haven't had any sleep since before we left for the Outside."

An overwhelming exhaustion seemed to hit him all at once. He *was* tired.

"What about you?"

"I'll keep working a little longer."

Gardiner was awoken by a less-than-gentle shaking from Jakop. The man tried to remain outwardly calm, but Gardiner could tell that he was agitated. While the doctor had a bit of breakfast he was treated to a tour. From a great height, Naples was easy to pick out in the view through the portal. After moving to a lower altitude, Jakop pointed out the recommended route to Gardiner. Starting in the town of Portici, west of Vesuvius, the road was relatively straight on the lower portion, then it meandered back and forth with switch-backs where the going was steeper.

"You want me to walk all the way from Portici to the top?" asked Gardiner.

"To the Observatory."

"That'll take hours."

"About six hours, yes. It might be best to lengthen it even more though, with rest stops."

"Why not start at the top? Won't the ceremony need to be conducted near the summit?"

"Going directly there may alert him."

Gardiner frowned and shook his head.

"It's a waste of time."

"If after four months the worst hasn't happened, investing the time in a scouting trip like this is worthwhile. The potential exists to learn much." It sounded as if Jakop was putting every possible bit of effort into serene persuasion, but his expression was at war with those words.

"I suppose one day of hiking won't kill me," Gardiner begrudgingly conceded.

Jakop handed him a few lira and placed the portal in a wooded area with no one in sight. Gardiner stepped through into the Italian countryside.

Surrounded by greenery, and blue skies overhead speckled with clouds, Gardiner could feel his irritation lessen, his body begin to relax. The fresh air was far more enjoyable than the dusty desert he had grown used to, or the Outside, or the desolation where Shub-Niggurath dwelt, or most recently, grey, urban London.

Following a path eastward, he found a cobblestone street and began his trek toward the lower slopes. The sun had begun to peek out from behind the bulk of the volcano, dispelling the shadows through which he walked.

Before long, he came upon a town of farmers and herders, now well awake. The fact that he understood a new language with the ease of a native was so gratifying that he soon forgot the last of his objections to this trip. Languages and magic had always been weaknesses for him; regardless of how much time he devoted to their study, very little of it lodged in his brain. Now as he walked, he could hear snippets of conversation about weather, goats, cheese, recent rumblings of the mountain, and on and on. Nothing of what he heard had any bearing on his mission. On a few occasions someone posed the question "Who's that?" as he passed by, but there was nothing but innocent curiosity in those voices.

He passed out of the village and began his ascent. As he climbed, he glanced back often to look at the *turchino* of the Mediterranean through gaps in the foliage. The smell of the sea needed to be imagined, as the odors of fires and the foods they cooked easily overpowered the subtlety of a salty breeze. Twice along the road he stopped, poking his head into small cafés for a bite, pointing to order and saying only "Grazie." He listened intently as he ate, but heard nothing of note.

Pockets of civilization grew increasingly sparse as the road wound up and up. Near the top, in the midst of a series of switchbacks, the heat of the day became too much. He stopped and waved an arm to attract the attention of Jakop, whose disembodied head appeared in mid-air, a few feet away.

"Some water please."

Jakop had seemed to anticipate the need, and handed through a metal canteen.

Gardiner took a long, refreshing draught from it.

"I've learned nothing," he said, handing back the container. "Isn't it time to end this?"

"Not yet. I was watching a cart farther up the road not long ago. It seems to be out of place. I'm going to disable it. Help the driver and see if you can learn anything."

Gardiner shrugged, and resigned himself to finishing what had turned out to be a pointless exercise.

After a relatively long, straight section of the road, a hard turn nearly back upon itself to the right, then a sweeping turn to the left, the cart was there. One of the rear wheels was wedged into a crack. The driver was very old, hair and beard fully grey. He was trying to encourage the pair of mules to pull, but they were doing their best to ignore him. As he got up close, the aroma of food from the cart was very strong.

"Sir, can you help? My wheel is stuck."

It was then that Gardiner remembered one fairly important detail: Though he understood everything he'd heard, he didn't know how to speak even a half-dozen words of Italian.

"Si'," he replied, then got down on hands and knees to get a closer look, but also to avoid interaction.

The old man had plenty to say for both of them, however.

"I delivered lunch for a group of students. My wife made a nice seafood stew, like a cioppino, but it's her recipe. It cooled off on the way up, but it still tastes good after reheating. Better, I think. I don't know what she's making them for dinner. I know that I'm in the mood for some scialatelli with shrimp, especially after smelling that stew all morning."

Gardiner was able to ascertain that the gash in the road was narrower on the downhill side, and deep enough that the weight of the cart and the force of the mules was enough to wedge the wheel in tightly.

"I know my eyes are getting old, but I swear it appeared from nowhere. Of course, we get cracks like this from time to time when the giant grows restless and flexes his muscles. We all live with it."

Gardiner tried to push the cart back up the road by himself, but there wasn't enough slack in the yoke.

"My mules are generally nice, but some days they don't listen. This is one of those days. Especially Maria, here. Oh my, she was stubborn right from the crack of dawn. I think she wanted to sleep a little longer." He looked at the animal and lightly petted the top of its head. "I'm sorry, Maria, but we all have a job to do. My Sofia cooks, I deliver, and you pull the cart. That's the way of the world. That's the way it must be."

Gardiner was getting tired of the man's yammering, and almost began to regret his new gift. He came to the conclusion that the old man, the mules, the food were all merely that. Jakop had disabled the cart for no reason.

No, there's a reason.

Jakop needed him here—or maybe not *here* so much as not *there*, with him in the underground storehouse.

But why?

Gardiner wanted to be on his way, but he couldn't simply abandon the old man and his mules. If he could just get him to stop talking...

"Sir, please," interjected Gardiner politely. "If you could get the mules to—"

"To what, sir? What about the mules?"

I spoke Italian!

Gardiner was delighted at his newfound skill.

"Back up," he said experimentally, then, "Have them back up a little bit."

"Okay." The man hobbled around to the front of the animals. Alternating between the two, he implored and gently pulled. Soon, there was some slack to play with. A hard shove on the cart by Gardiner unwedged it, but the wheel stayed down in the hole. Positioning himself at the rear of the cart, Gardiner pulled up with all of his strength.

"Got it. Now take them forward a bit." As the cart moved forward, Gardiner held the wheel out of the hole. "Stop. That's good."

The man was effusive with his gratitude, but gratitude turned into stories of similar situations, the mules, the cart. When he started enumerating his children and grandchildren, Gardiner found an excuse to interrupt him.

"Sir," he said. "Will you have to deliver dinner as well? Please don't waste any more words on me. Best to be on your way. Your wife will be waiting."

"And don't I know it," he said, climbing onto the cart. "Again, kind sir, you have my thanks."

"And don't I know it," murmured Gardiner to himself in English as the cart began moving down the road.

THIRTY-SIX

REVELATIONS

As soon as the man was out of sight, Gardiner put his hand up again to signal Jakop. There was no response. He tried repeatedly, walking a while between each attempt, growing ever more frustrated.

By the time he reached the Observatory, his anger had become a quiet indignation. He looked at the door, wondering what to do, and if there was any point in going inside.

A voice came from behind, one not unexpected.

"He abandoned you, didn't he, Doctor Gardiner?"

Gardiner turned to face Frances. The scars around her mouth had healed a bit during the intervening months, but were still visible. Her hair was a few inches long.

"You seem to be no worse off than when I last saw you," he said. "Did you stage your own kidnapping?"

"I did not. That was real."

"You're telling me that Kannit finally got from you what he wanted, and simply let you go?"

"So, Jakop did feed you that story—and you bought it." She laughed.

Gardiner felt redness setting in, but took some comfort that the heat of the day and his exertions would help disguise it. He got the impression that she was waiting for him to ask or beg, but he refused to give in.

"Let's take a walk, Doctor. There's a place to sit in the shade that has a nice view. I've spent a good bit of time there recently, waiting for one of you to show up."

She led him around back to a wooden bench that resembled a church pew. When she took a seat at one end, he chose a spot slightly beyond an arm-length away. The distance between them tickled the edges of etiquette, but trusting her would have been foolish. She'd had months to regain her health and make plans; there was no telling what she might do.

Frances was right about the view, though. Through a clearing in the trees, the top of the volcano rose up before them. In the relatively still air smoke could be seen seeping from a half-dozen cracks and holes. A group of adolescent boys came into view, moving away from them, up the mountainside. Some walked in a line along the clear path, and others clambered and jumped over the boulders it wound between.

"On my walk I met a man who had brought food for a group of students," commented Gardiner.

She didn't respond.

He waited.

"There is no Kannit," she finally said. "At least, not any longer. He died thousands of years ago, and is still dead. My kidnapping was staged by Jakop, with that man you met—Jazeer—hired by him. Jazeer had an above average aptitude for magic, but at the core proved to be an imbecile. Jakop told him, and paid him, to keep me unharmed and hidden, but never specified for how long. Based on the payment he'd received, Jazeer was under the impression that it would be for a week. A week turned into a month, then two. At that point he became exasperated, and I persuaded him to free me. We worked together, and he grew rich based on what I knew."

"You told him what the future would bring?" Gardiner asked angrily. "You do know how risky that is, don't you?"

"Only bits and pieces, Doctor. He was told just enough to make successful wagers and earn my trust. I needed time to learn how his network of contacts was set up. Once I had that information, he was eliminated, cleaning up any historical repercussions I may have introduced. Now I control his men."

"Why does that not surprise me? You think much like Jakop does with respect to life."

"Not really. He barks. I bite." She smiled, predator-like. "Did you know him to ever kill anyone?"

"No. He threatened me when we first met. He threatened you recently…"

"Despite the bluster, he consistently distances himself from any violence. I believe he'd never resort to it."

"Then he truly is fearful of changing the future."

"He may be, or up to a point. Whatever his motivations, they are his own and, we'll likely never know them."

"How did you know I would meet you here?"

"I didn't, but after I was kidnapped, I had a great deal of time to think. I compared my captivity with my previous experience with Kannit. They were completely unalike. Kannit abused and tortured me. Beyond the initial capture, Jazeer never even gagged me. Escaping from him and hiding would have been easy, but would have complicated the task of meeting back up with you. Because I hadn't been killed, it seemed a safe assumption we would be brought back together. I was also assuming that, once we were reunited, you would know how to get us back to our own time. That incentive, and the fact that I was treated with some courtesy, induced me to bide my time. When we began to work together, Jazeer admitted that Jakop had mentioned the name Kannit a few times. He was told to adopt that identity under certain circumstances."

"Which circumstances?"

"I never asked him. But upon learning that, I tried to imagine scenarios that included the presence of Kannit. His failed attempt to call down that entity made me think of volcanos—and I recalled mentioning this one to you."

She stopped while a light tremor shook the ground.

"They've been more frequent of late," she continued when it was still again. "I came here and spent as much time as possible out in the open, thinking that Jakop would use that device of his to spy me out. I had less hope each passing day that my strategy would work, but also had no better ideas. My agents were also watching for any of the three of you in London and Ischia."

"Did Bertram Hunt go back to London?"

"Not that I'm aware of. If he did, my agents missed that." The vengeful note with which he was so familiar crept into her words. "Why do you ask?"

"We used a Servitor to go Outside at the lunar eclipse, as we'd planned. Hunt called it. There was some confusion, and we were separated. Jakop and I continued on to the lair of Shub-Niggurath."

"For the second time. A rare honor."

"We only arrived back in this world yesterday. We didn't find Hunt, but saw no reason why he wouldn't have been able to return to London, or all of the way to America by this point."

"He may have done so before I installed my agents. And you say you arrived yesterday?"

"Yes. Subjectively, we were gone for six hours, if even that long, but the flow of time is far different there."

"And for all these months I thought you were avoiding me."

Still irritated over the amount of lost time, her attempt at humor was lost on him.

"Months, yes. Another month, and these blasted devices in our necks would have gone off."

"Perhaps. You may want to believe what Jakop told you, but at this point I refuse to."

"As you just said, he acts consistently. Strongly consistent within his words and actions is a fear of interfering with the sequence of events in time. To me, that implies that the things are real."

"That is a good argument, but there have been so many lies from him that I require proof."

A dry chuckle formed in Gardiner's throat, but he squelched it.

Lies? Are you the pot or the kettle?

"The ability to travel arbitrarily large distances is clearly some kind of advanced science," he offered.

"Trying to determine, without proof, what is truth and what is not is a foolish exercise. I don't care to waste any time on it."

Gardiner acknowledged that she had summed it up well. They had no proof, and further speculation and debate would be useless. As he wondered what else they could speak of, or what they should do next, he spotted the students through a different break in the tree cover. They had covered quite a distance and were now marching single file in a fairly orderly line; the trail looked to be too constricted to allow any roughhousing. It was also steeper, and even rambunctious adolescents wouldn't have extra energy to waste there.

"Doctor," began Frances, then stopped.

As he looked at her, he became conscious of an acute silence; even the birds had stopped their chirping. Then a new sensation—a deep, bass rumbling—intruded. Their eyes widened at the same time, as they both knew that the giant sleeping beneath their feet had awakened.

They were shaken off the bench, the quaking so violent they could do nothing but hope that the ground wouldn't open up beneath them. It didn't last long, but the damage had been done. As they righted themselves and stood, Gardiner saw that new gashes in the hillside had opened, many feet deep and spewing thick, deadly vapors. The students were safely above that, but their path back was gone.

"Do you think we can depend on Jakop to get us out of here?" she asked, the tone of her voice making her opinion clear.

Gardiner waved a hand in the air, hoping to see Jakop's head appear, or at least hear his voice. But neither happened.

"No," he said, galled that he now had to depend more on a woman whom he knew wished him harm than on someone who had been, to that point, an ally.

"Then I suggest we rescue ourselves. I can call a Servitor."

"Do we need to? The situation doesn't justify that drastic a measure yet."

As if in answer, shouts came from the other side of the building. The pair hustled around to the front to discover that things were worse than expected. The staff and some visitors were pointing at a stream of lava now issuing from a crack in the road a few switchbacks below them, destroying their exit. And another sizeable flow from further up was moving steadily downward. Fortunately, a large rock upslope was splitting that one in half, diverting it to either side. Or so it seemed.

"And now?"

"We're trapped, but still in no immediate danger."

She gritted her teeth.

"My goal was to meet up with you," she said. "I could have gone back to that chamber beneath the desert long ago, but was afraid that Jakop had laid a trap there, and so I waited. With the two of you back, I have no need to remain patient. Eruptions are beautiful things to behold from twenty miles away, but I don't need to see one this closely."

Gardiner looked at the lava and sighed.

They moved back around to the rear of the building. She laid down on the bench, and Gardiner positioned himself between her and the corner of the building, in the hope that he could prevent anyone from bothering her. It turned out to be necessary. A woman broke from the others out front and walked toward them, forcing him to invent a story on the spot. He placed a finger to his lips.

"My niece is troubled by this," he said quietly in Italian, "and needs a short while alone to recover."

The woman glanced over, nodded, and tiptoed away.

No one else came by as he waited. Eventually, he heard the sound he'd been dreading, and Frances stirred and sat up. In such an open space, and with all of the other chaos, it was doubtful that anyone else would even notice the thumping. Or, noticing it, they might dismiss it as being related to a volcanic process.

"Are you ready?" she asked as he approached.

Closer to the bench, Gardiner was in a position to see the students again, and he froze in horror. Another finger of lava had split off from the main flow and was headed for the group. They had only minutes left.

As he stared, the woman to whom he'd spoken j came up behind him.

"The boys," she cried. "I thought they were taking the trail down, not up!"

She couldn't contain her tears. One of the men from out front arrived and turned her away from the scene, holding her in his arms. The rest of the crowd showed up soon after. But Gardiner led Frances away from them.

"We can rescue them, can't we?" he asked when they were out of earshot.

"What?"

"We can rescue the boys." He listened for the thumping beat. "That thing can pick them up, take them Outside briefly, and deposit them here."

"You would subject the developing minds of young boys to that environment? That's not a good idea."

"It's better than letting them die."

"Must *I* be the one to tell *you* that we can't interfere with history?"

From this position Gardiner couldn't see the students, but the lava was unrelenting.

Damn!

Each second, precious area was lost to it. He imagined them coughing and gasping for breath as their island shrank, and hoped they would at least die of asphyxiation before being incinerated.

"I'm leaving" said Frances. "Are you coming with me?"

Forced to accept their deaths, he closed his eyes.

"Let's go."

The sole ray of light in that particularly dark scene came a moment later when he heard Frances speak the harshly garbled syllables of that alien language.

"Bring me and this other to you," is what she said—and he understood it!

Thirty-seven

THE CURSE

The trip from Italy to the Middle East was amazingly fast, but still too long. Though the thousands of miles were covered almost instantaneously, Gardiner was still able to *sense* other creatures populating that invisible region beyond. There were other Servitors, of course, both larger and smaller than the one transporting them. Other *things* seemed as inanimate as stone, but he knew they were alive, and driven by the needs and desires of anything living. A few were too fantastic to behold, and he hoped he would be able to expunge those memories from his mind one day.

But there was an anchor for his sanity: the realization that a complete mastery of that language had crystallized in his mind. As with the Italian, hearing a few words was enough to supply an enormous vocabulary, conjugation rules, and an understanding that the directions for the creature were based upon the locations and movements of stars—and Frances' commands jived with that. Most archaeologists had little need for a compendium of astronomical knowledge, but he had picked up far more than his fair share over the years due to his arcane delvings.

After arriving at the location of the underground chamber, they looked into it from their other-worldly vantage. There was no movement. The viewing window of the portal showed a scene of unbroken blackness, but Gardiner interpreted it as a visual distortion caused by the fact that they were still Outside. He looked at Frances and shrugged, but she was focused on something else. Something behind him. He sensed the presence right before it grabbed him by the shoulders.

"Get me out of here!" pleaded Bertram Hunt.

Gardiner loosened the man's grip enough to be able to turn around and take a look at him. Physically—if that word could be applied to the space they were in—he was none the worse for wear. Existing outside the normal flow of time, there hadn't been a need for food or water, his biological processes having been essentially frozen. His eyes, though—they revealed a stain upon his mind.

"You've been here all this time?" asked Frances. Incredulity was etched into her features.

"Yes! That bastard—wait. How long?"

He gulped, visibly frightened at what she might say.

"Four months."

"No, no, no." Hunt shut his eyes. "Has it really been that long?"

But his shock became outrage at a dizzying speed.

"He left me here! He trapped me! When we were trying to get through that membrane, he flew off. Do you remember?"

"I do," said Gardiner.

"He must have dismissed the Servitor, because it was gone when I got back to this spot. And he pushed me out of the way! Did you know that?"

Gardiner shook his head, stunned by the news. Jakop had gotten Frances out of the picture first, arranging for her kidnapping, then had Hunt trapped in this extra-dimensional prison. And finally, Gardiner had been abandoned on the volcano. He had disposed of everyone.

To be alone. To do what?

"He told me that he tried to bring you along, but missed," said Gardiner.

"I was pushed," insisted Hunt. "I was pushed away as he went by. Then the two of you were gone. And I had no way to leave. Perhaps I could have found another Servitor and commanded it to put me back. But I was afraid to try."

"And rightly so," commented Frances. "Without the sacrifice to guarantee its loyalty, you would have been attacked and eaten. Or worse."

"Worse?" His anger had dissipated. Now, he just sounded tired. "Can we please go?"

"Do you know where Jakop is?" asked Frances.

"He left through his doorway. I haven't seen him for…a while."

"Do you think it's safe?" she asked. "Would he have set traps?"

"I don't care. Let me go back first. I need to get out of here."

She shrugged and nodded. "Place this third one in the lesser world," is the command that Gardiner heard her speak. He was elated, as those words triggered even more insight into the language. The word *lesser*, for example, was a poor translation, but the best adjective in English to match the concept being conveyed, that of a *limitation*. It made sense for such a creature, though: a place of only three dimensions *was* limiting for it. But even more fascinating for him was *knowing* that the command had been spoken with a tone that was implicitly…soft. It was a command the creature was obligated to obey, but the language allowed for a subtle *stress*, something that Frances either did not know about, or chose to not use. The command she spoke that brought them into this realm was also missing that stress, he recalled. And as that fact registered in Gardiner's mind, the Servitor did what it had been told.

Back upon material that he could feel, Hunt dropped to his knees.

"Glorious gravity," he moaned, then lowered himself onto his right side, both laughing and crying, repeating "Gravity" over and over to himself.

"Place us both there also," commanded Frances, with Gardiner listening carefully.

Again, lacking that stress. She must not know of it!

They appeared behind Hunt, still on the floor. He ran his hands over his body, then the cold stone he lay upon. His mumbling stopped, and he took a deep breath and released it.

"Would you like some help up?" asked Gardiner, bending down and extending his hand.

Hunt turned around, looked up at Gardiner...and recoiled. He scurried backwards. A glimpse at Frances caused him to react even more intensely. His face became a mask of utter terror as he screamed, his eyes squeezed tightly shut.

"What? Did you see something?" Gardiner asked once he had regained his own composure. A glance at Frances showed that she had gone pale. Hunt shook his head several times, refusing to answer.

"Please get me some water," he gasped, still unwilling to look at anything.

The canteen from which Gardiner had taken his drink in Italy was sitting next to the portal, its viewing screen still showing only blackness, still giving no indication of where it was pointed. After emptying what remained of the water into his own mouth, he filled it with fresh water from the fabrication machine. He took it back over to Hunt, who sat up and clutched at it blindly. Gulping too much too fast produced a lengthy coughing fit, but he got it under control.

"I tried to visit my wife," he said abruptly. "Well, not visit her so much as just look at her. This episode has caused me to miss the birth of my child, and that, I think, is the most painful thing of all."

He stopped and massaged his forehead, looking as if he wanted to reach his hand through his skull, into his brain.

"You tried?" prompted Gardiner.

"Yes. I thought that I'd even be able to go all the way to America, given the speed it seemed possible to attain. I didn't get very far. Regardless of the direction I went, as soon I traveled a certain distance from this general area, I encountered too many other...things. Things I can no longer describe. Once, it was a very narrow escape. I stopped trying."

As Frances listened, the surprise and fear that had been instilled in her by his outburst was replaced by a look of disgust: Her patience had run out.

"Why will you not look at us?" she demanded.

Hunt grimaced and said nothing. After a while, still seated, he turned away from the both of them.

"Madam, please come around so that I can see you."

She did so.

He opened his eyes, looked at her.

"It's not as bad this time," he said, though not convincingly. "What I am seeing is more startling than anything else."

"Please explain."

"I see your death."

"What?"

For the second time, her face drained of blood, as if she had never conceived of the possibility that such a thing might happen one day.

"It's morbidly amusing, really," Hunt said with a vague smile. "I *did* want to learn about the future. I suppose that now I have. Would you lik—?"

Just the start of the question was enough to restore her senses.

"No!" snapped Frances, the word punctuated with a finality that made both men jump.

Gardiner broke the uncomfortable silence, speaking to the back of Hunt's head.

"But you looked at us while still Out—"

He stopped himself, conscious of the beating of the Servitor. Somehow, he had grown accustomed to hearing that abominable sound, something he didn't think would ever be possible.

"I'm sorry, but can we dismiss that thing?" he asked Frances pointedly.

"No, I like having it around," she said, her mouth twitching into a smirk. "Besides, having gone to the trouble of calling it, it's better to keep it here until we're sure that it's no longer needed. Jakop is still missing, and a known threat."

"You're right," he conceded bitterly. Trying to ignore the thumping, he spoke more loudly. "As I was saying, you looked at us while we were all still out...there." He waved his hand abstractly. "You didn't notice this effect then?"

"No," said Hunt. "It only became evident once here."

"Can you please turn around and look at me?"

When Hunt hung his head and made no move, Gardiner walked over to join Frances. There was a pause before Hunt looked up. He gasped and swallowed, then squinted while looking back and forth, back and forth, between the two.

"Is it..." Gardiner hesitated, not sure how wise it would be to learn anything. "Is it the same as what you saw before?"

"It is, but you..." Hunt pursed his lips and continued to compare the two of them.

"Never mind," Gardiner said. "Say nothing."

He walked away so that he wouldn't tempt the man into speaking some fact about the future that shouldn't be known. His echoing footsteps did nothing to disguise the audible presence of the Servitor, but still he tried to stomp or scuff his feet to give him something else to concentrate on. He was tempted to sing softly, or hum, but sound carried a long distance within the stone corridors, and an uncharacteristic nervous humming would have provided Frances with more ammunition: further proof of his already known fear.

Upset as he was, it was only when he reached the end of the corridor that he noticed that the storage chambers, normally sealed tight, were open. Looking back along the way he'd come, he saw that *every* chamber was open. He began to walk back at a faster pace. Most of the rooms were configured the same as the one Jakop had opened during his first visit to this place. Others contained machines of unknowable capabilities that barely fit within the available space. One was nearly empty, holding a squat, pentagonal pedestal with a marble-sized, shiny, golden ball perched upon it.

When Gardiner returned, he found Hunt on his knees, closely studying the bottom of the portal window.

"I thought I saw some movement within the doorway," he said. "A shadow, maybe. I was about to call you."

Frances was on the way back from her own investigation of another of the corridors, but still a good distance away.

Standing squarely in front of the portal, Gardiner studied the unwavering blackness. He tried to discern some variation, but couldn't. It seemed foolish to go through, or even put his head through, without a clue as to where it may lead. He didn't fully understand the instrument panel, with Jakop hardly ever volunteering information about the controls. The indicators didn't provide any information, although a covering panel on the back was slightly out of place. He nudged it, verifying that it was loose.

Hunt stood up and walked shakily to stand beside him.

"Before she gets back," he whispered. "Do you still intend to go back to 1925, to a point in time after you traveled into the past?"

"I do."

Hunt gritted his teeth, apparently distressed to hear that answer. Suddenly, his eyes flew open.

"Watch out!"

He shoved Gardiner backward as hard as he could—just as something emerged from the darkness.

Thirty-Eight

FINAL ENCOUNTER

Gardiner hit the ground hard on his left shoulder, but was able to turn it into a roll, keeping him from getting hurt. Prepared by the warning, he was ready for flight as he spun around to see—Jakop. Expecting to have to evade some kind of alien horror, he quickly reversed his decision: fight. As he charged forward, he stopped himself when he heard Frances give the command.

"Restrain the newcomer," she intoned in the language of the Servitors. Black, ropy tentacles materialized from thin air and wrapped themselves tightly around the body of Doctor Donau.

"Need I remind you that you cannot harm this body?" asked Jakop. The words were loud and clear, the intent likely being to cut through the strong emotions in play—each of them having been abandoned by him—and appeal to logic.

It worked. With a snarl, Gardiner turned away. He could never bring himself to strike his mentor, anyway. He didn't like the idea of Bertram Hunt beating on him either, but was willing to allow the man a small amount of revenge. As Frances walked over, he wondered if she had herself under control, or if she would command the thing to rip his arm off as punishment. The set of her mouth showed turmoil lurking just below the surface, but she said nothing, and looked at Hunt.

Is there an unwritten rule, a pecking order, for exacting vengeance?

Gardiner turned his attention to Hunt as well, expecting to see fury at the very least. Instead, there was a neutral blankness as he

306

looked closely at Jakop, followed by a few blinks and a shake of the head.

"No need for violence," he finally mumbled. More loudly, he commanded the Servitor in its language. "Release him and depart."

Frances grew furious as the tentacles unwound and vanished from sight. She glared briefly at Hunt, before finding an outlet for her anger in Jakop.

"What have you done?" she shouted. With the bass thumping fading away, each word ricocheted sharply off the stones around them.

"I've done what I came here to do," said Jakop flatly. "It took far longer than I envisioned, both in this current age and in the far past when you first met me. But it is done."

"Is it time to kill us then?" asked Gardiner. "Clean up the loose ends?"

"We *are* going to clean up loose ends," he said, "but there will be no killing. Things must be set aright. Time is not something to be trifled with."

"At this point, how do you expect us to believe anything you say?" asked Frances. "You're clearly not human. That is about the only datum we can trust. Where does the lying stop and the truth begin?"

Jakop didn't get a chance to answer as she plowed straight on.

"Kannit?"

"In this era, a charade," admitted Jakop. "The man who kidnapped you, Jazeer—"

"Is dead. And those devices supposedly in our necks?"

"They do not exist. I used a fine, sterile needle with a coagulant on the tip."

"But why such a cruel lie?" asked Gardiner, anger returning. "You used our deaths as motivation!"

"I needed your assistance," he replied. "We needed each other's help to discover the true dwelling place of Shub-Niggurath."

307

"So that we can return to our proper future, preserving the natural order of events," said Frances, resuming the interrogation. "Another fabrication."

"Not entirely."

"How so?"

"I did cast my mind into the future, and did make a valid attempt at the experiment that I described. However, the results were as inconclusive as other, similar attempts my people have made. Yes, I did lie, but only because that potential reshaping of reality is an ingrained belief, reinforced by our ability to travel through time. It grants a unique perspective on cause and effect. I would like to go into more detail, but cannot. Human languages are ill-equipped to express the full array of chronometric possibilities."

"I'll grant you that much," muttered Gardiner as he recalled his own difficulties just trying to think through events, let alone put them into words.

Jakop looked at each of the three in turn.

"But the integrity of the timeline has always been my priority," he said solemnly, "which meant that your safety was assured."

"And what about me?" demanded Hunt. "You left me trapped Outside. That is not safe!"

"But you couldn't die. Without my help, the only way for any of you to reach this chamber would have been through the use of a Servitor, such as you did. You, Mr. Hunt, would have wisely stayed in the vicinity of this underground chamber as your best chance of being rescued. And you have been. Had you not been here, my next task would have been to begin searching for all of you. You must believe me."

"You'll pardon me if I don't," said Gardiner bitterly. The other two frowned their agreement.

"Very well," said Jakop. "It's of no matter."

He walked down the corridor that Gardiner had explored earlier, stepping into one of the open doorways. Faint noises, which Gardiner associated with the movement of the storage units, drifted out to their ears. Jakop reemerged, carrying a mirrored mechanism that looked to be duplicate of the one he'd used right before his death in the desert, thousands of years before.

"I'll use this device to break contact with this body," said Jakop. "After my mind departs, Doctor Donau will be unconscious for several hours. At that point, you'll use the portal to take him to someone he knows in Mosul. They will see him safely home. He'll recover, remembering none of this. After delivering him, you'll have one minute to return here. The portal will automatically shift to the chamber of Shub-Niggurath, and you'll have one minute to go through a second time." He pointed at the blackness still visible within the frame.

"That leads back to that cavern?" asked Gardiner. "How is that possible?"

"Our time spent Outside granted me a new ability."

"That sense of location you mentioned?"

"That's the best word. But I'm not the only one affected by spending time there. Mr. Hunt now seems to have been changed as well."

Hunt's lip curled.

"Yes. You bastard."

"And what of you, G? Has your mind been influenced in any way?"

But you already know—

"Nothing of which I'm aware," lied Gardiner to the very best of his ability.

Why did he not mention my new gift of languages?

"Perhaps you will notice some difference soon," said Jakop with a shrug. "And you, F?"

Frances did not react to the question.

"In any case, my new ability allowed me to adjust the portal to transport across dimensions. Although the cavern is dark, the featureless blackness you currently see is due to the difference in the flow of time between here and there. But once you get there it will be up to the two of you to communicate with her and take care of the final details. Will you be able to handle that?"

309

"I can issue the commands," said Frances. "But why the urgency? Why two minutes?"

"As I told you when we first met in this era, I have duties. First, I must protect the integrity of this timeline. The portal will handle that by providing you passage to the lair of Shub-Niggurath. Removing you from this dimension to that one is really all that is needed. But you are both resourceful and I trust you to be able to return to your home from there. My other requirement is to ensure that the technology in this place does not fall into the wrong hands. Two minutes is more than enough for what you will need to do. After that time, the portal will shut down and this room will flood with water. The machinery here will become unusable. If it is ever located, nothing will be salvageable."

"And if you're lying about that?" asked Frances.

"I'm not," he said flatly. "And if you choose to not leave this room, your death by drowning also ensures that the timeline is not disturbed."

Gardiner saw the same logic, the same motivations that he had come to recognize as an integral part of Jakop. He was again threatening their deaths, but passively. They had a choice to leave. If they did not, they would die, but not by his hand. It all boiled down to a question of trust.

He didn't reveal my secret...

"We must trust him," said Gardiner.

"Then we are at a stalemate," declared Frances. "Because I will not."

All looked at each other, sighing and throat clearing the only sounds. Jakop, patient as usual, seemed content to wait. Bertram Hunt finally spoke up.

"I believe that I can resolve this," he offered. "If you do not trust him, then trust me when I say that I see...scenes."

"Scenes?" asked Frances.

"Yes, detailed. And through your eyes. I will not elaborate further."

Gardiner pondered that revelation. If Hunt saw the scene of his death, it implied that he would die at some point in the future, not drowned in this artificial cave, not in some inky, space-black place, but in a place that—to Hunt's eyes—was more like the 1925 that he was hoping to return to. At least, he hoped that interpretation was correct. He made eye contact with Frances, wondering if she would acquiesce.

"Fine," she said bitterly.

Hunt turned to Jakop.

"What about me?" he asked. "The sequence of events you outlined did not include me."

"You're first. I can send you back to the British Museum right now."

"Is it really April then?" He looked down and thought. "London isn't the best idea. Or rather, it is, but just for a moment. Place me in that same basement location we previously used."

Jakop's hands flew over the controls and the portal soon showed the familiar, dark hallway.

"Please wait for me," said Hunt. "I won't be long."

He stepped through and crept away, coming back not long afterward with a notebook.

"Okay," he said. "I'm ready now."

"Arkham?" asked Gardiner.

"Boston. The wharf area. My appearance there will be hard to explain, but I think easier than London."

After Jakop moved the portal to the general area of Boston, Hunt gave him instructions, using specific landmarks as guideposts. They found a quiet alley off of Commercial Street, a potentially dangerous spot at most times of the day, but relatively safe at sunrise, when even the hardiest of criminals needed to get some rest.

"I'd like you to come with me, G," said Hunt. When Gardiner eyed him quizzically, he added, "It'll be brief."

"All right."

"Madam," Hunt acknowledged Frances, who nodded back.

For Jakop, Bertram Hunt had reserved a long, frigid look.

311

"I know your fate," said Hunt, "and I'm not displeased." He then walked through the portal.

When Gardiner followed him through, Hunt sidled over to stand with his back to the invisible doorway. He studied the other man for a short while, then extended his hand. They shook, but Hunt held on a few extra seconds before releasing his grip.

"Pardon me for blathering on a bit now," he said. "This worrisome concept of influencing the future seems to have many…I don't know which is the best word to use. Implications."

"In what respect?"

"Cause and effect come into play. Some events need to come before others, of course. And like anyone who may be caught up in a situation like this, I do take it seriously—but not blindly. Most importantly, I strongly desire that my own future stays intact. Given that stipulation, I'm willing to roll the dice and perhaps change another's."

"Mine?"

"Yes. As you may have guessed, I also know my own death, and in great detail. It can best be described as a very well-defined image in my mind—and not a bad one, as things like that go: natural causes at a reasonably advanced age."

He gave a brief, sour smile before continuing.

"As I said, my death is singularly clear—so much so that it seems to be locked and unchangeable. Yours, however, is not." He shrugged and shook his head. "It may be because you're not in the correct time, but your fate is definitely blurred, while that of your female companion is not. As far as I currently understand this new ability, it seems possible that yours can be changed. Although, I don't want to stand here and try to divine the best path for you to take. It's best to not dwell on things."

He chuckled lightly to himself.

"I think I'm going to grow tired of telling myself that in the coming years."

The was a long pause before he continued.

"I haven't seen my wife for a long while. My child, of course, I haven't even seen once yet. It's going to be a struggle to somehow grow indifferent to their deaths. Even though I don't know your name, I want to exercise what remains of my humanity and save the life of someone I can call a friend. Remember that Jakop is watching you through the portal. Don't react too strongly to what I say next."

"Go on."

"You must consider changing your plans," he said. "If I'm correctly interpreting what I foresee, and you travel forward to 1925, a tall, bald man will gleefully tear your head off."

The words echoed in Gardiner's ears as he called to mind an image of the now-bald Jonathan Harris.

"I see," he responded calmly.

Then, without any additional farewell, Hunt moved around him and walked off down the alley. Gardiner stayed until the cursed man rounded the corner. Then he left the Boston of 1872 behind.

"What did he say to you?" Jakop asked as soon as Gardiner exited from the portal.

"Nothing of importance. A simple, but long, goodbye."

"I cannot say I believe that."

"I don't care what you believe."

Jacob's fingers hovered over the panel as he looked at Gardiner, deliberating over what to do or say. Finally, he acted. The scene changed to a hotel hallway.

"I verified that the contact is in room 202, there on the left. Everything is now preset. Once you step through to that hallway, you will have a total of two minutes."

"Before you go," said Frances, "Tell me. Whose side are you on?"

"I am on my own side, and if I may borrow a saying I know that Doctor Gardiner will appreciate, my needs trump yours."

Gardiner could see that the response upset her.

"But we're still willing to go through with this," he said, trying to calm her. It seemed to work.

313

Jakop seated himself on the floor, leaned back against the wall and set the mechanism down in front of him. A light touch on the bottom set it spinning, reflecting light all around the room. Minutes later, Doctor Donau's head tilted to the side. A wisp of smoke rose from the intricate machine, then it slowed and stopped.

Gardiner knelt down and checked Donau. His pulse and breathing were steady.

"Are you ready?" he asked.

She nodded and grabbed his feet. Their handling of the man wasn't exactly elegant, but they got him through the portal. In the empty hallway they placed their unconscious package directly across from room 202.

"You go," Gardiner mouthed. She left, and after he counted to thirty, he pounded violently on the door.

It was opened right away by a middle-aged man in native clothing, catching Gardiner off-guard. He shoved the man backward lightly, ran the short distance to the portal and through it. Back in the underground chamber, he spun around and looked back, hoping that he hadn't been followed. The man he'd pushed came out of the hotel room in a hurry, but stopped when he spotted the motionless Doctor Donau. As he bent down over the man, the scene turned black.

Gardiner felt a small amount of relief, though it didn't last long. His next action would be to walk into an absolute unknown, hoping that the being who had manipulated and betrayed him hadn't set a trap for him. He looked at Frances, feeling certain he knew what she was thinking.

"The portal's location did change automatically," Gardiner reasoned, "just as he said it would. I think we can believe him this once."

Evidence of the war within her was drawn on her features, but she didn't budge.

"And Bertram Hunt gave me a tiny bit more information to reassure me that we make it back."

She looked at him, but said nothing.

"If we don't leave in twenty seconds or so, we'll be trapped and drown."

She looked back and forth, still refusing to move.

"Live to fight another day," said Gardiner, wondering if he would have to pull her along.

"Damn him! Let's go."

And with that, they walked together through the portal.

Gardiner's eyes slowly dilated. He looked around, trying to find the bits of light he expected to find there. And before long, he did, as the fireflies of The Great Mother's eyes blinked into view. Doing his best to touch Frances politely and non-threateningly, he got her oriented correctly. They walked forward together slowly. The lights descended to eye-level, presenting a familiar sight.

"Hello," he said. "We're back again."

The tentacles only writhed in the air silently.

"How do we do this?" asked Frances.

"We need two things," he said. "That portal from the tepui needs to be set up to bring us here in order to begin this whole series of events. And we need to return to our own proper time. You can communicate with…her. Please do so."

"I really would prefer to see what the distant future holds, though. Don't you?" She looked at him innocently. "The ability to travel vast distances instantly, that mechanism that manufactures items from thin air. That is what I crave."

"I must say I'm curious," he said, "but it's not up for debate. We're going back to the twentieth century."

But even as he said it, his mind wandered back to the warning from Bertram Hunt. Distracted by the thought, he didn't notice the look on her face.

"Restrain him!" Frances shouted in the mangled language of the Ancient Ones.

Two of the floating appendages shot down and wrapped him up, pinning his arms. Knowing what she said, the experience was far less terrifying than it could have been.

"Doctor Gardiner. You are aware that I can give the command to kill you?" Her familiar smugness had returned.

"I am…"

Sorry, my dear.

It was time for his ace in the hole.

"Obey only me," he commanded Shub-Niggurath in that same language, but adding the extra *stress* he was now positive Frances didn't know about. "Release me, and restrain her."

The tentacles did just that. He couldn't tell what surprised Frances more: that he was as fluent as she was, or that he had been obeyed.

While she was still stunned by the turn of events, he weighed his options and took a chance.

"If she speaks at all, tear her head off."

A panic-stricken expression washed over her face, but didn't last long. She got control of herself and remained quiet.

Let's get this first thing out of the way.

He imagined the view of the stars from the area around the tepui in South America, recalled the technical drawings of Jakop, the measurements they'd made. It was a complex thing for sure, but when he felt he had the description accurate in his mind, he let loose with a paragraph of where to place it, how to orient it, how it should be keyed to his presence. A black circle appeared on the floor in front of him, and he firmly believed that the other end of was now also centered in that circular platform at the end of the causeway.

One detail left then.

He massaged his throat and pondered the final task…and it dawned on him that this wouldn't be so easy. He couldn't say, "Take me to 1925." The human calendar system made no sense to a being like this. The discrepancy in the flow of time between the two worlds further complicated matters; specifications based upon the time *here* would make no sense *there*. Somehow, he needed to give instructions using relative terms, but relative to what?

He thought and thought. Frances looked at him as if wanting to ask a question, but wisely said nothing. Doubt crept into his mind, but he fiercely drove it away.

I opened the outer door. I triggered the portal to bring the two of us here with Chico. It always comes back to me somehow. It must be relative to me—my age!

But how old was he now, really? He tried to calculate how much time he spent in Assur, then in 1871, 1872. After much thought, he arrived at a result he was fairly confident in.

Now he had to make a choice based on what Bertram Hunt had said. How much of an adjustment would be needed to avoid that fate? A month, a year, a decade? The language used a base of thirteen for the numbering system instead of ten. He played with numbers, trying to find a value that came out even with the conversion, and erring on the larger side.

Close enough.

"Frances, you're getting your wish about the future, to some degree. We're going to arrive in 1933, as best as I can calculate. And I have this feeling that, no matter where you wind up, you won't have a problem getting around. How about Paris?"

She stared at him, jaw clenched tightly shut.

"But I will not be following you. I have no desire to get stabbed in the back as soon as I do." He shook his head and sighed. "I have no proof for the authorities that you've done anything wrong, and so trying to charge you with a crime is pointless. I'm sure our paths will cross again."

Gardiner described in detail the landing place and time for the portal. Once it was there, suspended in the air, he gave the command to release her.

"Good-bye," he said.

Freed, Frances remained silent. She did not look back as she walked through that hole in the universe.

Now alone, Gardiner peered into the shadows around him, knowing who—what—was out there, and grateful he couldn't see the writhing mass of protoplasm that was the body of Shub-

317

Niggurath. He imagined the scene that would transpire here in about fifty years.

"I wish things were easier," he said in English. "But we all play our parts in the tapestry of events, making mistakes and correcting them when needed. Please remind me of that when we next meet."

There was no response. He didn't expect one.

After clearing his throat, he gave the commands for his own exit. Another shortcut through time and space blinked into being. He walked into it, hoping that his adventure was at an end.

THIRTY-NINE

HOME

Gardiner stood at the bottom of a steep hillside, vegetation clipped low by sheep. Their droppings were scattered around, but none of the animals were within sight at the moment. He surveyed the area with relief; it was at least the right spot. He'd only been here once, years before, but the memory of it was etched deeply.

Underfoot, the grass was still wet from a recent rain. Clouds overhead obscured the sun, but a steady breeze from the west would probably push them aside and dry things out before long; it looked as if it would be a clear evening.

Atop the rise, a lonely house stood guard over the surrounding area. The structure was exposed, but Gardiner was one of the few who knew its secret. It was a decoy. The owner spent enough time there to make it seem as if it was occupied, but his paranoia would not allow him to sleep in such a place. His true home was underground, well-disguised behind an overgrown patch of low bushes, and connected to the house via a winding tunnel. One had to be looking squarely at the hidden entrance and tiny window next to it to detect them.

Focusing on the house, he started up the slope toward it. But after a few steps the metallic sound of a rifle being cocked came from behind him. He stopped and called to mind the code words he was told would get him past any posted guards.

"Mind if I duck into your spittal, kind sir? We've some wolves on the prowl."

He heard cautious steps through the damp grass. The barrel of a gun touched him in the back.

"Hunds oot where I c'n see 'em."

Gardiner couldn't help but smile upon hearing the thick Scottish accent. He held his hands away from his body to be plainly visible.

"Wolves you say?" asked the voice. "Nearby?"

The final word had a heavily rolled *r*.

"Close enough to worry the shepherds." He waited for the gun to drop, but it remained. "James. You should know my voice."

"I know who you *sound* like, but you'll need to do better than that. That man died, eight years ago or so."

"That's what our enemies would have you believe, but I didn't." He paused to recall details that he really didn't want to. "The two of us met through Patrick MacNulty. He had immigrated to live in Boston, but had kept in touch with you. I'd been working with Higgins for a few years, and met MacNulty when he came to Miskatonic University to access the tomes in our library. He was doing research for the reputed monster of Loch Ness, or as much as he could on our side of the ocean. The three of us in America thought it to be a load of garbage, but your faith in the locals who lived in the area around the Loch convinced us to come across the pond and investigate. We almost went straight home because you and Higgins developed an instant dislike for each other, but cooler heads prevailed. We stayed for two weeks. With still no activity and very few facts, we were ready to leave, when a quake shook the ground here, though it was centered in Invermoriston. We met that odd young man Stuart there—"

"Odd? Ha! He's an idiot. To this day he won't even look at the Loch, though there's but one low knoll blocking his view of it."

"Still, he was an excellent guide. He got us into the cave system near the shore and only fainted when he saw the statue posted outside the innermost cavern—which, you must admit, was quite horrifying."

"Eh."

"It was you, me and Higgins in that cavern. Because MacNulty had badly twisted his ankle the previous day, he hadn't been able to get very far into the caves without our aid, and decided to go back to town to try to find more help. What we found wasn't the reputed Monster of Loch Ness, but it was monstrous in its own right: a gigantic worm-like thing with the distorted face of a man. It was quiescent and ignored us until Higgins got too close. How he avoided that first attack I'll never know. That massive tail ultimately caught him with a prodigious blow, but by then he'd put four or five bullets in it from close range. Your shots also found their mark, but it wasn't quick to die. Jebediah was still out cold when it spoke just one word, the voice thick with phlegm: 'James.' In the darkness I couldn't see your reaction, but I heard both anger and grief in your voice. You whispered to me, 'Never speak of this.' And I never have to anyone, until now."

The gun lowered. Gardiner turned slowly, his hands still held away from his body.

The brow of James Dunlevy first wrinkled, then smoothed, as he got a good look at the man.

"Quentin," he said finally. "You're gonna have to tell me what happened to you. And how you got to my front door undetected."

"I have a lot to tell you." He grinned broadly as he remembered a particular from his previous visit. "Do you still make your own whiskey?"

"Aye."

"Then let's sit down with a bottle."

"Aye. Or two."